(13)
A Fetishist's Dozen

First Edition

Published by The Nazca Plains Corporation
Las Vegas, Nevada
2012

ISBN: 978-1-61098-176-7
E-book: 978-1-61098-177-4

Published by

The Nazca Plains Corporation ®
4640 Paradise Rd, Suite 141
Las Vegas NV 89109-8000

PUBLISHER'S NOTE
(13) A Fetishist's Dozen is a work of fiction created wholly by Christopher
Trevor's imagination. All characters are fictional and any resemblance to any
persons living or deceased is purely by accident. No portion of this book reflects
any real person or events.

Cover, Ekh Photo
Art Director, Blake Stephens

(13)
A Fetishist's Dozen

First Edition

Christopher Trevor

Dedicated to my 13 Lucky Charms:

Alan (my husband forever)

Roberto (for being such a Superman)

Shaun (for never judging me and being such a great buddy)

Scott (for encouragement)

Rose (for being such a great and totally honest friend)

Debbie (thanks for being our matron of honor when Alan and I got married)

Donna (same as Debbie, thanks for being our matron of honor when Alan and I got married)

Charlie (for believing in my work)

Master Jeff (for being a spanking mentor)

Timmy Backman (for being such a willing and at times unwilling tickle victim)

Tickle Master Vince (for all the good times)

Logan Zachary (for your friendship and belief in me)

Nicholas Bowman (for lessons learned)

CONTENTS

INTRODUCTION

Tickling, spanking, bondage a go-go, kidnapping, erotic torture and all sexy and forbidden taboos, they are all the things we're outwardly afraid to know about, but inwardly we can't turn away from. We secretly want to see and know more, we want to experience more, and try more. Guilty pleasures…

When I see the name Christopher Trevor I think of steaming hot fetish sex and boiling hot fetish fiction at its best. With thirty and more books to his credit, Christopher has now picked the best of the best and put them all together in one collection, "(13) A Fetishist's Dozen."

So, whatever kink or curiosity you may have, sit back and enjoy Mr. Trevor's collection of short stories, a smoking hot baker's dozen. So, as the saying goes, if you can't take the heat, get out of the kitchen. If you can't handle the fetish, stay away from the bedroom, or the dungeon if you prefer, but oops, no place is safe and no fetish unearthed when Christopher Trevor is around and writing.

Logan Zachary
(Published author from Man Love Romance)

(1)

Licking Arthur's Feet

(From the book: *The Executive Guide to Foot Fetishism and Office Discipline*)

Welcome to my first anthology of short stories. After having had thirty books published, books of short stories, a few novels and even some that I edited I felt it was time for a collection of what I and some of my closest friends thought were my most thought-provoking works. And with that in mind I could not think of a better place to start than at the bottom, at the sole of it all, or, to be more precise, at the feet. I am happy to say that after all these years that this particular story still stands on its own (feet). I still receive e-mails about it from people who have read it for the first time and even from people who have read it for more than one time.

I chose this to be the first story in "The Executive Guide to Foot Fetishism and Office Discipline" because I believe it really says what "foot fetishism" between two guys is really about.

There's something to be said about a guy who wears OTC (over the calf) style dark colored dress socks. My personal belief is that a guy who chooses OTC style dress socks is what my buddy Rick calls "sock conscious." It shows me that the guy cares about his appearance, down to the smallest detail, his socks. It shows me that he is a gentleman.

For some reason my personal belief is that straight guys do not wear OTC style dress socks. I'm sure that assessment is not true, but how many straight guys would admit to wearing OTC dress socks?

Arthur, the character in the story who gets his feet licked and serviced was patterned after a gentleman I used to see on the train in the mornings on my way to work. I never got to talk with him too much, other than to find out that he was an attorney. I almost laughed when he told me he was an attorney because the way he would hike up his suit trousers when sitting on the train showing off those OTC black socks put some credence to a belief I have; that all lawyers wear OTC socks.

I think besides Bobby from my story "The Taking of Master's Boy", Arthur is one of the most paramount and outstanding characters that I ever brought to life.

Till this day I have no idea why I named the character Arthur. For whatever the reason the gentleman on the train looked like an Arthur to me. If I were to ever find out that his name actually is Arthur I think it would knock my socks off (pun intended...)

Besides making its way around the internet and finally finding a home in my book "The Executive Guide to Foot Fetishism and Office Discipline" this story had been published in a magazine called "ManTalk" in their May, 1998 issue. It has been resurrected yet again in the new MACH21 magazine that just came out via my publisher.

I like to think that this particular story will go down in gay history as one of the erotic classics.

If I recall correctly it took me less than two hours to write it... I simply envisioned the gentleman from the train in my mind and the words flowed out of me easily...

I have been asked if given the chance would I have licked the socked feet of the gentleman who I saw on the train that inspired the story "Licking Arthur's Feet." In response all I can say is, "Is the sky blue?"

The character of Arthur also appeared in my story "Tickling Arthur's Feet", but that story and "Licking Arthur's Feet" didn't intertwine at all. I just thought at the time that Arthur would make a good tickle victim for that particular story...

I work with Arthur at Chase Bank. We've known each other for five years. We're both married and in our mid-thirties. Neither of us have any children. Recently I had an experience with Arthur that I want to share with you. Coincidentally both of our wives were out of town on business for the companies they work for so with no plans for the evening I invited Arthur to come to my place after work for dinner...Chinese take-out of course. Dressed in a gray suit, Arthur in a blue suit we left the bank at five PM and rode the "F" train to my house in Brooklyn. When we got off the train I treated us to Chinese take-out from the place a few blocks from my house. Arthur dashed into a superette and emerged with a six pack of Coors light, his treat for the evening. When we got to my house we shucked off our suit jackets, loosened our ties, and undid the top buttons of our white dress shirts.

"Thanks for having me over Brad." Arthur said as he took two cans of beer from the six packs he had bought.

He handed me a can of beer and we both opened them, gulping them.

"Ahhhh!!" I said. "Nothing like a cold beer and good company to go with dinner."

"And, while we're eating we can talk about that new system we're having installed next week." Arthur said, taking me by my arm.

"Oh shit, come on Arthur, let's not talk shop." I said with a mock grimace as he walked me toward the dinner table.

While we chowed down on chicken with broccoli, fried rice, wanton soup, and our beers Arthur and I summarized what we had talked about in the recent meetings at work concerning the new computer system that was being installed in our department at the bank. We both agreed that it sounded great and should increase productivity dramatically. When dinner was over I suggested we watch some television in the living room. Arthur carried two beers with him as we walked to the living room. He placed them on the coffee table and sat down on the couch.

"Listen, make yourself comfortable." I said to him. "I'm just going to give Laura a call to see how she is. Turn on the TV, take your shoes off, relax…"

I trotted to the kitchen where the phone was as Arthur picked up the remote control and flicked on the television to CNN. The business report was on…Arthur's favorite thing to watch. The TV on, Arthur loosened his tie a little more, slipped his black slip-on wing tips off his feet and stretched out on the couch, his feet dangling off the end of it. He opened his second beer and sipped it as I spoke to my wife. When I was done talking to Laura I came into the living room. Arthur looked comfortable on the couch so being that he was the guest I didn't ask him to move. I simply sat down on the rugged floor, my back against the couch, and my head right next to Arthur's feet. He was wearing black nylon, ribbed, knee length, Gold Toe brand socks.

"Hey Brad, sit up here on the couch…" Arthur said, nudging my shoulder with his big toe.

"Nah, I always sit on the floor when Laura and I are watching TV." I said. "It's comfortable down here."

I tried to pretend I was interested in what was going on, on the TV but watching business after work is boring to me. But, Arthur was my guest so I didn't even suggest changing the channel. As we watched CNN Arthur sipped his beer. I hadn't started my second one yet. It was a few minutes later when I began to notice the smell of foot sweat coming from Arthur's socked feet. I didn't move head away because I didn't want to embarrass the guy after all. I leaned forward and grabbed my second beer off the coffee table. I popped it open, leaned back against the couch, and took a gulp of it.

"If you want to change the channel you can Brad." Arthur said, nudging my shoulder again with his big toe.

"No, it's fine…" I said and sipped my beer.

This time though Arthur kept his foot by my shoulder, his toe against it. I looked at that foot out of the corner of my eye.

"Do my feet smell bad?" Arthur asked me. "Sorry Brad, I've had these stinking socks on since early this morning…"

But he didn't move his feet away from me. I took a sip of my beer, placed the can on the coffee table, and leaned back against the couch. When I turned to look at Arthur and tell him that his feet didn't smell all that bad I found my nose pressed against the bottom of his left socked foot. I froze and inhaled deeply.

"Go ahead Brad; I have the feeling you want to…" Arthur said with a grin on his banker's face.

He looked so smug with his corporate haircut and big blue eyes smirking at me. I cupped his heel in my hand and with my other hand I curled my fingers around the gold material around his toes of his Gold Toe socks.

"Arthur, I don't understand…" I said, my nose still pressed against his foot.

But then my tongue came out of my mouth and I licked the bottom of Arthur's foot.

"Oh you understand perfectly Brad ol' boy…" Arthur said and crossed his arms behind his head. "Now, lick my socks clean for me."

"Yes Sir…" I whispered and held his foot tightly in my hands as I slowly licked the bottom of it, sucking on his sock at the same time, savoring the musty scent of it all.

"Oh yeah, always knew you had it in you to be a foot slave Brad ol' boy…" Arthur said. "You think I didn't notice all those times you came in my office when I had my feet propped up on my desk? Man, I knew you wanted to get those wing tips off my feet and lick em' right there in the office…"

What he was saying was true, so true, all of it true. For some reason I had always admired Arthur's black socked feet. It always intrigued me that he wore those knee length nylon socks. That way when he would cross his leg in a meeting there was no chance of Arthur showing any pale skin from his leg. And wing tips, Arthur always wore wing tips…lace up and slip-on. I continued licking the bottom of Arthur's foot, my dick getting hard in my pants. I toyed with the gold material around Arthur's toes, squeezing his toes at the same time, loving the feel of them… anticipating sucking on them.

"Yeahhh feels great Brad ol' boy…" Arthur said and reached down and hiked his pants up a little at the knees, revealing more oh his black knee length socks.

I moved my tongue from the bottom of his foot and licked along the side of it, moving upward.

"Yeah Brad, that's right, lick my socks, suck the sweat out of them for me." Arthur said. "So many times I've wanted my wife to do this for me but I guess only we men understand these things huh?"

"Yes Sir…" I said breathlessly.

I was shocked at myself when I kissed the calf of Arthur's sock.

"Okay Brad, get back down there and work on my foot, my toes, my heel, and later for the rest of my socks."

Seconds later I was kneeling in front of Arthur's feet as he lay on the couch. He had his socked toes in my mouth and was making me drool on the gold toe material and suck it off over and over. I held his foot in my hands, squeezing it gently as I sucked his toes…loving it…not getting enough of the taste. Then, I wrapped my mouth around more of his foot and swirled my tongue over it as best I could. When Arthur slowly pulled his foot from my mouth I kissed it all over. Holding his foot in my hands I looked up at him.

"Arthur, I still don't understand…" I whispered and kissed his toes.

"It's simple Brad." Arthur said as I hastily sucked his toes back into my mouth. "You have a foot fetish and I have a fetish for having my feet licked, sucked, kissed, whatever…"

"Simple?" I asked him, caressing his calf, moving my hands up his long sock. "We're married men Arthur…"

"Our wives don't have to know about this Brad." Arthur said. "It's our secret…"

I swirled the tip of my tongue around his ankle and over his heel. Arthur moaned contentedly and I could see the hard on in his suit pants.

"I need some beer." I said, reaching for my beer from the coffee table.

As I was putting the bottle to my lips Arthur placed his toes by my lips, just over the bottle.

"Why not drink your beer from my sock Brad ol' boy?" he suggested.

I gave Arthur's foot a hard kiss and then slowly and carefully poured beer over his foot, soaking his sock with it. Then, another idea came to me. I quickly pulled a hassock in front of the couch so Arthur could lay his feet out for me together. He turned on the couch, placed his feet on the hassock, and hiked his suit pants all the way up to his knees, revealing all of his socks for me.

"Oh yeah…" I said grabbing both his feet with my hands.

I again began sucking his left foot, loving the taste of beer, sweat, and saliva on his sock.

"Ohhh yeahhh Brad…imagine what you'll be having for lunch from now on…" Arthur said jokingly. My wife will always wonder how my socks stay so clean. She hates handling them when I take them off at the end of the day."

Actually, I was jealous of his wife in that respect. I would love to know how Arthur's socks smell at the end of the day…not to mention that I was thinking about rolling them onto his feet for him every morning.

Gads, I was falling in love with my CO-worker's socks and feet. I again sucked his toes into my mouth, sucking on the gold material, a feeling of ecstasy consuming me.

"You sure do love those toes of mine Brad..." Arthur said with a grin on his face.

I proceeded to kiss his feet all over, running my tongue over his arches, slightly tickling him. I ran my hands over the nylon material of his socks from his ankles to his knees and back down again, kissing his feet over and over and over. I then tongued the long ribs of his socks, kissing them as I went along. Done with that I placed the tips of my fingers under the tops of Arthur's socks and folded them down, kissing the inside of his socks now.

"Okay Brad, you're doing just what I had in mind next." Arthur said to me. "Roll those stinky socks of mine off me slowly, inside out. I have a real treat for you now. You're going to enjoy my feet...bare."

I hadn't really thought about that. It was actually Arthur's socked feet that were driving me crazy. But I did as he said anyway, slowly rolling those socks of his off him. When his socks were off his feet Arthur placed his bare feet on the rugged floor, spreading his legs around the hassock. I had his socks in my hands, inside out.

"Okay Brad, here's what I want you to do..." Arthur said to me. "Roll one of my socks into a tight ball, as tight as possible."

"Yes Sir..." I whispered and put one of Arthur's socks down on the hassock.

With trembling fingers I slowly rolled the other sock into a ball. Gads, I was holding Arthur's sock in my hands. Why was that driving me crazy??? When the sock was rolled good and tight I held it up for Arthur to see.

"Good." he said. "Now, open your mouth wide, and cram that stinker in as far as possible..."

I did as Arthur said, cramming his rolled up sock into my open mouth, the rancid taste of his feet sweat invading my taste buds.

"Mmmmfff..." I said when the sock was in, filling my mouth.

"Good boy." Arthur said. "You're an excellent foot slave if ever there was one. "Now, take my other sock and tie it over the one that's in your mouth...tight."

Once again I did as I was told. I was now gagged with Arthur's socks, chewing heartily on the one in my mouth. Arthur placed his bare feet back up on the hassock.

"Lastly Brad, I want you to take off your shirt and tie." Arthur said to me.

Moments later I was sitting in front of Arthur bare chested. He told me to lean back with my hands flat on the floor behind me. I again did as I was told. Arthur moved his feet against my big, pink, fleshy nipples and grasped them...with his toes.

"Mmmm..." I crooned as Arthur pulled on my nipples with his toes.

"Yeah, feels good huh Brad ol' boy?" Arthur asked me with a smirk on his face. "Like having my feet on your nips eh?"

I nodded that I did and he grasped my nipples again with his toes, pulled on them, and then let them go. He repeated this over and over again a few times till my nipples were erect, like my dick was in my pants.

Then, Arthur stopped teasing my nipples with his toes and propped his bare feet up on the hassock. That was my cue. I pressed my nose against the bottom of his bare feet and inhaled deeply. His feet really stunk and I guess it showed in my eyes because Arthur laughed at my expression.

"Okay Brad ol' boy, sniff at those feet of mine and my toes." Arthur instructed me as I did just that. "Then you can my socks out of your mouth and tongue my bare feet all over."

I sniffed his smelly feet all over. When he separated his toes I jammed my nose between them, taking in the scent of his toe jam.

"Mmmmfff..." I crooned, running my nose over the tops of his feet.

"Heh heh...yeah, that's it Brad ol' boy, sniff my feet." Arthur said and ruffled my blond hair.

A few minutes later Arthur said I could take his socks out of my mouth if I wanted to. I really didn't want to but I did as he said anyway, slowly untying the one that was tied over my mouth. I placed Arthur's socks on the hassock next to his feet and went to work on his smelly bare feet, beginning the way I did when he had his socks on...with the bottoms of them.

"Oh yeah Brad, lick my feet, suck the sweat out of them." Arthur said contentedly, leaning back on the couch. "They sweat so much..."

That much was for sure because with each lick I was being treated to a mouthful of rancid foot sweat. Holding Arthur's feet in my hands I began sucking each of his toes, one at a time. As I sucked his toes I pressed the tips of my fingers against Arthur's moist feet.

"Yeahhh feels great Brad." Arthur said. "And when you're done maybe I'll let you roll those socks of mine back onto my feet and you can start all over again licking them."

"Yes Sir..." I said eagerly.

After I had sucked each of Arthur's toes a few times each I ran my tongue over the tops of his feet, drooling over them and sucking up my saliva.

"Excellent foot slave you are." Arthur said happily. "Now, get ready to put those socks back onto my feet."

Moments later I was gingerly rolling one of Arthur's socks back onto his foot. I did the same with the other one, rolling them both up to his knees. Brad wiggled his toes under his socks as I wrapped my fingers around his feet and began licking his socks all over again.

"Can't get enough of my socks huh Brad ol' boy?" Arthur asked me.

"No Sir, I can't get enough..." I replied.

About a half-hour later Arthur told me to stop licking his socked feet, explaining that he had come up with another idea.

"How bad do your feet sweat?" he asked me.

"Probably worse than yours." I said, looking at him and kissed his socked toes.

Arthur smiled and took his tie off. Moments later we were standing side by side, both of us stripped to our white briefs and black socks. (My black socks were also nylon but calf length.) We were both hard as a rock in our briefs and oozing pre-cum. Neither of us mentioned that fact though as Arthur held me by my arm, running a hand over one of my erect nipples.

"Feeling good?" he asked me.

"Yeah, feeling great…" I replied.

"Okay then, here's my idea…" Arthur said and squeezed one of my nipples, giving it a twist. "I want you to take my socks off my feet…again…and then take your socks off your feet and put them on my feet. Then, I want you to service your socks while I'm wearing them."

"And I thought you were going to lick my feet…" I said with a smile.

"No way Brad ol' foot slave of mine." Arthur replied and squeezed my nipple again. "You're the foot boy in this situation. Now, let's get busy…"

Arthur let go of my arm and sat back down on the hassock, propping his feet up on it. I balanced myself on one foot and pulled off my left sock. Then, I did the same with the right one. My socks in hand I knelt back down at Arthur's feet. I gave each of Arthur's feet a quick lick each and then rolled his socks off them…slowly, so slowly, loving the feel of Arthur's socks in my hands. Moments later Arthur was wearing my day old socks and I was licking and sucking on them like crazy. The combination of his foot sweat mixed with my scent was somehow powerful and erotic at the same time.

"Oh yeah, you really are one hell of a foot slave Brad." Arthur said to me as I slurped away at my socks on his feet.

My socks on Arthur's feet…how great that sounded to me. I wrapped my fingers around the sides of his feet and slurped on his socked toes, drooling over them, and sucking up my saliva. I then moved my tongue over the tops of Arthur's feet, inhaling the scent of my smelly socks.

"Man oh man Brad, this shit has made me so horny…" Arthur said breathlessly. "Watching you lick my feet has sent me into a frenzy…"

"I couldn't have said it better myself…" I said, looking up at Arthur while holding his feet in my hands.

As I resumed licking Arthur's feet he reached into his briefs and pulled out his hard dick along with his balls.

"Oh yeahhh lick my feet Brad ol' boy…" Arthur said and began stroking his hard dick.

Pre cum oozed out of the piss slit of Arthur's dick. I moved my tongue over Arthur's socked heels, nipping at them at the same time.

"Ohhrrr yeahhh, bite on my heels Brad…" Arthur panted.

I could see he was taking his time in cumming, stroking his crank slowly, ceremoniously. I kissed Arthur's feet all over again, starting at his toes, moving to the fronts of them, and then down the bottoms. I licked and sucked the bottoms of his feet, loving the hot mixture of scents they were giving off.

"Oh shit Brad, oh shit…" Arthur crooned in ecstasy. "I'm going to cum Brad…now…Ohhhh yeah yeahh."

Arthur came in gushes, shooting rope after rope of creamy cum into his hand as he stroked himself. Some of it landed on his chest and dripped down toward his stomach. I licked his feet harder as he shot his load. When he was done he told me to stop licking his feet…temporarily. I watched as he moved his right foot toward himself and smeared his gobs of cum all over my sock that was on it.

"Oh yeahhh Brad ol' boy…" Arthur said with a big smile. "Now there's a real treat for you to lap up…"

He placed his cum smeared-socked foot back on the hassock in front of me and I looked up at him, unsure if I wanted this. I mean, I wasn't a faggot after all.

"Go for it Brad ol' boy…" Arthur insisted. "Lick up my goop…"

Slowly, I moved my face close to his foot and sniffed it. The first whiff of his cum on my sock drove me crazy and I eagerly opened my mouth, closing my lips around his toes, sucking up the cum that was all over them.

"That's it Brad ol' boy, eat it up, eat it all up…" Arthur said with a smile. "Feels great your mouth and tongue all over my feet…"

A while later I was done licking the cum off Arthur's socked foot. I looked it over, checking to see if I had missed any spots. I hadn't. Damn, I was a great foot slave. And then, without a word I pulled my hard dick out of my briefs, stood over Arthur's socked feet, and began stroking myself.

"Oh yeahhh, goin' to soak those socks with my cum now…" I said breathlessly. "Show *you* a real treat."

"Heh heh…" Arthur chuckled. "You fucking pervert…"

Arthur leaned back on the couch as I stroked myself, his hands crossed behind his head. Droplets of pre cum seeped out of my piss slit and slid down the fronts of Arthur's socks. I couldn't wait to start licking my cum off those socks on his feet.

"Fuckin' hot feet you got there Arthur my man…" I said breathlessly. "Fuckin' goin' to shoot my cream all over them!!"

"Yeah go for it you sleazy foot slave…" Arthur said to me.

Instead of this scene between my CO-worker and me calming down it was intensifying with each moment. But then, my thoughts were cut off for the moment as I felt myself about to cum.

"Oh yeahhh Arthur oh fuckin' A man!!" I panted and shot my creamy load of goop all over Arthur's socked feet.

My jizz dripped all over his socked toes, down the fronts of his feet, and all over the bottoms of them.

"Ohhhhrr yeahhhh…" I roared.

"Fuckin' big load Brad ol' boy…" Arthur commented.

When I was done I quickly settled back on my knees in front of Arthur, stuck out my tongue, and began at the bottoms of his feet, licking and sucking my cum off the socks he was wearing.

"Mmmm..." I crooned heartily, slurping away at Arthur's feet.

When I was done I rolled my socks off Arthur's feet, put his knee length black socks back on his feet, and rolled my socks back onto my feet up to my calves. As we packed our dicks back into our briefs we looked at each other and smiled.

"I better get dressed and be on my way." Arthur said, standing up and facing me.

"Want another beer before you go?" I asked him.

"Sure." he replied and gave one of my nipples a squeeze.

A few minutes later Arthur and I were sitting on the couch, sipping beers. Arthur was sitting stretched out on the couch, his socked feet in my lap. As we sipped our beers I toyed with his socks, tugging on the gold material over his toes.

"Nobody would believe this..." I said slowly.

"They don't have to." Arthur said to me. "It's our secret...our secret pleasure..."

I put my beer down on the coffee table in front of us and lifted one of Arthur's feet by his ankle and leg up to my lips. I ran my tongue over his socked toes and gave them a few sucks. Holding Arthur's foot up I caressed his calf and his leg, loving the feel of his nylon sock against his skin.

"Gads, I can't get enough..." I said breathlessly and kissed Arthur's foot. "Your feet are so fucking hot Arthur..."

Arthur smiled triumphantly and sipped his beer.

After we had finished our beers Arthur got dressed to leave.

"Well, I guess I'll see you tomorrow at work..." Arthur said as he pulled on his suit jacket.

"Yeah..." I replied, standing there in my socks and briefs. "Tomorrow..."

"Can't wait to get that mouth of yours all over my feet again eh Brad ol' boy?" Arthur asked me, giving one of my nipples a squeeze.

"Arthur, you can stay if you want too..." I said breathlessly.

"I would love to Brad, but if I did we wouldn't get any sleep at all..." Arthur said, now toying with both of my nipples.

"Yeah...we'd be up all night..." I said.

"Sure would, and then we'd never be able to get to work in the morning..." he went on, twisting my nipples.

"True." I said, smiling. "We would have to take a personal day."

"And if we did that you would probably want to spend all morning licking and sucking my socked feet." Arthur said. "Probably I would make you pour coffee all over my socked feet and slurp it up."

We looked at each other and smiled. Arthur gave my nipples a final twist and then let go of them.

"Tell me Brad, how many pairs of nylon dress socks do you have in your sock drawer?" Arthur asked me.

"Enough so we can play all fucking day tomorrow Arthur." I replied breathlessly. "Get that suit off…"

A few minutes later Arthur and I were in the bedroom. He was stretched out on the bed wearing just his socks and briefs. I was squatting on the floor at the foot of the bed…licking Arthur's feet.

(2)

The Abusive Wager

(From the book: *The Abusive Wager*)

    The character of Daniel in this story is a real person, another that I met while riding the subway to work. He affected me very differently than the guy named Dominick who was the model for the main character of my story "The Taming of Dominick." Dominick was a construction worker who wore jeans, work boots, sweat shirts, tee shirts, flannel shirts and dungaree jackets for work while Daniel looked like a guy who had just stepped out of the pages of GQ magazine in his suits; ties dress shoes, dress socks, and fashionable overcoats.

    Admittedly what Dominick and Daniel have in common in the two stories I wrote where I used them as the models for the lead characters is that they both fall victim to an abusive wager.

    While the gentleman who inspired the character of Daniel in this story is a real person and we were train buddies, most of what happens in this story is fiction. The conversations on the train that I relate in the story are pretty much non-fiction, but I honestly don't remember if we had a conversation where Daniel pulling his dress socks up after he sits down on the train actually took place. At this point it was rather long ago, seeing as when we discuss what was in the news the Michael Jackson molestation trial is mentioned.

    Daniel is the sort of guy who has style, real style. It shows not just in how he dresses, which I describe in vivid detail in this story, but also in the way he carries himself. He has an image. An image and a good look can get a person into the room, but something has to keep them in the room. I believe it's a sense of individuality that I'm talking about here, and Daniel has that.

Daniel doesn't go out of his way to make statements with the way he dresses; it's his demeanor that simply says it all. I loved when he would wear designer dress boots with his suits and ties and the way his suit trousers seemed to run up and stick into the tops of his boots as he walked. What attracted me to him I think was his original sense of style. He fit perfectly as the character for this story.

When I see someone that I think would make a good model for a story I act out of instinct, just like an animal I suppose. Even if I don't get to speak to the person I will make an imprint of them in my memory and get the story started as soon as possible. I don't want to lose that spark. Daniel was kind enough to be my friend for a short time... and this story is the result of that.

While Daniel's image is of the conservative my image is a natural extension of what I write about, the inner me though I have to say. I am not deliberately sexual; it just sort of seems to run in that direction when I write.

It's evident in the story that Daniel is straight, yet because like another of my characters in another book I wrote, he is a man of his word, which is why he does not resist my character's advances in the story.

I mentioned some old superstitions and beliefs in the story. As for the one about squeezing a man's nipples bringing him and the person squeezing the nipples luck, well, to be honest I made that one up simply for the story, as is said on the internet, LOL (Laughing Out Loud.).

———————

"OOOOHHHHHHHHH!!!" my new buddy Daniel moaned, deeply and throatily as I again squeezed his very jutted up nipples, followed by giving them yet another good twist each just for good measure (and for good luck as well.) "OHHHHHHHHHH FUCK MAN!!!"

"Feeling good buddy?" I whispered in his ear, my lips grazing his earlobe as I spoke, sounding as sadistic and menacing as hell as I leaned up against him from behind, my arms wrapped lovingly and crossed around his upper, fairly muscular torso, my thumbs and first two fingers of my hands gripping his gorgeous, bulbous and plumped pink nipples.

The way I was working Daniel's nipples was causing the sexy nubs to jut up more and more with each passing second, getting them harder and harder as I twisted and squeezed the life out of them...or perhaps I had that in reverse, perhaps I was squeezing life *into* those oversized nipples of his... It was amazing really, how receptive the handsome guy's nipples really were! When we had gotten started on this little voyage his nubs had been fleshy and all squishy, but the moment I had begun squeezing and teasing them they came to erect and rigid life. And not only was it his nipples that were jutted up. He had a real plumped up chub tenting his sexy (tighty whiteys) white boxer briefs. It looked to me like I had chosen well for my game where Daniel was concerned. Just as I had hoped the handsome stud had very sensitive and *very* responsive nipples.

"Fuck, fuck, *double fuck,*" Daniel said breathlessly in his half Asian half New York sounding accent. "When you invited me here for a game I didn't think for a second that it would be *my tits* that would become the main event man…"

"Welcome to my world," I laughed meanly and twisted Daniel's nipples hard.

"AAAAAWWWHHHH GOD!!! Double fucks again!!" Daniel blurted and for a moment arched his upper body real sexily, jutting his bulging cock forward, fucking the air, and then settling back as I again twisted and tweaked his nipples. "AAWWWWWHHHHH!!!"

"I find that a pair of nipples like these makes for a great game buddy boy!" I chuckled meanly. "And like I said earlier, squeezing a good pair of tits and working them over this way is really good luck."

"Yeah, good luck, *sure, good fucking fucked up fucking luck,* but for whom?" Daniel squeaked. "God man, my poor tits…"

"For both of us," I laughed. "Firstly, for you, because you're getting all horned up for free and secondly, for me, 'cause I just love playing with and torturing a meaty pair of nubby nipples!"

"OOOHHHHHHHHH fucking fucks Fucker, nubby nipples, what a hell of a fucking way to refer to my goddamned tits!" Daniel chirped throatily as he stood in front of me, totally helpless (yet inwardly loving the trip I had taken him on) with his hands roped tight behind him. "God almighty and all the angels in heaven, you're sending chills through me buddy… I got friggin' goose bumps all the fuck over me!"

"Yeah, I can sure as hell see that, I never saw a guy with such bubbled up goose flesh before," I guffawed and squeezed his nipples tighter, getting a few good loud moans and groans out of him. "And those friggin' goose bumps just seem to be multiplying with each passing second bud…"

"I'm feeling crazy here Chris," Daniel panted.

Dressed in just his white (tighty whiteys) boxer briefs style underpants and calf length nylon navy blue dress socks the handsome Asian guy made a real exotic and pretty picture let me tell you… Getting his hands roped behind him had been a bit of a chore but when I reminded him of the rules of the game that he had agreed to he gave in. (I'll tell you more about that very soon I promise.) Breathing heavily now I tweaked the very tips of Daniel's meaty nipples a few times (that really got him dancing in his socks for me), then tugged at them, then grabbed the beef of them again, and continued tugging on them, enjoying the nubby hardness of them between the rough skin of my fingertips. Daniel's nipples were like magic. I would squeeze the hard nubs down, squishing them between my fingers and then instantly they were hard again, ready for more tweaking and squeezing. I could actually do this all night if I wanted to I thought.

16

A Boner Book

"AAAAARRRRHHHH man, th-this is too much now buddy, I'm all worked up and steaming in my damned boxer briefs!! Fuck, a little more and you'll see my crotch smoking!" Daniel grunted, leaning his head back a bit. "FUCKING *totally fuck!!!* Never knew that my damned tits were so fucking sensitive!! *And I'm a guy!!* Fucking fuck, I thought that just women had sensitive tits!! RRRRRRRHHHHHHHHHH!!!"

"Looks like we learn something new every day huh?" I teased him and rubbed savagely at the sides of his nipples in a very fast and very circular motion. "And if your crotch were to start smoking I'm sure that would be a sight and a half to see…"

"AAAYYYYYY, yeah, and what an education I'm getting where my tits are concerned," Daniel reeled.

He pulled himself to his socked toes and danced real stupidly and sexily for me as I pointed his nipple tips upwards at the ceiling, stretching them far for him, squeezing the tips of them real hard as I did so, him looking down and seeing the fleshy and juicy skin of his nubs being elongated with each squeeze and tug I gave them.

"L-looks like you're planning on tearing my tits from my chest buddy," Daniel panted.

"Nah, I wouldn't do anything that extreme," I laughed. "You'd be surprised though just how much these nubs of yours can handle."

"I-I guess I'm finding that out now huh bud?" he asked me, gasping as he spoke. "L-like you just said you learn something new every day…GODS!!!"

"You should have your girlfriend do this for you once in a while buddy," I laughed and whirled his nipples with my fingers. "You really do seem to be enjoying it. I mean, like you just said, you're steaming in your boxer briefs!"

"OOOOOOOOOOO man, fucking totally fucking totally fuck!!!" Daniel cried out, swearing in that unique style of his, sounding like he was in a state of total disbelief as I whirled and twirled his nipples like they were a windmill. "Like that old song says, "What a feeling!!!"

"Yeah, what a feeling is right," I chuckled and squeezed his nipples harder yet, causing my new friend to clench his teeth. "Man, I would bet money that if I keep this up long enough these leathery feeling man tits of yours would spurt milk!"

"What a twisted fucking thought," Daniel grunted and lowered himself to his feet as I twisted his nipples like they were two old fashioned television knobs. "Fuck man, if my tits squirted milk we could both make good money, me because they're *my* goddamned tits and you for discovering that my goddamned tits had milk in 'em! D-did you just call them man tits buddy?"

"Yeah, a guy's nipples are his man tits, to call them just tits would imply woman's tits," I said right into his ear, the hardness in my pants caressing the back of Daniel's white boxer briefs as I teased and tormented him in a totally erotic fashion. "But I will say that there are some guys out there who would indeed call these jutted up nubbies of yours womanly, very womanly man tits indeed! Does it bother you that it's a guy doing this to you buddy boy?"

"I-I highly doubt that a woman would want to do this to my tits, sorry, *my man tits,* I doubt that a woman would want to do to my man tits what you're doing to them right now man," Daniel spouted breathlessly. "Al-although you never know right man? I mean, I got to tell you, I've dated some freaky women! M-maybe the next woman I date, I'll do this to her tits, yeah!! She'll fucking love it! Gods' man, *I need to cum*!! All this work you've been doing on my goddamned tits has really got me all worked up in my briefs! How about untying my hands and letting me use your facilities huh buddy?"

"Not for a while Daniel," I chuckled. "I want to see just how long I can keep you balanced but teetering on the edge..."

"OH FUCKER!!!" Daniel cried out as I again yanked his meaty nipples forward, stretching them out far. "Well man, I got to tell you, you really know how to fucking balance another dude. Y-you got me balanced and teetering real perilously here bud, but I feel like I'm about to fall off the edge! I feel as though I can fucking fill my damned boxer briefs to overflowing with my sexy mess right about now!"

"Now *that* would be something to see," I laughed, let go of his nipples and stepped in front of my very tortured, much worked up buddy. "If you could cum without touching your cock that truly would be a money maker I would think buddy! And not to mention how the girls would love using these nubs of yours as the control knobs for your cock, ha!"

Looking down I saw that Daniel's cock was truly hard and plumped up in his boxer briefs. He was gyrating real sexy in front of me, his nipples jutted up and real sore looking, but that was okay by me, seeing as those nubs of his had a lot more to endure before this day was out. His white boxer briefs showed a few stains where he had tricked and seeped some pre cum.

"Yeah, that's it Daniel, keep dancing for me," I teased him meanly as he hunched his upper body slightly forward. "Fuck man, I'm not even touching your man tits at the moment and you're dancing as if I was."

"FUCKER man, holy fucking fuck, look at me here, dancing for you to no music playing, fucking fuck fucker, so glad I'm so entertaining to you, but what a game this turned out to be huh?" Daniel asked me, sniveling as he spoke, glancing over at the couch where his discarded suit, tie and shoes were all strewn. "Wh-what do you suppose we should call this game man? Fuck, every game needs a name after all..."

Smiling fiendishly I said, "Let's call it Daniel's Man Tits" and then I reached forward and grabbed the guy's nipples from the front this time.

"OOOOOOOOOO FUCK, g-got my man tits in your clutches again buddy!!" the handsomer than handsome Asian guy ranted. "Fucker you are man, you got me feeling all sensitive and real fucking sexy here in my damned boxer briefs and dressy socks!"

Again he pulled himself to his socked toes as I played his nipples as if they were a musical instrument of some kind.

"C'mon bud, let's see you walk on your toes and play "Daniel's Man Tits" at the same time," I laughed, sounding campy and cruel as I tugged real hard at his nipples, yanking him forward with them. "It's kind of like walking and chewing gum at the same time wouldn't you say?"

"OHHHHHHHHH…wh-what a fucked up way to get a game named after me," Daniel said and plodded along slowly up on his toes. "N-now you really have me balanced real perilously buddy…"

"Just don't fall off the edge Daniel," I chuckled meanly and yanked harder yet on his man tits, forcing him along.

Holding his nipples extremely tight I pulled him forward a bit further and then using them something akin to a leash I turned him in a circular motion, causing him to face in the opposite direction of the room we were in, specifically my living room.

"AAAYYYYYYRRRR easy man, take it easy huh?" Daniel cried. "Th-that's starting to hurt now…"

"And that's the key word here Daniel boy, *started,* we are just getting started here," I said as he now faced the opposite direction of my spacious living room.

"J-just getting started?" Daniel croaked. "Y-you have got to joking man! We, we, OHHHHRRRRRRR fucking triple fuck; but we've been at this for almost an hour now!"

"Yeah, and that's just the warm-up buddy," I said and this time pointed his nipples downward and rubbed the sides of them vigorously.

"OOOOOOOO man, if, *if* my damned man tits could talk they would ask what the fuck has gotten into me and what the fucking fuck they did to deserve this crazy treatment," Daniel sputtered, sweating a bit now, his goose bumped riddled, smooth fairly muscular body glistening real nice with a sheen of funky smelling man sweat.

"If your man tits could talk *then* we would really make some good money," I said and we both laughed.

I was glad that Daniel was being a good buddy about all this and taking all that I was dishing out on his nipples. I just hoped that he continued in that vain, seeing as I had lots more planned where the handsome Asian stud was concerned. Working his nipples was just the beginning of what I intended to be a long and grueling day for him. Working a handsome guy over in an erotic fashion is one of the things I love most. But if this got to a point where he demanded that I untie his hands and leave his nipples the fuck alone I would of course have to abide by his wishes. All of this was just in good sleazy fun after all and the guy was a buddy, granted, he was a new buddy, but all the same he was a great guy and I didn't want to lose his newly found friendship. And not to mention how I didn't want this to be the first and only time that I got to work him over in this very erotic fashion…

"C-c'mon man, I gotta cum, *at least give me that much buddy,*" Daniel pleaded as I pointed his nipples forward again and tweaked the life out of (into?) them. "Un-untie my hands and let me at my raging tube steak buddy. I mean, just look at that fucking goddamned tent in my sexy boxer briefs man! You gotta let me shoot a load man! I swear, when I'm done cooking my meat I'll let you re-tie my hands again, then you can play "Daniel's Man Tits" some more, *I fucking promise,* I just really, *really* gotta cum! I've never felt so worked up before in all my thirty something years! FUCK, I gotta cum so bad it hurts! Getting a poor fucking guy all worked up the way you have me now and then not letting him have a cum is really crappy bud! So please, just one cum huh?"

The way he was describing his feelings of lust was moving me like I cannot tell you. His pleading and the way he had concluded his tirade I was thinking that he thought he had convinced me to untie his hands…

"Nah, *nah,* not yet Daniel," I said and the look of misery that came over his face was totally sexy and actually heartbreaking in a way.

"OHHHHHHH man, what a shitty ass way to treat a guy you call a buddy, that's all I gotta say," Daniel huffed, swallowed real hard and endured the erotic torture as I squeezed the sides of his nipples, the tips of them jutting up real hardcore at that point.

"Man, look at this shit, your man tits are pulsing," I commented, grinning at the same time.

"Yeah? That is pretty amazing I will admit, seeing as those nubbies of mine never pulsed before! But seeing as they are pulsing let me tell you so is my cock man," Daniel pleaded. "Fucking fuck, wish I had some sweet pussy to bury my big hard guy into at least."

Then, to Daniel's surprise I again let go of his nipples, only this time I did not grab them again (at least not yet) this time I walked away from him, turned a corner in my apartment and proceeded into my kitchen.

"H-hey, what are you doing?" Daniel called out. "*Where the hell are you going?*"

Without thinking Daniel followed me into the kitchen, padding real swiftly on his socked feet…

"C'mon man, you can't just play a guy's man tits that way and then leave him all worked up and scorching in his under shorts," Daniel said loudly as he headed toward my kitchen.

He entered the kitchen and as he did so I very quickly stepped in front of him and before he knew what had happened I snapped a pair of sharp teethed tit clamps onto his jutted up nipples, clamping them tightly at the sides.

"AYYYYYYYYYY ohhhhhhh h-holy fucking fucks, holy fucking shit," Daniel grunted, looking down in disbelief at his now clamped nipples, his jaw dropping in shock.

"Double and triple fuck at that Daniel?" I asked him teasingly. "Always adding up and counting your fucking fucks huh buddy?"

"Quadrupled fucking fucks is more like it man!!" the poor Asian guy moaned and slammed his back up against a wall in my kitchen. "OOOOOOOO GODS, y-you got my goddamned man tits in a pair of tit clamps! This ain't sweet buddy, *not sweet at all!"*

He clenched his teeth, squeezed his eyes shut a bit and did his best to endure the erotic agony... I was glad that having his hands tied behind him had been a prerequisite for the game of "Daniel's Man Tits" that I had invented.

"Pl-please man, how much more of "Daniel's Man Tits" are we going to play here?" he asked me, sounding desperate by then.

"Well, seeing as we both left our offices after lunch today and took the rest of the day off I would say we can play till our hearts are content," I laughed and grabbed the thin chain that was attached to the tit clamps. "Maybe after the game is over I'll order some dinner and beer sent in and we can talk about what a great time we had here today, but for the moment I say, onward with the game."

"Yeah, a real great fucking time, fucking fucks man!" Daniel said sarcastically. "God, the fucking pressure on my man tits is awful bud..."

I gave the chain attached to the tit clamps a few twists around my fingers and yanked it gently forward. Daniel's nipples burned and he screeched through his clenched teeth.

"F-F-FUCKER, what a way to dress up a poor sap's man tits," Daniel cried.

"And the clamps are just the first item of attire that will adorn those luscious nips of yours buddy," I chortled meanly and pulled a bit more on the chain.

"OOOOOOOO fuck man, what the hell am I in for here?" Daniel garbled miserably and pressed his back against the wall, looking as though he wanted to somehow escape from me through that wall.

I looked down at his boxer briefs and saw that he had really dribbled a goodly amount of pre cum at that point. At least my new buddy was enjoying all this in a masochistic sort of way...

Then, I let go of the chain attached to the tit clamps, reached into my pocket and brought out a length of rope, squatted in front of Daniel and proceeded to tie his socked feet together in a crisscross type of fashion.

"H-hey, what are you doing now man?" Daniel asked breathlessly. "GOD almighty, but you really have put the hurt on my poor man tits now bud!!"

"What does it look like I'm doing Daniel?" I asked him and snapped the elastic in his socks against his calves after I was done tying his feet.

"Fucking fucks, it looks like you tied up my goddamned feet! What's the point of all this man?" Daniel squawked as I stood up in front of him, grabbed the chain attached to the tit clamps and gave it a fast tug, sending searing and burning sensations through Daniel's very being.

"AAAYYYYYYYY, SHHHIITTTT!!!" the handsome Asian guy reeled.

I let go of the chain and opened a drawer in my utensil cabinet. I took out four very small egg shaped weights, each of them hooked onto a thin metal chain.

"OH MAN, OH NO," Daniel said after swallowing another big gulp. "Oh come on, I really fucking hope you're not going to do what I think you're going to do, and FUCKING FUCKS FUCKER!"

"These weights weigh about a quarter of a pound each buddy," I said, stepping in front of Daniel and holding up the egg shaped weights. "I'm going to hang them one by one on that chain on your tit clamps."

Poor Daniel pursed his lips together, heaved himself up to his toes and sheer agony showed on his handsome face.

"I gotta cum," he squeaked. "Please man, I'm fucking begging you now, at least give me one goddamned fucking fucked cum…"

Chuckling meanly I responded to Daniel's request by hanging the first of the four metal egg shaped weights on the chain on his tit clamps, dangling it dead center.

"OOOHHHHHRRRR," Daniel panted and heaved himself up higher on his socked toes, pressing his back against the wall, his chest jutted out real nice and invitingly.

"Ready for the second one buddy?" I asked him.

He simply nodded his head and involuntarily thrust his crotch forward; fucking the air it seemed…

I hung the second weight on the left-most end of the chain on his tit clamps.

"OH MAN, oh fuck, oh fucking totally fucks," Daniel seethed, his lips trembling and spittle flying from the sides of his mouth.

The weight in the center of his tit clamp chain pulled down on both of his nipples simultaneously while the one on the left side added agony to his left nipple.

"Now for the right side buddy," I said gleefully, holding up the third weight, swinging it on its chain, taunting the guy even before I set it on the tit clamp chain.

"OOOOOHHHHHH!!!" Daniel cried and now the weights combined were really yanking the poor Wall Street guy's nipples in all directions.

I held up the fourth and final egg shaped weight and set it dangling alongside the other weight that was hanging in the center of Daniel's tit clamp chain.

"There we go, look at that, just look at that shit man, you've got a pound's worth of weights on you along with the tit clamps and their chain," I said, sounding like a proud parent.

"OHHHHHH yeah, fucking bully for me huh?" Daniel asked and un-pursed his lips clenched his pearly white teeth and gyrated again real sexily for me on his socked toes. "FUCKING FUCKS, what an experience, *what a day I'm having!!*"

As the tit clamps hugged and squeezed and bit down on the sides of Daniel's beefy nubbins I marveled at the sight of his nipple tips as they protruded large and real pointy through the front section of the clamps. Smiling meanly I took full advantage of that by pressing the pads of my thumbs against the very tips of the guy's nipples.

"AAAHHHHHHHHH," Daniel heaved still with his teeth clenched. "I just don't get it man, torturing a guy's nipples are real fucked up if you ask me…"

"Totally fucking fucked up huh Daniel?" I asked him and we both laughed as I teased him about the way he swore. "But I beg to disagree, seeing as I think that working a guy's nipples over is great fun. I mean, come on buddy, we're having a great fucking time here today!"

I laughed and yanked the weighted chain on Daniel's nipples slightly forward, getting another good squeal of erotic agony out of him…

"FUCK man, fucking fucks, untie me and let me have one goddamned cum," the young executive pleaded yet again as he pressed himself up against the wall on his tied up socked feet, still balanced up on his toes.

"Nah, like I said, I think you're enjoying this too much Daniel," I replied. "Letting you cum would only put an end to the fun don't you think?"

"Maybe not," the guy croaked and as I looked him over I realized that maybe, somehow, I was falling for this newfound buddy of mine.

Holding the weighted tit clamp chain in my hand I forced the guy to turn himself around on his crisscross tied up socked feet till he was facing the wall, his back to me, giving me a real nice view of his coconut shaped ass globes in his tight sweaty boxer briefs. Moving on his tied up feet was no easy chore for the poor guy but being on his toes helped a bit… And being that I had chosen to tie his feet in a crisscross fashion did allow him some mobility. He was meanly hobbled but he could walk slowly, *very slowly* if I wanted him to. And that seemed to be key here, if I wanted him to, I had the guy in such a way that he had to do anything that *I wanted him to.*

"Wh-what's the point of all this buddy?" Daniel murmured breathlessly, lowered himself to his feet and I sat down at the kitchen table and simply took in the glorious sight of him.

He was beyond sexy, beyond beautiful, and to think that I had met him on the train only less than a month ago at this point. Less than a month now that we had become buddies and luck had really smiled upon me in finding someone so open minded and willing to play my sadistically campy games… I propped my feet up on the table and drank him in, the sight of him, the allure of him, I breathed in the sweaty sexy scent of him, and the overwhelming beauty of him… Trust me on this, the handsome Asian Wall Street stud was not the only one who was plumped up and throbbing in his under shorts at that moment…

"I'll let you stand there and enjoy the pressure on your man tits for fifteen minutes buddy," I said to him. "Then after that we'll resume the game of "Daniel's Man Tits.""

"OOOHHHRRRRR fucking fuck," Daniel squealed and thrust the hardness in his boxer briefs toward the wall he was facing, making his succulent looking ass globes twitch real sexily. "FUCKING fifteen minutes will seem like an eternity for me buddy…"

"Well, from what I read you shouldn't keep a guy's nipples clamped for more than that time," I replied.

"FUCKING FUCKS, you mean to say that you've read up on this shit?" Daniel chirped. "There are books out there on cooking a poor slob's man tits???"

"Yeah, let those man tits of yours really cook for me buddy," I said fiendishly. "I got more plans for them coming up…"

From the side I saw how Daniel's face scrunched up, he clenched his teeth and murmured the words "AAAAYYYYY GOD," in a very high pitched tone of voice…

"Yeah, lots more on the horizon for you and your man tits Daniel boy," I laughed.

My mind wandered to how Daniel and I had first met on a train platform when headed to our jobs in Manhattan…

It was a Monday morning like any other; I had gotten to the Bay Parkway train station (in Brooklyn) exactly ten minutes before my train was scheduled to arrive. I work very early hours at my office job as an inventory supervisor so I always catch the five fifteen AM train, which gets me to my job a half hour before I have to start work. I like those ten minutes on the train station to catch up on whatever current book I am presently reading and to sip my usual cup of coffee that I get at the Dunkin' Donuts which is located just downstairs from the train station. While I stood there reading my book and sipping my coffee that Monday morning I saw the usual crowd of commuters. The guy named Paul who is a religious fanatic and always reading some literature on how to be a better catholic. The young lady who is now thin as a rail but used to weigh at least three hundred pounds, I wonder which diet she used. She could be an inspiration to so many people. The guy named Bill who always eats an apple while waiting for the train and so many of the usual nameless faces that I see every morning, but at that time of the day very few suits and ties on the train. Although my job is an office type of job my company relaxed our dress code years back so like any other day I stood waiting for the train clad in khakis, polo collared shirt and slip-on loafers with black socks, my usual. While I waited for the train I watched the blue collar construction workers standing at their usual spots on the platform while waiting for the train to arrive. The train platform is a bit territorial, with everyone standing in the same spot every morning until the train got there. On that particular Monday morning was when I first saw Daniel, although of course upon first seeing him I didn't know his name. He was clad in a navy blue suit, a white shirt, a light blue taffeta tie and lace-up well shined wingtip shoes. He ascended the stairs of the train station and walked to where I usually stand on the platform after I have finished my coffee. He strode past me and the other people on the platform with a swagger of confidence in his step. He was about five feet ten inches tall with black silky hair and beautiful Asian looking eyes. I guessed that he was Chinese and I guessed his age to be in the mid to upper thirties. I wondered what kind of a job a suit and tie guy could possibly have that he needed to be at work so early in the morning. He carried with him a bottle of Volvic brand mineral water and he sipped it vigorously while waiting for the train. The way the clear plastic bottle was beaded with perspiration I guessed that the water was ice cold, which was good, seeing as it was pretty hot and humid that summer morning, the humidity being what would cause our first chat to happen a few days later. The first few times I saw Daniel on the train we didn't speak to each other, but we did steal glances at each other. I finished my coffee, dropped the empty plastic cup in a trash receptacle and walked down to the front end of the platform, right where Daniel was standing and stood a few feet away from him. He was fiddling with the knot in his tie, sweating in the early morning heat and humidity and a few moments later the "D" train barreled into the station. I and all the other passengers boarded the train and sat down in our usual seats. (I was sure that the handsome Asian suit and tie guy was relieved to sit in the cold air conditioned train.) Like the train platform the train itself is territorial, with commuters sitting in or as near to the same seat as possible every day. As luck would have it Daniel sat down directly across from me and the first thing he did was to put his mineral water bottle down on the seat next to him for a moment while he reached down to pull his socks up. As a foot fetishist (among other fetishes) I always found that to be very erotic for some reason, to see a young handsome guy pull his thin dress socks up right after sitting down. Daniel was wearing thin navy blue dress socks that climbed as high as his calves. (Actually they could be the same socks he was wearing the day we played the new game called "Daniel's Man Tits.") And Daniel wasn't the type of guy who pulled his socks up while gripping the tops of them around his suit pants, no way; Daniel hiked up his socks by reaching under his suit pants, showing off some leg skin and then pulling up those fallen socks. I have to say that when it comes to handsome Asian guys I have always, for some reason enjoyed tickle torturing them. There is something so hot and amusing about hearing a studly Asian guy laugh his head off and sweat while his bare feet are tickled. I guessed Daniel's feet to be around the same size as mine, nine, or perhaps a tad larger, judging from the way his feet filled his shoes. When I saw that he favored thin nylon dress socks the desire to tickle torture the soft bottoms of those feet while he had his socks on (and then off of course) filled my head with gleeful visions. At that moment I didn't for a second entertain thoughts of torturing the guy's nipples, no, that came a bit later. But I would tickle him as well, and spank him, although those stories are for later. While we rode the train I concentrated on the current book I was reading. Daniel disembarked the train at Pacific Street, a pretty normal station for lots of commuters to make connections to local trains, downtown trains and the Long Island Railroad. I wondered if I would see the handsome Asian guy again or if perhaps like so many other people on the trains he was someone I would see only that once. I concentrated on my book for the remainder of my ride to my stop, which would be West Fourth Street in Manhattan.

The next day Daniel was there again, this time clad in a black suit and wearing a lightweight overcoat and carrying an umbrella, seeing as it was raining that morning. Once again he strode past me, walking with that air of confidence about himself that I had noticed the day before. When the train arrived we again sat in the same seats, him taking the seat directly across from me. Like the day before the first thing he did was to reach down and pull his socks up. That day he was wearing black nylon dress socks and like his navy blue socks they climbed as far as his calves. Through the years I have noticed this phenomenon so much that it's uncanny, how when a suit guy sits down the first thing he does is to reach down to pull his thin dress socks up. Even in meetings they do this, it's kind of a ritual I think. And even if their socks are not fallen that far most suit guys will take a moment to hike those stinkers up when they sit down. I think that the manufacturers of calf length dress socks make them with the elastic real thin on purpose, just so the poor guy wearing them will be forced to pull his socks up every time he sits down, that's my theory at least. There's some kind of sadism in that although, granted, not a hardcore one. The thought that went through my head as Daniel pulled up his black socks that day was of his navy blue socks from the day before more than likely all crumpled and bunched up, moist, and sitting in a hamper or laundry bag somewhere waiting for the laundry day, sleazy thoughts indeed. Once again while riding the train Daniel and I stole glances at each other. A few times he stretched his legs out in front of himself and crossed his sexy looking feet at the ankles. His socks were thin enough that I could see the outline of his ankles under them... It was the third time that I saw Daniel that we would begin speaking with each other and a friendship would be born...

The next day I did not see Daniel on the train, seeing as I took the train that came directly after the one that I usually take. I don't recall why I ran a tad late that morning but it really was no big deal, seeing as I still got to work on time. The next day it was miserably hot and very humid. New York City was having one of the worst summers that I could ever remember. I was standing at my usual spot in the front section of the train platform when Daniel strode up the stairs, just as the train was pulling into the station. As on the last two times I had seen the handsome Asian guy we sat directly across from each other. On this day he was wearing a pinstriped navy blue suit with a burgundy silk tie, looking real suave. As he sat down the first thing he did this time, rather than reach down to pull his socks up was to pull his shirt collar away from his neck to alleviate some of the way he was sweating under there. (Nothing is worse for a suit guy on a hot summer day than to be sweating under his shirt and tie collar.) As we looked at each other as he tugged at his shirt collar I saw my opportunity and went for it. I had to get him talking to me if I wanted to know this handsome guy.

"It must be awful to have to wear a suit and tie in this weather," I said to him as he straightened his tie.

"Yeah, the humidity makes it real uncomfortable for me, but this is a summer suit so it's not all that bad," he said and let go of his tie, grabbed his jacket lapels and waved them a bit, trying to cool off his upper body as well.

As he waved his lapels was when I was treated to the sight of his big pointy nipples pressed against his white dress shirt. I quickly stifled a gulp at the sight of those over-sized man nipples and politely told him how my company used to require us to wear a suit and tie everyday as well, but about three years ago upper management had let all us managers and supervisors vote on a relaxed dress code.

"Obviously we all voted in favor of it," I said with a smile as the handsome Asian guy settled comfortably in his seat, not having taken a moment to pull his socks up that day…

"You're lucky that your company did that," he said to me, smiling across at me as he spoke.

"Yeah, it also saves me a lot of money on dry cleaning bills," I said and we both laughed.

At that point he settled his head back and I quickly immersed myself in my book…

As we rode the train I stole glances down at the guy's feet and saw that his socks were a bit slouched down around his calves, real sexy looking navy blue nylon socks with wide ribs in them, definitely not the same navy blue socks that he'd had on the first day I had seen him. Between his very sexy looking feet and those nipples of his the way they pressed against his dress shirt had my mind awhirl with very nasty and very erotic ideas… I imagined that he had to be wearing a white tee shirt under his white dress shirt and if his nipples pressed against both those shirts and were accented in such an obvious fashion they definitely had to be of the oversized nubs that so few men are blessed with…

The next day when I walked to the front end of the train platform Daniel was there before me, which was sort of unusual seeing as I always got there first since I had first seen him. As I strode up next to him he smiled at me and said "Good morning."

"Good morning," I replied as he held his hand out.

I shook his hand and took note of the fact that his palm was kind of cold and moist. In his other hand was his ever-present bottle of Volvic mineral water.

"It's kind of humid again today," he said as he let go of my hand.

"Yeah, it sure is," I replied.

"My name is Daniel," he said to me.

I told him my name was Christopher and that it was very nice to meet him. He replied by saying that it was nice to meet me as well. When the train arrived we sat next to each other this morning rather than across from each other.

"Would you mind holding my water a moment?" he asked me and handed me his bottle of mineral water. "I need to pull my socks up."

"Sure," I said through trembling lips and watched as he pulled his black socks up to his calves, me glorying in seeing that patch of skin on his calf for that moment.

"I honestly think that someday someone is going to invent a pair of socks that don't fall down on us poor guys," Daniel chuckled, looking at me as he sipped his water after I had handed him back his bottle.

"Yeah, I totally agree," I said, not believing what we were talking about.

"I notice that you don't pull your socks up every morning like I have to," he laughed, sounding a bit self-conscious.

"I wear OTC socks; that means over the calf," I replied. "They don't seem to fall down as much as calf length socks do."

"Hmm, maybe I should invest in some of those huh?" the guy mused.

"Yeah, maybe you should," I said agreeably.

Daniel then told me that he worked for a bank on Wall Street and the reason that he had to be in so early everyday was that he was a security supervisor and that it was his job to open certain highly secured offices before the bank personnel arrived. I told him that I worked as an inventory control supervisor for a jewelry company and that as the supervisor I also had to be in early before other personnel. The next time Daniel and I saw each other on the train we talked a lot about all the celebrity gossip that was in the news lately. The Kobe Bryant trial, the upcoming Michael Jackson trial, the Martha Stewart sentencing and other very important issues. While Chatting with Daniel I didn't get to read too much but I did get to take in the sight of his beautiful brown eyes while we talked and I also told him how I had recently become a published author. He seemed genuinely impressed by that and asked if writing was something I did for relaxation or because it was challenging or both. I told him that I did it for both reasons. I followed that up by asking him what he did for relaxation and for something challenging. He smiled and said that he liked playing card games, old fashioned Chess and even up to date video games. I saw my next opportunity and did not let it get away. Since becoming a published author I have learned never to let a good opportunity pass me by... I asked Daniel if he would like to meet for a beer sometime after work and perhaps we could set up a card game date. I told him that I liked a challenging old fashioned card game of "War" with nasty but fun consequences for the loser of the game.

"Now that sounds like it could be really interesting and something that I can really sink my teeth into," Daniel said, looking at me quizzically. "I never played a card game like that before..."

We set up a night after work where we would meet for a couple of beers so we could get to know each other a bit more and then while having the beers we set up a day when we would both leave work early and head to my place for a card game of "War." Daniel seemed really confident in the fact that he was going to win the game, citing how he planned to make me, as the loser, really pay. Chuckling a bit I asked him what he planned to do to me if I lost the game. He said that he planned on putting me through a heavy-duty regiment of sit-ups, push-ups, and other drawn out sessions of backbreaking exercises. He told me how his dad had been in the army years ago and had told him all about basic training and the horrendous exercise routines that all soldiers are put through. Daniel said how he always wanted an excuse to put someone through a real hardcore exercise routine. When I asked him if he wanted to hear what I had planned for him if he lost the game the handsome Asian stud sipped his beer and said that there was no need for me to tell him because he did not plan on losing the game. Smiling sadistically he leaned back in his seat in the booth we were sitting in and spread his long arms out a bit. He had taken off his suit jacket before we sat down so when he spread his arms out those bulbous nipples of his pressed against his white dress shirt. I hungrily drank in the sight of them and took a hefty swig of my beer…

The Day of the Card Game…

"God damn it, God damn it and fucking fuck," Daniel said as he threw down his last card, having lost the game of "War" inside of only an hour and a half.

It was a Friday afternoon. We had decided on a Friday for the card game, Daniel citing how I would need the weekend to rest up after all the push-ups and sit-ups he intended to force me through once I had lost the card game. We both left our offices at lunch time that day and met at my apartment for the agreed upon game. After a light lunch we began the card game, me allowing Daniel to deal the cards. We sat across from each other at a card table that I had set up in my air conditioned living room. Daniel got comfortable by shucking off his suit jacket, loosening his tie, rolling up his sleeves, and unbuttoning the topmost button of his white dress shirt. When he asked if it would be okay if he took his shoes off I stifled another gulp and told him that it would be fine, adding how my floors were very clean and that his socks would not get dusty at all. Smiling sadistically as he sat across from me at the card table he unlaced his wingtips and got them off his feet.

"Thanks man, I appreciate that," Daniel said. "I always get my shoes off first thing when I get home from work. Now, let's play cards buddy, and I really hope you're in good shape for when I win this little contest…"

And so we played the old fashioned card game called "War."

The rules of the game of "War" are very simple actually. You play by throwing down a card each. The player with the higher value card wins the card toss by taking both cards from the table. If both players throw down a same valued card then a "War" has occurred. When that happens each player must throw down three cards, face down and then toss out one more card each, face up. Whichever player has the higher value card that time wins the first hand that caused the "War", plus they win the cards that were thrown down face down and they win the new cards that they just threw out face up, ending the "War." This happened three times during my card game with Daniel and he lost all three "Wars." At the end of the game the player who achieves the entire deck of cards wins the game. While he played I noticed that he wiggled his toes under his thin socks and pressed his toes against the floor as well, a definite nervous habit I supposed.

"I can't believe I lost that goddamned game," the handsome Asian stud said miserably, leaning back in his chair as I held the entire deck of cards in hand, me being the winner. "I was so sure I had it in the bag!"

"Well, it looks to me my new buddy that what's now in the bag is you," I laughed. "Are you still ready to adhere to the rules of our game?"

"Sure thing man, I am a man of my word, and trust me on this I can do endless fucking push-ups and sit-ups," Daniel said, practically sneering at me.

"Well, push-ups and sit-ups really aren't what I had in mind for you buddy," I said with a sly looking grin on my face.

"Wh-what do you have in mind for me then?" Daniel asked, the sneer slowly leaving his face and being replaced with what looked like some kind of anxious fear.

With that sly looking grin still on my face I folded my arms, leaned back in my chair and said, "Seeing as you just said that you're a man of your word let's start with you getting a bit more comfortable shall we?"

"Sure, I guess," Daniel replied, sounding perplexed.

"Let's pretend we're at the doctor's office and you're about to have a procedure of some kind okay?" I asked him. "What's usually the first thing that you have done in a doctor's office buddy?"

"I, uh, I get weighed usually," Daniel said, obviously wondering where the hell this was going.

"Before that, what happens?" I asked him, starting to sound impatient.

"Well, usually I sit in the waiting room for about a half hour and then the nurse calls me to the examination room where I wait another ten minutes or so for the doctor to get there and..." Daniel gibber jabbered.

"Okay, in between having the nurse call you in and waiting for the doctor to come to the examination room, what happens?" I asked him, sounding very impatient now.

"Well, I usually strip out of my clothes down to my underpants and socks and..." Daniel began and I held up a hand, halting him in mid-sentence.

"That's it, you strip down to your underpants and socks," I repeated him.

"Holy fucking fucks, you want me to strip down right here for you???" Daniel squawked in a high pitched tone of voice. "Fucking fuck, you're joking right? Strip down to my goddamned boxer briefs and sexy socks like some sexy male stripper or something?"

"You did say that you're a man of your word Daniel, and you did agree to the rules of the game," I reminded my new buddy as he sat there nervously tugging on his necktie, a look of total dismay etched on his exotically handsome face. "But if you want to back out of it at this point I understand and..."

"Let me ask you this Christopher," Daniel said, him cutting me off in mid-sentence now, that look of disbelief on his face growing more intense. "If I had won, would you have agreed to all the push-ups, sit-ups and other intense exercises I was going to put you through?"

"YES!" I replied my eyes open wide.

"I was planning on working you over in a gym, you would have agreed to that? You would have come with me to the Bally's over here on Nineteenth Avenue and taken all that I would have dished out on you?" Daniel seethed, looking intently at me from across the table.

"YES!" I replied again, my eyes opened wider now.

"And in front of all the people there you would have allowed me to humiliate you that way?" he asked, sounding unsure of himself.

"YES!" I replied again.

"Why man? Why would you have agreed to all that?" Daniel asked me, seeming to be looking for a way out of this mess that he had gotten himself into, sweating in his socks as I would call it.

"Because like you I'm a man of my word," I began in reply. "And I would have agreed to it because I find that I like you a lot and I like being your friend..."

"Okay man, *okay,*" Daniel said, standing up and undoing the knot in his necktie. "But please, please man, tell me at least this much, once I'm stripped down to my boxer briefs and socks what are you planning on doing to me then?"

"That is still not for you to know buddy," I laughed meanly, trying to sound as sadistic as possible. "Let's just take one thing at a time shall we?"

"Okay man, just that I really don't have a sweet feeling about all this," Daniel said as he slid his tie off his shirt and dropped it on the couch. "I am definitely not getting a sweet feeling about all this..."

I watched as my buddy unbuttoned his crisp white dress shirt, shucked it off and I saw how his luscious nipples were pressed hard against the white tee shirt he was wearing under his dress shirt. I had been right; his nipples appeared to be of the very over-sized sort that so many men are not blessed with. Daniel on the other hand seemed to be very, very blessed in that area. He placed his dress shirt on the couch where he had put his tie and then shucked off his tee shirt.

"Enjoying yourself so far?" he asked me, looking at me straight ahead, his semi muscular and smooth chest staring me in the face.

His nipples were as pointy as two pencil erasers and just as pink buds. If the guy didn't know it, it amazed me, that his nipples needed some real passionate attention.

"Oh yes, I'm having a great time," I replied, still seated as my new buddy slowly stripped down for me. "And so will you once I get going on you..."

"Yeah, that's what the fucking fuck I'm afraid of," the handsome Asian stud said and undid his belt buckle followed by unbuttoning his suit trousers.

I chuckled a bit meanly as the guy's suit trousers fell down around his ankles. There's something so comical about how most guys look when they are standing with their pants down around their ankles. The sight of the guy with his pants down around his ankles, his socks peeking up out of the pants, his underpants totally on display, a possible erection tenting said underpants, all of it combined is just too humiliating for the poor guy and just too funny for anyone lucky enough to be seeing it...

A few moments later I got up and out of my chair, and stepped over to my buddy as he now stood there clad in just a pair of the sexiest looking white boxer briefs I had ever seen and his navy blue nylon dress socks. A look of utter and total humiliation was all over his handsome face... His cock was semi hard in his boxer briefs already. (It always amazes me how when a guy is feeling fear filled, humiliated, or totally embarrassed for whatever the fuck the reason most of them get totally hard in their underpants. You would think that that cock would shrivel up, but it does seem that most guys out there get off on this kind of being worked over.) Once I got started on Daniel's over-sized man tits that erection of his would be demanding attention…

"Okay man, you satisfied now?" Daniel asked as I drank in the sight of him. "Just like at the doctor's office…"

"Yeah, but with only one difference that I'm about to put on you" I said, reaching into my deep pants pocket.

"What's that buddy?" Daniel asked me, sounding very apprehensive now, obviously feeling very vulnerable as well.

When I brought out the long length of rope from my pocket Daniel's eyes opened wide in shock and his jaw seemed to drop to the floor.

"H-holy fucking fucks, you, you're planning to tie me the fuck up man?" he asked, taking a few involuntarily steps back away from me on his socked feet. "Come on man, you won the game, you got me to strip for you, tying me up is a horse of a totally different goddamned color here buddy!"

"Spoken and said like a true Wall Street bull," I commented slyly and Daniel then saw how I was looking hungrily at his pink fleshy nipples.

At the moment his nipples were real squishy and squashy looking. Once I got started tweaking and squeezing and really working on them they would be as hard and as pointy as two bullets.

"I could have had you strip totally raw for me buddy," I said, holding up the rope. "But I did give you breaks by letting you keep your underpants and socks on…"

"Jeez, some break," Daniel said miserably and his cock engorged to a bit more than semi hard in his boxer briefs.

"So, are you still going to abide by the rules of our game?" I asked him.

"OH fucking fuck, *fuck me,"* Daniel sputtered, pressed his wrists together and held them up in front of his chest. "Go ahead man, do your worst. But I'll tell you, next time we play cards I WILL WIN!"

I was so glad to hear him say that there would be a next time. I smiled and said, "Hands behind you buddy boy…"

His face sank a bit more but again he did as he was told. He took short sounding miserably breaths as I stood behind him roping his crossed wrists behind his back.

"So tell me something here buddy, what was the kinkiest thing that a date ever did to you in the bedroom arena?" I asked Daniel as I secured his wrists with double knots each time I looped more rope around and around and around his wrists.

"Well, some feisty chick I dated once or twice asked me if I liked threesomes, and she invited two girlfriends of hers over and those three horned up bitches took turns sucking my cock," Daniel said, sounding real proud of himself.

"Fucking fuck man, I purposely took forever to shoot my load that time. I made those bitches really work for my cream soup you know?"

"Yeah, that does sound really intense," I said, finishing tying his hands, but not moving from where I was standing behind him.

The sight of his ass globes was like two coconut shaped melons in his sexy white cotton boxer briefs… When I accidentally on purpose glided a hand over his tight butt cheeks he didn't say one word of protest. So far I was sailing on calm seas it seemed…

"And you fucking fucked all three of those bitches Daniel?" I asked him and swatted his ass cheeks with the back of my hand. "You bad boy, did you fucking fuck all three of them?"

I swatted his ass again…

Daniel simply grinned and said, "Like I said, I really made those bitches work for my soup buddy!"

"Have you ever had a date do this to you?" I asked him and then reached my arms around him from behind, hugged him against me as I crossed my arms over his upper torso and with my thumbs and first two fingers of each hand I grabbed each of his plump nipples, squeezing down hard.

"HUUUUHHHHHH!!!" the handsome Asian stud gasped at the suddenness of his nipples being grabbed that way.

I rubbed the sides of his nipples in a vigorous fashion, really getting the guy started on his sexy dance for me.

"HUUUUUHHHHH, n-no man, *no date ever squeezed my nipples,*" Daniel panted. *"Holy fucking shit here!!"*

His nipples felt real sweet and all rubbery in my fingers as I squeezed and mashed them up to an erect and hard state…

"I didn't think so, not too many women know how a guy's nipples can be real sensitive and sexy feeling," I commented, increasing the pressure as I worked and worked his nubs.

"F-fucking fuck, *I* didn't know just how sensitive and sexy my goddamned nipples could feel buddy," Daniel grunted and swayed on his socked feet in front of me, me loving the way his sexy butt rubbed against my crotch as I worked and worked his nipples, just getting started actually. "H-holy fucking fucks man, wh-what are you doing to me here?"

"Just having some mean and sleazy fun with you buddy," I replied. "The first time I saw you air out your suit jacket on the train I couldn't help but notice the way your nips were pressed against your dress shirt. It made me really want to get at them, and other parts of you as well, but we'll get to all that later on…"

"Ah, so now the puzzle pieces start falling into place," Daniel laughed, clenched his teeth and endured the ecstasy I was forcing on him. "Fuck, fucking fuck, and double fucks, looks like my nips have become the main attraction here, serves me right for being cursed with such big fucking tits!! (GASP)

"I would call it blessed is more like it buddy," I laughed also, squeezing the sides of his nipples tighter and tighter as the tips of them bubbled up and got hard.

"EEEEEEEHHHHHRRRRR GOD OF GODS!" Daniel seethed through clenched teeth.

I squeezed them tighter yet...

"So, so you noticed the way my big ol' tits pressed against my shirt while we were on the train huh?" Daniel squeaked, gyrating now as I squeezed and teased the fuck out of his man tits, loving the way they seemed to be swelling up between my fingers with each passing second. "That makes me wonder what other parts of me you're planning on getting at, as you so pointed out, *buddy!*"

"Oh, not to worry Daniel, all in good time, all in very good time you will find out," I said chidingly and then tweaked the very tips of his nipples, whirling my fingers over and over and over them. "I see this as good luck Daniel, sort of like its good luck to find a four leafed clover or the way it's good luck to dream of a blue cross. I think it's good luck to squeeze a nice pair of nipples."

"OH GAWD MAN," Daniel seethed in his part Asian, part New York sounding accent.

With my fingers whirling over Daniel's nipple tips the guy was obviously in a sort of orbit.

"F-fuck man, it feels like you have bionic fingers or something," the Asian stud said breathlessly and at that point his cock was totally erect and tenting his boxer briefs...

So that's how I met Daniel and how I managed to coax the handsome Asian guy into the position he was presently in. What he didn't know at the time that I was working his nipples was that I also had two other tribulations to put him through before the day was over. And seeing as it was only the early afternoon we had plenty of time...

My mind returned to the present moment as I sat glorying in the sight of Daniel standing with his back to me in my kitchen. He was seething and grunting as the tit clamps and the weights I had hung on them tortured him endlessly, tormented him actually in a twisted mixture of pain and seventh heaven.

"So, tell me, are you feeling good buddy?" I asked him about fifteen minutes later, stepping over to him and grabbing his upper arm in my hand as he faced the wall.

"Y-you've asked me that so many damned times now that I think I've lost count," Daniel seethed through clenched teeth, glancing at me and then facing the wall again. "Fucking fucks man; my poor man tits feel like they're on fire and just about ready to explode, and not to mention my seven and a half inch guy too!"

"Ah, so you're a man who measures his manhood and his ecstatic agony by the inch huh Daniel?" I teased him and squeezed his arm tighter. "Okay, once your man tits are really cooked up for me I'll take the tit clamps off them and that should be pretty soon now."

"Th-thank you man, *thank you,* " Daniel spouted, his lips trembling as he spoke.

"Okay, back around and facing me again buddy," I said, gripping his arm tighter and moving him around on his tied up socked feet.

"H-holy fucks man, if you planned on spinning me like a goddamned top why did you tie up my feet?" Daniel ranted, hefted himself again to his toes and almost like a ballet dancer balanced himself and turned facing me as I held his arm tight, keeping him well balanced.

Once he was facing me he leaned himself up against the wall, heaved his crotch forward and his erection was enormous by then. The tit clamps and the weights dangling on them looked torturous to epic proportions by then. The look of sensual agony in his beautiful eyes was heartbreaking and it nearly drove me over the edge. Drinking in the sight of him in his erotic agony I boldly reached forward and with my fingers and thumb I caressed his bulging and chock filled balls in his sexy boxer briefs. The way his underpants were all moist and sweaty made a nice outline of his juicy balls let me tell you. They looked like they were swollen to the size of two kiwis in his sexy underpants. He didn't seem to mind that I was handling his precious family jewels at the moment. I really expected him to tell me to get my hands off his most private of areas. They felt totally hard and tight in his boxer briefs those luscious testicles of his. I rolled them a bit in my fingers. They were obviously beyond chock filled with his Asian man juices.

"OHHHHHH GAWD man, y-you're making more chills eat me up here doing that to my nuts," Daniel reeled and danced real sexy for me against the wall, standing flat on his tied up feet again.

If he didn't mind me playing with his balls I was sure that he would not mind what I was about to do to him next, or perhaps he would mind.

"Fuck man, one cum, one goddamned cum, please man, *please,* " Daniel begged and all I did was chuckle as I stopped toying with his balls. "FUCKING FUCKS, I should never have let you get my hands tied behind me man…"

"Okay buddy, I think your man tits are cooked and ready at this point," I said and took the tit clamps along with the weights hanging on the chain of them off the guy's nipples at that point.

"AAAAYYYYYYYYYRRRR GOD!!" Daniel screamed as the blood rushed back into his nipples at what had to have felt like a thousand miles per hour.

"Yeah, I know, it feels worse now that the clamps are off your man tits huh?" I asked him meanly.

"OHHHHHHHRRRR fucking fucks, totally fucked up fucking fucks!!" Daniel squealed and squalled, his eyes squeezed shut, his teeth clenched and his man tits all jutted up and ready for what I had in mind next. "God man, I didn't realize how awful it would feel once you took those devices from hell off me, SSSHHHHIIIIITTTT"

I stepped in real close to him, reached around his lower body, grabbed his coconut shaped ass globes, squeezed them tight and leaned down.

"Wh-what now buddy? What the fucking fuck now???" Daniel asked me as I hefted him a bit upward by holding real tight to his silky and succulent feeling ass cheeks.

I leaned down and with my tongue out slurped one of his jutted up man tits into my mouth...

"OHHHHHHHH fuck, holy fuck, goddamned fuck," Daniel snorted, looking down at the top of my head, disbelief showing in his beautiful eyes as I sucked, chewed, and slurped his jutted up nipple in my mouth, squeezing his delectable ass globes at the same time. "OH GAWD, it must be lunch time 'cause you're eating my man tit!!"

His nipple felt so hard and durable in my mouth and when I slid the tip of my tongue over the very tip of it Daniel swayed and rocked in my tight grasp. I clenched his ass cheeks tighter and yanked him up higher onto his toes. His nipple in my mouth was jutted up like a pencil eraser and the way Daniel was swaying in my grasp and swooning was sheer ecstasy, for both of us... I felt his cum oozing erection gliding back and forth over my crotch area as I sucked and slurped at his man tit in my mouth.

"OOOOOOHHHHHH fuck, what a buddy you are Christopher, fucking best buddy I've ever met," Daniel spouted breathlessly. "Fucking fuck, stripping me was a bit embarrassing but I can deal with that buddy, tying my hands, well, that was kind of shitty I got to tell you!"

He seemed to be going on and on and reeling in the forced throes of ecstasy that I was heaping on him. I had him practically lifted off the floor by his ass cheeks as I abandoned his nipple that was in my mouth and quickly slurped the other nub into my mouth.

"YYYAAAAAAHHRRRRRR," the handsome Asian Wall Street guy croaked loudly, looking down at the nipple that I had just finished sucking the fuck out of. "FUCK, just look at my nipple man. I never saw it so sore and pink looking! My poor man tits will never be the same after all this..."

"Oh they will, in a few days they will," I said and quickly swigged his nipple back into my greedy mouth, wrapping my lips around it...

A while later I said, "In a few days they'll be as good as new buddy," laughing meanly as I said it...

"So tell me man, was this what you had in mind for me the first time you saw me on the train platform?" Daniel asked, still kind of breathless.

"This and a few other things," I replied and then stopped kissing his jutted up man tits. "Man, I sure did a hell of a job on this nipples of yours huh buddy?"

"Yeah, you sure as fucking fuck did," Daniel chirped, looking down at his nipples as they were swelling up bigger and bigger it seemed. "God almighty, I have huge nips!"

We both laughed and then in a fast motion I slung the handsome guy up across my shoulders and lugged him toward my bedroom where part two of my day with Daniel was waiting...

"Hey, put me down man!" Daniel hemmed loudly. "What now??? What the fucking fuck now???"

(3)

Welcoming the Marine Home

(From the book: *Executive Ties That Bind*)

I wrote this story along with a spanking buddy of mine on the internet. His name is Elvis and he loves spanking black guys and getting spanked himself by black guys. The story not only explores my spanking fetish but it also explores a fetish I have for hunky black guys wearing military uniforms.

The story was entirely my idea. Elvis did not seem all that interested in writing when we worked together on it. I got the feeling that Elvis is more into experiencing spanking in real time rather than in a fictional sense. I practically begged him to help me with this story though, seeing as he is so much into the spanking and discipline scenes. I don't think he found it difficult to do, I just don't think he knew that he had it in him to do something like this and bring a piece of fiction to life.

A lot of the sinister dialogue in the story was penned by my buddy Elvis. He had me hysterical with a lot of the things that his character and mine said to the marine who got spanked in the story.

Lately, I have been exploring a part of my life that I really do not share with many people. Writing this story helped me to deal with some of the not so fun stuff that is locked away inside me. I suppose that it was always there but I never had an avenue, other than therapy to bring it out somehow.

The other stories in these books mostly dealt with guys being pretty submissive when stripped to their dress socks. In this story the guy, he being a marine, stripped to his socks (and briefs) is anything but submissive. He submits in a tough guy sort of way to prove his worth as a marine and his machismo as to how much he can take when two good buddies dish it out on him.

The overall emotional content of the story is about discipline, but in an erotic arena. A lot of the spanking images portrayed in the story I drew on from my time when growing up. I suppose it can be said that I am still growing up…but now I am doing it through what I write about.

I would have to say that out of all the stories I wrote about discipline and spanking "Welcoming the Marine Home" ranks up there as one of my favorites. I loved every moment of working with my buddy Elvis on this one and the character of Joe the marine that we brought to life was extraordinary.

I have to wonder though how many marines in real life would agree to a session like the one Joe is put through in the story.

This story is of course very wishful thinking. I am sure that most of us would love to put a marine through the trials that the one in the story endures. It's an illusion really. I realize of course that in real life the chances of this happening are a million to almost none…but one never knows for sure does one?

My buddy Joe had been in the Marine Corp. for the last three years, it was that long that Elvis and I had seen him. He had kept in touch with us via letters and e-mails while he had been stationed overseas and other areas of the world that I'm not allowed to mention here. When Elvis and I each received the e-mail from him that he was coming home for a week and a half worth of leave time we decided to welcome him home in a way totally befitting that of a rugged hard-core United States Marine. Our buddy Joe, Lance Corporal Joe Grant to be exact is a twenty-three year old African-American man and damned proud of his heritage let me tell you buds. He is equally as proud of being a marine. When we were teenagers the thin and scrawny handsome black guy used to tell us how he was going to join the Corps, pass their horrendous boot camp training, travel the world and really prove to himself and us that he could take it, *that he could take it all.* I would think that part of his reason for wanting to make it was the way we used to tease and razz the poor scrawny dude every chance we got. Since becoming a marine Joe has short cut cropped (marine style, high and tight) dark brown hair, his body is now extremely muscular and hard as a fucking rock bud. Our good buddy is more than well-toned from the daily regiment of exercises that marines are put through on a daily punishing basis bud. Actually, to say it bluntly, since becoming a marine Joe is built like a goddamned brick shit house. In his e-mails and letters to us he always gloated over how muscular and well-toned the marines were making him, how hard they made him workout and even how his good buddies worked him over as a bonus every once in a while. He would tell us how he would be ready for *us, when the time came that is.* His shoulders are as broad as a doorway; he has stomach muscles as tight as knotted rope, long muscled arms with biceps the size of medium sized bowling balls and big hands bud, real big fucking hands. His hands are big enough to make fists big and hard enough to punch holes in walls. His legs are long and powerful, nothing like the scrawny legs he had back in the high school days. But all that muscle and all that brawn was not going to keep Elvis and I from welcoming the handsome black guy home in a proper fashion. And we knew, knowing Joe that he would take all we could dish out to welcome him home in the proper fashion. It had been three long years of intense marine time for the guy and we were sure he wanted to show us "just what the fuck he was made of now." Yeah, he would deal with it and then some, Elvis and I knew that for sure. Joe has dark chestnut colored eyes and stands five feet ten inches tall in all his muscular magnificence and really does justice to his marine uniform. But alas, for what Elvis and I had in mind for our "good" buddy he wasn't going to need his uniform that day...

It was Joe's second day home when I pulled up in front of his mother and father's house where our buddy grew up. It was nine thirty AM on a seasonably cool September day. Elvis and I figured that we would give the marine a day to settle in and see his family before we went to work on him for the better part of his second day of leave time. I shut off the car's ignition and walked up to the front door to ring the doorbell. Joe was expecting me as Elvis had called him the night before to see if he would want to spend a few hours with us the next day, so that the two of us could welcome him home properly. Joe had instantly agreed to a visit with us at Elvis's apartment, but cited how he had to be back at his parent's house by early evening, seeing as they had other relatives coming who were anxious to see him. With a mean looking grin on his face Elvis told Joe that he would be home in plenty of time and hung up. Elvis and I gave each other a high-five and laughed and cackled meanly...

Joe's mother opened the front door a few moments after I rang the bell.

"Good morning Mrs. Grant, I'm here to pick up Joe," I said to her in a friendly tone of voice. "I'm going to drive us over to Elvis's place for a visit."

"Good morning Chris, it's good to see you," Joe's mother said. "I'm so glad that you three are still all good friends since you were children."

"So am I Mrs. Grant," I replied, her not knowing just how very glad I was that we were all still good friends.

"Would you like to come in for some coffee or something?" she asked me pleasantly. "Joe is just getting his shirt and tie on."

"Uh, no, thanks," I said. "I had breakfast earlier."

"Okay then," she began and at that moment Joe appeared behind his mother in the doorway wearing his olive colored formal marine uniform.

"Hey there buddy!!" Joe called out loudly to me, stepping past his mother and out of the house.

"How are you Joe?" I asked him happily as we hugged each other tight.

His hug was like being locked into a vise and I have to say as I said earlier that he filled out his marine uniform perfectly, really doing justice to it, up to and including his tightly knotted tie and his spit shined lace up marine issued shoes.

"Man, it is so good to see you buddy," Joe said, releasing his hold on me and I took in the sight of him in his entire splendor.

Even from a simple glance I was able to see that his muscles were bulging and straining in his uniform jacket.

"I'll see you later Mom," Joe said to his mother, giving her a kiss on the cheek.

"Okay Joe, enjoy your visit with Elvis and Chris," his mother said, turning her attention to me. "If you and Elvis want to come back later for dinner we're going to have a lot of company Chris. You guys are more than welcome to join in the "welcome home" festivities for Joe."

"Thanks Mrs. Grant, that's very kind of you," I replied. "Maybe we will come over at that, as soon as we have some "welcome home" festivities of our own for Lance Corporal Grant here."

At that Joe chuckled happily and he and I headed toward my car as his mother closed and locked the door behind us.

"Where's Elvis?" Joe asked me. "Didn't he come too?"

"He's waiting for us back at his place buddy," I said, opening the passenger side door for him.

Joe climbed in and I quickly got in the driver's seat.

"So, you glad to be home?" I asked him. "Even if it's going to be for less than a couple of weeks?"

"Sure am man," Joe replied. "The neighborhood still looks the same even after three years, but gads man, my two little brothers sure grew up fast and my sister too."

"Yeah, time has a way of getting away from us I suppose," I said agreeably. "I'm just wondering about one thing though buddy."

"What's that?" Joe asked me.

"Why you decided to stay at your parent's house rather than in a hotel in the city," I said. "I mean, you could have spent your days and nights in the arms of beautiful women."

"Yeah, and caught God knows what and spent thousands for a hotel room and so on," my marine buddy said. "Staying at home with the family suits me just fine and I can still spend my nights in the arms of women when I get back to the base."

"Suit yourself buddy," I said with a smile, plucked his hat off his head and perched it up on mine. "I'm just so fucking glad to see you and Elvis can't wait to see you either."

"I'll bet," Joe snickered as I drove.

It was about five minutes later when I pulled up in the parking lot of the building where Elvis lives. Joe plucked his hat off my head and placed it on the dashboard, saying to me, "Gimmie my damn hat white boy, you ain't worthy enough to be wearing a marine's hat." We both laughed in a friendly way as we got out of the car...

We rode the elevator to the fourth floor where Elvis's apartment is.

"Man oh man, I cannot believe that it's been three years since I've seen Elvis," Joe said, smiling real big, about to knock on the door.

I quickly grabbed his big beefy wrist and told him to wait, telling him that I had to prepare him for the visit.

"Prepare me?" Joe asked, looking at me quizzically as I took a long white cloth blindfold from my pocket.

"I'm going to need to blindfold you for a while buddy," I said to him, holding up the white cloth.

"What's up with that?" Joe asked me, grinning snidely. "Blindfold me? *Blindfold me?* You and Elvis got something cooked up for me in there?"

"You might say that," I replied fiendishly.

"Might say that?" Joe asked me, looking at me intently as I held up the white cloth blindfold.

"It's a great surprise bud," I said insistently. "You'll see."

"Heh, *blindfolded I won't see*," Joe chuckled with a smirk on his face.

"Just for a few quick minutes," I said to him reassuringly.

"Okay bud, I'll play your game *and Elvis's*," Joe said and my heart beat a little easier. "Seeing as this is a "welcome home" for me."

"It sure is buddy, it sure as shit is," I said as I tied the blindfold on him, knotting it behind his nearly baldhead, wallowing in the sight of his big bull-like neck.

Once blindfolded the marine knocked on the door.

"Can't believe this shit, got me wearin' a damned blindfold," Joe muttered. "No wonder you took my hat off me in the car. Gads, whatever you two jokers got cooked up for me it better be good buddy."

"Oh, it's better than good," I said. "Actually, it's great."

Elvis opened the door, a handsome white guy with dark brown hair, chiseled features, a muscular body and twenty-five (good) years old. At the sight of me with our blindfolded buddy Elvis's eyes lit up big and wide.

"Here he is," I said to Elvis gleefully.

"Come on in," Elvis said, his face more than lit up and smiling.

"Our buddy is home from the Marine Corps," I said happily.

"And that's a great thing," Elvis said, now smiling sadistically, he took Joe by his upper arm and led him into the apartment as I closed and locked the door. "Welcome home Joe."

"Thanks man," Joe said to Elvis as he was guided through the apartment. "Wish I could say that it's great to *see* you Elvis, but our buddy Chris here insisted on putting this blindfold on me for some reason or other."

"Trust us, it's for a good cause," Elvis said.

"What do you dudes got cooked up for me huh?" Joe asked Elvis as we both positioned him in front of a table where a leather paddle, a hairbrush, a ruler and a wooden spoon were all set out. "Some sort of "welcome home" surprise for me?"

"A very good surprise," Elvis said and he and I looked at each other and snickered.

Joe simply grimaced behind his blindfold as Elvis tugged his tie a few times, no doubt recalling the mean things and tricks we used to heap on our good buddy. (Tricks like for instance the time we put itching powder in Joe's underpants in gym class while he was showering. Tricks like the time we put Crazy Glue on his chair in science class before he had gotten there. Tricks like the time Elvis had somehow gotten his hands on Joe's lunch bag before lunch period and unwrapped his chocolate bar and replaced a few pieces of it with Ex-lax. Poor Joe never made it to his next class seeing as he spent most of that period in the bathroom. And yet even after all the mean tricks we'd played on him he still thought of us as his two best buddies. Despite the tricks we were all pretty much very good to each other.)

"Okay, lower his blindfold Chris," Elvis said fiendishly, still tugging at Joe's tie.

I quickly did as Elvis asked and the first thing Joe saw before even saying a proper hello to Elvis was the stuff strewn out on the table. Standing there almost at attention with the blindfold now dangling around his big neck Joe took in the sight of the spanking utensils and gulped hard, a look of dismay coming into his handsome eyes.

"Holy shit," he whispered, simply looking down at the stuff, licking his big lips real moistly. "Oh gads you guys, I get the feelin' I should have stayed home."

"Too late for that," Elvis said, hooking a hand around one of Joe's muscular arms. "It's time for a *good* ass whipping."

"Y-you guys are goin' to *spank me* welcome home?" Joe asked, nearly choking on the words as Elvis held his arm tight.

"You got that right, buddy," Elvis quipped, leaning in real close to our marine buddy and giving the knot of his tie a squeeze.

"Fuck, *fuck,* that's how my marine buddies *welcomed* me *to* the damned Corps," he said to Elvis. "Fucking guys took turns tanning my damned behind blacker than it already was. Now I'm goin' to be spanked welcome home to??? Gads…fellas just love spanking my black ass."

"Too damned bad," Elvis said. "It's the way Chris and I decided to welcome you home."

"Okay buds," Joe said after licking his lips hard a few times and seeming to consider what he was in for. "Like I said when Chris blindfolded me in the hallway I'll play your game here. *And fuck,* I will show you what I'm made of. Now that I'm a damned marine *I will really show you what the fuck I'm made of!*"

As Joe spoke he clenched his teeth.

"Fuck it all, my buddies in the Corps spanked me and I took it," Joe went on confidently as Elvis began brazenly loosening his tie for him.

"*Fuck man, you plannin' on stripping me too?*" the hard-core marine asked in disbelief.

"Well, this is an ass whipping after all, not just a spanking, buddy," Elvis said. "You need to be in your underwear. Yes, we plan on stripping you."

"*This is a marine uniform I got on,*" Joe said sternly, getting his tie off after shooing Elvis's hands away.

"Heh, not for long will you have it on," Elvis laughed, stepping next to me.

"Okay buds, *okay,* I see where this is goin'," Joe said almost miserably but sounding determined at the same time, shucking off his marine uniform jacket.

Elvis and I watched as our buddy slowly stripped out of his uniform, folding it perfectly and laying it neatly on a chair till he was wearing just his marine issued white briefs and calf length black nylon dress socks.

"Fuck, *fuck,* lookit this shit, got me in just my damned under shorts and dressy socks," the marine quipped angrily, standing there in all his muscular glory, his marine body more than a work of art. "What a way to treat a hard-core marine…"

"Very nice," Elvis murmured. "What you said in your letters was so true Joe; the marines really did a job on you. But now it's our turn."

Joe looked at Elvis with anguish in his eyes but remained standing at attention.

"Should we tie his hands behind him?" I asked Elvis with a grin, reaching into my pocket and bringing out a long length of white cotton clothesline.

"I would think that's a good idea," Elvis laughingly replied as I quickly stepped behind our marine buddy, gently took him by the wrists, pulled his arms behind him and crossed his wrists at his lower back.

"Tie me up?" Joe asked in shock as I wound the rope tightly around and around his big wrists, knotting it as I went. "Gads man, this is a shitty thing to be doing to a marine of my stature Elvis. When my marine buddies spanked me welcome to the Corps *they didn't tie me up bud.*"

"We're not your marine buddies Joe," Elvis replied, stepping up real close to our marine buddy, taking in the sight of Joe's massive pecs and his huge fleshy and overly pointy nipples. "And you're very wrong on another count buddy, this is not a shitty thing that we're doing to you here, it's a good thing, *a great fucking thing.* Chris and I are working hard to make sure you're welcomed home in a proper marine fashion."

"Huh, could have just toasted me with some champagne buds," the marine quipped, hunching his shoulders farther back, jutting out his chest as I roped his hands behind him.

"Well, we are going to toast you Joe, but not with champagne," Elvis said and then he and I both laughed fiendishly. "We're going to toast your hard marine butt…starting with a few rounds using a leather paddle."

Joe simply stared forward and gulped hard. I took in the facts that Joe hadn't stopped me from blindfolding him before bringing him into Elvis's apartment. He hadn't resisted the order to strip out of his uniform down to his marine issued white briefs and black socks when he learned he was going to be given an ass whipping. All right, he dished out some machismo marine attitude but had he actually resisted? And he didn't resist or fight me off as I tied his hands behind him. (God knows he could have told me to go fuck myself where the blindfold was concerned. He could have told Elvis there was no way he was stripping down to his briefs and socks. He could have left on his own power after finding out that we were going to whip his ass welcome home. There was no way, *no* fucking way that we could have stopped him from leaving if he wanted to. Built like he now was Joe was like a human tractor that would simply mow down anything that stood in his way. And he could have knocked me into next Tuesday before I even started tying his hands behind him.) But he didn't stop Elvis or me from any of those things. He just went along with it all, seeming to relish the memories of the spankings he'd endured at the hands of his marine buddies, seeming to take pride in telling us about the spankings he'd endured from his marine buddies. Yes, I (and Elvis too I am sure) got the distinct feeling that Joe *was* enjoying all this, showing off in a way for his two buddies, showing off that new marine machismo that had been pounded (spanked? Whipped?) into him. And yes, stripped to his underpants and socks he was able to show off that hard-core well-muscled body he had achieved being a marine.

"Okay buddy, his hands are tied good and fucking tight," I said to Elvis.

"And you know that's a good thing," Elvis said, brazenly taking Joe's fleshy nipples between his thumbs and first two fingers, squeezing and twisting them. "Say Joe, I don't recall you having such big fat titties. What happened here? It looks like someone's been sucking these babies. And sucking them for great lengths of time I might add."

"Ohhhhhhhh fuck man, d-don't be playin' squeeze and tease with my man tits Elvis," Joe gasped through clenched teeth, his cock growing hard in his marine issued white briefs. "Fuck, my man tits are more sensitive than a woman's bud."

"Yeah, and that's a good thing too I have to say," Elvis said, still twisting and squeezing our marine's nipples. "But you didn't answer my question buddy. How'd your titties get so big and fat?"

"M-my buddies in the Corps again man," Joe replied almost breathlessly. "B-besides spanking me welcome to the Corps they would hang things on my man tits and leave 'em there for a goodly length of time. It was another test of a man's endurance bud, to torture and haze his damned man tits. After a while my man tits were real big and plump. Call 'em marine's man's tits bud."

"So I see," Elvis mused and squeezed Joe's nipples harder.

"Yeah, and just like the spankings they gave me and just like the one you and Chris here are going to give me I took it, *I took it all Elvis,*" Joe said angrily, grimacing in erotic pain as Elvis squeezed and twisted the fuck out of his nipples. "But they didn't tie me up for it bud."

"Well, we did tie you up and you know that's a great thing buddy," Elvis said and let go of Joe's nipples.

Joe breathed a loud gasp and I noticed that the tips of his nipples now looked even more erect and sensitive to the touch.

"Okay buddy, let's go to the spanking couch," Elvis said, taking our marine by his upper arm and picking up the leather paddle. "It's time to get this show on the road."

"Shit, shit," the marine muttered somewhat bitterly as he trudged next to Elvis on his black socked feet, his cock rigidly hard in his white briefs and bulging big, his testicles outlined nice and plump in there as well.

I could not help but notice that the marine's hardness was oozing pre cum, staining the front section of his underpants. Obviously I had been right in my observations. *He* was inwardly enjoying this trip that Elvis and I were taking him on, although he wasn't about to admit that out rightly.

"Say Elvis, should we tell him about the dice?" I asked as my buddy sat down on the spanking couch and positioned our marine over his knees and lap.

"He's going to need to know," Elvis said, hooking an arm over Joe's muscular body as he got him situated on his lap and over his knees.

"The dice?" Joe asked, his head hanging down and his socked feet balanced up on his toes as he was now positioned over Elvis's lap, his white briefed butt cheeks pointing straight up, a ready target for Elvis's paddle. "What's up with the dice?"

"We're going to roll dice to determine how many swats you'll get for each round of spanking," I explained, holding up a pair of dice. "And if we roll double digits you'll get double the amount of swats shown on the dice."

"So in other words, if we roll two five's you'll get twenty swats, rather than ten," Elvis said, rubbing his round leather paddle over Joe's briefed butt cheeks.

"And I suppose that's a good thing huh Elvis?" Joe asked, looking down at the floor as he spoke.

"It's a great thing," Elvis said and then looked at me. "Chris, the first number if you would."

"Sure thing," I said anxiously and began shaking up the dice in my hand.

"Fuck, my marine buddies never used dice," Joe said softly as I threw the dice on an end table.

My eyes opened wide in sheer delight.

"Ha, two sixes," I said sadistically.

"A great number and a great beginning," Elvis said and raised the paddle over Joe's briefed cheeks. "Twenty four swats just to warm you up buddy. And to make it easier on you at the beginning I'll leave those briefs of yours pulled up… for now…"

"G-gads, don't think my little cotton briefs are goin' to absorb a lot of the swats Elvis," Joe said miserably, squirming on his buddies' lap. "I get the distinct feeling you spank hard."

"Count 'em off Marine," Elvis said with total authority and brought his leather paddle down hard on Joe's upraised butt cheeks.

WHAP WHAP WHAP WHAP WHAP was the sound of the leather paddle connecting with our marine's butt cheeks…

"Uhhhhhhhhrrr f-fuck, counting now bud, one, t-two, three, four," Joe barked, sounding like the real hard-core marine he had become.

"And by the way, if you miss a number or repeat a number we start back at the beginning," Elvis said meanly as he swatted our marine's butt harder.

WHAP WHAPPP WHAPPP WHAPPP WHAPPP

"F-five, six, seven, eight, ohhhhh God, and nine," Joe sputtered, tottering awkwardly on his raised toes. "Gads, but that paddle hurts!!"

Elvis held tightly to our buddy with an arm hooked around him, almost lovingly I thought as he administered the swats harder and harder to Joe's butt cheeks. Joe counted loudly and properly each time the paddle connected with his butt cheeks.

"And, fifteen, sixteen, and seventeen," Joe barked mightily. "Goin' to show you guys just what the fuck a marine like me can take buds!"

"More counting and less complaining Marine," Elvis said and delivered two fast hard swats to Joe's butt cheeks. "Goin' to break you of that arrogant marine attitude as well during your time here being spanked welcome home."

"E-eighteen, nineteen, twenty, ohhhh fuckers," Joe seethed. "Took the marine's less than six months to build this attitude in me Elvis, you won't break me that easily…*buddy…*"

"You know buddy, five or six hard swats with a leather paddle is enough to have a guy's ass cheeks really stinging," Elvis said and swatted our marine's butt hard. "But we're not going to be all that stingy where you're concerned Joe. No way buddy, we're going to make sure you get plenty and then some. And that is a good fucking thing!"

WHAP WHAP WHAP

"Tw-twenty two, twenty three and fuck it all, twenty four!!! OWWWWW!!!" Joe recited loudly, sounding more than delighted at the number twenty-four. "Ohhh man, my poor butt cheeks…"

"And we're just getting started Marine," Elvis said, giving one of Joe's spanked butt cheeks a squeeze through his white briefs.

"My turn," I said anxiously, stepping over to the spanking couch.

Elvis helped our marine buddy to his feet and stood him at attention while I got comfortable on the couch next.

"It's a good thing being able to do whatever we want with a marine huh Chris?" Elvis asked me snidely, holding tight to Joe's upper muscular arms while the marine stood rigidly at attention in his briefs and socks, his cock rock hard.

"Sure as shit buddy," I said agreeably. "Now, get him over my lap and roll up those dice."

Elvis and I snickered meanly as we got Joe into position over my lap and knees.

"Fuckers, make me sound like I'm some damned toy that you can play with and use however the fuck you want," Joe muttered. "Huh, wonder if any of my good buddies in the Corps ever got welcomed home like this, shiiitttt…"

"And I want a good high number just like you got," I said to Elvis as he picked up the dice and started shaking them up.

"We shall see," Elvis said.

"Gads, what a fucked up position you guys got me in," Joe muttered with his head hanging down by my feet, his socked toes again raised and his briefed butt jutted up over my lap.

I rubbed Joe's butt cheeks in anticipation with the leather paddle as Elvis threw the dice down on the end table.

"Five," Elvis said sadly.

"Ha, not that many swats this round huh you mugs?" Joe laughed.

"It can still feel like more than twenty-four like you got the first round," I said and raised the paddle high. "Count 'em off Marine."

WHAP WHAP WHAPPPP

"UGHHHH, o-one, two, three," Joe sputtered angrily. "Fuck, you spank hard Chris!!"

"And that's a great thing, seeing as you drew such a low number," Elvis said.

WHAP WHAPPPP

"F-four and five fucker!" Joe barked, his voice hitting a high crescendo at the fifth and hardest swat.

"Great!!" Elvis said and stepped over to the spanking couch.

Once again he and I helped our marine to his socked feet. Without even being told to do so Joe snapped to a stance of rigid attention, his chest jutted out, shoulders thrown back and his feet slightly parted.

"Okay Chris, roll the dice," Elvis said, sitting down on the spanking couch and helping Joe over his lap and knees, picking up the leather paddle quickly.

Smiling wickedly I shook up the dice in my hand.

"Fuck man, hell yeah, we're going to whip this hard butt of yours so bad that you're not going to be able to sit comfortably for a week buddy," Elvis said, rubbing the paddle hard over and over Joe's jutted up briefed butt cheeks.

I threw the dice on the end table.

"A six and a five," I called out. "Eleven!!"

"Much better number than I got for you Chris," Elvis chuckled and raised the paddle high.

"Count 'em off Marine," Elvis commanded and brought the paddle down hard and stingingly on our marine's butt cheeks.

"OWWWWWW!!! One," Joe called out loudly and Elvis wasted no time, whapping Joe's butt cheeks harder and harder with each blow. "T-two, three, and four, five, owwwwwwww!!! G-God…"

WHAP WHAP WHAP WHAP

"Six, seven, eight, nine," Joe counted, his tied hands opening and closing, balling them into a big meaty fist as Elvis administered the last two hard swats.

"T-ten and eleven! ARRRRRRRHHHH!!! G-Gods man…" Joe bellowed through clenched teeth.

I quickly stepped over to the spanking couch and Elvis and I got our buddy to his socked feet, hauling him up by his massive biceps. Joe again snapped to a stance of attention in his briefs and socks, jutting his massive chest way out.

"Hope you boys are enjoying yourselves here," Joe commented bitterly, his cock now more than rock hard in those white marine issued briefs of his. "Hope you're enjoying it all, seeing as it's not every day of the week that you get to work over a marine, not to mention any marine either buds, but a marine of my caliber and stature."

"Hmmm, looks to me like we're not the only ones enjoying this," Elvis said, placing the palm of his hand over the rock hardness in Joe's briefs and giving it a squeeze or two.

Joe grimaced in what looked like ecstasy and curled his toes back under his socks.

"That hard on is telling a story huh Elvis?" I asked my spanking buddy snidely.

"Sure is, and that is a great thing," Elvis said squeezed Joe's hard cock again through his briefs, this time giving one of those big marine nipples of his a squeeze as well. "True story marine? You enjoying all this shit that Chris and I are heaping on you?"

"No fucking way man, that's a natural hard on I got," Joe grunted. "Marines are always rock hard buds. Ain't got shit to do with what's happening to me here."

Elvis simply smiled sadistically and squeezed Joe's nipple harder, giving the beefy hard on in his briefs two good tugs.

"OHHHHHHHHHH shiiiiitttt man, FUCKKKK!!!" Joe suddenly grunted breathlessly and shot a load of what looked like three days of stored up marine spunk in his white briefs. "Ohhhhh come on buds, th-this shit ain't funny now!!! Arrrhhhhhhhhh yeah, fucking A, real fucking A, got me creaming in my damned under shorts!!"

"I knew it man," Elvis quipped as Joe's mess stained and soaked the front section of his marine issued briefs. "Bet we can squeeze a lot more out of him as the day goes on Chris."

"A lot more as the day goes on???" our marine asked in a high crescendo and Elvis let go of his crotch and his nipple. "J-just how long do you fuckers plan on keepin' me here today? Gads, spanking and jacking off a marine in his underwear is real humiliating guys…"

In response to Joe's question Elvis simply squeezed the marine's biceps real hard…

"Your turn to spank our buddy here Chris," Elvis said, turning Joe toward the spanking couch.

Joe's mouth dropped open as the last remnants of his slop oozed from his slit and stained the front section of his briefs. Seconds later I was sitting on the spanking couch with Joe over my lap and knees as Elvis shook up the dice.

"Two threes," Elvis called out happily after throwing the dice on the end table. "That's a good number for you Chris. You get to give him double that amount."

"Gads," Joe muttered as I raised the paddle high. "Good number for him but a lousy and fucked up one for me!"

WHAPPP WHAPPP WHAPPP

"Count 'em off Marine," I ordered.

"One, two, and three," Joe called out and I brought the paddle down hard again and again. "Four, five…"

Joe clenched his teeth and his butt cheeks twitched erotically under his briefs in anticipation of each swat to come.

WHAP WHAP WHAP

"And six, seven, eight…" Joe barked loudly.

I gave him the last four of the twelve allotted swats, he called out the numbers loudly and in pain and then Elvis and I got him to his feet, positioning him in a stance of rigid attention. Unbelievably the marine's cock was again rock hard in his briefs. I guessed that it was true what he'd said, that a marine was always rock hard in his briefs. Elvis and I took in the sight of Joe's new boner and we both grinned meanly.

"Time to get the briefs off him," Elvis said, stepping behind the marine and hooking his fingers around the sides of Joe's underpants. "Two rounds each of spanking him with his briefs on and pulled up in back is enough. This grunting and kick-ass marine can take it bare assed now."

Joe grimaced more than self-consciously as his briefs were pulled down and landed with a bit of plopping sound due to them being soaked with his cum around his black socked ankles. Still standing rigidly at attention he unceremoniously stepped out of them and Elvis picked them up, placing them under the chair that his uniform was neatly folded up on. None of us could ignore the massive and cum slicked boner that popped up big and freshly rigid and beyond stiff between the marine's powerful tree-trunk like legs. Joe's muscle pipe was easily a bit more than seven inches of pure African-American choice meat, thick and veiny and totally beefy all around the shaft. We were all momentarily stymied as it twitched with a life of its own, bouncing back and forth against his washboard stomach, his big black balls hanging down real fucking low and sweaty in his sexy sac like two overly ripe olives in his scrotum. A small tuft of black hair adorned the bottom of his big balls and a thick tuft circled his cock erotically. The marine's cock was so fucking hard and throbbing like crazy, even after he'd shot a load like the one Elvis squeezed out of him just a few minutes earlier. Fuck, the guy really was enjoying all this. Were Elvis and I the ones being played here?

"All righty then!!" Elvis piped up in his best Jim Carrey impersonation. "Let's get this show back on the road."

That said Elvis sat down on the spanking couch, Joe gulped hard and without being told to splayed himself over Elvis's lap and knees and I picked up the dice. As I shook up the dice I could not help but notice that Elvis had pinned the marine's hard cock between his thighs, his big black balls visible between his thighs as he lay across Elvis's lap.

"Give me a good number Chris," Elvis called out, running a fingertip up and down the crevice of Joe's ass crack, sending obvious chills and thrills through the hands-bound marine.

Joe shuddered on Elvis's lap…

I shook up the dice and threw them down on the end table…

"Double threes, just like what you rolled for me on the last round," I called out happily.

"And you know what that means right Marine?" Elvis asked Joe.

"It, it means I get double the amount shown on the dice," Joe said with his head hung down low by the floor. "Shhhhhiiiitttt, another twelve swats with your damned paddle."

"Hell yeah, a great thing Marine," Elvis laughed. "And we still haven't gotten to the other items, the hairbrush, the wooden spoon and you can't even imagine what we're going to do with the ruler buddy."

"I shudder to think," Joe said nearly in a whisper as Elvis raised the paddle high.

"I assure you it'll be a good thing Marine," Elvis said sadistically. "Now, get ready to count 'em off!"

"Yes, yes Sir!" Joe called out loudly.

His calling Elvis "Sir" made me think that perhaps we were breaking him of that marine attitude and machismo after all…

WHAP WHAP WHAP WHAP came the resounding sound of the leather paddle as it connected with Joe's naked black butt.

"OWWWW, shit, one, two, three, and four," Joe counted as Elvis paddled him and squeezed his thighs tighter around Joe's hard and throbbing slimy manhood.

WHAPPP WHAPPP WHAPPPP

"F-four, five, six!!! Oh shit, no!!" Joe called out, too late realizing his mistake of repeating the number four.

"Oh man, some marine you are, can't even count," Elvis said disgustedly. "Looks like we'll have to start these twelve good swats back at number one again. You ready Marine?"

"Shit, *shit,* do I have a choice?" Joe asked.

"None at all," Elvis laughed. "Count 'em off buddy boy…"

WHAPPP WHAPPPP WHAPPPP

"Ugggghhh, one, two, three," Joe counted. "I'll get it right this time buds."

WHAPPP WHAPPP WHAPPPP

"F-four, five and six, gads, halfway there with this round already," Joe croaked.

Elvis gave Joe the last six swats in fast and hard succession all on the same naked butt cheek. That really had the marine howling let me tell you, and to quote Elvis, "That was a great thing." The tied and stripped to his socks marine literally cried out the last numbers as quickly and as desperately as possible. So far he had suffered a mere sixty-four swats plus the five bonus swats he had earned when he'd fucked up on the count and had had to start over…and there were still plenty to go.

"G-gads, if my marine buddies and my family could see me now," Joe quipped angrily as he again stood at attention in between the spanking rounds.

It seemed that marines were trained to stand at attention whenever they were awaiting orders, unless told to do otherwise. It was doing Elvis's and my hearts good to see our marine buddy standing at attention for us.

"Oh, I'm sure they'd be more than proud of you," Elvis said, sidling up to Joe's left side and hooking a claw like hand around his upper arm, squeezing his biceps hard and teasingly. "Taking all that we're dishing out on you is a great thing bud, your buddies and your family would be most impressed."

"Fuck all that Elvis my man," the African-American well-muscled marine bitched loudly. "Couldn't you two have just taken me out for a few beers to celebrate my damned homecoming?"

"Sure, but after that we would have just brought you back here and spanked you welcome home anyway," Elvis said, grabbing one of Joe's nipples with the thumbs and first two fingers of his other hand while he held tightly to his muscular arm at the same time.

"And even you have to admit that is all more fun than scoffing down a few beers," I said, stepping to Joe's other side and brazenly grabbing his hard slimy cock.

"Ohhhhh, f-fuckers got me by the man tits and cock," Joe grunted throatily. "Ohhhhhh sh-shiiiiittt, I told you mugs what the fuck that does to me..."

"Fucking great thing," Elvis said teasingly.

Elvis and I smiled meanly at each other across our marine's massively muscled torso as he squeaked out his words of anguish mixed with heated passion. He tried his best to remain standing balanced at attention as I gave his cock a few tugs.

"F-fuck, fuck it all you mugs, I-I can't believe what's about to happen here again buds," Joe gasped breathlessly as I again gave his hard stiff cock a few tugs. "And this time I ain't got my damned briefs on to catch the mess... ARRRHHHHH yeah, fucking A, here we go again!!!"

I held Joe's rock hardness real tight and Elvis twisted and squeezed his nipple as the marine shot a second load of thick creamy sperm, this time all over his massive chest, pecs and stomach areas.

"Oh man, what a nasty thing to clean up," Elvis laughed as Joe bucked madly, trying to keep his stance of attention as he shot his load.

"Ohhhhhhhhrrr gads," he panted madly. "Fuck, lookit this shit, got me cummin' again buds. Fuck, my girlfriend wouldn't believe this shit if she saw her hero marine now, gads, stripped to his socks and bein' jacked off and havin' his man tits worked over... ARHHHH yeah, fucking A buds...not to mention how'd she'd feel seein' her marine being spanked "welcome home" by his two best buddies..."

"Actually she might like it Marine," Elvis laughed and let go of Joe's nipple as I released my hold on his cock.

"Fuck, what a sight," I said to Elvis as we watched Joe's mess drip down his chest and stomach areas.

Joe stood at attention and watched miserably as Elvis picked up his cum sopped marine issued briefs and used them to wipe his mess off him. Joe's cock twitched semi hard between his muscular legs...

"Ohhhhhh man, that's a shitty thing man, to use a marine's under shorts to wipe his mess off him," Joe muttered angrily.

A few minutes later we had our marine propped up at attention standing against a wall, blindfolded again for the moment. We had tied two lengths of thin rope snugly around the shaft and just under the crown of his cock, wound the rope around his waist and tied them off behind him, thus hoisting his semi hardness straight up and making his sweaty ripe-olive sized balls real visible. Actually his balls were nice and tight and jutted out.

"Wh-what's goin' on now buds?" Joe asked, standing at attention but obviously not thrilled at the fact that his cock was tied up the way it was. "Fuckers got me blindfolded again too. Come on you mugs, I don't like bein' without my sight here."

"Well, once again it's for a good cause," Elvis said, standing next to Joe, holding a thin ruler in his hand while I stood nearby with the dice in hand.

"Heh can't spank my hard muscular ass the way you got me standing here against a wall Elvis my man," Joe chuckled.

"Who said we were going to spank your ass for the next few rounds?" Elvis quipped and rubbed the ruler of Joe's tight and jutted up balls.

"What???" Joe squeaked and then Elvis took the blindfold off him.

Joe quickly looked down at his tied up cock and gulped hard when he saw Elvis rubbing the ruler over and around his balls.

"Rulers are nice marine," Elvis said sadistically, taking Joe by his upper arm and holding it tight, keeping the guy balanced as he teasingly ran the ruler over his balls. "And they can hurt like a bitch."

"Ah no buds, you guys got to be kiddin' now," Joe nearly cried. "You ain't planning on whippin' my nuts are you?"

Elvis simply went on rubbing the ruler over Joe's exposed testicles and the poor marine hunched his broad shoulders up real tight in anguish.

"Spanking a marine's ass welcome home is one thing," Joe grunted desperately. *"But Gods; now you're talkin' about my nuts here."*

"That's a good thing to do to them," Elvis laughed, holding tight to our marine's muscular biceps as he rubbed the ruler over his balls. "Actually it's a better thing."

"Maybe for you bud, but it's my poor nuts on the line," the marine said miserably, trying to remain standing at attention despite his obvious terror.

"That has nothing to do with me," Elvis laughed.

"Man, this is worse than the shit you used to heap on me in high school buds," Joe said softly.

"Are we going to use the dice Elvis?" I asked my spanking buddy. "Or are we just going to tease and razz him for the rest of the day?"

"Of course Chris," Elvis replied and we both laughed as Joe tried to get his hands untied. "Roll 'em up Chris."

I shook the dice up in my hand.

"Come on Chris, let's get a real low number here huh buddy?" Joe asked me desperately. "We're old friends here after all."

"Only the dice can decide," I said laughingly and Joe turned his head to look at Elvis.

"Fuck man, lookit my poor hard cock all tied up the way you got it," Joe nearly whimpered and a few droplets of pre cum oozed from his wide sexy slit.

"But isn't that a good thing?" Elvis teased our marine.

Elvis and I knew that our marine was secretly enjoying all this attention that we were lavishing on him. The way his cock kept getting hard and oozing pre cum even after we'd jacked him off twice was evidence of how much he was enjoying all this. I shook up the dice a little more and then threw them on the end table.

"What's the number buddy? Elvis asked me.

"Double sixes," I called out and Elvis and I both guffawed triumphantly.

"Fuck, *fuck, double digits again,*" the marine said in total anguish. "And this time it's my balls on the line."

"Double digits are right buddy, that means twenty-four swats," I said to him as Elvis rubbed his testicles with the thin metal ruler.

"Yeah, this might hurt a bit," Elvis quipped, sounding real humorous yet sadistic at the same time. "Start counting 'em off Marine."

Elvis began lightly swatting Joe's testicles with the ruler.

"OWWWWWW, o-one, two, three," Joe called out as Elvis delivered the blows.

"Elvis, if he misses a number I don't want him to have to start over this time," I said, sounding somewhat concerned as my buddy swatted our marine's nuts. "These are his nuts after all..."

"OWWWWW!!! F-four, and five, six..." the marine counted on

"Okay, I guess that's fair enough," Elvis said, sounding almost as concerned, but not quite as much as I.

"OWWWWWW, seven, and eight," the marine grunted, nearly jumping out of his socks as Elvis swatted his balls a bit harder. "N-nine and ten!!! OWWWWWWW!!!"

"Yeah, sure enough, I think that does hurt," Elvis laughed, holding tight to Joe's upper arm to keep him balanced and at attention as he swatted his nuts.

"You bet your white ass it hurts man!!" the marine nearly cried, standing there with his teeth clenched, his muscles flexing like crazy as he endured the swats to his nuts. "Like I said hell of a way to welcome me home. OWWWWWW!!! Eleven man!!!"

"You mean the best way to welcome you home," Elvis corrected Joe harshly. "And after all, it is *your* black ass and balls suffering."

"Sure as shit bud, OWWWWW!!!" Joe bitched. "Wonder how many of my other buddies who are on leave are being spanked welcome home."

"Just the lucky ones like you I'm sure," Elvis said and gave Joe's nuts a few whacks in fast succession.

"OWWWWWWW!!! Twelve, thirteen, four-fourteen," Joe seethed, his muscular black body glistening beautifully with sweat at that point. "Yeah, when I get back to the base my buddies and I can compare notes on how we were spanked welcome home. OWWWWW, fifteen, sixteen, seventeen!! And I got no doubt that when I get back my best buds in the Corps are going to spank me welcome back, gads!!!"

When Elvis finished administering the twenty-four swats to Joe's nuts it was then my turn.

"Okay Chris, your turn to swat our marine's big balls," Elvis said as we switched places and he now picked up the dice after handing me the thin metal ruler. "Then after that I'll decide what to do next with him."

Standing there at attention with tears glistening in his eyes Joe simply gulped hard at Elvis's words. I stepped next to our marine and rubbed the metal ruler under and over his wounded and aching testicles.

"You ready to swat his balls Chris?" Elvis asked me, shaking up the dice.

"You know it buddy," I said anxiously. "Get me a good number this time."

Smiling, Elvis tossed the dice on the end table.

"Ha, double five's," Elvis cackled happily and our marine squeezed his eyes shut and looked up at the ceiling in anguish.

"Fuck, I can't watch," Joe whispered.

"Great number for us buddy," I said to Elvis.

"Yeah, but it's not a great number for him," Elvis laughed. "But like a good marine he'll take it all of course, as he should..."

"Count 'em off Marine," I said with total authority in my voice. "Twenty good hard swats coming up."

Looking up at the ceiling Joe blurted out, "OWWWWWW, one, t-two, ohhh G-god, thr-three..." as I began whapping his balls good and hard with the ruler.

"St-still can't look buds," Joe grunted miserably as I whapped his balls harder. "OWWWWWW shiiiitttt, f-four, and five, and six, OWWWWWW...seven, eight..."

When I was done giving our marine's balls the twenty swats Elvis and I agreed that one round each of swatting them was more than enough. We were simply having some nasty "welcome home" fun with our good buddy and we had no intention whatsoever of doing him any permanent damage.

"OHHHHRRRR gads man," Joe sputtered as Elvis did the honors of untying his semi hard cock and letting it hang freely again over his whapped and aching balls.

"OHHHHHhhhh my poor balls you fuckers," the marine whimpered as Elvis and I took him by his upper arms.

"Back to the spanking couch for him?" I asked Elvis.

"You know it man," Elvis laughed as we trudged Joe slowly back to the couch on his socked feet.

"*B-back to the spanking couch?*" the marine, asked us in total surprise. "Y-you mean you guys are planning on whipping my ass some more???"

"Sure as shit," Elvis said, sounding almost angry at that point. "I don't see any tears and I haven't heard any words of remorse for that marine attitude of yours bud."

"Fuck man, you keep paddling and whipping my naked butt you're going to see tears," Joe pleaded as Elvis sat down on the spanking couch and I helped Joe get himself splayed over my buddies knees and lap. "Gads, this really is a shitty thing to be doing to a United States marine you guys!!"

"Doing this to an arrogant United States marine calms him down and puts him in check," Elvis said, sounding like he was correcting our buddy again and rubbed a hand over Joe's wounded and bruised butt cheeks.

Elvis smiled wickedly as he ran his hand over our marine's wounded butt cheeks.

"Fuck man, we're working hard for him here to welcome him home properly," I said to Elvis. "He should be thanking us, don't you think?"

"Sure thing Chris, but he isn't," Elvis replied as I handed him the hairbrush. "Just roll the dice buddy."

"I'll thank you when you're done and when you two clowns untie me, damn, a hairbrush this time???" our marine grunted.

"Still no respect," Elvis said and grinned as I shook up the dice. "And I don't like that..."

With his head spinning Joe watched from over Elvis's knees with his head slightly raised as I rolled the dice...

"Oh fuckkkk, here we go again," Joe said miserably.

Elvis looked at me in anticipation of a high number or double digits as I rolled the dice and he rubbed the wooden side of the hairbrush over Joe's highly raised succulent looking butt cheeks. Joe grimaced and tottered on his socked toes over Elvis's lap...

I threw the dice and snapped my fingers, grinning over at my two buddies...

"Double threes," I said ecstatically.

"That's twelve Marine," Elvis laughed. "Seems like the double digits are in love with you today..."

"Yeah, and I guess for you that's a great fucking thing huh Elvis my man?" Joe asked miserably and his head shot slightly up as Elvis brought the wooden side of the hairbrush down on the marine's raised ass. "OWWWWW, shiiiittt, one!!!"

Elvis and I grinned and laughed as the marine counted off twelve "really fucking hard" swats, all administered to the same butt cheek with the wooden side of the hairbrush.

"FUCK, twelve!!" Joe barked loudly and in searing pain as Elvis gave him the last swat. "What's up with that shit Elvis? Beating on just one of my ass cheeks???"

"I'll let Chris have the other one," Elvis chuckled and helped our marine to his feet, standing him momentarily at attention.

Elvis and I switched places again and Joe got himself again situated across my knees and lap. As Elvis picked up the dice I picked up the hairbrush...

"A five and a four," Elvis called out after rolling and throwing the dice. "Nine hard hairbrush swats to one ass cheek if you would Chris."

"Sure thing buddy," I said happily and brought the wooden side of the hairbrush down twice real hard on Joe's left-sided butt cheek, the one that Elvis had not paddled with the brush.

"OWWWWW shit man, one, two," Joe blurted loudly. "G-gads, if those first two swats just stung like the devil I can fucking imagine what the last seven are goin' to be like buds..."

I paddled his left-sided butt cheek two more times, harder with each blow.

"...th-three, f-four," Joe announced almost breathlessly.

I paddled his left ass cheek again and again; the sound of the wooden hairbrush was like a dull thudding sound as it connected with our marine's butt.

"F-five, six," Joe called out. "And fuck, all on the same damned butt cheek..."

I gave Joe the last three and hardest of the nine paddles with the hairbrush and then it was again Elvis's turn to paddle our marine's butt with the hairbrush. By now Joe's butt cheeks were pretty bruised looking and Elvis was pretty happy about that as he got the marine over his lap and his knees. I rolled a real low number, a four, and not even double digits. Elvis saw that as a waste of time but administered four real hard swats with the hairbrush side of the brush this time to Joe's right-sided ass cheek.

"OWWWWW shit, whappin' me with the damned hard bristles," Joe bitched loudly. "One, two, OWWWWWWWW!!! And three, four!!!"

For my second round of hairbrush spanking the marine I was much luckier than Elvis had been where the dice were concerned. When Elvis called out "double sixes" after throwing the dice my eyes lit up and I raised the hairbrush bristles over Joe's left-sided ass cheek. Joe however, over my knees and lap was not as thrilled as I was.

"Oh fuck, no, no, twenty-four swats on one ass cheek with a damned hairbrush bristles???" the marine croaked, tears finally welling up in his eyes.

"Looks like we're about to break him of that arrogant marine attitude now," Elvis quipped. "And *that* is more than a great fucking thing. Begin thrashing his ass Chris."

"Sure thing," I said with total enthusiasm. "Count 'em off Marine!!"

"Y-yes Sir, Sirs, I mean," Joe whimpered and I brought the bristles of the hairbrush down on his left-sided ass cheek.

"One!!!" Joe blurted miserably and this time in between spanking his ass left-sided cheek I saw how it twitched and jerked in anticipation of each impending blow...

"T-two, three, f-four, owwwwww!!!" our marine sputtered as the tears finally rolled down his cheeks as he lay splayed over my lap and knees...

After I gave him the allotted twenty-four swats with the hairbrush bristles Joe stood at attention with his lips pursed in a mixture of anger and pride as Elvis and I rubbed a goodly amount of aloe cream over his wounded butt cheeks. The cream slightly soothed the marines spanked and bruised ass cheeks and was also preventing them from bleeding from the swats we had given them and the ones still to come. With his massive chest and fat nipples jutted out Joe stood as rigidly at attention as possible as we smoothed the cream over his ass cheeks, his cock rock hard again, his wounded balls hanging down real low... He nearly jumped out of his socks when we each slid a cream slicked finger up his warm ass hole and prodded around in there for a few seconds each.

"Ayyyyyrrr shiiiiittt, get your damned fingers out of my raunchy hole you mugs," Joe grunted. "Spankin' my hard marine ass is one thing but diggin' for gold in my hole is totally another!!"

At that point the marine had suffered one hundred and eighteen swats to his butt cheeks and forty-four swats to his balls. When Elvis pointed this out to him Joe asked if we were done...

When Elvis glanced at the wooden spoon on the table where the spanking utensils were and when I picked up Joe's blindfold the marine gulped real hard...

"Fuck, wonder if I'll make that party my parents are havin' for me tonight," the marine whimpered.

"Oh you'll make the party, don't worry about that, that's a great thing after all," Elvis laughed as he squatted down and tied the marine's black socked feet tightly together and I tied the blindfold over his eyes.

"Wh-what now buds?" the marine asked nervously. "T-tyin' my feet now and blindfolding me again???"

"Got to get you ready and positioned for the next round of spanking bud," Elvis laughed, snapping the elastic in Joe's black socks against his calves after getting his feet securely tied.

"Oh gads Sirs, my poor ass cheeks," Joe whimpered as Elvis and I each grabbed one of his arms and upper legs.

"Not your ass cheeks this time Marine," Elvis said, looking at me across our tied and blindfolded marine. "And up we go into the wild blue yonder..."

That said Elvis and I hoisted the muscle-heavy marine off the floor by his arms and legs in a prone position.

"H-hey, what's up with this?" the marine barked as we lugged him over to a long table at the other end of the room. "Fuckers, put me down, gads, carryin' me like I was a sack of laundry or something..."

Moments later we had Joe stretched out atop the table, leaning back on his tied hands, his chest area jutted up and a poor ready target for what we had in mind next.

"What now Sirs?" Joe asked almost desperately. "Haven't you guys had enough of spanking me at this point?"

"Marine, you know that we could never get enough of spanking a guy like you," Elvis replied for both of us, grabbing one of Joe's fat nipples and jiggling it hard, twisting it too.

Joe grimaced behind his blindfold.

"Fuck, at least get this damned blindfold off me, hate this shit when I can't see," he complained miserably. "I keep getting the feelin' that you two are goin' to sucker punch me in the gut like my Marine Corps. Buddies did during hazing and initiation."

"That sounds interesting," Elvis said, still holding tight to our marine's nipple, twisting the bejesus out of it, causing Joe's cock to grow rock hard between his legs again. "How did that work?"

"The poor guy being hazed was tied and blindfolded, just like you mugs got me here now," Joe explained. "Then his buddies would take turns giving him good hard marine-like punches to the gut. The tied up and blindfolded dude's job was to tighten his gut fast enough before the next blow *and* to guess correctly who it was that had delivered the punch. If he guessed correctly the guy who gave him the gut punch was out of the game. If the marine being hazed guessed incorrectly the guy got to give him more gut punches, until the poor marine guessed correctly. Only difference being that the marine being hazed had to be standing at attention, not hoisted up on a table and stretched out like a buffet at a wedding."

"Fuck, that sounds hot bud," Elvis said almost breathlessly. "Sounds like a great fucking thing…"

"Sure as shit was for the guys giving the tied and blindfolded marine the gut punches," Joe said and this time all three of laughed together.

"Okay, time to show our marine here what he's in for, for the last round of spanking here," Elvis said and took the blindfold off Joe.

Joe looked up from the table he was stretched out on and saw the two of us standing over him, holding a wooden spoon each in hand.

"Oh man, of fuck," Joe said softly as he looked at the wooden spoons in our hands.

"Just like mama used to whip your ass with Marine," Elvis teased our bound up buddy, rubbing the back of the spoon against one of his pecs, swirling it over the nipple he'd just squeezed and playfully tap tapping him with it.

"Yeah, sure thing Elvis, but mama never whipped my damn pecs and big marine tits," Joe said almost pleadingly as he sat up on his tied hands atop the table, his chest and pecs jutted up real big.

"Then, it's a real good thing we're doing here bud, seeing as you obviously missed out on it years back," Elvis laughed and then looked across at me. "Chris, the dice if you would."

"You got it buddy," I said and picked up the dice, momentarily putting my wooden spoon down.

"The number that Chris rolls will be the amount of swats that we each give to each of your pecs," Elvis explained to the marine.

Joe simply nodded that he understood while looking straight down at his bound socked feet, wiggled his toes under his socks and his cock grew harder still...

I shook up the dice and threw them down on the side of the table Joe was on...

"A six and a five," I said as we all looked at the pair of dice, Elvis and I in delight and Joe in agony.

"Take it easy buds, if I remember right those wooden spoons can hurt like the devil," Joe grunted as Elvis and I took our positions on the sides of the table.

"Yeah, and isn't that a great fucking thing?" Elvis laughed.

Joe leaned his head back, looked up at the ceiling and stuck his chest out real wide and massively...

WHAPPP WHAPPP WHAPPP WHAPPP

"OHHHHHHH FUCCCKKK, fuck it all buds, that's my damned pecs you're whippin' the tar out of now," the marine seethed. "And okay, one, t-two, three, four..."

Joe grunted out the numbers of swats we gave him across his pecs, even aiming for his big fat nipples in between, really getting some howls of pain out of our marine. He told us how that was an awful thing to do to a marine's man tits and even worse to be beating on and bruising his massive pecs. When Elvis rolled the dice for the next round of pecs and man tit swatting the number was six, double threes actually. Joe whimpered miserably and grunted in pain through twelve more swats to his man tits and muscled-pecs. A few times his pecs bounced real erotically as we swatted underneath them, that's the most sensitive section of a guy's pecs, if you didn't know that already bud...

When it was all over it was almost three hours later. Being that Joe had been more than a good sport about it all Elvis and I told him how we would treat him out to a few beers at a neighborhood watering hole before heading back to his parent's house for the welcome home party they were having for him.

"I doubt that my parent's party will be anything like this one was buds," Joe said, climbing down off the table after we'd untied his hands and feet.

We all laughed at his comment as he shucked his socks off his feet and stood before us in his entire naked and muscular splendor.

"If it's okay with you Elvis I'm going to take a shower before I get back into my uniform," Joe said. "After all that spanking and whipping I'm all sweaty and smelly."

"Help yourself buddy," Elvis said, holding out his hand and Joe shook it. "You did well buddy, I'm proud to know you and proud that you're a hard-core marine. I just hope you're not too pissed off at us."

Joe simply smirked at Elvis as he shook his hand. I was sure that if the marine were pissed with us for stripping him, for tying him up, for blindfolding him and of course for spanking him we would know it. I shook his hand next, he thanked me for the most interesting welcome home he could ever have imagined and trotted off to the bathroom to shower...

Elvis gave Joe a fresh pair of briefs and kept the marine's cum sopped ones as a sleazy sort of souvenir of our spanking session... When Joe was again impeccably dressed in his uniform we drove to a nearby neighborhood bar where we treated our marine to a couple of cold tall beers. Being that I was driving I drank club soda while Elvis and Joe enjoyed the beer. People from the neighborhood who knew Joe came over to shake hands with him and to say "Welcome Home" as well. A few of the girls looked Joe up and down lustfully and so did a few of the guys actually. Joe had been right earlier, he didn't need to rent a hotel room if he wanted to spend the nights in the arms of beautiful women while he was home on leave. I was more than sure that some of the girls would have jumped at the chance to spend the night with Joe by inviting him to their places. A few people offered to buy him a beer but he politely declined, citing how Elvis and I had bought him a few beers to welcome him home...

We arrived back at Joe's parent's house an hour before the party in his honor was to begin. When we got up to the front door Joe's mother opened it and stopped us in our tracks.

"Joe, I have the most wonderful surprise for you," she said, smiling from ear to ear as she took in the sight of her handsome son, Elvis and I. "You will never believe who's here for your "welcome home" party."

"Who is it Mom?" Joe asked anxiously.

"I know, I know, let's blindfold him and you two can lead him into the living room," Joe's mother said, handing Elvis a long white cloth.

Joe turned and looked at us with dread in his eyes, until Elvis tied the blindfold on him...

Moments later Elvis and I were leading our blindfolded marine into his parent's house and toward the living room as his mother led the way. Standing in the living room were three tall, rugged looking marines, all dressed in their formal uniforms, just as Joe was. The guy marine standing in the center had an unlit and stinky cigar wedged in the corner of his mouth.

"Okay, one of you take the blindfold off him," Joe's mother said giddily.

I took the blindfold off our marine and at the sight of his three buddies Joe whooped it up like crazy.

"Holy shit, holy cow!!!" Joe blurted in total delight.

"How're you doin' buddy?" the tallest and most rugged of the three marines asked Joe, his arms open wide. "Welcome Home!!!"

"I do not believe this shit!!!" Joe laughed like crazy and ran into his marine brother's arms.

With no effort whatsoever the guy hoisted Joe off the floor in a bear hug and spun him around a few times...

"How'd you know where my parents lived?" Joe asked his buddies and it was explained to him that his mother did all the inviting for the party.

Joe told Elvis and me how these were his good buddies and his hazing buddies...

Elvis and I smiled wickedly at his three buddies, a knowing look in all of our eyes...

Joe's mother explained how she and Joe's father and siblings had more setting up to do before the party and that the five of us could relax down in the basement till the party was ready to start...

Looking at his marine buddies and Elvis and I, I got the feeling that Joe knew what he would be in for down in the basement... It seemed that the spanking welcome home that Joe received that day was far from over and Elvis and I were glad we had brought the dice along with us...

(4)

Tickle Challenge for Julius

(From the book: Timmy and the Hong Kong Tailor)

This story was inspired by a rough and tough Brooklyn dude who lives across the street from me. What really gets me where he is concerned is the Guido way he sits out on his front porch in the summer time in shorts, no shirt, (his flabby belly and big tits hanging out for all to see) and thick white or black socks with slippers. His name is John, why I called him Julius in the story I will probably never know.

Obviously I made the character of Julius in the story very gullible. I am sure that my neighbor who I modeled the character after is not as gullible to allow himself to fall into such a ticklish predicament. I am sure that I would be extremely disappointed if I tried to talk him into such a thing... but then again, as I have stated in the past, one never really does know, does one?

I was real positive when writing this story. I liked the idea of having the rugged tickle victim's feet skin softened up with the lavender lotion and then blow drying them with a heated hair dryer. I know for a fact that that really does make a guy's feet all the more sensitive to touches... and of course all the more sensitive to being tickle tortured.

The book itself has received very good reviews. I loved being the character in the story that sort of fell in love with the guy across the street and got to work him over a bit. I do not think that my character was inherently evil, but he was quite accomplished in villainy. Basically though, like me, he is a good person.

Is this a love story? I'm really not sure. Can a person show how much they love another person by tying them up and tickling the daylights out of them? Again, I'm really not sure, but I do know that it works just fine for me.

What's the point of writing a story like this if you are not going to embellish the characters a bit? Then it wouldn't be a story right? I know I embellished the character of Julius on a lot of levels, but as for my character, I would say that I am pretty much like that. I can talk most people into things...when I am feeling real persuasive that is.

Some of the incidents mentioned in the story were real, like how me and Julius first got to know each other, the time he offered to buy me coffee when he and his buddies were heading over to Dunkin' Donuts, etc. But Julius falling into my ticklish clutches and being tickle tortured were all figments of my twisted imagination, or, perhaps to say it in a different way, the tickle scenes were all wishes from my creatively twisted imagination.

It amazes me how I took the real-life person of my neighbor John and transformed him into a gruff but gullible tickle victim named Julius in this story. It was a great thing for me and taking the traits of his personality that I knew and adding the ones that I created worked pretty well for me. I know I am good at that, when it comes to creating fictional characters out of people I know in real life.

It's a sort of power that I feel I have when I create a fictional person out of a real person. It's like I am giving birth to the fictional character and in a way so is the real person. I also have to wonder if what I see in a person in a fictional sense is somehow underlying in them. There is truth in jest and fiction, as I have found out over time.

———————————

Julius and I live directly across the street from each other on a quiet street in Brooklyn, New York. We have never been close when it comes to the term "neighbors", but we always politely wave at each other across the street if we happen to be coming out of our houses at the same time, we always say "hello" to each other if we pass on the street and we always ask if the other needs anything if we're headed to a store. In fact, one time Julius was getting into a car with a bunch of his buddies as I was passing by headed to my house and as I waved a "hello" greeting to him he told me that he and his buds (that's what he called them, his buds) were heading down to Dunkin' Donuts to get some of their famous coffee, asking if I wanted any. I thanked him but said, "No thanks, I only drink coffee in the early morning and its past afternoon now." He smiled his pursed lips together smile and climbed into the backseat of the car along with two of his other buds. It amazed me that he was able to fit in that backseat as Julius is a mountain of a guy, at least two hundred to two hundred and fifty pounds of sheer muscle. I know Julius works as an iron-worker because a few years back when he had just moved into the neighborhood we ran into each other on the train on the way home from work. He was sitting one seat away from me and to be perfectly honest I didn't recognize him. As I was putting my paperback book away in my attaché case he looked over at me from where he was sitting, clad in big clunky mustard colored construction boots, scuffed blue jeans and a heavy parka jacket over a sweatshirt, (it was during the winter months when we met on the train) smiled with his lips pressed together and said "Hello." He had a deep baritone sounding voice, a real fucking grunt of a guy. I looked at him a tad mystified and fleetingly wondered if I was about to be picked up by a real rugged nearly bald, six foot or more construction worker.

"You know, I see you practically every day when you leave for work in the morning," he said to me and I looked at him even more mystified. "I live right across the street from you. I'm Julius…"

"Oh, yeah, now I recognize you," I said, sounding real stupid as his deep dark brown eyes seemed to bore into me.

"We live right across the street from each other, I bought that house about a year ago, me and my wife I should say," he went on. "We just had a baby girl…"

"Congratulations," I said, recalling seeing the giant pink plastic stork outside the house on the lawn with the words "It's A Girl" stenciled on it in giant letters.

I stood up and sat back down next to him in the seat for two passengers as the train barreled along.

"I'm Christopher," I said and held out my hand. "It's nice to meet you Julius…"

"Good to meet you too Christopher," he said and shook my hand, his giant ham-sized and calloused hand dwarfing mine as we shook and then released each other's hand. "Yeah, every morning one of my buds picks me up and drives me in to wherever we're stationed to work that week or month. Being that it's so cold out I wait inside the house by the door. I see you when you leave the house all doodled up in your suit and tie and you're heading for the subway."

"Oh, okay, no wonder I don't see you in the mornings then," I said.

"I would offer you a ride to the subway but my bud's car is a bit dusty from the work we do," Julius said with a smile. "He's real lazy about vacuuming out his car…and uh, I wouldn't want you getting your nice suit all dirtied up. We work for Green and Sons, the construction and Iron Company."

"I've heard of them," I said. "And it's no problem at all, I don't mind walking to the train station, it's not that far from the house after all…"

"Thanks man, I didn't want you to think I was a rude neighbor," Julius said. "I like to be friendly with everyone in the area if I can…where we used to live that's how it was. But when me and the wife decided we wanted kids it was time for a bigger house…"

"I see…" I said.

"So what about you Christopher?" Julius asked. "You married or what?"

My heart pounded because I was not ready to tell Julius that I lived with a male partner, had lived with Alan for the last thirteen years to be exact, although I was pretty sure Julius knew I was gay and was just riding me for information.

"Uh, no, I'm not married, my uh; roommate and I share the upstairs apartment in the house directly across from yours..." I replied, stretching my legs out in front of me and crossing my wing tipped and dress socked feet over each other.

"Yeah, I know your landlords, nice Italian couple, the Signora's," Julius said, suddenly having an Italian accent when he said the word "Signora's."

"Yeah, they're real nice," I said, trying not to sound too sarcastic as I said it.

I was thinking how if it weren't for the very cheap rent Alan and I would have been out of that apartment years ago. Dealing with an old fashioned Italian landlord and his wife, both of whom barely speak a shred of English is not that easy...

"So now we know each other and we can say "Hello" to each other when we see each other in the neighborhood," Julius said and held out his hand to shake again. "In the winter months I hibernate, being that I mostly work outdoors. But in the summer I like to sit out on the porch so we'll probably see each other a lot then..."

"Or here on the train..." I said as I shook his hand again.

"Nah, I'm only takin' the train tonight because my bud that usually drives me home was out sick today..." Julius explained as he pumped my hand, once again dwarfed in his huge one.

I saw him glance down at my crossed feet for a millionth of a second and then as he let go of my hand our train barreled into the "Bay Parkway" station.

"Well, here's our stop Christopher," Julius said and stood up, towering over me as I still sat.

He was easily a tad better than six feet tall...

I wondered what size his giant feet were...

I also could not help wondering if he had a cock the size of a horse's in those scuffed up jeans of his...

"Yep, time for us to get off the train," I said, me getting to my feet next and standing next to him as he still towered over me.

"I have to stop in the supermarket by the station," Julius said. "What about you?"

"No, I don't need anything; I'm just going to head on home..." I said as we disembarked from the train.

"Okay then, it was great to talk with you Christopher," Julius said. "Maybe I'll see you soon in the neighborhood..."

"Take care man," I responded and Julius quickened his step to head for the supermarket, swaggering as he walked toward the flight of stairs that led out of the train station.

I took in the sight of his big ass as he climbed the steps and my heart leapt in my chest…

As time passed and winter turned to summer, as Julius had said on the train, he always sat outside his house on the raised porch, I would see him sitting there on a yard chair most summer evenings when I got home from work, and his big feet propped up on the railing of the porch. He always waved "Hello" at me and called out "How's it going bud?" I always politely waved back at him and said "Hello" as well and said that it was going just great. Julius always had a cigarette in one hand as he sat there relaxing on his porch, clad at the end of his workday in knee length shorts, a string tank-top with his huge buffalo-sized arms sticking out of the thin sleeves and what had to be his leftover sweat socks from the workday tucked down around his ankles. Seeing those damned sweat socked feet of his propped up on the railing of his porch sent chills through me. He always favored both black or white thick cotton socks and the way they were scrunched down around his ankles told me that he had most definitely started his day with those stinkers pulled up over his iron-like calves. As the day wore on Julius's socks, like most guys socks out there found their way to his ankles. And like most guys who wear construction boots for their jobs he didn't give a fuck about pulling them back up. It's not like he was in a suit and tie after all and he would have those stinkers on display when he sat down… What really got me though were the times I passed by when getting home from work and Julius would be standing out on the sidewalk rather than sitting on his porch, chatting with neighbors while smoking his cigarette. Always at the end of the day he would be clad in knee length shorts, his string tank-top and those damned sweat socks down around his ankles. But it was when he would be standing on the sidewalk was what really sent chills through me, because unlike most guys who would be wearing sneakers Julius had his socked feet in slippers, and not just any slippers mind you, but the type where the toes stick out the front. There was something feminizing and vulnerable, yet totally fucking sexy in that look for a huge grunt of a guy like Julius if you ask me. Now, mind you, Julius is not the best looking guy on God's green earth. Granted, he's built like a bull and nearly as bald as an eagle but he's not exactly Cary Grant handsome. But even though, seeing him in those damned slippers with his mangy sweat socks from his sweaty workday piled down around his ankles just got to me and the wicked thoughts took root in my mind. As always Julius waved "Hello" at me. One night while walking down the street toward my house I saw Julius sitting on his porch, but his big old socked feet weren't propped up on the railing this time and as I got closer I saw that the reason for that was that he was holding his baby daughter in his lap. She was absolutely an angel… He looked up, saw me as I passed by and waved a quick "Hello" this time, his attention returning instantly to the baby in his lap. As I worked on the "Tickle Story" that I was writing at that time for my publisher Julius's face kept popping into my mind… My tickle story centered around two buddies in a New York neighborhood. One of the guys in the story challenged his buddy to a tickle bet, gambling one hundred dollars that he could make his cocky buddy laugh while tickling him crazily. The buddy insisted he wasn't ticklish and would win the bet hands down... Sitting there writing that story Julius's face again came into my mind and I wondered if he was ticklish...

During that first summer when I got to know Julius through our passing each other in the neighborhood and saying our quick "Hello's" to each other my partner Alan had to go on a three day business trip. I was on my two week vacation at the time from my full time job, and as I found out and as luck would have it, Julius was on his two week vacation as well. It seemed that lots of companies closed for vacation during the first two weeks of July. I was sitting outside the house on the front stoop sipping a beer on the second night that Alan was away when Julius came sauntering down the block, clad in his usual uniform of string tank-top, knee length shorts, slippers and sweat socks, although this time Julius's sweat socks were the short style that reach just above a guy's ankles *and* they were dark grey with a thick black stripe going around the top of them... I was totally astounded that Julius had changed his style of sweat socks. It was about seven o'clock so the sun was still shining and it was still pretty warm out that summer evening.

"How's it goin' Christopher?" Julius asked in greeting, his baritone voice booming as he spoke, and held out his hand.

"Pretty good," I replied and reached out to shake his giant hand, holding my beer bottle in the other hand. "I'm enjoying two weeks of vacation, my roommate is out of town, I got the whole place to myself...could not be better... And you?"

"Same man, same," Julius said and propped one of his slippered and sweat socked feet on the step just below the one I was sitting on, his foot right between my legs actually. "I'm on vacation, the wife is away with my daughter at her mothers, like you I got the whole damn place to myself...could not be better... Every once in a while I need that..."

"Here, here," I said and raised my beer bottle. "Say, can I get you a beer?"

"Uh, no, I'm not real big on beer," Julius began.

"I have Diet Coke and iced tea as well..." I said, seeing how he was sweating a bit from the summer heat.

"Iced tea sounds good," Julius said and smiled his pursed lips smile.

"Come on upstairs, we'll have it in the air conditioned living room, it's too hot out here," I suggested, thinking for sure he would decline that end of my offer.

"Now that sounds like a plan..." the huge grunt of a guy said and for the first time ever smiled from ear to ear.

He actually had a beautiful smile and I wondered why he didn't smile that way more often. As we walked up the flight of stairs to my upstairs apartment Julius's giant feet made stomping sounds. My heart made its own stomping sounds, but of course Julius was unaware of that...

"Sorry about the noise man, these size twelve feet of mine do it every time..." Julius laughed as I opened the door to the apartment.

"Not a problem," I said as we stepped into the apartment. "Living room is that way, make yourself comfortable."

"Thanks man," Julius said and sat down on the couch in the air conditioned living room.

"Hey, real nice place you and your roommate got here!" Julius called out as I poured a tall glass of iced tea for him.

"Thanks, we like the conservative look I suppose you could say..." I said as I entered the living room with his iced tea and my half empty bottle of beer.

I handed Julius the iced tea and sat down a few feet away from him on the couch. We clinked my beer bottle and his glass and in unison said, "To friendship..."

"Thanks man, this is real nice of you I gotta say," Julius said and sipped the iced tea.

"No problem, it was nice of you to offer to bring me coffee that day," I reminded him.

"Oh yeah, I forgot about that," Julius said and sipped his iced tea as I sipped my beer. "When you said you didn't want coffee I should have offered you ice tea...dumb of me..."

"Don't worry about it," I repeated. "It really was nice of you to offer..."

Julius sipped his iced tea and then slipped his slippers off and set his socked feet atop them, wiggling his toes...

"So uh, size twelve feet huh?" I asked him. "It must be kind of difficult for you to find shoes and socks in your size..."

"You could say that, but I thank God for the store in lower Manhattan that sells what's called over-sizes in work boots," Julius said. "I buy three and four pairs of boots at a time so I always have them on hand... or on foot if you would..."

"I see," I said and we both chuckled a bit at his comment.

"I tell you though, having big feet like mine sure ain't easy," Julius said.

"What do you mean?" I asked and sipped my beer.

"Well, for one thing, like you said, finding a store that sells my size in shoes and socks ain't easy," he replied. "My wife though, she manages to find me my socks. But when a guy has huge feet like mine they tend to cramp a lot..."

I looked down at his gray and black socked feet and saw that he was again wiggling his toes...

"You ever get a Charlie horse in one of your arches during the night Christopher?" Julius asked me and I nodded "yes." "Well let me tell you bud, when you get a Charlie horse when you have size twelve feet it's a real bitch and a half. One night it woke me up, it was so fucking painful and I screamed so loud that my wife thought I was fuckin' dying!"

"Man that sounds awful..." I said, not believing that we were actually talking about his big feet.

"It is, I even woke the baby that night, for that I really felt awful," Julius said and took a big gulp of his iced tea. "Poor little girl cried like she was terrified. I couldn't believe you didn't hear me all the way across the street, that's how bad it hurt that it made me scream like a goddamned banshee, shit! But when it happens my wife is able to massage it out for me, even though she complains about how my feet stink, hardy har, har!!"

Smiling from ear to ear Julius lifted his feet off the floor, held them stretched out a bit and wiggled his toes under his socks again.

"Wigglin' my big cock sized toes helps some too, but for the most part I'm just prone to Charlie horse cramps man," he said dejectedly. "With my wife out of town I really pray I don't get a Charlie horse during the night. No one there to massage it out so I would just have to ride that Charlie horse through…"

"That's too bad," I said and saw that his glass was just about empty. "Let me get you a refill on that…"

"Thanks man," Julius said and handed me his glass.

I went back out to the kitchen to refill his glass and was back in moments…

"It sounds like those cramps, what you call Charlie horses are a real challenge for you Julius," I said, pulling up a chair and sitting down in front of Julius this time.

"Yeah, they sure as shit can be," Julius said as I handed him the re-filled glass of iced tea. "Thanks man, this iced tea really hit the spot…"

"I'm glad," I said. "Yes, cramps in your feet sure can be a challenge Julius. Have you thought about going to a foot doctor for it?"

"Actually, it's funny you should mention that because my wife suggested the same thing the other night, the last time I woke up screaming in pain," Julius replied. "I just might go you know? I mean, I'm not all that thrilled to have some guy handlin' my damned smelly feet, but fuck, if it'll stop the Charlie horses and my wife won't have to massage them it'll be awesome. Plus I won't have to hear my wife complain about the smell of my feet when she takes my socks off me before massaging them when the Charlie horse hits…"

"Ah, you sleep with your socks on eh?" I asked him and by now with all this talk of his feet and their scent my cock was hard and doing a rain dance in my jeans.

"Yeah, the way my feet tend to sweat and stink I need to…" Julius said and took a gulp of his iced tea. "Jeez, never talked so much about my damned feet before. I sure do hope though that I'll be okay if the foot doctor is a guy and he handles my big dogs you know?"

"You uh, have a problem with a male doctor handling your feet?" I asked, my heart pounding by now.

"Only if he's gonna massage them you know?" Julius asked. "I mean, that's something that so far in my life only my wife has done…"

"I see," I said and watched as he sipped his iced tea.

"Although I will tell you a real funny bitch of a story," Julius said, sitting back on the couch and crossing one of his legs across his knee and letting his grey and black socked foot dangle downward. "If you have the time to hear it that is…"

"Sure, neither of us are working tomorrow, tell me," I said.

"One time my work buds and I were on lunch break in the basement of this building that we had been assigned to work in," Julius said. "We had been hired as part of a job to renovate the concourse area of an office building. Anyway, we were all sitting on the floor chowing down on our lunches when one of those goddamned Charlie horses decided to take me by surprise at that very moment... Well, I dropped my sandwich and started ranting in agony, my left foot thrashing outward in front of me. Needless to fucking say all my buds thought I was havin' a heart attack or something. But when I started bitching the words "My Foot, my foot, my goddamned foot" one of my more intelligent buds, this guy Tom, he knew just what the fuck to do."

"And what was that?" I asked and before he resumed his story Julius sipped more iced tea.

"Tom told my other buds to stand back, tellin' them that I was sufferin' a damned Charlie horse," Julius continued. "I screamed out "No fuckin' shit Sherlock" and Tom quickly went to work getting my boot laces undone. He got my boot off my foot followed by peelin' my smelly sock off afterwards. He knew just the fuck how to massage the Charlie horse right out of my foot, teasing me about how rancid my bare foot smelled as he worked. I guess he didn't want the guys thinking that he was enjoying massaging my damned stinkin' foot you know? Well, when he was done and while I was getting my sock and boot back on the other guys were all breathing sighs of relief that it was nothing critical and Tom told 'em and me how he suffered Charlie horses once in a while too, tellin' them how they mostly hit during the night and his wife has to massage them out. Tom and I found out that day that we have something in common, hardy har, har. We both have stinkin' rancid feet and we both suffer Charlie horses. Anyway, one of the guys said that Tom should have tickled my damned foot as payback for scaring them that way."

"Now that would be a real challenge," I said quickly, my hard cock twitching in my jeans at the word "tickle."

"Not really, because even though my buds thought it would have been funny as all hell to watch me laugh my head off I told them all that my feet may smell like yesterday's laundry but they were not ticklish," Julius said with satisfaction.

"Now that would be a real challenge, but more for me I suppose," I said, pretending to be mulling something over as I spoke.

"And what does that mean Christopher?" Julius asked, holding his once again half empty iced tea glass in hand.

"Well, let's say we would make it a bet between two buddies," I said, getting to my feet. "Here, let me refill that iced tea for you again."

Julius quickly scoffed down the rest of his iced tea and handed me the glass.

"A bet?" he asked his eyes nearly all aglow. "What the fucking fuck kind of bet do you have in mind? And where my damned feet would be concerned at that?"

"Let me get you more iced tea and then I'll tell you..." I said, quickly stepping out of the living room and leaving him wondering.

This time I took my sweet time refilling his iced tea glass...

My hands were shaking as I refilled Julius's glass for the third time...

Would I be able to pull off the stunt that I was considering???

I took a long enough time in the kitchen refilling Julius's glass for him to consider leaving my apartment before I told him what the bet was that I was considering presenting to him. I didn't hear him headed for the door so I supposed that meant he was intrigued. I picked up his once again full glass of iced tea and walked back into the living room. Without a word I handed him the iced tea...

"So, what's this bet between two buddies that you have in mind for me Christopher?" Julius asked me as I sat in the living room chair directly across from him again.

Glancing down quickly I saw that he had slipped his slippers back onto his grey and black socked feet.

"It uh, has to do with what your buds at the jobsite said to you the day you got the Charlie horse in your foot," I replied. "And what I said about it being a challenge..."

"Okay," Julius said, retracing our conversation before I had left the room to get him his third glass of iced tea. "You had said that it would be a challenge when I told you that I told that bud of mine at work that my smelly feet weren't ticklish...when he had suggested that Tom should have tickled my foot for having scared them when I got the Charlie horse and Tom massaged it out for me and... HOLY CRAP MAN!!!"

Julius's eyes had opened as wide as saucers as he looked at me.

"You mean to say that you want to try to find out if I was telling those buds of mine the truth???" Julius barked at me, sounding incredulous. "You mean to say that you want to...holy CRAP again man..."

Suddenly, Julius's face lit up like a beacon and he was chuckling... When he stopped laughing he sipped his iced tea...

"A hundred dollars says I can make you laugh your head off if I tickle your feet Julius," I said, narrowing my eyes and looking at him intently, still scared though that he would bolt to his slippered feet, stomp me, and then stomp out of my apartment.

"A hundred fucking dollars???" Julius echoed me. "Man, you really want to lose that kind of money Christopher?"

"I'll take that last question as a testament that you have just accepted my bet Julius..." I said with a grin.

I reached for my bottle of beer, held it up and Julius and I clinked his glass and my bottle together again...

"My feet are not ticklish man," Julius insisted a few minutes later as we walked toward my bedroom, after he had gulped down the rest of his third glass of iced tea. "You are about to lose one hundred dollars..."

"Well, I placed the bet so now I guess I'll have to just see it through…" I said as we entered my bedroom.

"Why in here man? Can't we just do it out in the living room?" Julius asked me as I reached under the bed for a cardboard box.

"It's better in here, you can lye stretched out on the bed, plus it's easier to tie your wrists to the bed board than it would be to tie you to the couch…" I said, reaching into the box and bringing out a length of rope.

"T-tie my wrists???" Julius blurted. "What do you mean tie my wrists?"

"That way I can really tickle test you Julius," I explained. "Let's face it, that guy that you work with, if he had started tickling your bare foot you could have simply swatted his hands away. Tied up here you won't have that chance, it gives me more of a chance to try to break you into laughing and it gives you the chance to really prove that your feet aren't ticklish…"

"Okay, I suppose that makes some kind of sense," Julius said and looked despondently at the length of rope I was holding.

I told him to take off his tank top and to lie down on his back with his wrists crossed above his head.

"Get comfortable buddy," I said with a grin as Julius did my bidding.

A few seconds later I was busily tying Julius's huge wrists to the bed board behind him in a crisscross type of fashion. His head was propped up on three pillows and his enormous muscular body was goose bump riddled as I tied him, taking my time about it.

"Fucking shit man, can't believe I accepted such an easy bet and I can't believe I'm letting you tie me to your damned bed…" Julius mused and wiggled his toes under his socks.

As I tied him the musty and funky scent from his hairy and furry armpits wafted up at me. The smell was somehow intoxicating. I figured that if I lost the bet and could not get him to laugh while tickling his feet I would simply tickle his armpits then, hardy har, har, as Julius would say…

"And to think all I did was accept an invitation for some iced tea…" Julius said as I finished tying his wrists to the bed board.

He watched as I stepped to the foot of the bed, slid his slippers off his feet and then took his socks off him, slowly peeling them off his feet…

"Ah man, hardy har, har, you are in for it now Christopher," Julius said with satisfaction in his voice. "When I mentioned that my feet were really rancid and stinky I wasn't just blowin' smoke! My wife really does insist that I wear my damned socks to bed…clean ones at that!"

"Whoo, you're right, you weren't blowing smoke," I said, waving a hand over my nose and mouth as the smell of Julius's giant feet assaulted my nostrils. "You sure are blowing foot stink though…"

"Ha, ha, looks like the jokes on you after all buddy," Julius said sounding triumphant.

He then watched as I deposited his rancid socks in a zip-lock plastic bag that I had had in the box along with the rope and other tickle supplies I keep on hand.

"What the fuck are you doin' with my socks man?" Julius asked as I picked up another length of rope.

"Not to worry Julius, I'll give you socks to wear for when you go home later," I said to him teasingly. "But I'm keeping these as a souvenir of this experience…"

"Jeez man, that has to be the shittiest thing you could do to a guy, to steal his goddamned socks, of all things," Julius said in disbelief.

Then, I sat down at his smelly size twelve feet, pushed them together at the ankles and began winding rope around and around them…

"Hey, you didn't say shit about tying up my feet too Christopher…" Julius complained. "God, if my wife could see me now…"

"Just getting these big feeties of yours ready for my challenge Julius," I said and after his feet were tied I lifted them to my nose and mouth and took a hearty sniff of them.

"WHOA!!! You really do have a big guy's foot stink, looks like I'll have to do something about that huh?" I asked my now captive.

"Fucking fuck man, what are you doin' sniffin' my dogs?" Julius ranted at me. "And what the hell do you mean do something about the way they smell? Just start ticklin' my feet, I won't laugh and I'll walk out of here a hundred dollars richer than when I came in and with new socks on to boot…"

"Like I said Julius, I'm just getting your feeties ready for my challenge, tying them up will keep you still when I start tickling you…in the meantime let's do something about the way they smell, yes?" I teased him meanly.

I turned on the air conditioner to a low setting in the bedroom and then reached into my box again. This time I brought out a bottle of moisturizing lotion and a hair blow dryer.

"Holy fuck man, what have I gotten myself into here?" Julius asked, looking up at the ceiling as I squeezed a goodly amount of the moisturizing lotion into the palm of my right hand.

"This lotion is lavender scented," I said to Julius as I put the bottle down and rubbed the lotion onto both my hands before applying it to my captive's feet. "It'll help to lessen the rancid scent of your feet plus soften them up a bit for you… and me…"

"Soften 'em up?" Julius asked. "Why the fucking fuck do you need to soften up my danged dogs Christopher?"

"You'll see, you'll see," I mused, sounding totally sadistic as I knelt down on the floor at Julius's bound up feet and gripped them at the sides and then began slathering and rubbing the lavender scented lotion onto them.

"Oh man, yeah, I gotta admit that does feel great at that," Julius remarked a few seconds later as I massaged the lotion deeply into his arches, all over the tops of his feet, of course against the meaty beefy bottoms of them and well in between his toes.

My hands made squishing sounds against his huge size twelve's as I coated them liberally with the lotion.

"Smells nice too," Julius commented. "Maybe I'll have my wife buy some of that lotion you got there and she can rub it on my feet every night before we go to sleep. That way I won't have to wear my damned socks to bed…"

I massaged the lotion onto his rough feeling heels with the palms of my hands pressed hard against them, my fingertips working the sides of his ankles at the same time, coating them as well with the lavender lotion.

"Okay, that's enough for now, now let's dry 'em up a bit yes?" I asked Julius.

"Huh? What do you mean dry 'em up?" Julius asked as I was wiping my hands on a cloth.

Then, he watched as I plugged in the hair blow dryer, set it to a medium heat setting and began blow drying his lotioned feet.

"Hey, what're you doin' man?" Julius asked, sounding totally confused as I blew the warm air all around and around his lavender smelling feet.

"Like I said buddy, you'll see, you'll see," I mused sadistically again.

When Julius's feet were dried up I turned off the hair blow dryer, knelt back down at his bound up feet and slathered a second goodly helping of the lavender scented lotion into the palms of my hands.

"Hey man, when are we goin' to get down to you tryin' to see if my feet are ticklish man?" Julius asked as I began again massaging the lotion onto his bound feet. "I really want my hundred dollars and new socks…plus I want to be untied real soon at that…"

"We're getting there Julius, we're getting there," I said, doing my best to sound like the villain in one of those old-time movies.

This time as I slathered the lotion over Julius's tootsies I could not help but notice that he flinched a few times as my fingers trailed upward along the bottoms of his feet. I smiled a bit with satisfaction. Yes, as I had said, we were getting there…

"HUHHH!!!" Julius sighed loudly as I purposely ran my fingertips upwards along the bottoms of his feet.

"Was that a laugh I heard just now Julius?" I asked him, my face very close to his feet now, my nose taking in the scent of his lavender scented cock-sized toes, as he had so aptly called them earlier.

"N-NO man that most certainly was not a laugh…" Julius replied, sounding a tad nervous by then.

I smiled meanly and gripped his toes with the palms of my hands…

Once again my hands made squishing sounds as I really applied a goodly amount of the lavender lotion between each of Julius's toes, really getting the cheese between his toes smelling real nice at that point. I purposely squeezed his toes with the palms of my hands as I did my work, bending them back and forth a bit. Then,

I massaged back down again along his arches, the bottoms of his exquisite size twelve's and along the tops. I put a lot of elbow grease into it when I lotioned up his heels the second time...

"Damn, my feet smell real pretty here Christopher..." Julius said heartily. "If I make my wife do this for me every night going forward from now on she'll never complain again about my smelly dogs..."

"Perhaps not..." I replied, wiped my hands off on the cloth and picked up my hair blow dryer for the second time.

Julius watched as I aimed the hair dryer at his lotioned feet and turned it on again to a warmer setting than the first time I had blown dried his slicked feet.

"I really don't know what all this lotion and blow drying on my feet is going to accomplish," the giant grunt said.

"You'll see, you'll see very soon," I teased him and spent a tad longer blow drying his feet this time.

When I was done blow drying Julius's feet the second time I picked up the bottle of lavender scented lotion for the third and final time...

"More lotion?" Julius asked as this time I held the bottle upside down over his toes.

I squeezed the bottle and let the lotion pour liberally over his gigantic feet.

"One last time buddy," I chuckled. "And then you'll see why I slicked and heated your big dogs.

Watching the lotion drip over his massive sized feet drove me wild. It actually looked like globs of cum coating his big tootsies. When his feet were liberally slathered once more with the lotion I put the bottle of lotion aside and again began massaging and squeezing Julius's feet...

"Ah man, that really does feel awesome bud," Julius commented and I saw the big plumped up bulge in his knee length shorts. "Jeez man, I just might start coming over here on a weekly basis for a nice foot rub you know? Not to sound all faggy or anything Christopher but your feet massage is givin' me a rage in my shorts here..."

"Yeah, I can see that," I said as I massaged the giant's arches, squeezing them both with the palms of my lotion slicked hands.

When I was done greasing up Julius's feet for the last time I put the bottle of lotion back in my box of supplies, wiped my hands on the cloth and aimed my blow dryer at his feet. I turned the blow dryer onto the highest setting and began drying his feet again...

"Hey, that's really hot this time..." Julius said and squirmed in the tight bondage. "Say man, what's the point of all this anyhow?"

"Just a few more moments and you are going to find out," I said fiendishly, gripping him by five of his toes as I blew dry his feet.

When his feet were thoroughly dried I put the blow dryer away and then knelt down at his very tightly bound, very slicked up and very sensitized feet, although Julius didn't know yet just how VERY sensitized I had made his feet with the lotion and the heat...

"Unt now Julius, eet ees teekle time for you," I said in a fiendish sounding yet comical German accent.

Julius raised his head above his arms and looked down at me as I reached into my box of supplies. I held up a long, stiff, white goose feather...

Julius wiggled all ten of his toes and nervously said, "Uh, look man, I told you, I'm not a ticklish guy...and...PWAHHHHHHHHHHHH!!!"

Julius screamed like an out of control hyena when I touched the tip of the goose feather to the bottom of his left foot.

"OOOHHHHRRRRRRR!!!" he screamed a second time as I trailed the goose feather upwards against his meaty foot.

His tied feet bobbed up and down on the bed as I tickle tortured him...

"Is that laughter I hear Julius?" I asked him and glided the feather alternately along his arches.

He pursed his lips tightly together and a look of total bewilderment came over his face...

"AAAARRRRRHHHH!!!" he roared loudly when he could no longer keep his lips pressed together as I slid the feather down the bottom of his left foot to his heel and then up his right foot and back down the left foot.

"Sounds like laughter about to happen if you ask me Julius..." I teased him.

"I-I won't laugh man, I ain't gonna lose that damned bet..." Julius ranted. "B-but fuck man, fuck it all, what the fucking fuck did you do to my damned feet???" What was in that goddamned lotion??? OOOOOOOOOOOOOOO!!!"

His head arched back and rested against his crossed arms, his tied hands struggled in the bondage and he looked up at the ceiling.

"Nothing was in the lotion but lotion Julius," I said to him as I teased his toes with the feather and strummed my fingertips against the bottoms of his feet. "It's just that that particular lotion is for highly sensitive skin. So, I softened your feet skin and then by blow drying your feet of the lotion I really *"softened"* your feet skin or perhaps the right word I'm looking for here is sensitized. Yeah, that's it; I sensitized your skin..."

"Th-that's cheatin' man," the giant grunted and looked back down at me as I swished the feather over the tops of his feet and around to the backs of them.

"Now, now Julius, we never said that I couldn't do something to help my cause," I said meanly with a smile as I trailed the feather again along his arches. "You told me that your feet weren't ticklish, I said that I could get you to laugh if I tickled your feet...we never agreed to me not doing something to help you along..."

"H-help me??? PWAHHHHHHHHHHHHHHHH!!! Y-you call this helping me??? You call tying up a guy and slicking his feet with lotion and heat helping him??? OHHHHHH GAWD MAN!!!"

"Almost there Julius and I'll be one hundred dollars richer..." I said.

"We-we'll just see fucker, PAHHHHHHHHHHHHHHHHH!!!" Julius screeched. "I haven't laughed yet.

Smiling meanly I reached into my box and then held up a sharp plastic toothpick...

"Wh-what are you planning on doing with that Christopher?" Julius asked miserably, starting to sweat at that point, even though the room was air conditioned.

"You'll see..." I said and with one hand I glided the goose feather against the beefy soles of his feet and with the other hand I started inserting the toothpick between his toes, working my way slowly across his big piggies.

"AAAAAWWWWWWWWWHHHHHHHHHHH!!!" Julius hyenaed. "N-not my toes man, oh God, *not my toes...*"

I used the toothpick like a saw between his toes, even running it against the sides of his toes a few times.

"OHHHHHH GAWD, I-I didn't count on this man, I-I think..." Julius began.

"Yes Julius?" I asked. "What do you think?"

"I-I think...AAAAAWWWWWWWW!!!" he screamed as I feathered and tooth-picked his feet. "I think I'm gonna fuckin' laugh man, I think I'm gonna lose that damned bet!!"

I smiled wickedly and goose feathered his right heel while at the same time sawing between the toes of his left foot. Julius's feet bobbed around like crazy as I worked my tickle magic on them...

"PWWAAHHHHHHH, HA, HA, HA, HA, HA, HA, HA, HA, HA, HA, HA, HA, HA!!!" he suddenly guffawed, letting loose with a torrent of baritone sounding laughter.

I wondered if my landlords, what Julius had referred once to as "The Signora's" could hear him all the way downstairs...

"OHHHHHHHHH, ha, ha, ha, ha, ha, ha, ha, ha, and there goes a hundred smackeroos right down the toilet man!!!" Julius bitched as he laughed and laughed.

"Don't be so hard on yourself Julius, you did give it your best shot after all," I chided him and sat down on the bed, grabbed his big feet in my lap and held them tight as I goose feathered and tooth picked them some more.

"H-HEY!!!" he ranted at me as I held his tied up feet tight, keeping him totally immobile now as I tickled him. HAHAHAHAHAHAHAHAHA!!!"

"Fucking hundred dollars gone, ha, ha, ha, ha, ha, ha, ha, ha, how'll I explain that to the wife???" Julius cackled.

"Well, you are getting a fresh pair of socks out of the deal Julius," I teased him and tickled between his toes with the toothpick some more.

"Oh yippy do, new socks, big, HAHAHAHAHAHAHAHAHA, big fucking deal bud...HAHAHAHAHAHAHAHA!!!"

Finally, after what seemed like an eternity to the poor guy I stopped tickling him with the goose feather and the toothpick. He stopped laughing and breathed a sigh of relief as I dropped the two tickle items back in my box of supplies.

"Oh man, th-thanks for stoppin' bud...th-that was unbelievable," Julius said. "I-I never laughed in all my life from havin' my damned feet tickled... I suppose you learn somethin' new every fucking day huh?"

"Yeah, I suppose you could say that," I said and held up a high-speed battery operated toothbrush.

Julius's eyes opened wide in terror as I clicked the brush on and the bristles started spinning and vibrating at what had to have appeared to him to be at least one hundred miles per hour...

"HEY, hey now wait a minute here bud..." Julius pleaded as I pressed the spinning bristles against the meaty bottom of his left foot and then over to his right foot. "WHOOOOOOO, HAHAHAHAHAHAHAHAHAahahhahahaha!!! HOLY FUCKAROO man, what, what's the goddamned time limit on ticklin' a poor guy's feet huh???"

"Well, now that I won my hundred dollars I want to make sure you get your money's worth of being tickled Julius..." I chuckled and pressed the spinning toothbrush bristles against Julius's toes, strumming them along slowly, while at the same time using my fingertips to tickle the bottoms of his feet. "I'm working hard for you here bud..."

When I again brushed the bottoms of his feet I tickled his toes with my fingertips...

"OOOOOHHHHHHH th-this is awful man..." Julius ranted and squirmed atop the bed in the bondage.

The tent in his shorts had really plumped up at that point and I could even see evidence of pre cum and beads of piss staining the front of them, not surprising considering all the iced tea he had drunk...

"I-I hope you-you're enjoyin' yourself here bud, because I want a chance to get even, ha, ha, ha, ha, ha, ha, ha, ha, ha, ha, ha, ha, ha, ha, ha, ha, ha!!!"

"Hmmm, now how do you suppose we're going to go about arranging that Julius?" I asked him, trying to sound as dumb as all possible.

"Just like this man, just like this, a goddamned bet... HAHAHAHAHAHAHAHAHAHAAHAAAAAA!!!" Julius responded laughingly.

"Now that does sound interesting indeed," I said, still trying to sound like a fool. "But Julius, if you lose whatever the bet is you could wind up tickle tortured a second time..."

"I fuckin' doubt that man..." Julius grunted. "HAW, HAW, HAW, HAW, HAW!!!"

I trailed my battery operated toothbrush along the tops of his feet, over his arches, (that really got him hitting the high C's I must say) and around and around on his heels, holding his tied feet tight in my lap. But then, a short while later Julius screamed the words I knew would be coming soon, "Oh God man, I gotta piss!!! All that iced tea you fed me wants out now!! Shiiiiitttt, I gotta fucking piss like a racehorse!!! Stop ticklin' me man, stop ticklin' me and untie me!!! HAHAHAHAHAHAHAHAHA!!!"

"Oh I'll let you piss but you're not getting untied for a while Julius," I said, sounding real sinister at that point. "You still have more tickling to endure for me... I want to make sure I really earn those hundred dollars..."

"Oh you son of a bitch, HAWHAWHAWHAWHAWHAWHAW!!!" Julius half laughed half cried. "I somehow, HAHAHAHAHAHAHAHA, get the feelin' that you had all this in mind the second you asked me up here for a cold drink... HA, HA, HA, HA, HA, HA, HA, HA, HA, HA, HA, HA!!!"

"Good thinking," I chuckled and turned off the battery operated toothbrush.

"Oh thank you man, thank you, oh man, I n-never thought that my damned feet were so ticklish," Julius said more to himself than to me as I got to my feet, resting his tied and tickled feet back down on the bed. "Amazing what a few globs of lotion and a hair dryer can do..."

"Yeah, and now those big dogs of yours are starting to sweat Julius," I said, giving his right foot a squeeze. "I guess all that laughing I made you do really got you all worked up huh bud?"

"I-I suppose so," Julius agreed. "Jeez man, I gotta fuckin' piss Christopher..."

"Soon, but not yet buddy," I said with a grin.

That said I reached into my box of tickle supplies and held up two long stick cotton swabs, two oversized Q-tips if you would...

"H-hey, what the fucking fuck are you planning on doing with those man???" Julius asked, sounding almost as if he were in a panic, which in a way he was.

I mean, it's not every day that a big rugged iron-worker like Julius finds himself to be in the position that I had him in... And not to mention that he himself had agreed to be in that position...but I'll mention it anyway...

"As if you didn't know what I was planning on doing with these," I said, squatting down at Julius's tied feet. "Like I said Julius, your feet are getting sweaty here; I'll use these to dry 'em up a bit..."

"AW no man, NO!!!" Julius ranted as I propped his feet up on some pillows and reached into my box for some more rope.

I tied the extra rope around Julius's upper calves, then around the pillows I had propped his enormous dogs on, and extended the slack of the rope downward and under the bed, tying it off around one of the wooden bed slats, totally immobilizing his feet now...

I began by trailing the long stick cotton swabs between his mangy toes...

"WHOOOOOOOOO!!! HAHAHAHAHAHAHAHA!!! And here we go again huh fucker???" Julius laughed miserably. "Like I said man, ha, ha, ha, ha, ha, ha, ha, ha, ha, ha, ha, ha!!! I want a chance to get even here!!! God, but I gotta piss though!!! HAHAHAHAHAHAHAHAHA!!!"

"We'll get to both those things soon enough buddy," I said, grinning at my captured tickle prize. "Let me just get your feet wiped up a bit though, they're really sweating here..."

"HAW, HAW, HAW, HAW, HAW, HAW, HAW, HAW, HAW, HAW!!!" Julius laughed, sounding real rugged now somehow as I trailed the long stick Q-tips up and down the bottoms of his huge feet.

His feet made a wonderful spectacle the way they were snared in all the ropes, tied down to the pillows and to the slat under my bed. They bobbed up and down a bit taking the pillows along with them just as much as the bondage would allow.

"Easy buddy, easy, I'm only trying to wipe some of the sweat off your feet here, I don't mean to be tickling you this time…" I teased my buddy.

"HAHAHAHAHAHAHAHA!!!" Julius screamed. "Yeah, right, and if you think I believe that I'll buy the Brooklyn Bridge from you… HAHAHAHAHHAHAHAHAHAHAHAHA!!! Oh GAWD man, s-stop ticklin' me just long enough so I can go and piss…"

After I had swabbed Julius's feet all around numerous times with the cottony end of the long swabs I did the unthinkable… I turned the swabs over and began trailing the wooden stick ends up and down the bottoms, along the arches and over the heels of Julius's tied and pillowed feet…

"AAAAAARRRRRRRHHHHHHH NO, NO, OH GOD NO!!! HAR, HAR, HAR, HAR, HAR!!!" he guffawed and by now it wasn't just his feet that were sweating.

"Okay Julius, just a while more of this and then I'll let you piss…" I said as I slid the thin sticks between his toes. "But you have to agree to something first buddy…otherwise I'll just keep tickling your feet here. And trust me on this Julius, I am not beyond lotioning and blow drying your tootsies a second time to make them even more tickle sensitive…"

"OKAY, OKAY, what do you want me to agree to??? Fucking fuck, look at me here, tied up like a goddamned steer in a rodeo…" Julius screamed. "HAHAHAHAHAHAHAHA!!!"

"After I let you piss I want you to agree to let me tickle those hairy armpits of yours…" I said and Julius's face turned to a mask of pure and unadulterated horror.

"M-my armpits???" Julius stammered a look of total fear and trepidation in his eyes. "Whatsamatter with you man??? Tickling a poor guy's feet ain't enough for you? You gotta go after my smelly armpits too???"

"Either you agree to that or you don't piss and I just keep on tickling your feet here…" I said.

"HAWHAWHAWHAWHAHWHAWHAWHAWHAW!!!" Julius suddenly hooted loudly as I increased the tempo with the long sticks against the arches of his feet.

"Okay, okay, my armpits it is man," Julius said in between laughing his bald head off. "J-just stop tickling me and untie me so I can use your bathroom…"

I stopped tickling his feet and held up the two long swab sticks…

"Untie you? Who said anything about untying you?" I asked my tickle captive and when I stepped out to the living room and returned with my empty beer bottle Julius's chin nearly dropped to his stomach area.

"Wh-what are you up to here Christopher?" Julius asked me apprehensively. "I uh, I gotta tell you man, I don't like the looks of things here now…"

Smiling, I looked at the now huge tent in Julius's knee length shorts and said, "Actually, I like the way things look here Julius…"

I put the empty beer bottle down on a night table next to the bed and then began slowly pulling Julius's shorts down…

"H-hey, wh-what the fucking fuck man???" Julius ranted. "Don't be strippin' me down to the bare essentials here Christopher!"

"Well, how else are you going to piss?" I asked him mischievously.

"Holy fuck man, holy fucking fucks!" Julius seethed. "What the fucking fuck have I gotten myself into here???"

He wiggled his toes as I got his shorts down around his knees… It's worth mentioning here that the guy wasn't wearing any underpants. He was totally freeballing in those knee length shorts, in commando if you would…

The sight of his mammoth sized cock caused a lump to form in my throat. It was at least eight or nine inches long, thick veined, and portly, if you can believe that, a true blue muscle pipe if ever I saw one. It was hard as goddamned steel, (or as my good buddy Timmy Backman would say, he was hard as Chinese arithmetic) throbbing and beads of piss and cum were forming on Julius's wide sexy slit. His balls were the size of kiwis and like kiwis they were really hairy. Needless to say Julius noticed the look in my eyes at the sight of his pride and joy.

"Yuh like that huh? Yeah, you like my goddamned cock!" Julius grunted. "Fucking fucks man, one time I was takin' a piss at one of the jobsites that me and my buds had been sent to. There were three of us in that stinkin' bathroom, three of us lined up at the urinals relievin' ourselves, me in the middle, my bud Stevey on my left another guy named Dan from one of the other construction and iron companies on my right. It was Stevey who noticed that guy Dan stealin' glances at my huge meat stick while it was reposin' in that urinal. Stevey laughed real meanly and told me that it looked like Dan over there had a thing for my big fuck wad."

"What'd you do?" I asked, already knowing what Julius was going to tell me though.

"Well, I'll tell you man, I gave Dan what he wanted," Julius chuckled meanly. "I stopped pissin' and asked the guy if he'd like to be my goddamned toilet… fuck man, he was on his knees faster than you can say your name Christopher. Not only did that fucker drink what was left of my rancid and sloppy yellow stream but he sucked two gushy loads of spunk outa me too…fuckin' married guy and all… made me cum two fuckin' times in that filthy bathroom. And with Stevey watchin' no less…"

"So you're not beyond letting a guy work you over in that arena once in a while...or in this one..." I said, gesturing around the room and picking up the empty beer bottle.

"Hey man, who the fuck am I to turn down a blow-job you know?" Julius laughed meanly and then without another word I gently grabbed my tickle captive's balls in one hand and placed the mouth of the beer bottle over his wide sexy cock slit.

"AW man, d-don't be depositin' my baby maker in a beer bottle man..." Julius panted as I handled his huge and hairy family jewels.

"C'mon man, you said you had to piss, make like a racehorse and do your stuff..." I teased him. "Then I want to get back to tickling the crap outa you..."

"AW man, fucking shitty ass things to be doin' to me here Christopher," Julius said. "And we're neighbors after all..."

"Now we're more than neighbors," I replied, rolling his balls in my hand, keeping the beer bottle mouth balanced over his slit. "Piss Julius..."

"Fucking totally fucks, but it ain't easy to piss with a goddamned boner the size of what I got here Christopher..." he said and if that wasn't an invitation I didn't know what was.

"AAAAAAAAAHHHHHHHHH!!!" Julius was moaning a few seconds later as I sucked his huge cock, my head bobbing up and down on the colossal sized beef stick.

Fuck, I have to admit that I wasn't able to get Julius's entire girth into my craw, but I sure as fuck was having fun trying.

"Oh yeah, fucking fucks man, everybody loves my huge baby maker..." Julius groaned.

What Julius didn't know was that after a guy shoots his pent-up load it makes him even more tickle sensitive. And believe you me I intended to take full advantage of that.

"Oh fuck man Christopher, you want to tickle me some more, you want that hundred dollars, well, it looks to me like you're earnin' it all..." Julius panted, feeding me his huge manhood and squirming in the tight, tight bondage.

"NYYYYUUHHHHHHHHHHHH!!! UUUHHRRRRRRHHHHH!!!" were the sounds of a man in passion a short while later as Julius shot his load like a banshee.

He reeled and rocked on the bed, his tied feet bouncing up and down on the pillows as he seemed to cum and cum, and a never ending rivulet of jism it seemed. He jammed his cock deeper into my gullet and force fed me every drop of his pearly man juices. He tasted sweet somehow and I wondered what his diet consisted of to cause that...

When he was done I let his cock slip from my mouth, giving it a few last sucks, and seconds later it started to go flaccid.

"There you go bud, now you'll be able to piss," I said and again gently grabbed his balls and held the empty beer bottle over his cock slit.

"OHHHHHH man, easy there Christopher," Julius breathed heavily as I slid the bottle over his slit. "I'm all slimy and sensitive there now you know…"

"Oh yeah, I know, and you're going to find that you're all sensitive in other spots too…" I said, glancing at his very on display armpits.

"Oh no man, you don't mean…" Julius said and then began a yellow stream of pissing into my empty beer bottle.

"You got it my ticklish bud," I laughed and held the bottle steady as he pissed and pissed into it, sounds of relief emanating from him at the same time. "Bet you didn't know that for whatever the fuck the reason, a guy becomes a lot more tickle sensitive after he shoots a huge load. And man, you just fed me a nice gushy one…just quoting you there bud…"

"OOOOOOHHHHHHHHH NO NO NO NO NO!!!" Julius said miserably, nearly crying now.

When he was done pissing I quickly poured his piss deposit in the toilet in the bathroom and when I returned once again to the bedroom I picked up my bottle of lotion…

"Ready for round two Julius?" I asked him. "This time starring those mangy and hairy armpits of yours…bud…"

"Christopher, please, no more ticklin' me here…" Julius begged. "Now I know that I said if you let me piss I would agree to more ticklin' but I was delirious with the need to piss…and not to mention that you had tickled me into a state of nearly incomprehension…"

I chuckled meanly and sat down on his crotch area, straddling his torso actually. Oh, did I mention that I hadn't pulled Julius's shorts back up? His cock went semi rigid as I straddled him and squirted a goodly few dollops of the lavender scented lotion into my palm. I then put the lotion bottle aside and slathered the stuff in my hands, really getting them slicked up for the laughter to come…

"Oh no, no, look man, I didn't admit that my feet were ticklish, okay, you nailed me there bud…I mean, fuck, I didn't know they were ticklish you know?" Julius began bargaining like a desperate salesman. "But I know, I DO KNOW that my armpits are ticklish man! There's no need to go there to find out you know?"

"What, and miss out on all the fun and comedy that's coming?" I asked Julius and in a fast motion I slapped my open palmed hands into his very visible armpits.

"OHHHHHHHHH NO NO NO NO NOOOOOO!!!" Julius cried and I hadn't even started tickling him yet.

With a twisted looking grin on my face I really slathered the lavender lotion in Julius's burly armpits. When I was done soaking them up real well I gave them one more helping of the lotion.

"OH MAN, this ain't fair Christopher, this ain't fair at all," Julius said, his lips very close to mine as I was leaning down and coating his armpits with the lotion. "I'm all tied up here, that doesn't even give me a fightin' chance bud…"

"And that's the general idea…bud…" I replied, moving my mouth closer to his so that our lips grazed a tad as I spoke. "Now I want you to think about what I said Julius, how a guy becomes even more tickle sensitive after he's shot a load…"

As I spoke I moved closer to Julius and by then my lips was most definitely touching his as I spoke. His lips trembled and he didn't try to pull away from me.

"F-fucker…" Julius said softly, closed his eyes for a second and pecked my lips.

I grinned in a tomfoolery way and held my lips gently pressed against his… He pecked me again… Then, without warning, I leaned back, still straddling his torso and gripped the inside of his lotioned and slicked armpits with my fingertips, my thumbs pressed hard against the section just under his shoulders…

"OOOOHHHHHHHHHHHHH!!!   HAHAHAHAHAHAHAHAHA!!!" Julius screeched at the suddenness of my onslaught. "OHHHHHHHH GAWD!!!"

"Was I right Julius?" I asked him teasingly as I squiggled my fingertips deep into his hairy and scruffy pits. "Are you even more tickle sensitive now that I made you cum?"

"F-FUCK that, I didn't need to cum to be more tickle sensitive in my dang pits you bastard!!" Julius cried out. "HAHAHAHAHAHAHAHAHA!!! My scrungy pits are normally ticklish!!! HAWHAWHAWHAWHAWHAWHAW!!! And oilin' them up with that lotion was dirty pool man!! HAHAHAHAHAHAHA!!!"

Julius leaned his baldhead against his stretched up arms and howled up at the ceiling as I did my dirty work in his armpits. After squiggling my fingertips around in his pits for a good while I dug in with my thumbs as well.

"HAR, HAR, HAR, HAR, HAR, HAR, HAR, HAR, HAR!!! Oh good GAWD, the neighbors are gonna hear me at this point!!" Julius pleaded, sweating like crazy now.

After I had finger and thumbed his armpits for a half hour I next used the stick ends of the cotton swabs to tickle them with. Poor Julius was pleading with me beseechingly at that point to stop tickling him. In his tickle delirium he even offered to double the amount of the money he had lost at our bet if I would just stop tickling him…

Finally, after another fifteen minutes of stick tickling his armpits I did stop, but I didn't agree to the doubled amount of money… Julius had been a real good sport about it all after all. I mean, he even let me suck a load out of him and he kissed me on the lips, although I doubted we would be talking about those things any time soon. I untied his wrists and feet from the bed and he sat up, massaging his wrists as he did so.

"Man, what a great time this was huh Julius?" I asked him teasingly.

"Yeah, great for you maybe bud…I'm the poor guy who wound up tied and tickled, jeez…" Julius said as he swung his long muscular legs over the side of the bed, pulled his shorts up and sat there catching his breath.

I brought him a glass of cold water and he sipped it slowly…

"I gotta tell you though Christopher, you are sadistically creative when it comes to the art of ticklin' a guy…" Julius said.

"Thanks, I'll take that as a compliment," I said with a grin as he handed me his empty water glass. "Now, where's my hundred dollars?"

"Where's my socks?" Julius asked, glancing at his slip-on slippers on the floor.

We both laughed…

I gave Julius a pair of my black nylon dress socks. Needless to say they were a couple of sizes small for him so he had to struggle a bit to get them onto his giant feet.

"Jeez man, you're really gonna keep my goddamned socks that I had on when I came up here?" he asked me as he slid his slippers onto his feet and stood up. "Fuckin' dressy socks you give me here…fucking fuck…"

"Sure am man, I earned those after all…" I laughed. "Now, my money?"

"It's in my wallet back at my house…I'll get it for you and come back…" Julius said. "But man, like I said while you had me all tied up there and tickling me, I want a goddamned chance to get even here… I'll still pay you the hundred but I wanna give you a taste of your own medicine Christopher…"

"Hmm, you really seem hell bent on that Julius…" I said musingly. "And we did agree that it would be a bet to decide who would get tickle tortured in the next round… Any ideas on how you want to pull off this next bet?"

"You got a deck of cards lying around here anywhere?" the giant guy asked me.

"Sure, why?" I asked in reply.

"Whoever draws the higher card wins the tickle bet; lower value card gets tickled…" Julius said.

"Now that is a bit scary Julius," I said advisedly. "I mean, what if you draw a lower value card?"

"I don't plan on having that happen…bud…" Julius said, grinning sadistically at me. "Now, get the goddamned cards…"

A few minutes later we were sitting back in the living room where all the tickle madness had begun. I was shuffling the cards. When I was done I handed the deck to Julius and he shuffled them next. We each shuffled the cards three times each to insure that the deck was not fixed in favor of either of us…

"Okay man, like I said, higher value card wins, lower value card gets tied and tickled…" Julius said, sitting there still with his chest bare.

I had taken note of the fact that the guy had really bulbous and delectable looking fat nipples…

Each of us with our hands shaking a bit drew a card from the deck, Julius from the middle of the deck me from the very top… We held up our cards… The next sound that was heard was Julius saying, "FUCK!!! FUCK!!! Of all the rotten luck, goddamn it all!!!"

I laughed meanly when I saw the three of clubs that Julius had drawn against my king of hearts...

As we walked back to the bedroom I held tight to one of Julius's upper arms, he looking totally despondent...

"Don't worry your baldhead too much over it Julius," I said teasingly and soothingly at the same time. "I promise to only tickle your nipples for an hour... each..."

"M-my nipples???" Julius cried out and I pushed him down onto the bed and started tying his wrists back to the bed board...

(5)

Bondage Buddies

(From the book: *The Gym Instructor*)

     This is yet another story of a wager between two friends, like with the stories "The Abusive Wager" and "Tickled Yuppie" a game of cards determines the fate of the loser of the game. I hadn't realized how many times I had used this method to invite bondage games and other erotic scenes into my stories. And in all the cases where I used the card game as the method of coercion so to speak, the bound up victim is always a straight guy in the clutches of a Gay guy. I suppose that's one thing worth analyzing somewhere down the line.

     I once heard that marines are totally submissive, even though they are the most boorish and macho guys in all of the branches of the United States military. I suppose that having to take orders all the time just makes them that way after a while. When I wrote this quick story I wondered if it was possible the same thing could be said of soldiers. I decided to run with it and I have to say that the story was quick but it turned out good and said a lot in a short time.

     I think also that this story is essentially about trust and how much fun two buddies can have when they truly do trust each other. As is shown in the story no harm whatsoever comes to the soldier after he loses the card game and is tied up by his buddy, unlike in my story "The Taming of Dominick."

     I've realized that I go to different extremes in my fiction when it comes to binding a muscular guy up really tight. One of the things I love most when it comes to tying a guy is that look in his eyes when he realizes he's basically helpless. That look of vulnerability is so sexy to me. But in some stories the bound up guy winds up being really worked over...whereas in this story he is worked over too, but in a more sexual way. I think in "The Abusive Wager" Daniel was worked over by being edged. In this story the tied up soldier is not edged, he is made to cum rather quickly.

I love the ironic ending. It is something that I am known for as well as my fetish for the well-dressed man and the man in uniform. A lot of my stories have what I call the twisted ending, just as this one does. I also like bursting a confident macho man's bubble. I did this in "Tickled Yuppie" and I did it here as well. A lot of my stories end on a cliffhanger but rarely do I write a sequel. With my story "Larry Captured by Cleeve and Otis" I had written a few sequels but they have yet to see the light of day.

The original inspiration for this story "Bondage Buddies" was an old porn film I saw years back where two cowboys played a game of cards to decide who would be the bottom boy when they had sex. I don't recall the name of the film, what I do recall is that both the actors were extremely hot looking, muscular and very sexy. I also recall the bad acting when the guy who lost the game of cards tried to play it off like he was so disappointed that he was about to be the bottom guy.

Another factor that I brought into this quick story was my fetish for army socks. Besides men's navy blue or black dress socks, I find a soldier's olive green socks to be most enticing for some reason. I often wonder who came up with the idea for making a soldier's thick combat socks such a drab color, yet so erotic looking for some reason at the same time.

"Royal flush!" I said, throwing down my cards, smiling from ear to ear. "I win, and you lose, again..."

"Goddamn it man, this is the third fucking time," my buddy Bill said miserably, throwing down what was left of his cards as I leaned back in my chair feeling real satisfied and fat-headed.

"It seems like the damned fates are really against me lately," Bill said, looking at me across the table, his eyes filled with mock despair.

"Either that or they're smiling down on me," I said, getting to my feet. "Come on; let's get you prepared while I get the box."

"Yeah, the box, the fucking box," Bill whispered, knowing all too well what "the box" meant.

I stood up, sauntered into the living room and came back with the box that we kept filled with rope and other bondage paraphernalia.

"Shit man, I really thought I had it in the bag this time," Bill said, stood up and began unbuttoning his fatigue style shirt, slipping it off followed by his olive colored tee shirt.

He neatly folded his shirts and placed them on the extra chair we kept for just that purpose. With his dog tags dangling around his neck he bent down to unlace his bog clunky combat boots, shucked them off his size eleven feet and placed them under the chair. Watching him bend down to get his boots off always sent a shiver or two of ecstasy through me, seeing as Bill has one of the best proportioned and well-muscled backs I had ever seen. The way his ripped muscles bulged and flexed while he bent over was pure magic to see.

"Looks like you win underpants again bud," he said, starting to unbutton his fatigue style pants, still all rolled up at the knees from having been tucked neatly into his boots.

"And seeing as you lost you really should be calling me Sir Soldier boy Billy," I said meanly, getting into my role rather well.

"Yes Sir, as you say Sir," Bill said. "But shit, it's sure going to feel strange going home later without my under shorts on again. Fuck man, how am I going to explain that to the wife a third goddamned time?"

"Ha, just tell her the truth," I laughed. "Tell her that you bet your under shorts in a card game and lost."

"Phooey man, I can't tell her that I gambled away my damned shorts," he said and we both laughed.

Bill had recently been honorably discharged from the army after four years and was a newlywed of only four months. Our card games however had been going on like this since we were teenagers... We always gambled on the most unusual and sleazy things that guys possibly could gamble on. When Bill told me how in the army he and his buddies had gambled on each other's under shorts I could not believe it, but decided it would be fun to humiliate the hunky soldier boy, if I won that is... We made a deal that whenever we got together for our card games that Bill would come attired in his military fatigues. Whenever he lost the game I got to play POW.

A few moments later Bill was stripped to his white briefs and calf length, olive colored military issued cotton socks. From where I was standing I could tell that those socks were pretty moist having been in those boots of his for so many hours. Also, from where I was standing I could tell just how awesome they smelled as well. His muscle pipe was tenting his briefs as if Ringling Brothers had pitched a tent in his crotch area. He placed his hands behind him and stood rigidly at attention.

"Ready for your orders Sir," he said in a deep soldierly voice, the bulge in his BVD briefs starting to ooze droplets of pre cum.

"Hmm, I think that this time I'll keep your socks too Soldier boy," I said with a grin.

"Oh please Sir, how will I explain losin' my socks as well?" he grumbled miserably, beads of sweat appearing on his forehead, just under his very short cropped dirty blond hair.

"Just tell the wife that after losing your under shorts all you had left to gamble with were your smelly socks," I replied.

"Lousy way to refer to a guy's socks, shit man, third fucking time in a row that I lost at our damned card game," Bill complained.

His body was a work of United States army magic, totally rock hard and muscular, totally fucking hard bodied. The army had really turned my scrawny buddy into a brick wall. Being that Bill is a fair haired blond had no hair on his muscular torso to speak of, save for his blond pubic bush and somewhat bushy armpits. He told me once that while he was in the army he had not done well on his morning exercises and his drill sergeant had meanly shaved his pits for him as punishment. Bill recounted, sounding miserable, about how the drill sergeant had strung his wrists tight above him and tied them to a ceiling beam and then slowly and methodically shaved his pits raw. The hot water washcloths and steaming shaving cream, the highly sharpened razor, all of it still gave my buddy nightmares. It gave me a hard-on to hear him tell of it. His chest jutted out muscular and huge enough to eat a three course meal off of, that chest adorned by two big pink nipples that were always hard as pencil erasers.

"Sit down," I said sternly.

Doing as he was told Bill sat back in his chair, his hands and arms behind him and draped over the back of it. I got busy very quickly roping him to the chair.

"Shit, shit, like I said Sir, I really thought I had it in the bag this time," he said forlornly as I tied his wrists together behind him, looping the rope around and around his huge lower arms.

"The only thing in the bag Billy boy is you," I said, winding a good length of rope over his upper torso, under and over his huge male cleavage, pinning him securely to the chair.

We had been doing this sort of thing since we were teenagers, as I mentioned. Actually, it was Bill who had come up with the idea for the loser of our card games to be tied up and left that way till the winner said he could be released. I think Bill always enjoyed the fantasy of roping a guy up and then making his life miserable. I don't think however that Bill realized just how easily he could wind up the loser of the game as well. Although, as time went on I sort of got the feeling that Bill liked being tied up as well as tying me up. Each time we played he was always confident of winning. Ha, nine fucking times out of ten the poor fuck lost and lost miserably I might add. It was my idea to have the loser strip to his underwear and socks before being roped up. Bill was not crazy about that part of the game but if it meant him being able to tie me, his good buddy up, he was willing to go along with it. The first time I jacked the guy off while I had him tied up he complained and ranted like crazy, saying that that was not part of the game, stating how we had not agreed on such folly. But after I got him off more than a couple of times he agreed to that as well, realizing I suppose, that being in bondage really floated his boat a lot more than he cared to admit.

When I finished tying his upper body to the chair Bill's muscles strained beautifully. I had left his nipples real visible and the rope tied real tight under and over them, making a nice showcase of them.

"Gods in the heavens, as fucking usual you roped me the fuck up real goddamned tight Sir," Bill seethed, straining to get himself untied but to no avail.

"Yeah, I really do love tying you the fuck up Soldier boy Billy," I said breathlessly and gave him a quick peck on the cheek, squeezing one of his erect and hard nipples real meanly as I did so.

"Hey man, hey there bud, don't be kissing me," Bill said. "This is all in good mean fun Sir. We ain't faggots here you know."

"Of course not," I said sarcastically and got busy roping his feet to the legs of the chair, spreading his legs good and fucking wide.

Bill decided to join the army when he was eighteen years old and fresh out of high school. His girlfriend Linda was sad to see him go as I was. He had been dating her for the past three years of high school and our card and bondage games had been going on for just as long. When he came home on leave the first time we played our usual game of poker. I lost once and Bill lost twice. Watching him strip out of his uniform nearly drove me over the edge. The army had done wonders in getting Bill into amazingly good muscular shape, as I pointed out; I really love pointing that out. Tying him up had never seemed more inviting at that point. I teased and taunted him about having a real POW in my clutches as I tied him up that time. When I started jacking him off he begged me to only do him once, explaining that Linda was waiting for him and she was as horny for him as a bitch in heat. I got him off twice that time and he told me afterwards that when he fucked Linda later on his cock had never felt so sore. He always dreaded losing the card games because he knew that I liked keeping him tied up for long periods of time, knowing that any excuse he offered to shorten the length of bondage time would be totally ignored by me. Inwardly I knew that he loved our games. He had invented them after all. A few minutes later I had Bill's socked ankles tied to one of the chair legs each. The swelling in his white briefs was now enormous and oozing pearls and pearls of pre cum through the thin cotton fabric.

"Oh fuck man, I really cannot believe I lost that goddamned game," Bill said, straining and sweating against the ropes. "When we started I was doing so well too."

"Just goes to show what could happen Billy boy," I said and squatted down in front of him.

He watched helplessly as I slowly pulled the fly opening of his under shorts apart and almost ceremoniously brought out his rage hard cock and his big juicy peach fuzzed balls.

"OHHHH fuck, just once man, please, *just once,* " Bill pleaded as I handled his gargantuan meat pole. "Linda is really, really in the mood today. I promised her that after my card game we would have an all-day fuck marathon."

"Yeah, if she could only see her soldier boy husband now," I said mockingly and spit a few times onto his hardness as it pulsed like a thing alive in my hand.

Bill squirmed miserably and in ecstasy at the same time under the ropes as I began stroking his now slimy and hard meat stick

"Fuck man but my wife loves my big soldier-sized cock," Bill panted as I stroked and stroked him. *"And so do you buddy...so do you..."*

Bill's cock was of the soldier-sized as he had just referred to it, all thick, long, beefy and veiny. He never failed to shoot big hefty creamy loads for me, even after I'd jacked him off more than a couple of times. Bill married Linda shortly after his honorable discharge from the army. I was a little concerned that that would be the end of our card games. But Bill assured me that our card games were our secret and he could never give them up, always hoping against hope that he would win more often. Unfortunately for him he didn't.

"OHHHHH GODS, I-I'm getting there already buddy," Bill garbled. "Fuck. I had a goddamned hard-on while we were playing that damned game."

"Yeah, a hard-on because you thought you were going to win and tie me the fuck up," I said mockingly. "But look at you now..."

"Yeah, fucking look at me now..." Bill grumbled. "OOOHHHH FUCK, I-I'm cumming buddy, pl-please untie me when I'm done, OHHHHH FUCKING FUCKS!!!"

He threw his head back and writhed in ecstasy as I stroked his cock and squeezed his balls, getting every possible drop of soldier boy jazz from him.

"Okay Bill, I'll untie you on one condition," I said, still stroking him, getting still more jazz to erupt from his wide sexy slit.

"WH-what the fuck condition now bud?" he asked me, still panting and gasping after I'd let go of his meat stick.

His mess of cum dripped down his roped up chest to his stomach area, settling on his under shorts.

"I've already agreed to give you my damned underpants and military socks," he seethed. "WH-what more do you want?"

"Another card game," I said.

"Fuck yeah, FUCKING A MAN, and this time I will win for sure," Bill said eagerly. "And then we'll see how you feel when I force you to cum more than a few times. Being jacked off is great bud, but squeezing three loads out of a guy can really get to him you know?"

I looked up at my bound buddy in shock. It would be the first time in all the years of our card games that he would jack me off.

"Don't be so sure of winning so quickly," I said, starting to untie him. "Just call Linda and tell her that you'll be a little later than expected."

"Sure thing bud," Bill said. "Right after I'm dressed."

"Well, if I were you I would stay just as you are," I said with a grin. "You never know what might happen."

"What's going to happen is I am going to win this time," Bill said with the utmost confidence, standing up and facing me.

"Whatever," I said and gave the elastic waistband of his under shorts a snap. "But I still get your under shorts and socks."

"Yeah, yeah, damn but you got a fetish for my damned funky scented under shorts and socks," Bill mused and walked over to the phone on the wall.

He looked beyond sexy and vulnerable standing there talking on the phone wearing just his underpants, socks and dog tags. His cock was semi hard as it hung freely out of his underpants along with his big succulent balls. He explained to Linda that our card game had gotten really intense and that he would be home a little later than he had expected. After he hung up he didn't get dressed. Instead we played a second game of cards...

"Goddamn it all, *fuck, fuck,*" Bill ranted horribly and miserably a while later as I again tied him tightly to the chair.

This time to really grate on his nerves I had tied a blindfold over his eyes as well...

"Can't believe I lost again..." he seethed.

(6)

Terry's Appointment

(From the book: *Terry's Appointment and Other Spanking Tales*)

This story is fiction; however, it is a story of true bonding between two men. It shows complete trust, compassion and a certain brutality all at the same time. Terry Dean Bradshaw is every disciplinarian's dream...He is a man consumed with rising in the corporate world, yet unaware of his own inhibitions and shortcomings that hold him back from achieving his truest potential. He is a topnotch executive, yet he lacks that push, that drive so desperately needed to propel him to the position of Vice President in the corporation where he is employed, a position he desperately craves, for various reasons other than for himself. It is at the center of his core the reason that this man's man covets such a high position in the corporate world... Enter Disciplinarian and stickler for rules Master Jeff and Terry Dean Bradshaw learns the errors of his ways...the hard way...so to speak. Master Jeff takes the no-nonsense topnotch executive under his wing (and places him under other devices as well) and with a hardhearted commitment from Terry Dean Bradshaw; Master Jeff becomes the executive's mentor, confidant and strictest of authoritarians. Terry Dean Bradshaw shows his nobility and stature as a man's man by standing by his commitment to Master Jeff, realizing that once a deal is made "there is no turning back."

The listing of questions that "Master Jeff" puts to Terry Dean Bradshaw on the night of their meeting I lifted directly from a questionnaire that "Master Jeff" himself was kind enough to give me. It is a listing of questions that all men should think about and reply to at some point in their lives... It is the listing of questions that brings Terry Dean Bradshaw and Master Jeff together in their truest of bonds...

The story is also for the curious little "whacker" who wants to look into the secret life of what might be going on in the person of power's daily ritual, mannerisms and practices. It offers the reader a view of what a session with a motivational psychologist could be like and how the person turns into someone with blind obedience. The exaggerated mental and physical characteristics that makes these characters different, yet similar to most others is to see the change of the general antagonist, Terry, when he steps into the office and has to deal with his wanting inwardly to see what it might be like to be on the other end for a change. This is shown in a very provocative and exaggerated fashion.

Note from consultant, Master Jeff:

Christopher is very observant and paradoxically can make his characters very realistic as well. He is a prolific writer and good friend, as well as a workaholic who takes his writing seriously. He makes all his stories so realistic that at times it's hard to tell that they are mostly fictitious; also Christopher's stories are original and highly convincing. He will make you hang on as he is a sound writer with conviction.

He also writes with a style that is all his own as well as acute realism and in my opinion, a very entertaining storyteller, giving the reader a "fly on the wall" view into what can go on in the minds of his protagonists. He is a good listener and observer of human nature who works well with his many characters and their development, with his own creative "inner voices" and keen awareness. Thus he is a pleasure to work with. He mixes his talents of the written word with the factual and delicious fiction. Christopher does a lot of free association of what people think and should act like as well as extrapolation so that the characters truly stand out.

Terry Dean Bradshaw, homeowner, staunch corporate executive, a man on his way up the professional ladder with no intention whatsoever of stopping at just Vice President, family man, a guy who has it all, and some secrets as well, one in particular that *only* his good buddy, a man he calls "Master Jeff" can be of assistance for where a certain *need* is concerned. Terry Dean Bradshaw, five feet ten inches tall, he has wavy salt and pepper colored hair cut and styled neatly in a classic banker's style, matching neatly trimmed thick mustache, gleaming blue eyes that could seduce just about any woman, or man if you should so prefer... Terry Dean Bradshaw, ruggedly handsome and a senior corporate executive with a top of the line brokerage firm in New York City, the financial capital of the world. Terry Dean Bradshaw, a man's man in his early forties, well-toned and muscular and in well-developed shape from his daily workouts at the health club four nights a week after work and once on the weekends. Terry Dean Bradshaw, praying to be promoted to Vice President, a promotion he believes is long overdue in coming... Terry Dean Bradshaw, happily married for better than twenty years at this point in time, he and his beautiful wife Wendy have two children, a son, Terry Junior and a daughter, Amanda... Terry Dean Bradshaw, deep voiced, is a Brooks Brother's suits, Hermes shirts and ties and Gold Toe socks wearing gentleman. As pointed out he is a man's man. A man's man who on this Friday night after work arrives at "Master Jeff's" home in the Greenwich Village area of Manhattan. He goes to "Master Jeff's" home every other Friday night for his expected "appointment", his "sessions" as they are called as well...his sessions in discipline and self-control, along with the ability to contemplate well under pressure without showing what he is thinking and feeling. The handsome executive lives with the fear that "Master Jeff" will increase his sessions to every Friday rather than every other. Terry Dean Bradshaw's wife and children think that he has a meeting with his superior manager every other Friday and in a way he does...*he really does*...

"Good evening Master Jeff Sir," Terry said, his voice deep and rugged sounding, yet with a nervous twinge to it as well as he walked into his good buddy's home that Friday night, clad spiffily and sharply in a navy blue pinstriped three thousand dollar Brooks Brothers suit.

"You are three minutes late Terrance and promptness is a valued trait," Master Jeff said in stern response, closing and locking the door after admitting his guest into his home. "What do you have to say for yourself, anything? Anything at all?"

Terry knew that he was three minutes late, but inwardly had hoped that Master Jeff would have either not noticed or would have let it slide this time, no such luck though. The man that Terry called "Master Jeff" was militant when it came to the rules of punctuality. Actually, when it came to "the rules" Master Jeff was militant with everything. Any rule broken even slightly could cost Terry and he knew it, *God almighty but he knew it.*

"I'm sorry Master Jeff Sir, the train delayed and then I got stuck waiting for a light to change as I crossed the street," Terry explained as Master Jeff rolled his eyes in his head in disbelief that he had to listen to the executive's boring excuses. "I didn't want to walk out into traffic and risk being hit by a car Master Jeff Sir... and you and I both know Master Jeff Sir that I can't use a company car to get to our meetings, too much would have to be explained and..."

"Yeah, yeah, yeah, excuses, excuses, blah, blah, blah, and yadda, yadda, yadda," Master Jeff said, sounding irritable as he walked toward the bar in his living room, Terry following slowly behind him, almost like a shamed puppy, his big meaty hands crossed behind his back. "You want a drink before we get started tonight Terrance?"

"Only if you're having one Master Jeff Sir," Terry replied, standing in the center of the living room at that point, watching Master Jeff as he poured half a glass of red wine for himself.

It was Master Jeff's favorite drink, red wine, a nice soothing merlot that he favored, always had, *always*, since that night when Terry had met the man he called Master Jeff. Terry stood practically at soldierly attention with his hands crossed behind his back…sweating, the armpits of his dress shirt damp with his manly perspirations. He knew well to stand in that position, seeing as Master Jeff insisted upon it. Terry's cock also began to stand at attention in his suit trousers. Truth be told, Terry's cock had started to stiffen in a mixture of fear and ecstasy since he had left his office to head to Master Jeff's home.

"Well, I am having one, but I just decided that you're not after all," Master Jeff said, held up his glass, mock toasted his guest, said "Bottoms up Terrance", laughed meanly and sipped his wine. "Consider it punishment for your tardiness. A corporate executive such as you should know better when it comes to promptness."

"Yes Master Jeff Sir," Terry replied, sounding totally humbled. "You are correct as always. And just to reiterate I am very sorry for my tardiness Master Jeff Sir."

"Okay, no time like the present to get started," Master Jeff then said, putting his wine down on the bar. "Got to get you disciplined and then back home to the little wife and kids after all…"

Terry looked apprehensively over at the coffee table where all of Master Jeff's "equipment" was neatly laid out and lined up. The executive stifled a gulp of fear and quickly turned his gaze back to the man he called "Master Jeff."

"Well, you know Master Jeff Sir, I was sort of thinking about our session all day today and even on my way over here on the train and…" Terry began, sounding nervous as all hell.

"You were thinking?" Master Jeff asked the handsome and striking executive, sounding totally mocking as he took a sip of his wine. "I do suppose that there's a first time for everything then huh Terrance?"

"Well yes, yes, I suppose there is Master Jeff Sir," Terry replied as he was ridiculed, his hands crossed behind him starting to feel as sweaty as his underarms. "But, as I said Master Jeff Sir, I *was* thinking how I really did do very well these last couple of weeks, since our last session that is. I was kinder to staff members at work, I treated my vice president with the utmost of respect and I even treated a good buddy of mine to an expensive cigar."

"And your point is?" Master Jeff asked and took another sip of his wine, staring steely eyed and impatiently across at Terry as he stood there looking handsomely regal in his suit and tie.

"Well Master Jeff Sir, I was thinking, and my point is this, being that I've behaved exceptionally well these last couple of weeks, I was thinking that perhaps we could skip tonight's session, you know, postpone it till the next time…"

Master Jeff's eyes rolled in his head, a look of total disbelief filling his face...

"Again Terrance?" Master Jeff snapped. "Again we have to go through this prattle of yours?"

"Well Sir, I mean, *Master Jeff Sir, oh God, Master Jeff Sir,*" Terry said beseechingly, already knowing that his request had fallen on deaf ears. "I just thought that maybe...*maybe...*"

"You are not here to think, are you Terrance?" Master Jeff asked in reply and Terry slowly nodded "no." "Don't you even remember the rules that you, YOU, agreed to or do you need a refresher course in listening? We each have a role here that we both firmly agreed to. At this moment I am adhering to my role. You, my numb nutted executive are not! I am really starting to be surprised on how you made it up the corporate ladder so far. You stop thinking right after you leave that fancy office of yours. Do you remember the last time you asked me to postpone a session?"

By now Master Jeff sounded totally angry.

"Y-yes Master Jeff Sir, I remember," Terry said through trembling lips.

"What did I do in response to that request you so called high and mighty executive?" Master Jeff asked.

"Y-you gave me, I mean, oh God, I did it again, Master Jeff Sir, you administered to me forty extras just for asking a stupid question and..." Terry babbled.

"Exaaaaaactly," Master Jeff said, making it sound like Terry was the dumbest corporate executive to ever grace God's green earth. "Now, it seems that lately every time you come here I have to listen to how good you've been, how wonderful you've been, how fucking thoughtful you've been..."

"Well, no, Master Jeff Sir, not every time," Terry said as Master Jeff put his wine glass down, held up a hand halting Terry's talk and stepped over to his handsome charge.

"Now, let's get this straight shall we Terrance?" Master Jeff asked, twining his fingers around the top part of Terry's expensive silk necktie, right under the well done Windsor knot. "You are not here to try to convince me to postpone sessions. You are here for your sessions. You are not here to tell me how wonderful you've been to people you work with or people who work for you or to your wife or even to your kids. That stuff is no matter to me. What matters to me is that you are here for sessions. I am here for sessions. That is what *we* are here for Terrance. You and I are here for our agreed upon sessions. Sessions Terrance, sessions, *sessions...*"You got all that so far?"

"Y-yes Master Jeff Sir, so far I've got it," Terry replied as Master Jeff tugged on his tie a bit and held up his other hand again, silencing Terry's talk again.

"Good, I'm glad to hear that we're on the same page at this point," Master Jeff said sarcastically. "You are simply here to do as I tell you, *that*, and nothing more! Is *that* clear??"

The threatening tone of Master Jeff's voice sent a chill of expectancy, (of ecstasy?) as well as fear directly up Terry Dean Bradshaw's spine. He felt himself starting to twitch uncontrollably with the knowledge of what would soon be in store for him.

"Yes Sir, Master Jeff Sir, it's clear," Terry said, sounding totally defeated yet he repeated the memorized litany that the man he called Master Jeff had taught him…painfully. "Master Jeff sir, I am here because I agreed to accept you in full as my disciplinarian and to assist in relieving me of two weeks' worth of built-up stress from my corporate job. I am here because I agreed to hand myself over to you for these sessions, knowing how much you truly care about me Sir. I am here Master Jeff Sir because you are a true disciplinarian and I am in much need of the services you render upon me."

"Good, now unlike last time for making such a stupid request I'm not going to give you forty extras," Master Jeff said and Terry looked somewhat relieved for a second. "I'm going to give you fifty extras."

The look of relief that had been on Terry's handsome face a second ago quickly evaporated. He balled his big hands behind him into a huge fist of apprehension. He could actually feel his ass cheeks tingle at the thought of fifty extras…

"And besides fifty extras perhaps you should spend some time in the corner," Master Jeff said, sneering like an angry parent at his handsome executive. "Because of your repeated tardiness and your apparent mindless questions and excuses *you will* stand in the corner. You will stand at military attention, in just your socks and underpants, with your eyes blindfolded for fifteen minutes of reflective thinking, totally without movement."

Terry swallowed hard…he came to realize that Master Jeff was going to be extra severe with him during the upcoming session. And in a way it was his fault and his alone. What had he been thinking asking Master Jeff to postpone a session? Yet as fearful as he was feeling a very deep and secret part of him was feeling overjoyed at this turn of events. His cock tingled in his suit trousers. Tonight Terry would be able to give up control totally and let Master Jeff do all the work…as it were and so speak.

"Now, climb out of this corporate uniform of yours and down to the uniform you wear for me," Master Jeff said, letting go of Terry's tie.

"Y-yes Sir Master Jeff Sir," Terry said, reaching with his shaking hands and fingers to start undoing the knot in his tie first.

"And you know the rules Terrance, tell me what happens once that fancy tie is off you," Master Jeff commanded.

"Master Jeff Sir, once my tie is off me there is no turning back, once my tie is off me you own my ass and every other part of me until you decree otherwise," Terry said, repeating what he said each time Master Jeff had him in his home, repeating the words that he knew so well by now, slowly undoing his tie as he said his mantra, looking like a man who has made up his mind about his present situation. "If I decide to leave now I am free to go Master Jeff Sir, but, once I slide this tie off my shirt collar the rules are all yours."

Master Jeff nodded with total satisfaction and finished off his wine as Terry got his tie off... As Terry put his tie down on a nearby living room chair Master Jeff prided himself on how well he had trained the handsome corporate executive. He watched lustfully as his charge shucked off his suit jacket, hung it neatly on the back of a chair and began unbuttoning his crisp white dress shirt, his big hands and fingers seeming to tremble as he did so. The wedding band on Terry's ring finger of his left hand was a mocking symbol of part of who the man was. As he undid his expensive gold cufflinks and got his shirt off Master Jeff took in the sight of the executive's robust chest under his white tee shirt. The way Terry's plump nipples pressed against his tee shirt was beyond erotic in the sadistic yet loving master's eyes. Terry laid his shirt on the chair and quickly shucked his tee shirt off, revealing a hairy, muscular barrel like chest and huge, well-proportioned massive pecs, two of the plumpest pinkish brown nipples and a flat washboard stomach region. Terry's shoulders were nearly as wide as a doorway; his arms were long, sinewy and muscular, adorned with biceps the size of two bowling balls. His hands, when fisted were big enough to punch holes through walls with, yet his long well-proportioned fingers showed the inward sensitivity of a piano player, a writer, or perhaps where Terry Dean Bradshaw was concerned, a painter. Master Jeff could tell that besides the discipline he endured at his hands the handsome executive punished himself extensively at the gym as well. Master Jeff wondered how many times a night Terry Dean Bradshaw's wife wanted him. He wondered just how much sleep the beyond handsome executive actually ever got. As the ruggedly good looking executive bent down to unlace his highly shined lace-up black wingtip shoes his luscious melon shaped ass cheeks outlined beautifully and erotically in his suit trousers. It was those ass cheeks that were Master Jeff's pride and joy. It was those ass cheeks, shaped like two round hard melons that Master Jeff had (secretly?) fallen totally in love with. It was those ass cheeks that Master Jeff loved so much, loved to torture most of all with all, not some, *all* of his implements. And Terry Dean Bradshaw was his truest dream made flesh. The man had proven time and again just how much he could endure being disciplined (tortured?) with ALL of Master Jeff's implements. The man was a staunch executive in every respect of the word. Terry got his shoes off his feet, placed them neatly under the chair where he'd piled up his clothes and then stood up straight, unbuttoning his suit trousers as he did so. The look of fear and apprehension on his face was incomparable. He was such a willing submissive and Master Jeff had to thank God for having brought Terry to him, although he would never let Terry Dean Bradshaw know that, at least not during one of their sessions. In his heart Master Jeff truly loved this man and if he couldn't have Terry Dean Bradshaw as a permanent lover then he would settle for the every other week sessions that they both played their parts for. Master Jeff had come to realize how both he and the handsome corporate executive played their parts very well indeed. Master Jeff chuckled as he thought of the times when he had threatened to increase

Terry's sessions back to every week rather than every other week. Terry slid his suit trousers down and stepped out of them, folded them neatly, placed them on the chair with the rest of his clothing and then stood almost at attention before Master Jeff in just his Brooks Brothers burgundy silk boxer shorts and OTC (over the calf) Gold Toe brand navy blue nylon dress socks.

"Now you're in uniform for me," Master Jeff chuckled, noting how Terry's cock was hard as a rock, the tip of it just about peeking out of the fly opening of his boxer shorts, his big juicy balls outlined just inches lower in the boxers.

"Y-yes Sir Master Jeff Sir," Terry said, quickly placing his hands behind his back and standing up even straighter, jutting his massive chest outwards.

"How does it feel being stripped of your corporate uniform, your power suit as you call it, and standing there in just your damned underpants and socks?" Master Jeff asked Terry.

"Master Jeff Sir, it feels humiliating, totally humiliating," Terry replied, his gruff voice belying his underwear and sock clad appearance.

Besides his cock being hard and beefy in his silk boxer shorts Master Jeff took note of the fact that Terry's bulbous nipples had become erect and hard. They were the size of two pencil erasers on the executive's massive chest. It seemed to Master Jeff that whenever Terry stood before him in this manner he was always plumped up big and hard in his executive style silk boxer shorts and his nipples followed suit as well... Master Jeff marveled at how Terry Dean Bradshaw had been blessed with two such oversized and luscious looking nipples. The way they pointed out from his hairy chest was erotic in every sense of the word. This was the uniform that Master Jeff decreed his charge should wear, because nothing humiliated a man more than to be seen in just his underpants and dress socks.

Terry Dean Bradshaw, a man very used to giving orders all day to staff and colleagues, a man very much used to being totally in charge in his domestic home, now stripped of his pride and manhood as he stood before the man he called "Master." Yes, Terry Dean Bradshaw was a man VERY, very used to giving orders on a daily basis both in his professional and domestic lives. He was also a man used to having his orders followed to the T. But here, in Master Jeff's universe all of that power the man imbued went out the window. In Master Jeff's world Terry Dean Bradshaw was able to relinquish all control one hundred percent. For the time he spent with Master Jeff the feeling of relinquishing control was both headily wonderful and awfully painful, an erotically delightful mixture to the corporate executive. Being a corporate executive carried with it a lot of responsibility and power. Wearing what Terry Dean Bradshaw called his "power suit" emanated that power to his underlings. Never did he remove his suit jacket at work like his office underlings. He felt that his complete suit was his armor, but now, stripped to his silk boxer shorts and socks he felt that shield of armor was gone. He had literally been stripped of his power (suit). Truthfully he had stripped himself down to his boxer shorts and socks but at his master's orders it was as if Master Jeff himself had stripped the executive down. When Terry and Jeff (at the time they met that was how they addressed each other, the title of "Master" for Jeff came when they had decided on their first session together) had discovered a while back how this kind of relationship could serve both their secret needs a friendship so trusting, a friendship like no other was born for both men. With a look of trepidation on his face Terry again took in the sight of the equipment on Master Jeff's coffee table. Lined up neatly and ready for use was a round leather paddle, (Master Jeff always began the sessions with that damned paddle) a wooden rectangular shaped paddle with small holes drilled into it (a fraternity paddle Master Jeff called it, a superb device to remind the executive of his college days while in his fraternity active's clutches), a hairbrush, an old fashioned large wooden spoon, a leather strop, and last, but certainly not least an old belt that had once belonged to Terry's step-father, a man who at one time instilled fear, loathing, raw lust and a strange hunger at the same time in the man who was now a corporate ladder climber. When Terry had reached his early twenties he had moved out of his mother's and step father's house. He lived in the dorm of his college campus (another place where he continued to endure having his ass reddened it seemed). His stepfather hadn't seemed to notice that the prized belt that he used to whip Terry's ass with a few times a week when the young man's mother was not around had gone as absent as his handsome stepson. Terry had taken the belt with him and kept it as a reminder of the man who had come into his and his mother's lives and had somehow mastered him. Terry kept that belt close at hand to remind himself of what he had suffered at the hands of his wicked stepfather, to remind himself that no one, no one would ever have him in such a fashion again. But as time went on and the dreams haunted him it seemed that Terry Dean Bradshaw realized that there was a secret and very deep part of him that craved and hungered for the discipline his stepfather used to mete out on him. Even though he was paddled by the actives when he pledged the college fraternity he did not see that as discipline. That was part of being able to endure so that he could become a member of the elite fraternity. It was also a college-boy ritual that he somehow looked forward to. Discipline would come again years later. It wasn't until Terry and Jeff met on a fateful night when Terry's secret needs would be fulfilled once again and he would give his newfound master his stepfather's belt as a symbol of his devotion. Master Jeff decreed how being worked over with an instrument that had been yours and your stepfathers before you made the experience that much more intense and that much more humiliating. Terry was inclined to agree as he recalled how when he was a teenage jock his stepfather reddened his ass for him at least twice a week, sometimes more than twice a week with that very belt. Terry, standing there scantily clad also recalled how his step dad had always, for whatever the fuck the reason made Terry leave his socks on for his ass whippings. Sometimes he was allowed to leave his underpants on, most times they were off, to really get at his meaty jock ass as his step dad used to call it, but his socks, always he was left clad in just his damned socks. (Terry always recalled his stepfather seething as he spanked him with that belt and saying things like, "Yeah boy, nothing teaches a lesson better than having your meaty jock ass reddened like a tomato huh?

Fucking meaty jock ass you got here boy! Bet you inherited this meaty ass of yours from your Dad huh? 'Cause sure as shit rolls downhill your mom doesn't have a meaty ass like yours Boy!") As the memories played havoc with Terry's mind he glanced down at his navy blue dress socked feet and nervously wiggled his toes. When he was a teenaged jock it was predominantly white sweat socks that he wore, but now, as an adult, as an executive it was these dress style stinkers he wore. Being stripped down at his stepfather's orders and then having the man whip his ass with that belt made Terry feel worse than violated yet sleazily aroused somehow at the same time. He came to believe that the arousal had more to do with his strength in being able to take what his step-dad dished out on him. When it came to his sexuality Terry Dean Bradshaw prided himself on being a real ladies man. But his stepfather whipping his ass… It was a memory and a need that would follow him for his entire life it would seem. Amazing to him though how his stepfather in the past and Master Jeff now in the present made him strip down to his underpants and socks for his sessions.

"Okay, now that you've stripped down and bared yourself to your uniform of humiliation and humbleness for me go and find your corner," Master Jeff said sternly. "You'll spend fifteen minutes standing at attention in your corner and reflecting and then we shall proceed as we usually do."

"Yes Sir Master Jeff Sir," Terry said, hunched his broad shoulders out and padded on socked feet across the room to a corner of his choice.

Choosing the corner he would stand in like a child was one luxury Master Jeff allowed his charge…

Terry stood in front of the corner of his choice, faced it, took a deep breath, stepped as far into the crack of the wall as possible and with his cock now totally erect in his silk boxer shorts he balanced himself at a stance of soldierly attention…

"Good boy," Master Jeff said from across the room, once more taking in the sight of Terry's delectably shaped ass globes as they filled out the back of his under shorts.

Master Jeff adored how this rugged, masculine man had so trustingly handed himself over to him where his "secret" needs were concerned, his needs also being a desire for "stress relief." Making the corporate executive stand in a corner like a misbehaved child was very humiliating, granted, but that is why Master Jeff insisted on it where his handsome charge was concerned. Stripped to his underpants and socks and humiliated Terry was, yet at the same time fully and wholly erect, his cock straining in the confines of his silk boxer shorts as he obeyed his master's commands. It is always the given Master Jeff thought, how the excitement of the challenge that the topnotch guy had accepted could cause that, as well as his latent submissive nature. Terry knew what he was in for each time he reported to Master Jeff at his home. Being treated in such a way at these "disciplinary" sessions was a reminder for the executive of his carelessness in the past that would stop him from achieving his personal best, his true potential.

As Terry stood with his nose pressed against the corner and as his cock turned to concrete in his underpants the corporate executive found that in this moment of his ordered time of reflection he recalled the night when he and the man he had come to call "Master" first met. Funny, Terry thought now, how when he first met Master Jeff he would not have in a million years thought about addressing him by that title. Now, he could think of no other way to address the man who'd had such a profound effect on his life. To help his charge to reflect and meditate properly Master Jeff stepped behind Terry and tied a soft white cloth blindfold over the executive's eyes.

"Thank you Master Jeff Sir," Terry said, even though in truth he hated being sight-hindered.

Master Jeff gave Terry's backside an openhanded swat and then poured himself a second glass of wine…

"Fifteen minutes Terrance," Master Jeff said softly.

Terry nodded and in his mind saw the bar a few blocks away from the Wall Street office where the company he worked for was located. It was a Friday night, six PM and it had been what most executives would call "A week from hell." Terry Dean Bradshaw, an up and coming vice president could think of no better way to end the hectic week than with a couple of what he called "stiff ones." Clad very sharply and spiffily in a charcoal colored Armani suit, a crisp white custom made shirt, a black silk necktie and a pair of Kenneth Cole highly shined black loafers Terry Dean Bradshaw sauntered into the Wall Street bar, aptly named "The Wall Street Local" in honor of the fact that it was frequented by the locals of Wall Street, or to be more appropriate, the "Bulls" of Wall Street. The place was dimly lit and decorated tastefully and elegantly ala Wall Street. Small round tables adorned one side of the bar where after-work business could be discussed if the executive patrons desired it. A pool table dominated a second room where young "Wall Street" bulls challenged each other and gambled away thousands of dollars on a game or two, their suit jackets off, their shirt sleeves rolled up and their ties pulled down as they engaged in some intense games of Pool. The front of the establishment was where the main bar was, where Terry Dean Bradshaw was headed for his after work "stiff ones." Terry made a commanding appearance as he sauntered up to the bar, carrying his attaché case. He placed his attaché case on the floor under the straight-backed barstool where he always sat when frequenting the bar, it was his usual spot.

"Good evening Mr. Bradshaw," the middle aged bartender said as he placed a square napkin on the bar, in front of where Terry would be sitting.

"Good evening Craig," Terry said as he shucked off his suit jacket and draped it on the back of the barstool.

As he did so he said "Good evening" to the gentleman who was seated next to his usual spot at the bar. The man was about five feet eight inches tall, he had short cut brown hair and brown eyes and was wearing what Terry would call "Harold Lloyd" spectacles. He appeared to be of average build and was clad in a brown suit, a white shirt opened at the neck with no tie and brown slip-on loafers. Terry guessed the newcomers age to be in the mid-forties or thereabouts. The topnotch executive did not (yet) know this man but he had said "Good evening" to him anyway, he was a proper exec after all.

"Good evening to you too," the gentleman said to Terry as he sat down and hefted his feet onto the rung of his barstool.

The man raised his glass to Terry and took a sip of what appeared to be red wine.

"The usual Mr. Bradshaw?" Craig the bartender asked Terry as the man sitting next to him said, "I'm Jeff" and held out a hand, in Terry's opinion, a very big and meaty sized hand, a hand that seemed over-sized for the man's height and build.

"Uh, good to meet you Jeff, I'm Terry, Terry Dean Bradshaw," Terry said and shook hands, Jeff's big hand gripping his good and tight.

"Interesting name," Jeff said as he pumped the executive's hand real hard, taking in the sight of his gold cufflinks with some kind of a company logo etched into them, a definite proclamation to his stature at whatever he did and wherever it was he worked, also the monogrammed custom made white dress shirt.

"Thanks, I'm uh, named after my dad," Terry said and as Jeff held tight to his hand he turned to the bartender.

"I'll have a..." Terry began and without thinking why he glanced at Jeff's glass of red wine on the bar.

"It's red wine, merlot," Jeff said and finally let go of Terry's hand.

"Yes, red wine sounds good Craig," Terry said to the bartender.

"Coming up Sir," Craig said and turned to fetch the executive his drink.

Terry fleetingly wondered why he ordered red wine in place of the usual scotch on the rocks that he usually had. It was obvious to Terry that Craig had been totally prepared to serve him his "usual."

"You seem to be pretty well known here," Jeff said and sipped his wine, facing forward as he spoke. "The bartender greeting you by your name and you by his, pretty impressive."

"Pretty well known I would say, I come here fairly regularly," Terry replied, looking at the man as he spoke. "I know this sounds a lot like a cliché but I don't recall ever seeing you in here Jeff."

"That's because it's my first time here Terry," Jeff said. "I'm meeting a client. What is Terry short for?"

"Uh, Terrance," Terry replied. "I like being called Terry though."

"Fine, I'll call you Terrance," Jeff said, sounding almost sarcastic as the bartender placed the glass of red wine in front of Terry.

"Um, okay, sure," Terry said and picked up his glass of wine. "To new friendships Jeff..."

"To new friendships Terrance," Jeff said and clinked his glass against Terry's.

"Yes, to new friendships," Terry replied, thinking, "I suppose..."

"So, what sort of client are you waiting for?" Terry asked after taking a long and satisfying sip of his wine. "What business are you in?"

"I'm a behavior modification therapist," Jeff said. "I specialize in stress control…"

"Ha, bingo!" Terry said and leaned back on his barstool. "You win the prize Jeff…"

"I am guessing you are a stressed out executive," Jeff said, turning and facing Terry, a stern expression on his face. "And a family man no doubt…"

"Bingo again Sir," Terry responded, not knowing at that moment that he would eventually be addressing Jeff as "Sir" on a regular basis.

"What do you do?" Jeff asked raw lust and some sort of primal desire filling him as he took in the sight of the regally handsome man seated beside him.

"I work as a corporate executive for a brokerage firm here on Wall Street," Terry replied and sipped his wine. "I'm in charge of two departments, lots of money involved, and it's pretty heady stuff all day."

"I bet it is," Jeff said.

"So uh, what kind of therapy do you use for your clients?" Terry asked. "Maybe I'll come to your office sometime for a session or two…"

"I require a commitment of more than just *a session or two* Terrance," Jeff said, sipped his wine and knew that he had just hooked another frontrunner.

"Well, I suppose that would be okay, seeing as I'm always stressed out after a long hard day at work," Terry said, seeming to be surmising his timeframe.

As Terry sipped his wine Jeff noticed the wedding band on his ring finger. The man had a wife. He was right when he'd said that he was a family man. That always made it more intense and more interesting, both for him and for his charge. In Master Jeff's opinion there was nothing more intensely intriguing than having a married man, some woman's husband under his control.

"Okay, let's say I make a commitment of five sessions," Terry began and chugged down what was left of his wine.

As he set his glass down Jeff raised a finger at the bartender and almost instantly two more glasses of red wine were set down, one in front of Jeff and one in front of Terry.

"I require a commitment of at least ten sessions to start with Terrance," Jeff said, reaching into his pocket and producing a business card. "The kind of therapy I treat my clients with is seriously intense, very hard-core and to some *very* terrifying, yet, if you are a person of substance and inner strength it can be the most rewarding of experiences you ever submit to."

"Wow, now you really have my curiosity piqued Sir," Terry said, turned on his barstool facing Jeff and lay one foot over his knee. "I consider myself to be very strong both mentally and physically. With what I do for a living I better be strong, sharp and focused. But at the end of the day the stress just seems to crawl all over me…and…"

"...and that's where I would come in..." Jeff said and handed Terry his business card.

Terry looked at the card which depicted a muscular man in his thirties or thereabouts with his pants yanked down in back slung over the knees of an older man and being spanked with a leather paddle. Terry's chin dropped as he stared at it, his other hand pausing as he was raising his glass of wine to his lips. Under the picture of the man being spanked was Master Jeff's e-mail address and phone number.

"What in hell is this?" Terry asked, holding the card between his thumb and first two fingers of one hand as he sipped his wine.

"That is my business card Terrance," Jeff replied sternly. "The kind of therapy I mete out is not the Freudian or Jung or new age methods. I don't use religion or any of that mumbo jumbo to treat my clients with. I dish out strong discipline. I demand total obedience and from that you will learn true self control. I am a strong believer in the healing powers of serious "spankology."

Terrance, still looking at the card, glanced up at Jeff and looked back at the card again. His hand seemed to be trembling all of a sudden as thoughts of his stepfather filled his mind.

"S-spankology?" Terry asked, almost in a whisper. "Y-you mean you spank your clients?"

Jeff simply nodded "yes" slowly and sipped his wine.

"And *that* relieves them of stress?" Terry asked. "Being spanked relieves them of stress???"

"Yes, as it would you Terrance," Jeff replied. "It would relieve you of stress, cause you to learn self-control, AND, and, at the same time I would force you to stretch your limits."

"Spank me? Spank me???" Terry asked, sounding shocked at the fact that Jeff had even suggested such a thing, yet for a fleeting moment seeing his stepfather's face in his mind. "Man, you have got to be kidding! The last person that ever spanked, paddled and whipped my poor ass was my step dad when I was a teenager! Okay, when I pledged a fraternity in college I was paddled but that was different, that was all college hi-jinks!"

"So what you're saying is that at this age a therapeutic spanking would not benefit you," Jeff said, staring forward. "In my opinion it would benefit you greatly Terrance."

"How, how so?" Terry asked.

"Terrance, if we are going to continue this conversation I will insist on something right here and right now," Jeff said, looking into his glass of wine as he spoke.

"What's that?" Terry asked.

"You begin addressing me as "Sir"," Jeff said sternly. "Being the disciplinarian I am it's only proper that I should be addressed as such. I'm sure you're properly addressed by your underlings where you work."

Terry looked at Jeff in disbelief, pursed his lips tightly for a moment and huffed, but for some reason heard himself saying, "Okay, Sir it is, if you insist on it, Sir."

"Insist I do," Jeff said.

"But I'm not your underling, Sir," Terry said and took a gulp of his wine, not believing that he was actually having this conversation.

"Not yet you're not," Jeff chuckled and Terry winced for a moment.

"Okay Sir, now, if you would be so kind as to answer my question," Terry continued, still looking at the card in disbelief that he had been handed. "How would *you* spanking *me* relieve stress and force me to stretch my limits? What limits are we talking about here, Sir?"

"Well, have you ever felt that you have not reached your fullest potential in certain areas of your life Terrance?" Jeff asked.

"Uh, yes, in way I feel like that sometimes, Sir," Terry replied.

"How so?" Master Jeff asked.

"Well, I feel that where I work I should be a vice president at this point, Sir," Terry replied. "And with the way I work so hard I think I am being shafted."

"My form of therapy would help you to realize the error in that line of thinking and I would force you to see how it's you and your own ineptitudes that are holding you back from achieving that much coveted title in your workplace Terrance."

"M-my ineptitudes? Now hold on there Jeff, Sir," Terry said through clenched teeth. "I am not inept...at all..."

"Then why aren't you a vice president where you work?" Jeff asked and sipped his wine. "Since we started talking here why have you been so defensive?"

Terry simply looked at the man as he sipped his wine, took a deep breath and whispered the words, "oh shit." Jeff, facing forward, set his wine glass down and nodded "yes."

"Ten sessions Terrance, *to start with*," Jeff said and as he said it Terry felt that he should bolt from the bar, to get away from this strange man he had just met, instead he sat as if fastened to his seat.

"To start with Sir?" Terry asked sounding totally nervous yet he could not believe that his manhood was stiffening in his suit trousers.

His curiosity was more than piqued at that point...

"Yes, it appears to me that you are a very highly competitive, stressed out, high socked executive who is in dire need of regular sessions with me," Jeff said. "I specialize in only highly competitive people who can thrive on discipline and control...to be able to relinquish their control to me for the duration of spanking sessions."

"High socked," Terry chuckled. "I like that for some reason Sir. Uh, if that's your professional opinion..."

"It is..." Jeff replied quickly, cutting off Terry's words while at the same time praying that this beguilingly handsome man would submit to him.

The thought of having this rugged and masculine married man under his control was the headiest of feelings he had had in a long time. He could tell from the look on Terry's face that the man was terrified yet intrigued at the same time.

"Ten sessions to start with, once a week," Jeff said. "Then after that I will have you report to me every other week on an agreed upon day and time. When you agree to that day and time you will adhere to it religiously. Part of training you will be to teach you the value of being prompt and always, ALWAYS on time for your appointments."

Terry nodded, not believing that he was actually agreeing to all this. *Was he agreeing to all this?* He squeezed his black socked ankle as it rested on his knee and realized that *yes, he was* agreeing to this. Somewhere deep inside him he knew this need resided…and Jeff seemed to be the man to serve that need for him.

"Okay then, once a week Sir," Terry said, gulped his wine and found he was fighting tears as they filled his beautiful eyes. "What uh, what day are we looking at, Sir?"

"Terrance, now that you've agreed the rules will become even more rigid," Jeff said. "From this moment onward you will address me as "Master Jeff Sir…" Is that clear and understandable to you?"

"Y-yes, I suppose so," Terry said, his lips trembling and he quickly finished his wine. "Master Jeff Sir…"

"Very good Terrance, very good," Master Jeff said.

To Terry it at first sounded totally ridiculous, but somehow, as he said it, looking at the man he had just addressed as Master, he felt a stirring deep down in his loins. He had not felt like this since the days of his stepfather… Obviously, the high-powered executive realized, there was still some deep seeded need within him for discipline.

"Master Jeff Sir," Terry said again. "What day would I be required to meet you for…uh, to report to you for sessions?"

"Does Friday nights work for you Terrance?" Master Jeff asked and reached forward to take Terry's left wrist in hand, eyeing his wedding band. "Did you call your wife tonight to tell her you would be home late, seeing as you're here in "The Wall Street Local" bar?"

"I, uh, no, Master Jeff Sir," Terry replied. "She uh, she can't know about this, ever…"

"That Terrance, is not my problem nor did I question that, I simply asked if you had called her to tell her you would be home late," Master Jeff said, holding Terry's wrist tight, taking in the sight of his cufflinks, his wedding band and the Rolex watch under his shirt sleeve.

"The only time I call her to tell her that I'll be late is when I get stuck working on special projects or if the computer system where I work goes down Master Jeff Sir," Terry said shakily. "Those are things that would keep me at work longer than usual Sir. She works part time for a jewelry company and Friday nights are usually her late nights. If not she'll just get home and think I'm still at work. I would think that Friday nights would be satisfactory then Master Jeff Sir. I could tell her that going forward I'll be working late for about one..."

Master Jeff held up two fingers on his other hand as he caressed Terry's sleeved wrist with his other hand.

"Two...two hours every Friday night for the next ten weeks Master Jeff Sir," Terry said, his tears filling his eyes to nearly overflowing at that point. "And then every other week after that."

"Good man," Master Jeff said and his heart thundered in his chest at the sight of the crystalline-like tears that had flooded his new charge's eyes. "I assure you Terrance, this is the best decision you will have ever made for yourself... You see my executive, discipline derives from *disciple*-disciple to perhaps a philosopher, disciple to a set of principles, disciple to a set of values, disciple to an overriding purpose, to a super ordinate goal or in this case, me, a person who represents that goal."

"Yes Master Jeff Sir, if you say so," Terry said and snuffed back his tears.

"Well, shall we be on our way to my place then?" Master Jeff asked. "I don't live too far from here."

"N-now Master Jeff Sir?" Terry asked. "But I thought you said you were waiting for a client."

"I was, you're here now," Master Jeff said and let go of Terry's wrist. "I'll meet you outside. Pay for the drinks and order a car for us. I live on Fourth Street and Avenue B. Also, be sure to call your wife and let her know that you'll be late in getting home tonight...and for the next nine Friday's as well."

"Y-yes Sir, Master Jeff Sir," Terry said and sprang to his feet.

He stood there paying the tab, watching out of the corner of his eye as the man who he would from that moment on call "Master" strode out of the bar with a confident swagger in his step. As Terry waited for his change from the bartender he again looked at Master Jeff's business card. He gulped hard...wondering what in the Sam hell he had agreed to here tonight...yet somehow he could not (did not want to?) turn back; inwardly he knew that as well as he knew his own name...

A short while later Terry stepped out of the bar called "The Wall Street Local" and stood beside Master Jeff.

"Did you do as I instructed you Terrance?" Master Jeff asked as Terry stood, shifting his attaché case around in his hand.

"Yes Master Jeff Sir, I did as you instructed," Terry replied. "I paid the bar tab, I used my cell phone to call my wife to let her know that I would be late tonight and a cab is on the way Sir."

Master Jeff nodded, looked at Terry and said, "Very good, very good so far Terrance. Perhaps as it is your first night in session I'll just hold onto you for an hour and a half rather than the allotted two hours."

"That uh, that is up to you Master Jeff Sir, it is not for me to decide," Terry said and then a fancy service car pulled up in front of the two men...

Before the driver could get out and open the door for Terry and Master Jeff Terry did the honors of opening the car door for his newfound friend, mentor and master…

"Yep, you do learn fast Terrance, I will give you that," Master Jeff said as he stepped into the car and settled into the plush seat.

"Okay, let's begin the usual way," Master Jeff said now, jarring the blindfolded Terry back to the present as the executive stood in the corner, reflecting on the past.

Stepping over to his stripped down handsome charge Master Jeff hooked a hand around one of the man's upper arms, his hand of course not making it all the way around Terry's huge bicep. "Let me tell you what you're in for this time you numb nuts executive. Let me show you just how stupid you were to hand yourself over to me tonight."

"Y-yes Sir Master Jeff Sir," Terry said, the feeling of Master Jeff holding tight to his arm almost claw-like.

"I'm going to begin by giving you the fifty extra swats you earned by asking me a stupid question," Master Jeff said in an explanatory sounding manner. "That will be a reminder to you as an executive to never, NEVER ask stupid questions, whether it's here or in your world of work. Those swats I will administer to your hairy ass cheeks with my leather paddle, twenty-five consecutive swats to each cheek. After that warm-up I'll give you ten swats with the leather paddle again, those for your tardiness. Five swats to each ass cheek this time. Once those hot ass cheeks of yours are warmed up and primed the way I like them we'll get down to the regular business for your session. Any questions so far you numb nuts executive?"

"N-no Sir Master Jeff Sir, no questions," his eyes filled with tears behind his blindfold and his lips trembling as he tried to speak clearly.

It had only been a short fifteen minutes that he had stood in the corner but the tension was showing. Terry's muscular body was perspiring more than ever from the feeling of dread mixed with anticipation. Master Jeff took his charge's blindfold off him and still held tight to Terry's arm.

"Okay Terrance, time to go to the spanking couch and get this show on the road what do you say?" Master Jeff asked Terry.

"I, it's not mine to say Master Jeff Sir, it's yours to say and yours only," Terry said softly as he walked on his socked feet beside Master Jeff to the spanking couch.

Master Jeff sat down and pointed at the leather paddle…

Without a word of resistance or complaint Terry picked up the leather paddle, kissed it twice, once on each side and handed it to Master Jeff. The regal looking corporate executive then got himself situated over Master Jeff's lap and knees, his socked toes pressed hard against the floor as he balanced himself in the most humiliating of positions. He folded his arms and pulled them up behind him. He was glad for small favors as Master Jeff didn't tie him this time… But the session hadn't actually begun so he could still wind up tied the ruggedly handsome executive thought somewhat miserably…

"Okay Numb nuts, count off the swats for me," Master Jeff said, rubbing the leather paddle against Terry's silk boxer shorts covered ass cheeks. "For the warm-up rounds I'll leave your fancy shmancy silky boxers on you. After we're done though you're going through the regular session bare assed."

"Y-yes Master Jeff Sir," Terry said, his head hanging down, looking at the floor as he spoke.

Inwardly it amazed Master Jeff that this strong minded and very take charge corporate executive could put himself in such a mortifying and degrading position. But the boner that Terry was sporting in his boxer shorts as it pressed against Master Jeff's lap told him that Terry was right where he was meant to be at that moment. Master Jeff had to wonder what the executive's wife would think seeing her man this way. It seemed that many, many Wall Street corporate executives craved this kind of treatment at the end of a long and hectic week. Giving orders and being in positions of command eventually took their toll and it was good therapy to let go and allow someone else to take charge once in a while. Master Jeff was pleased that Terry had found him…and he planned to have "sessions" with the handsome executive for as long as time would allow.

"And you'd better count correctly you numb nuts," Master Jeff said with total authority in his voice, moving the leather paddle over Terry's hairy and muscular thighs and upwards over his melon shaped ass cheeks. "Tell me what will happen if you miss a number or stupidly repeat a number…"

"Master Jeff Sir, if I mess up on the count we will start back at number one," Terry stated, repeating still more of the rules that he had been taught during his times with Master Jeff.

"Very true story," Master Jeff said, loving the way Terry's ass cheeks looked so beautifully and delectably outlined in his silk boxer shorts.

Master Jeff raised his leather paddle and brought it down hard on Terry's left ass cheek… It made a sound like **WHAPPP**

"OWWWWW!!!" Terry hollered. "ONE!!!"

WHAPPP WHAPPP WHAPPP WHAPPP WHAPPP

"ARRRRRHHHHH, and two, three, four, five, six!!" Terry called out loudly, his hands holding tight to his folded arms behind him as he lay across Master Jeff's lap.

"You know Terrance, ten to twenty swats with one of these leather paddles is enough to have the boldest of men sniveling like when they were children," Master Jeff said sarcastically.

WHAPP WHAPP WHAPP WHAPP WHAPP WHAPP WHAPP

"OWWWWWWW!!!" Terry cried out through clenched teeth. "S-seven, eight, nine, ten, eleven, twelve, thirteen…G-GAWD!!!"

"But I don't plan on being stingy with you like that, "Master Jeff said meanly. "In your case I'm being really generous here and giving you fifty good hard ones!"

"Y-yes Sir Master Jeff Sir, thank you Sir!!" Terry bantered.

As Master Jeff swatted Terry's left ass cheek over and over and over and over again the corporate executive counted diligently as his cheek seemed to be heating up and stinging more and more with each blow. He kept the count true, gritted his teeth, and held his folded arms tight. For the moment he choked back tears as the blows from Master Jeff's paddle pummeled his ass cheek…but soon enough the superlative executive knew he would be sniveling and crying like a little kid.

"OWWWWWRRRR!!!" Terry ranted and screamed out the numbers. "Twenty, twenty one, OWWWWWWWWRRR my poor ass globe Master Jeff Sir, twenty two and twenty three!!"

When Master Jeff administered the twenty-fifth and final swat to Terry's left ass cheek Terry screamed out the number twenty five like he was filled with joy, glad that that part of his punishment was over. Master Jeff wasted no time however in getting down to the business of swatting Terry's right sided ass cheek.

WHAPP WHAPP WHAPP WHAPP WHAPP WHAPP WHAPP

"OHHHHHHHHRRRRR oh fuck," Terry cried out, wondering on one hand why he had ever agreed to all this, while on the other hand overjoyed as the man he called "Master" doled out the discipline. "One, two, three, four, five, six, seven!!!"

When Master Jeff completed the twenty five swats to Terry's right ass cheek he congratulated his charge on having counted so well, saying it sarcastically however. Both of Terry's ass cheeks felt like they were crimson, more than likely already matching the color of his silk boxer shorts.

"Th-thank you Master Jeff Sir," Terry gasped, trying desperately not to reach down and rub his stinging ass cheeks.

He knew that if he moved his hands from the position they were in Master Jeff would waste no time in tying them tightly behind him… It had happened so many times in the past. Terry wanted so much to obey his master's orders and keep his hands clasped tightly behind him, but reaching down and rubbing one's wounded ass cheeks after being spanked good and red was a natural response Terry had found over time. But Master Jeff would simply tie him if he did so. And Terry had to admit that he hated being tied. (Maybe not?)

"Okay, those were for your stupidity, now for your tardiness," Master Jeff said and brought the paddle down good and hard on Terry's left ass cheek, beginning there again.

WHAPP WHAPP WHAPP WHAPP WHAPP

"OWWWWWCCCHHH!!! One, two, three, four, five!!!" Terry called out.

"Will you be tardy for our next session you numb nut executive?" Master Jeff asked Terry.

"N-no Master Jeff Sir, no way Sir!!" Terry cried out loudly. "It won't happen again Master Jeff Sir!!"

"I didn't think so," Master Jeff chuckled and brought his paddle down hard five times on Terry's right sided ass cheek.

Terry called out the numbers from one to five correctly and wondered if his ass cheeks now matched his silk boxers. He recalled when his wife had bought him the burgundy silk boxer shorts for his last birthday and she said how very sexy he looked in them when they had gone to bed that night. If his wife could see him now in his sexy boxers she would not believe it Terry thought, unaware that Master Jeff had just thought the same thing just a few minutes ago... Actually, for whatever the reason, Terry thought at that moment how his wife purchased all his socks and underwear for him, just like most married guys out there it seemed...

"Okay Numb Nuts, that was a good warm-up," Master Jeff said.

"I-I agree Master Jeff Sir," Terry said, sounding stupid.

As Terry lay across Master Jeff's lap, squirming slightly, he felt the paddle being rubbed over his reddened wounded ass cheeks, and he knew that the warm-up was nothing compared to what Master Jeff would have him endure as the session progressed...

A few moments later, per Master Jeff's orders Terry was standing next to the spanking couch with his hands crossed up behind his head. He had only suffered a total of thirty five swats to each ass cheek so far but being that Master Jeff was expert when it came to the art of spanking the corporate executive was already feeling the burning sting and searing sensations. Master Jeff having ordered him to cross his hands up behind his head insured that he would not reach down to rub his wounded ass cheeks. (Plus, having had Terry cross his hands up behind his head really forced the stripped down executive to show off his beautiful musculature. In Master Jeff's opinion Terry Dean Bradshaw had one of the best bodies he had ever seen. Every inch of the man was solid muscle, barely an ounce of fat on him anywhere.) Master Jeff wanted Terry to thoroughly enjoy and benefit from every moment of the searing hot pain. Plus it was after being well-spanked that the searing sting set in a little more with each passing moment, Master Jeff called this the baking part of one's ass cheeks. Roasting those cheeks came as the session progressed. Terry then watched as Master Jeff placed his leather paddle back down on the coffee table and then picked up the wooden fraternity paddle with the holes drilled into it... Terry nervously wiggled his toes in his navy blue socks, recalling how in his college days those kinds of paddles had been used on him when he was a fraternity pledge and then in turn he used those kinds of paddles on pledges when he became an active. During Hell Week he was paddled at least two to three times a day and he made sure to do the same to his pledges when his turn as an active was finally at hand. He recalled having endured being spanked and paddled in college when he was what was called a "frat pledge" but now he would be enduring it from a true spanking master, not some college boy wanna be master.

"Now Terrance, walk to the spanking table," Master Jeff said commandingly. "And bring your arms down, but be sure to keep them positioned at your sides."

"Yes Sir Master Jeff Sir," Terry said and slowly brought his arms down.

Once Terry was standing beside the spanking table Master Jeff slowly slid down Terry's silk boxers to his ankles, resting his hands on the executive's flaming ass cheeks with a light pinch to induce more anticipation. Terry stepped out of his boxers and tossed them over to the chair with the rest of his discarded business attire. Terry's hard cock pointed straight out, rigid and thick veined, his plump cum filled balls hung down real low, low hangers his wife sometimes called them when she would play lick and slurp with them. Master Jeff made no mention of Terry's erection; he simply stepped behind his charge with the wooden fraternity paddle in his hand and followed Terry toward the huge dining room table of his home... As he walked wearing just his navy blue OTC socks Terry had to admit to a feeling of total and complete humiliation and degradation engulfing him. His cock strummed harder in front of him as he thought of his underlings at work and how they would feel if they saw their manager in this position. His red ass cheeks stung and he knew they would be on fire before the evening was over...

The elegant dining room was dominated by a large oak table in the dead center of the room...

Terry did not need to be told what to do as he stood at the end of the table, awaiting Master Jeff's orders... The table, where in the past numerous dinner parties had been held, had been completely cleared for the spanking occasion... Master Jeff had one time in the past allowed Terry and two of his subordinates to use his home as a meeting place, seeing as their conference room at the bank was booked for the day by other departments. The two underlings enjoyed the fact that they were able to have a meeting in a less business-oriented atmosphere, somehow they were both more productive at that particular meeting, but for Terry it held more meaning than they could ever know. Terry, seated at Master Jeff's dining room/spanking table with his two subordinates, one male and one female and knowing that this was the table where he was spanked sent a chill of elation and dread through him during that meeting...if only they knew he kept on thinking and his cock churned in his suit trousers like crazy at that meeting.

As Terry stood there naked but for his socks he thought how for all the times he was spanked in the past, whether it was his stepfather dishing it out or perhaps an active in college he was always stripped down to his socks. He was always ordered to strip to socks.

"Always spanked in my socks, ALWAYS in my damned socks..." the topnotch executive seethed inwardly as he felt Master Jeff's hands on his red butt cheeks and his mind once more wandered to the past, to that first night when he met Master Jeff at the "Wall Street Local" bar and how he had unexpectedly wound up accompanying Master Jeff home to his luxury apartment. Of all places that he would have thought he could have possibly wound up winding up in that Friday night after work, a spanking master's apartment was the last place he would have thought of…

"Welcome to my home Terrance," Master Jeff said as he guided his blindfolded and well-dressed charge into his apartment.

"Th-thank you Master Jeff Sir," Terry replied sheepishly, holding tight to his attaché case as he was led into the pleasantly scented home.

He detected a scent like lavender in the air and Terry wondered if Master Jeff enjoyed scented candles the way he and his wife did. Master Jeff let go of Terry's arm long enough to lock the door to the apartment. Terry stood docile as he waited to be led further into the place. It was when he and the man he would from then on call "Master" had stepped into the elevator that Master Jeff had said he was going to blindfold him. Terry took a deep breath as his eyes were covered with the soft white cloth and he heard Master Jeff say reassuringly, "Don't be afraid Terrance, this is all part of your training which will begin tonight."

"Y-yes Master Jeff Sir, I mean, no Master Jeff Sir, I won't be afraid," Terry replied.

As he stood there now in Master Jeff's apartment Terry realized that by allowing the man to blindfold him he had shown that he would permit him to take control of him. He had also shown Master Jeff that he trusted him implicitly…and in such a short manner of time at that. Master Jeff took Terry's attaché case from him and set it down in a corner.

"This way Terrance," Master Jeff said, clutching his charge's upper arms in his hands and guiding him into the living room.

Moments later Terry was seated in a straight backed cushioned living room chair, clad in just his blindfold, a pair of plaid silk boxer shorts and his black OTC nylon dress socks. Stripping down out of his suit while blindfolded had proved to be a tad taxing for the corporate executive, but in the end he had managed. His cock was betraying him by plumping up in his silk under shorts, plumping up, and chubbing up, what his wife called it when he became erect in his silk boxer shorts. She claimed that that was part of the reason she purchased them for him. She loved how whenever her handsome hubby wore silk boxer shorts it never failed to cause him to really become erect. She figured it was the feeling of the silk against his thin skinned huge cock that set him in motion where that was concerned. As he sat there blindfolded awaiting his master's orders Terry wiggled his toes nervously in his black dress socks.

"Would you care for a drink Terrance?" Master Jeff asked his newfound "client."

"Only if you are having one Master Jeff Sir," Terry replied.

Master Jeff pursed his lips and an expression of pride came over his face as he stepped to his full wet bar.

"You learn fast Terrance," Master Jeff exclaimed as he poured two glasses of red wine, merlot style.

He handed Terry the glass of wine and told him to sip it slowly. As the blindfolded and stripped executive sipped his wine Master Jeff sat down across from him on the couch, what would be called the "Spanking Couch" in time to come.

"Comfortable for the moment Terry?" Master Jeff asked, facing his charge, taking in the delicious sight of him there in just his underpants and socks and blindfolded.

"Y-yes Sir Master Jeff Sir, I'm comfortable for the moment," Terry replied and carefully sipped his wine.

"The way you were dressed when you came here, in your suit, your tie, your highly shined shoes, that's considered your Wall Street uniform for the day," Master Jeff said. "When you report to me for your sessions you will be clad in the uniform you wear now, just your under shorts and socks. I find that being stripped down the way you are now truly humbles a man. Is that understood so far Terrance?"

"Yes Master Jeff Sir, it's understood," Terry replied and licked his lips.

"When you report to me for your sessions you will always, ALWAYS be on time," Master Jeff went on, sounding stern then. "Any tardiness will not be accepted, nor will any excuses for tardiness be accepted. Promptness is a virtue and one that must be adhered to. Tardiness of any kind will be met with extra swats added to your punishment for that week's session."

Terry nodded and sipped his wine…

"When you arrive here for your sessions you will have time to strip down to your socks and under shorts for me," Master Jeff continued. "Until you take off your tie you are free to leave, in other words you control the situation for the moment when you first arrive here. Once you take your tie off it is a signal to me that you have relinquished control and that I am now fully in charge."

As Master Jeff spoke Terry's cock was by then fully erect in his silk boxer shorts. He could feel it dribbling pre seed and staining the front section of his boxers as he listened intently to his "Master." If Master Jeff noticed the erection that Terry was sporting he made no mention of it.

"I understand Master Jeff Sir," Terry said and sipped his wine.

It was all too much for him Terry thought in disbelief, it could not be him seated there in just his silk boxers and black dress socks, yet it was. All too much to be believed yet he would not get up to leave…not just yet anyway. Fear filled as he was he was also intrigued to the point that he was erect and throbbing in his silk boxers…

"Good, now in order for me as your behavior modification therapist and to assist you in relieving the stress and anxieties you feel I need some information from you Terrance," Master Jeff stated. "For this part of our session tonight you will remain blindfolded for a while. Any time I blindfold you it is to assist you in reflecting on something or perhaps to help you meditate to a state of mind in preparedness for your spanking that night. Do you understand?"

"Yes Master Jeff Sir, I understand totally," Terry replied and gripped one of the arms of the chair he was seated in.

"Good, now tell me, as a manager at the bank you work for how do you treat your subordinates?" Master Jeff asked. "Not how you treat them once in a while, but for the most-part, how do you treat them?"

"Well, Master Jeff Sir, I'm very stern, very uncompromising," Terry said. "But that's only because of the pressure that I'm under from my vice president and..."

"I didn't ask you about the pressure you're under Terrance," Master Jeff interjected, sounding harsh. "Answer the question and only the question..."

"Yes Sir Master Jeff Sir," Terry said sheepishly, thinking of how just recently during that past week he had reprimanded a young female subordinate for making a very small mistake and how she had cried as he reprimanded her in front of the entire office staff.

His cock churned in his silk boxers...

"Do you sometimes belittle the people that work for you Terrance?" Master Jeff asked.

"Y-yes I do Master Jeff Sir," Terry replied and wanted to say how at times it was necessary in order to get things done in a demanding atmosphere but followed orders and answered only the question he had been asked. "I admit that sometimes I treat staff like they were gofers."

Terry found that when Master Jeff asked a question it was best to simply answer the question and not try to add other embellishments to what he said in his reply.

"Do you feel that it's right that you belittle them?" Master Jeff asked.

Terry pursed his lips and grimaced a bit behind his blindfold.

"Terrance?" Master Jeff prodded him.

"I, Master Jeff Sir, I'm not sure how to properly answer that question," Terry said.

"Do you think it's right that you treat staff like gofers?" Master Jeff asked.

"Master Jeff Sir, I'm, I'm not sure how to answer that question either,' Terry responded and nervously licked his lips.

"Terrance, the fact that you belittle your staff members and the fact that you treat them like gofers shows me part of the insecurities you have," Master Jeff said. "It is also by belittling them that makes you feel a bit better about yourself, but not by much, it's that insecurity you hide that keeps you from achieving your true potential as a vice president..."

"If you say so Master Jeff Sir," Terry said.

"I say so Terrance, but here, in my private home I will assist you in overcoming those insecurities," Master Jeff said, again sounding reassuring.

"Th-thank you Master Jeff Sir," Terry said and felt tears once more that night filling his eyes, this time behind his blindfold.

Master Jeff stood up, stepped beside Terry's chair and rested a hand gently behind the back of Terry's neck.

"Take off your blindfold Terrance," Master Jeff said.

Terry reached up with one hand and pulled his blindfold off, setting it on the coffee table in front of him. On the coffee table he saw the leather paddle, the fraternity paddle, the hairbrush, the large old fashioned wooden spoon and the leather strop. With his hand trembling he raised his glass to his lips and sipped more wine.

"Those are my tools Terrance," Master Jeff stated as Terry stared straight ahead as his eyes adjusted back to the light and he took in the sight of what Master Jeff had just called his tools. "Each time you come here I will use each of those tools on you, or, to be more precise, on your ass cheeks, and at times when I feel you really need punishment I will also tan the backs of your thighs."

Terry grimaced and gulped hard, feeling like the captured super-hero in one of the comic books he used to read when he was a child. He sipped his wine and enjoyed the warm and mellow feeling it gave him as it slid over his palette down his throat.

"Tell me Terry, when you were young did your father discipline you by spanking you?" Master Jeff asked, his hand still resting gently on the back of Terry's neck.

Master Jeff stroked the executive's soft wavy salt and pepper colored hair. He loved the way it felt so silky against the back of his "bull" sized neck. It was going to be his pleasure to spank this handsome mountain sized muscular executive.

"Uh, yes Master Jeff Sir, but it was my stepfather who spanked me," Terry replied, sounding a tad miserable as he said it. "My uh, my parents divorced when I was a kid and my mom married Glen when I was a teenager."

"And it was Glen who spanked you?" Master Jeff asked.

"Yes Master Jeff Sir," Terry said. "As I mentioned earlier I was actually named for my father, his name having been Terrance that is…"

"Why did Glen spank you?" Master Jeff asked his charge, taking his hand off the back of his neck and sat back down across from him.

"To uh, keep my grades in check, to push me to be a better athlete, to pound respect into me Master Jeff Sir," Terry responded, his eyes filling with tears yet again.

"You hated your stepfather for doing that to you Terry?" Master Jeff inquired, staring intently across at the robust executive.

"I, sometimes Master Jeff Sir, but for the most-part I loved him," Terry said, his tears flowing slightly. "You see, my real dad was not a good provider Sir, whereas Glen my stepfather was. He always took good care of me and my mother. I loved him for that but I hated him for spanking me…he spanked me two times a week, sometimes three."

"How old were you when he did this?" Master Jeff went on.

"Through mostly all of my teen years Master Jeff Sir," Terry replied.

"And you never told your mother?" Master Jeff asked.

Terry nodded "no" and said, "I felt it was something that was just between us men, just as this will be here, just between you and me Master Jeff Sir."

"Terry, look at my tools lined up in front of you," Master Jeff said and Terry did as he was told. "Those are *my* tools, as I've pointed out to you. You will provide me with one more."

"I don't understand Master Jeff Sir," Terry said, but did not look up at Master Jeff as he said it; instead he kept his eyes riveted to where his master had instructed him to.

"Each person I treat with spankology provides me with at least one tool of their own that they will be spanked with," Master Jeff explained. "Usually it's a leather strap that their dad, step-dad, mom, step-mom or guardian used to use on them or perhaps a fraternity paddle that they were made to make while in college and then spanked with by their pledge master. It could also be just an instrument that they bought say in a utensils store, such as a wooden spoon. Some people have memories of childhood and will bring me a wooden paddle that used to have a rubber ball on a string attached to it. I think you get the idea Terrance…Bringing me an object that you were pummeled with in the past will show your devotion to me in what I am administering to you."

"Master Jeff Sir, I'll bring you my stepfather's belt," Terry said. "It's the one he used to use on me."

"You have this belt in your possession Terry?" Master Jeff inquired, his curiosity piqued off the Richter scale at that moment.

"Y-yes Master Jeff Sir, I have it," Terry responded. "When I moved out I took it with me. It's a reminder of what I went through at the hands of my stepfather. It was also a reminder to me that I would never allow somehow to have me that way again."

"Hmm, and here you are after all Terrance," Master Jeff said with a grin.

"Yes Master Jeff Sir, here I am after all," Terry said and gulped down the rest of his wine. "Master Jeff Sir, may I set my empty glass down on the coffee table?"

"You may Terrance," Mater Jeff replied and again felt a sense of pride in how quickly this charge was learning.

Terry placed his empty wine glass on the coffee table alongside Master Jeff's "tools."

"Terrance, before you leave here tonight I plan to spank you," Master Jeff said. "I want you to start getting used to what you will be enduring at these sessions. We will always begin with the leather paddle to redden and warm your ass."

"Yes Master Jeff Sir," Terry replied respectfully but not without a hint of fear in his tone.

"Before we get to that however I'm going to put a series of questions to you," Master Jeff went on. "You'll answer the questions quickly and honestly. Is that clear?"

"Yes Master Jeff Sir, it's clear," Terry said.

"And you do not have to say "Master Jeff Sir" when you reply to each question," Master Jeff stated. "That would take too long seeing as there are a lot of questions. Do you understand Terrance?"

"Yes Master Jeff Sir, I understand," Terry replied and Master Jeff smiled thinly.

Master Jeff's questions will be written in **bold** type and
Terry's responses will be in regular type.

Master Jeff reached under the couch he was seated on and produced a sheaf of papers that were stapled together. He began reading the questions that were listed there...

How old are you? I am in my forties.

Where were you brought up? Here in New York City.

Do you feel you are too defensive? Sometimes.

Do you feel that your life is now too stagnant? Yes, even though I am making it in the corporate world I sometimes feel that there is something more that I want.

Do you feel that you need pressure and structure in order to function to your fullest capacity? I really don't like pressure on me at all. Maybe a prod once in a while to get me moving, but no pressure. Structure, yes, I like structure. I like the expected and mostly the routine; although this experience has really thrown a monkey wrench in there I would say.

Would you consider yourself to be unreliable? No, I am very reliable... when I make a commitment I see it through to the end. Just like I'm going to see this through to the end...wherever that end is going to be that is...

Do you feel that you don't think before you act? No, I generally think first.

Do you feel that you get embarrassed much too easily? Oh yes, that is a fear.

Do you feel that you have a hidden "dark side?" Yes, there are times when I have a temper.

Would you consider yourself to be a quitter? No…I will tend to struggle through.

Do you usually look for immediate gratification? Yes, especially when I have done a good job or seen something difficult all the way through.

When you were growing up were you allowed to develop at your own pace? Yes and no. My stepfather always pushed me to succeed so there was some stress there. My mother was not as pushy, although she was always happy when I did well. She wasn't aware that it was my stepfather was literally beating successful motivation into me, via my ass cheeks.

Do you feel that athletics was "over stressed" in your upbringing? Oh yes, I was heavily involved in athletics when I was a teenager, my stepfather made sure of it and then on my own until nearly thirty. Now the only athletics I engage in is at the gym on a regular basis, if you want to call that athletics that is.

Are you seeking more stability in your life? Yes…sometimes at work I feel very unstable even though I put forth a very stable persona.

Do you feel that you need more realistic goals to follow? No, I just need to focus and pursue the ones I have.

Are you prone to mental or creative blocks where you just can't seem to function? Sometimes, although being the manager I am at the brokerage firm where I work it's hard for me to admit that.

Do you feel that you are a hotbed of tensions, fears and anxieties? No…but at the moment I think I am.

Do you become irritable or annoyed much too easily? Yes…I think it is because I have not made vice president yet at the brokerage firm.

Do you often obsess about death? No, not at all.

Does it really bother you to be alone for long periods of time? I don't like being alone but I am not sure what you mean by long periods of time. I can't say I have ever really been alone for long periods.

Do you often feel that you lack follow through? Sometimes, but not often. Hmm, maybe that's why I haven't been made a vice president yet where I work.

Would you consider yourself to be a sore loser? More of a bad loser not a sore loser…but, if I can lose in the right way it can be exciting.

Do you feel that you are too introverted? I used to be a very shy person but my stepfather managed to beat that out of me as well, again, via my ass cheeks.

Do you often fantasize about violent acts? No.

Do you often feel that you lack common sense? Not at all.

Do you feel that your curiosity often gets you into trouble? It looks like it might have tonight, seeing as I am going to be spanked on a weekly basis from now on.

Do you feel that you are too complacent and laid back? No, I am anything but.

Are you often bothered by feelings of being too self-destructive or self-abusive? Not at all.

Were you often punished for doing poorly in an athletic event (parent, coach, whomever?) I generally excelled, as I have stated already my stepfather made sure of that. When I did not do well he brought me home and as long as my mother was not there he tanned my rear end for me. Doing fairly well was not tolerated either.

Are you bothered by self-doubts almost every time you make a decision? Inwardly yes, I can say that is generally the case.

Do you often feel that you are too incompetent? Maybe just not competent enough, maybe that's another reason why I'm not a vice president yet at the brokerage firm.

Do you feel that academics or achievement was "over stressed" in your upbringing? Oh yes, just read the question about succeeding in athletic events.

Were you <u>ever</u> stalked, or did you <u>ever</u> stalk anyone? There was a girl in high school that seemed to be always after me…but nothing ever came of it. I am not that bold or stupid enough to stalk someone. If they are not interested in me…then I just let them go.

Do you like to seek attention, even if it is negative? No, not negative, although I do like attention brought to me if I have done a good job on a special project at the firm where I work.

Do you feel that self-reliance was <u>not</u> stressed enough in your upbringing? No.

Do you often feel paranoid or afraid? Not paranoid but sometimes afraid.

Does it really bother you to be kept waiting? A bit…I can be impatient. That is an area at the firm where I work where that really comes through. When I put an order to an underling I want it carried through as efficiently and as quickly as possible. If it is not I can be a bit unruly to the person who works for me.

Does it really bother you to have others look over your shoulder? Yes, now that is annoying. It makes me lose my concentration.

Do you feel that you "burn out" much too easily? No.

Would you consider yourself to be very moody, with sharp highs and lows in mood swings? No.

Were the arts or creativity stressed enough in your upbringing? No, not really. As it turns out I am a very artsy person, but because of what my stepfather forced me through in my youth I did not have much time for art. I love painting and I love paintings by the masters.

Do you now have a steady girl, lover, or wife? I have a wife. **If so, are you happy with this situation?** Yes, she is a good partner. We've been happily married through our better than twenty years together. Other than the usual arguments, stuff about finances, things where the kids are concerned and regular day to day events we're still there for each other. And we've never cheated on each other…at least I never have. I'm sure I can say the same for my wife.

What area of your life do you feel was most stifled in your upbringing? My artistic ability…it was not really stifled, more like just not fostered because I was never really able to express how much I loved art. I spent most of my time at athletics and then over my stepfather's knee.

Do you feel you often try to hide your sensitivity and emotions from others? Yes. I can be very emotional, I will admit to that here and now.

For your age, would you consider yourself to be physically immature? No.

Do you find it really hard to express your emotions? No…not really.

Did you often move while you were growing up? Not at all.

Did you _ever_ seek punishment just for the attention it would put on you? No, not on a conscious level, but it looks as if tonight that subconscious desire has been brought to the surface. I do like seeing a haughty person being punished though.

"Okay Numb nuts, assume the position," Master Jeff said, jarring Terry back to the present for the moment while reaching into his pocket at the same time and bringing out a pair of dice.

"Yes Sir Master Jeff Sir," Terry said and did as he was told.

The handsome corporate executive leaned down over the table, his chest area resting atop it as he did so. He spread his muscular legs as wide as possible and then gripped the sides of the sturdy oak table... Terry's most private crevice, what Master Jeff called to his humiliation his shit chute, his pink valley, his chocolate channel, his anal canal was now on total display along with his low hanging balls dangling between his choice looking muscular thighs. Terry's red hairy butt cheeks were pointing totally upwards and were ready for another good paddling. Chuckling meanly Master Jeff shook up the dice in his hand...

"Recite the rules where the dice are concerned my numb nut executive," Master Jeff said meanly.

"Yes Sir Master Jeff Sir," Terry said. "You will roll the dice and I will receive the amount of swats shown on the dice."

"Hmm, very good so far Terrance," Master Jeff said, sounding again as if Terry was the dumbest man in the world.

"If you should roll double digits Master Jeff Sir, I get double the amount swats shown on the dice," Terry went on. "As an example, as you always say to give Master Jeff Sir, if you roll double sixes I'll be given twenty-four swats with your paddle rather than twelve."

"Amazing, totally fucking amazing that a numb nuts like you can keep all this straight in that limited mind of yours," Master Jeff said sarcastically.

"I-I do my best Master Jeff Sir," Terry replied, sounding like a little boy trying to please his mother. "Okay, the rules Master Jeff Sir, you will roll the dice three times for three sessions, which means I will be walloped for a total of nine rounds.

"You got it Terrance," Master Jeff chuckled and bent down and gave one of Terry's socked feet a squeeze, showing him just a tad of affection.

"And like when you paddled me with the leather paddle Master Jeff Sir, if I fuck up the count we begin back at the beginning..." Terry said, completing his usual prattle where the dice were concerned.

Terry then took a deep breath as Master Jeff stepped behind him at the end of the table and took up position behind his spread legs. Terry knew that even though he was facing away from Master Jeff and would not be able to see the numbers on the dice as they were rolled he knew that Master Jeff would be honest. It was the sure thing the two men knew they both shared, their honesty. They knew from the start of all this that they could trust each other implicitly where certain things within their sessions were concerned, the number on the dice being one of those things. Master Jeff reveled in the mortifying sight of Terry Dean Bradshaw's luscious looking ass and his hole as it stared up at him it seemed, totally on display on his table. The way Terry's muscular legs shimmied down to his sexy huge sized feet, the way his socked toes curled back in anticipation of the upcoming swats, the way the executive's gaping rosebud of an asshole flicked at Master Jeff, the way his sweaty and juicy low hanging balls dangled like Christmas tree balls hung too closely together, all of it spurred the man on the more where spanking his handsome subject was concerned. Terry then heard the sound of the dice being shaken up in Master Jeff's hand. The corporate executive took a deep breath and clenched his teeth as he heard the dice hit the table between his spread legs…

"A five and a one numb nuts," Master Jeff said and aimed his fraternity paddle true against Terry's target of an upturned ass.

WHAPP WHAPPP

"UHHH, one and two Master Jeff Sir," Terry seethed through his clenched teeth.

"Aren't you lucky at the outset of this end of your session?" Master Jeff asked.

WHAPPP WHAPPP

"Yes, yes Master Jeff Sir, very lucky indeed I am," Terry called out. "Three, four…"

WHAP WHAPPP

"And five and six Master Jeff Sir," Terry said, his voice belying the fact that he was already feeling the sting back there."

He heard Master Jeff shaking up the dice for the second set of the first three rounds…

"A five and two numb nuts, seven lucky hard swats coming up for you…" Master Jeff said.

"Y-yes Sir Master Jeff Sir," Terry said loudly and kept his teeth clenched.

WHAPPP WHAPPP WHAPPP

The sound and feeling of the fraternity paddle as it sailed through the air and then connected meanly with Terry's upturned ass was maddening to the first-rate executive.

"One, two, three," Master Jeff Sir," Terry cried out, starting to sweat at this point.

WHAPP WHAPPP WHAPPP WHAPPP

"F-four, five, six and seven…" Terry said glad that the second set of round one was over.

He silently prayed not to have double digits of any kind rolled (or maybe not…) He cringed as he heard the dice being rolled and then they hit the table again…

"Damn, a four and a one you numb nuts," Master Jeff said, rubbing the wooden fraternity paddle over Terry's ass cheeks as he spoke to him, taunting him. "It looks like the dice really love you tonight eh?"

"I-I think it's just dumb luck on my part Master Jeff Sir," Terry replied, his eyes filling with tears of awe as he called out the master's name.

WHAPPP WHAPPP

"One, two, Master Jeff Sir," Terry said.

WHAPP WHAPPP WHAPP

"Th-three, four, and five…" Terry called out triumphantly…

"Good boy so far numb nuts," Master Jeff said meanly and again squeezed one of Terry's socked feet.

Terry knew from past lessons and sessions that the squeezing of his foot meant that he was doing well so far…

"Let's switch to the wooden hairbrush for the next round of dice throwing," Master Jeff said stepping over to the coffee table and putting down the fraternity paddle and picking up the round wooden backed hairbrush. "How do you feel about that numb nuts?"

"Like earlier Master Jeff Sir, what I want or feel is not what matters here, it's all what you want Sir, Master Jeff Sir, and how you see fit to train and discipline me," Terry responded and Master Jeff chuckled, sounding totally sadistic.

"Coming up, round two of dice throwing and spanking," Master Jeff said and shook up the dice, throwing them on the table. "YES, HA!! A six and five numb nuts! Now we're getting to some good numbers huh?"

"Y-yes Master Jeff Sir, good numbers Sir," Terry said despondently at the thought of eleven more swats on his already reddened ass cheeks.

"Good for me but not for you, numb nuts," Master Jeff laughed.

This time he hooked an arm around Terry's mid section and faced away from him, the handsome executive's ass cheeks right in his line of fire.

"And away we go…" Master Jeff laughed and raised his hairbrush, wooden side aimed at Terry's ass.

WHAPPP WHAPPP WHAPPP

"UHHHHH!!! One, two and three, Master Jeff Sir," Terry said and reveled in the feeling as Master Jeff held him tight.

"Sing out you numb nuts executive," Master Jeff chided his charge.

WHAPPP WHAPPP WHAPPP was the awful sound as Master Jeff used the wooden hairbrush to thrash Terry's ass cheeks dead center…right over his gaping and sexy crack…

"Th-three, f-four, five, six…" Terry called out louder but too late realized his fatal error.

"Ah, ah, ah, Terrance, you bad, bad boy," Master Jeff laughed and tightened his grip on Terry's mid-section. "You repeated the number three you stupid numb nuts…"

"Oh God Master Jeff Sir," Terry reeled, his head hanging down as he spoke.

"What happens now you bad boy? Tell Master Jeff what happens now…" Master Jeff said, sounding totally fiendish.

"Please Master Jeff Sir, can't I have a break this one time?" the high socked executive pleaded miserably. "I've been so good so far tonight and…"

To cut off Terry's irritating tirade Master Jeff swiped his red ass with the bristles end of the hairbrush.

"AAAYYYYY!!!" Terry screamed. "OH, okay Sir, being that I fucked up the count we will begin this round back at the beginning…Master Jeff Sir…"

"Good boy," Master Jeff said and raised the hairbrush.

WHAPPP WHAPPP WHAPPP

"One, two, three, Master Jeff Sir," Terry counted well and true.

"Good boy let's hear it again," Master Jeff teased his charge.

WHAPPP WHAPPP WHAPPP

"F-four, five and six…" Terry seethed, feeling that each blow was harder than the one before it, causing his stinging ass cheeks to tingle.

WHAPPP WHAPPP WHAPPP WHAPPP WHAPPP

"S-seven, eight, nine, ten and eleven Master Jeff Sir, eleven Sir!!" Terry called out happily.

"Amazing the things that will make a numb nut executive like you happy Terrance," Master Jeff laughed and picked up the dice, giving Terry's low hanging balls a sniff as he reached for the dice.

Terry secretly grinned, despite the pain he was in, as the man he called Master Jeff sniffed his nuts, it showed him that the man really did care for him and all his insults and mean gibberish was all part of the game. But Terry didn't have long to think about all that as he heard the dice shaken up yet again for the second set in the second round… The dice hit the table and Master Jeff announced…"A five and a three you numb nut exec."

"Eight…" Terry said miserably.

"Eight is right," Master Jeff said and again gripped Terry around the mid-section with his arm held him close and raised his hairbrush, wooden side up. "No wonder you're hoping to be up for that promotion where you work…you really can count…"

WHAPPP WHAPPP WHAPPP WHAPPP WHAPPP

"RRRRHHHHHHHH!!!" Terry wailed as Master Jeff swung harder and harder it seemed with this round of swats to his poor ass cheeks. "ONE, two, three, four, five, Master Jeff Sir…"

"And three more to go," Master Jeff said, his own cock beginning at that point to grow stuff as Terry's delectable looking ass became more and more reddened.

To Master Jeff's eyes Terry's hairy ass was starting to look like an over-sized bowl of red cheery Jell-O.

WHAPPP WHAPPP WHAPPP

"Six, seven and eight Master Jeff Sir," Terry called out through clenched teeth. "OHHHHRRRR my poor ass…"

Master Jeff chuckled, gave Terry an extra swat with his hairbrush for good luck and laughed meanly before saying, "One more set for this round and then we move on to round three where your poor ass, as you so aptly called it, will get a break…"

"OH MY GAWD, no," Terry sniveled, droplets of moisture forming at the end of his nose as he managed to keep himself balanced on all fours up on the table.

By now the rigidly topnotch and no funny business executive was looking like anything but that…

"You know what I just said means eh Terrance?" Master Jeff asked as he shook the dice in his hands.

"I sure do Master Jeff Sir, I sure as all hell do," Terry said, nearly crying now. "When you say you're going to give my poor ass a break it means that you're going to lash and fire up the backs of my thighs…OOOOOHHHHH GAWD MASTER JEFF SIR!!!"

Master Jeff snickered meanly; Terry would get no compassion at that moment…

It wasn't at every spanking session that Master Jeff would lash and barbecue the backs of Terry's thighs, but when he did it was because Terry was overdue for some deeply needed discipline. Master Jeff also said that it was a good way to once in a while remind Terry Dean Bradshaw, powerful corporate executive just who the hell was in charge where this scene was concerned. In the corporate arena Terry was a man in charge, in the spanking arena Terry was not in charge at all. So while his poor reddened ass was getting a break from being spanked, it really was another torture that the stalwart executive would be enduring. What a double edged sword that was Terry Dean Bradshaw thought miserably.

"Let's get it done Numb nuts," Master Jeff said and threw the dice down on the table between Terry's spread legs and under his very red, cherry Jell-O like ass cheeks. "A six and a two…"

"Another eight Master Jeff Sir," Terry said despondently and Master Jeff raised his wooden hairbrush.

After Master Jeff had administered the last eight swats to Terry's now very red ass cheeks with the back of the hairbrush he ordered his charge down off the table and into a new position for the last three sets for round three of the dice deciding number of swats that Terry would receive. With his hands crossed behind his head and his mammoth sized erection saluting Master Jeff, Terry Dean Bradshaw awaited his instructions. If he could just rub his wounded ass cheeks it would mean so much to him he thought…but that was not to be, as Master Jeff wanted him to really feel the burn as it penetrated the skin of his luscious ass globes. It was what Terry needed to help him achieve in his life where he had under-achieved.

The instructions that Terry received were what he had dreaded hearing since coming to Master Jeff's home that night for his spanking and discipline session, Master Jeff was going to tie him, and to make the matter all the worse he was going to tie him to the "Block." With his hands still crossed behind his head, with his huge erection still swinging in front of him like a flagpole, Terry, naked except for his navy blue OTC socks followed Master Jeff most humbly to the sound-proof room. It was the room where the man that Terry called "Master Jeff" kept the "Block." Terry was literally shaking in his socks as he padded behind the man he had totally submitted to for these sessions. Terry's red ass cheeks stung more and more with each passing second, proof that Master Jeff knew just how to administer spankings…

In his hand Master Jeff carried a long leather strop, the next piece of his equipment that would be Terry's instrument of torture. The backs of the executive's thighs stung just thinking about what he was in for now… As they entered the room Terry gulped hard and took in the sight of the "Block" and in what seemed like no time Master Jeff had secured him to it, in one of the most humiliating positions that a man could be secured to a device of this sort…

"Okay Terrance, we'll continue with the dice for the thigh stropping as well," Master Jeff said to his charge.

"Y-yes Master Jeff Sir," Terry said miserably as Master Jeff dashed out of the room to retrieve the set of thrash-deciding dice.

As Terry squirmed sexily and miserably on the "Block" his mind once more wandered to the past, to the night when he and Master Jeff had first met. As he thought of that night his hard cock twitched under him and his cum filled balls churned. He recalled how Master Jeff had made him sit facing him, clad in nothing more than his underpants and black dress socks as he rattled off the questions to him. Terry felt as if he were in a situation between being interrogated and being interviewed somehow. Also, it amazed the superlative executive how at this moment in time, strapped down to the "Block" how he remembered so many of those mind-searching questions...

Do you feel you could use better stress control? Yes. This has been an issue for some time now I would have to say.

For your age would you consider yourself to be sexually inexperienced? No Sir. And I have to say that being spanked will somehow expand my horizons. I just get that feeling.

Do you feel that you are physically weaker than most other males your age? Definitely not Master Jeff Sir, the way I work out keeps me fit and strong.

Were you taught to do what you were told to do without questioning? Yes, but mostly from true authority...not just some asshole that walks up.

Were you taught, or did you experience that a male should not show his feelings, his sensitivity, or his creativeness? Well, not really. That was more of a societal thing that we guys picked up from our peers.

Are you too easily talked into things others want you to do? Yes...I sometimes find that I am rather submissive in that way. It boggles my mind, seeing as I am a strict and very demanding corporate executive...yet there's that submissive side to me as well.

Do you feel that you are compulsively neat and clean? Most times, yes.

What is one of your biggest complaints or gripes about anything? That I have not yet made vice president yet where I work and I work harder than most of the guys there.

Complete this: My life at present is: not what it should be. I have not achieved what I had pictured for myself to be financially successful. I still struggle financially at times.

Are most of your close friends male or female or about equal? Interestingly, I seem to get on with females better. But my friends are mostly male.

Does that make you think you might do better with a female disciplinarian? Not at all, I think the male bonding thing that will happen between you and I will work for both of our benefits.

Do you feel that you are too easily distracted? Yes.

Do you feel that your life is now too dull or routine? A bit. But after tonight and going forward I doubt that will be the case.

Do you feel you are not as responsible or as mature as most others your age? No.

Were you often complimented while you were growing up? Yes. Not to sound too vain but I was big, very handsome, fairly smart, artistic and as I have pointed out, athletic.

Complete this: I enjoy: I enjoy being with my family.

Complete this: I get nervous when: I get nervous when I have been put on the spot or find myself in a new situation. I also get nervous being made to sit wearing just my underpants and socks.

At that reply Master Jeff chuckled and ordered Terry to stand up and take off his plaid boxer shorts, adding that he had permission to keep his black OTC dress socks on. As Terry stood to do his new master's bidding he blushed sheepishly as his erect cock popped up in front of him, long, thick, beefy and throbbing as his two succulent hairy balls hung down low in his sweaty looking sac. Terry placed his underpants under his chair and sat back down, his legs slightly parted, his balls resting on the chair, his cock standing straight up, oozing pre seed and staring at the ceiling. Master Jeff had all to do to keep his gaze off his charge's most impressive manhood.

Do you feel you could use more discipline and control? If it's dished out by the right person, yes.

Were you ever in therapy? No.

Do you feel that you are under a lot of stress lately? Most definitely.

Would you consider yourself to be the "life of the party"? No, but I am a true participant.

Do you feel that too much was expected of you while you were a teenager? Yes. My stepfather's approach was too hard for someone my age.

Were you considered to be hyperactive while you were growing up?
No.

Do you feel that you could benefit from strong behavior modification?
Probably from some behavior modification. We will see how the next few
weeks go and how I do.

Is it very hard for you to really enjoy life? No.

**If you could do or change anything that has ever happened to you in
the past, or has ever affected you, what would you do or change?** I
would have been more truthful about my love of the arts. Instead I put up
with being spanked and forced to do things that I really did not want to.

Do you expect too much from others? Yes, I think I do at that.

Would you consider yourself to be a boat rocker? Sometimes.

Do you feel your life is in a constant struggle mode? Yes, more-so now
than ever before with the demands of job and family. But please don't get
me wrong, I love my family dearly.

Do you usually feel uncomfortable with the opposite sex? No.

Do you feel you are more conservative than most men your age? No, I
tend to be libertarian. I would be viewed by most as conservative but I do
tend to sometimes have some very different views.

Do you often feel that you are too excessive? Yes, sometimes.

Do you feel that you might be a dysfunctional person? No…not really.

Do you want to be less shy and more outgoing than you are now? Yes.

**Do you feel that you have to, or just want to test your pain, endurance
or embarrassment levels, even if it means crying or losing face?** Until
tonight I didn't think so, but now, sitting here in just my socks and ready
to be spanked I would have to say yes to that question.

**Do you feel that it is important to be accepted or to fit in, even if it
means going against your own values?** No.

Do you feel that you are prone to unfulfilling relationships? No.

Do you feel that you get upset too easily when things go wrong? Yes.

Who was stricter with you, your mother or father? As I told you, my stepfather.

Do you feel that you have trouble dealing with rage? Yes, sometimes.

Are you often afraid to show affection? No.

Do you feel that you procrastinate too much? No.

Do you often feel that you are too intense? Yes. As I've stated I can be very intense at my place of work.

Do you usually make the first move in establishing personal contacts? Yes, like tonight when I sat down next to you at the bar.

Do you feel you should be more adventurous? I'm about to be.

Is it overly hard for you to keep friends? I don't usually lose friends. The situations change and the relationships seem to become history.

Do you often feel so depressed that it is hard for you to function? No.

No…No…No…that was the word that was racing through Terry Dean Bradshaw's mind now as Master Jeff sauntered back into the soundproof room. In one hand the man that Terry had come to call "Master" held a pair of dice. In the other hand he held the long leather strop that for three rounds would redden the backs of the executive's muscular thighs. Terry squirmed miserably on the "Block" and held his tears in check…for the moment.

"How are you feeling there my numb nuts executive?" Master Jeff asked his charge, the look in his eyes one of absolute fiendishness.

"Apprehensive Master Jeff Sir, I'm feeling very apprehensive," Terry replied and squirmed on the block, his already reddened ass making a pretty picture in his master's eyes.

"Looks to me like this has been a very productive session so far," Master Jeff said and ran the palm of a hand over Terry's red ass cheeks.

Terry flinched a bit at Master Jeff's touch…

"Now, let's get the backs of those thighs reddened shall we?" Master Jeff asked and held up the dice.

"It, it's not for me to say Master Jeff Sir," Terry said, sounding miserable now as he recited his mantra.

Master Jeff chuckled and shook up the dice in his hand. Terry watched from his strapped down vantage point as Master Jeff dropped the shaken dice to the floor…

Terry's eyes nearly popped out of his head when he saw the double sixes staring up at him mockingly while staring up at Master Jeff triumphantly.

"Oh Good Lord," Terry whimpered, sounding totally fearful now.

"Double sixes my executive," Master Jeff said, taking up position beside the terrified Terry. "And you know that when double digits are rolled…"

Master Jeff paused in mid-sentence and pointed at his charge…

"When double digits are rolled I receive double the amount of swats shown on the dice, Master Jeff Sir," Terry recited, finishing Master Jeff's litany for him.

"Very good Terrance," Master Jeff chuckled. "And I'm sure that a first-rate executive such as yourself knows that twelve doubled is…"

Once more Master Jeff pointed at Terry…

"…t-twenty-four Master Jeff Sir…" Terry said shakily. "Tw-twelve doubled is twenty-four!"

"Very good Terrance," Master Jeff said. "Now start counting…"

That said Master Jeff swung his arm back and brought the leather strop crashing down on the backs of Terry's thighs.

"AAAYYRRRRR!!! One, Master Jeff Sir!" Terry cried out, sounding almost pitiful.

SWATTT SWATTT SWATTT SWATTT SWATTT SWATTT was the sound as the leather strop landed over and over across the backs of Terry's trapped thighs…

"T-two, three, four, five, six…S-SEVEN!!!" Terry screamed in a high-pitched tone of voice. "Oh God Master Jeff Sir. "Is this really necessary tonight???"

SWATTTT SWATTTT SWATTT SWATTT SWATTT SWATTT

"Eight, nine, ten, eleven, RRRRRRRRRR!!!" Terry cried, literally. "…twelve Master Jeff Sir…thirteen…"

As Terry lay there crying his thighs reddened with each forceful swipe of Master Jeff's strop. The ruggedly handsome executive clenched his bound hands into fists as he felt swat after swat against his thighs, screaming out the numbers now as they landed.

"AARRRRRHHHH, f-fourteen Master Jeff Sir," Terry screamed out, thinking how there were only ten more swats to endure for this round.

When Master Jeff reached the twenty-fourth swat Terry's face was drenched with tears and his lips were quivering as he called out the number twenty-four, followed by a litany of repeated "Oh God's" over and over.

"Easy my executive, easy does it," Master Jeff said soothingly, stepping behind Terry and running an open hand over the handsome exec's reddened thighs.

Terry blubbered and sobbed under the straps, his entire muscular body quaking. But Master Jeff knew that to stop now would be worse for the spanked guy. Instead, as Terry shook in fear in his bonded position the man he called "Master" shook up the dice. Terry's chin dropped and a look of disbelief filled his handsome face as he saw the second set of double sixes…

"Oh fuck me, oh poor me tonight," Terry whispered as his tears flowed.

"Hmm, seems to me that as tonight is wearing on the fates are turning against you and more in my favor yes Terrance?" Master Jeff asked his charge.

"It, it certainly would seem that way Master Jeff Sir," Terry replied through clenched teeth.

Master Jeff stepped beside Terry, raised the strop and brought it singing and screaming through the air till it connected hard with the backs of Terry's thighs…

"AYYYRRRRR!!!" One…Master Jeff Sir!" Terry squawked and cried.

The executive cried and sobbed but managed to keep the count true. He knew in his heart that if he screwed up the count during this intense part of his training tonight that Master Jeff would not make him start back at the beginning. In some ways the man he called Master was very considerate with him…

As Terry counted and cried his thighs turned redder and redder…his mind wandered back to the first night of his meeting with Master Jeff and the questions that were put to him while he sat wearing just his socks and sipped merlot…

Was it hard for you to cope with your punishments? Yes, sometimes my stepfather could be kind of cruel when thrashing my ass cheeks. There were times I found it difficult to sit down for the next day or so.

Do you often feel helpless or unsure of yourself? Sometimes.

Do you feel that you panic too easily? No, but I sure did almost panic when you showed me your business card Master Jeff Sir.

Is it overly hard for you to make long term commitments? Not so far.

Do you feel that you are too much of an "over achiever?" Not enough of an over-achiever actually Sir.

Is it hard for you to find solutions too many of your problems? Sometimes, but it sure looks like I might have found a solution to some of my problems tonight.

Do you feel there is now a lack of excitement in your life? Yes, but not anymore, not after meeting you tonight Sir.

Did you have many tantrums while you were growing up? No… because if I did my stepfather took his paddle to me.

Do you usually push yourself beyond your endurance, or until you drop or just can't go any further? No, I seem to know my limits.

Did your parents often help you with your homework? Sometimes.

Is it overly hard for you to start new things, even things you really want to do? Yes, I would have to say that it is indeed getting harder.

Does it bother you to be seen in the nude, even by another male? It's a little unnerving.

Were you considered to be cold or unfriendly, only because you were afraid to open up and express your feelings? No.

What is one of your best assets? On the whole I'm friendly and get along with most everyone.

Do you feel that most of your problems are self-induced? I think all my problems are self-induced.

Do you often feel that you make a fool out of yourself? No.

When others are getting "rattled" or upset do you remain fairly composed? No, I am just as upset and rattled as they are.

Do you feel that you have a very high tolerance for pain or endurance? Actually, I think I have an above average tolerance for pain but I am a bit impatient.

Do you like taking part in weird or strange things? I think I am right now doing that.

Do you often get headaches? No.

Do you feel that religion was "over-stressed" in your upbringing? No.

Do you feel that you are now a very religious or spiritual person? Yes, I am at times now.

Were you considered to be a trouble maker in high school or junior high? No, I knew what my step dad would do to me if I were.

Were you often embarrassed or afraid to bring your friends to your house? No.

Do you do many things that you regret doing later? Not really.

Is it often very hard for you to bounce out of depression? No.

Do you find it extremely hard to find solutions to many of your problems? No.

Do you often feel that you are too impulsive? No.

Do you often feel confused or uncomfortable about your sexuality or masculine/feminine persona? Not really. I would like to be more sexual…

I'm pretty much heterosexual in my personal life…but have become very stimulated by homosexual activity…mostly dealing with non-consensual stuff like tonight, as I am about to be disciplined and spanked, loss of control. There's a bonding between two men that I can fully understand.

Are your feelings too easily hurt? Yes.

Do you often feel disoriented? Sometimes.

Do you often feel confused or bewildered? No.

Do you often feel that you are too shallow? No.

Were you taught <u>not</u> to trust others? No.

Do you feel that most people don't really listen to you? Yes.

Do you feel there are no real challenges in your life? No, every day at the brokerage firm I work for is a real challenge.

Were your parents divorced or separated while you were growing up? As I mentioned they were.

Do you feel that you are too introspective? Yes.

Do you feel that whenever you did your best or tried your hardest, your parents would raise their standards and expect more? Yes, mostly my stepfather.

Did your parents believe in "tough love?" My stepfather did.

Do you often feel that you are too opinionated? No.

Do you feel that sibling rivalry was "over-stressed" in your upbringing? No.

Do you like to take chances, even with the odds against you? I think I did that tonight Master Jeff Sir, seeing as you have me sitting here in just my socks.

Do you feel that you are an overly rebellious person? No.

Do you often feel that you are too obsessive? I might be, at times that is.

Is it really hard for you to feel comfortable with your relationships? No.

Do you feel there is now too much pressure on you to perform or to do well? Most definitely, but that pressure is coming directly from me to me.

Do you feel that money or status was "over stressed" in your upbringing? No.

Do you feel that you project a poor image to others on first impression? No.

Do you feel that you need a sharper mind? Yes.

Do you feel that you are often too insensitive to other people's feelings? Sometimes, but mostly at work.

Is it overly hard for you to cope with new situations? No. But this new situation here and now might prove to be a tad hard, we shall see Sir.

Do you feel you should have been punished more while you were growing up? Well, I would have to say yes, seeing as I'm here now and about to be punished. Even though my stepfather dished it out, it seems a part of me was looking for more somehow.

Do you often find yourself in "compromising situations?" Not really.

Do you often wish that you were more spontaneous? A little.

What is one of your worst faults? I demand too much of my underlings at work.

Do you feel that you are too susceptible to peer pressure? A bit.

Were you often punished when you made mistakes or did poorly at something? Yes, mostly by my step dad.

Do you feel that most people don't take you seriously enough? Yes.

Yes, yes, yes, was the word that Terry was now saying over and over as Master Jeff undid the straps holding him to the "Block" in the soundproofed room. The stropping of the backs of his thighs was over, thankfully and the ruggedly handsome executive's mind was jarred back to the present yet again. Terry had counted well and true and once more proven to his disciplinarian that he could endure a horrific thigh thrashing. It wasn't at every discipline session that Master Jeff walloped the backs of Terry's thighs but the executive figured he needed the dose of harshness this time out. Yes, he was saying to the man he called "Master" in reply to Master Jeff asking him if he was glad that the present discipline session was done.

"Thank you Master Jeff Sir, thank you," Terry panted as Master Jeff rubbed a large ice cube over Terry's reddened ass cheeks and his now crimson thighs.

"Tell me why I'm coating your ass cheeks and thighs with ice my numb nuts executive," Master Jeff ordered.

Still sniveling Terry recited yet another mantra that had been taught to him by the man who had become to known to him as his "Master."

"Ice Master Jeff Sir, ice helps to heighten the skins awareness of sensations," Terry said, his fingers clenched into fists as his hands dangled free in front of the "Block" he was still splayed on. "It also acts as a pain reliever in the anti-inflammatory sense. It's soothing after the initial rubbing of the hot flesh."

"Very good Terrance," Master Jeff responded and rubbed another ice cube liberally over his charge's ass cheeks and down his thighs, after having deposited what was left of the first ice cube into Terry's hole, getting a real loud sounding yelp from the executive.

"Once you've rubbed ice on the parts of me that you've spanked and paddled already Master Jeff Sir my skin there will be even more sensitive and the pain of the next ass thrashing, if you decide to administer one to me will be more intense," Terry went on and before he could continue Master Jeff stepped in front of him, grabbed a handful of his wavy salt and pepper colored hair and yanked his head upwards.

As the two men looked into each other's eyes Master Jeff said, "Oh you know I plan to administer another ass burning thrashing to those cheeks of yours Terrance."

"Y-yes Master Jeff Sir," Terry whimpered, sopped in sweat at that point.

Master Jeff let go of Terry's hair. Terry hung his head back down and his master resumed rubbing his red flesh with the ice cube.

"Continue telling me the benefits of rubbing ice on your heated skin Terrance," Master Jeff said commandingly.

"Well, once iced a bit there will be less bruising the next time you spank me Master Jeff Sir," Terry said as he lay on the "Block." "Of course an alcohol rub can do the trick at times as well, but because you know that I have to go home to my wife and family I can't risk any telltale scents lingering on my person…and I appreciate your consideration in that area Master Jeff Sir."

Smiling broadly Master Jeff gave one of Terry's reddened ass cheeks a gentle squeeze…

"And lastly Master Jeff Sir, we cannot go on with uninterrupted discipline without a break, a break for both of us," Terry finished. "A break so you can get your second spanking wind and a break for me to revel in and enjoy the stinging pain of what you have put me through thus far…the pain I have endured so far tonight reminds me of my shortcomings of the last two weeks…"

"Very good Terrance, very good indeed…" Master Jeff said and like he did with the first ice cube he inserted the second one into Terry's asshole as well.

Master Jeff nearly laughed out loud at the way his charge's hole seemed to suck in and gulp down what was left of the cube... Terry yelped as his hole slurped up the ice cube and a chill coursed through him...

"Now, before we get to the wooden spoon part of tonight's session perhaps you'd like some cold water to drink," Master Jeff said a few moments later as he helped Terry off the "Block."

"Yes Master Jeff Sir, that sounds wonderful," the sweat sopped high sock wearing executive replied as Master Jeff walked him out of the soundproof room, holding his charge lovingly by the upper arm.

Terry was made to sit on a not so comfortable un-cushioned wooden chair as he sipped down a cool tall glass of water. Being that the chair had no cushion insured that the paddled executive would really feel the sting in his hindquarters as he sat there. Ice had been rubbed on his red and tender sections but when he sat the feeling was less than soothing, as Terry's strict disciplinarian said it should be. Master Jeff reveled in the sight of the well-toned muscular executive as he sat there naked but for his navy blue OTC dress socks, sipping his water and crying. Master Jeff knew at this point in the session that Terry was crying in a mixture of joy at what he had been able to endure thus far and fear at what was coming next as he looked at the wooden spoon on his master's coffee table. As Terry sipped the refreshingly cool water he slowly stopped sweating and his mind wandered once more to the night when he and Master Jeff had first met. Questions, so many questions the man who insisted on being addressed as "Master Jeff" was putting to him it seemed. Master Jeff claimed that these questions and the answers that Terry supplied to them would give him the information he really needed where the executives truest ineptitudes lied. Terry felt more like he was being intensely interrogated...

Do you feel that it is very important to have others look up to you? Yes, definitely, in what I do for a living I need to have leadership qualities.

Did you often "date" or just go out in high school or college? Yes, but I wish I had played the field more.

Do you often find yourself in "out of control" situations? No.

Is it hard for you to control your temper? Sometimes.

Was it hard for you to "break out of your shell" socially? No, I was nudged in the right places.

What is one of the best things that has ever happened to you or what were you most proud of taking part in? Well, I was most proud of getting the promotion where I work to being the manager that I now am and before that I was most proud of having finally moved out of my parent's home. At that time I felt as if I had escaped my stepfather's firm hand. But now it looks like I've traded his firm hand for another...in a way... I'm also most proud of the day I married my wife and of course on the days my children were born.

Do you feel that you are an overly self-conscious person? Yes.

If so, what are you most self-conscious about? Knowledge of a subject... and sometimes I have trouble remembering names.

Do you feel that you led too much of a sheltered life? No.

Do you get frustrated or uptight much too easily? Sometimes.

Do you often feel that you have no real outlets for your angers? No.

Complete this: I want to be more focused with: my artsy side of my personality.

Are most of your friends: A) Older than you? B) Younger than you? C) About the same age? About the same age.

Do you often find yourself getting drunk or high more often than you are really comfortable with? A little more now it seems...I go to "The Wall Street Local" a little more often than I used to.

Do you want to be more self-sufficient or independent? Yes.

What do you usually daydream or fantasize about? Being a vice president, being a great artist and sex.

What are you most sensitive about? What I don't know.

Did you ever run away from home? No, but I did think about it a few times while over my stepfather's knee.

Is it overly hard for you to control your spending? No.

Do you feel that you are too serious or too mature for your age? No.

Did your parents often fight or argue? Well, when my mother was still married to my father they argued a lot. But after she divorced him and married my stepfather they rarely argued or fought.

Do you often feel that others are staring at you? No.

Do you want to have a higher tolerance for pain or endurance than you do now? I think I already have a high tolerance for pain and endurance, being what I was put through by my step dad, but yes, I would like to have an even higher tolerance for it, physically and mentally I would say. (As

Terry answered that question he knew in his heart of hearts and at that moment that meeting Master Jeff had been a blessing that night.)

Is it hard for you to assert yourself or speak your mind in tight situations? Sometimes, yes.

Do you usually try not to let others know what you are really thinking? Yes.

Do you feel that you are too much of a showoff or that you brag too much? No.

Is it overly hard for you to really break loose and have a good time? No.

Do you feel that you are too sickly or prone to illness? No.

Is it overly hard for you to feel excited or enthused about things? I do tend to hold in my enthusiasm.

Would you consider yourself to be a "workaholic?" Sometimes, yes I am.

Do you usually "choke" or do very poorly under pressure or stress? No, quite the reverse, because of what my stepfather put me through I think I do better under pressure and stress.

Do you feel that you are too easily offended? Yes.

When you were younger did you have many practical jokes played on you? No.

Complete this: The image I project of myself is: a successful businessman, more so than I really am or more so than I really feel I am.

Do you often feel that you lack tenacity? No.

Do you feel that you are a very competitive person…perhaps too much so? Maybe not competitive enough.

Do you feel that you can be too self-absorbed? No.

Were you taught to keep problems to yourself? No.

Do you feel that you are often too cynical? Sometimes I find that I can be, yes.

Do you feel inwardly that you are less masculine than most other males? Not really.

Do you get angry at yourself too much for things beyond your control? Yes.

Do you feel that you could use more peace of mind? Yes, I think my mind could definitely use more peace.

Do you feel that you don't think before you act? No.

Does it really bother you to be interrupted? A bit.

Would you consider yourself to be very unstable? No.

Do you often feel that you are too docile? Yes, sometimes, like tonight. Although I think tonight my being docile is going to work out in my favor.

Does it really bother you to be careless or to make foolish errors or mistakes in front of others unintentionally? Yes.

Do you often do things without thinking about the consequences until it is too late? No.

Do you often feel that you have many self-destructive tendencies? No.

Do you often "over" analyze yourself or your actions? No.

Do you feel that you are not living up to your potential? Yes.

Do you often feel tired or run down with low energy levels? Sometimes.

Do you feel that you are an overly nervous, tense, jumpy or high strung person? No.

Do you feel that you are too sexually compulsive? No.

Do you now have a roommate or an apartment mate? Yes.

If so, are you happy with this arrangement? Yes.

Does confrontation generally scare you? No.

Do you feel that you are too much of a loner or anti-social? No.

Name one or two problems that you feel you need to be corrected or addressed, <u>but</u> are having trouble dealing with. My procrastination in trying for that VP job at the firm where I work.

Do you want to be more coordinated? Yes.

Are you often bothered by recurring dreams? No.

Do you feel that you are not really prepared to be on your own? No.

Do you like to play practical jokes on people? A bit.

Do you feel that you have done many spiteful things in the past? No.

At what age(s) did you get into the most trouble? Seventeen. When I was seventeen was when my stepfather seemed to thrash me the most with his leather belt.

Were you often afraid to express yourself at home? My true feelings, yes.

Do you feel that punishment and discipline was "over-stressed" in your upbringing? Well yes, the way my stepfather doled it out was sometimes over the top I would say.

Do you <u>ever</u> remember getting spanked, strapped or paddled or beaten (by anyone)? Yes.

Do you feel you were too old the last time you were physically punished? Yes.

How old were you? I was in my teen years and my step dad still thrashed me a few times a week.

Did you often feel you were abused while you were growing up? Sometimes. But in his heart of hearts I really think that my stepfather thought he was doing the right thing by me.

Is it overly hard for you to admit to your mistakes? No.

Do you often wallow in self-pity or self-hate? No.

Do you feel that you are an overly cautious person? No.

Are you often bothered by a fear of "losing face" or prestige in front of others? Yes.

Did you get into many fights when you were younger? No.

Did you often get into trouble for things you <u>didn't</u> do? No.

Do you feel it is a weakness to <u>show</u> that things are really bothering you? Yes.

Do you suffer from unexplained anxiety attacks? No.

Do you feel that you are too much of an under achiever? Yes, as I have mentioned I feel that I should be a vice president at this point where I work.

Do you feel that you might have an addictive personality? A little.

Are you now or were you ever in a 12 step program? No.

Do you want to be more refined than you are now? No.

Are you bothered by a lack of accomplishment? Yes.

Do you feel your life is going in the direction you planned? Only my married life, my professional life is not.

Were you considered to be weird or strange in high school or junior high? No.

Did you have many nightmares or bad dreams while you were a teenager? Amazingly, no. You would think the way my step dad doled out the punishments that I would have had bad dreams and nightmares, but I never did.

Do you feel your life is now at a turning point? In a way, as of tonight, yes.

What was one of the hardest things you have ever done, or one of your biggest challenges? Well, as of this moment I think just being here and what I'm going to endure will be pretty challenging. As for in the past I would say speaking at a high school rally when I was seventeen years old. I hadn't really wanted to speak at the rally and when I told my stepfather as much he treated me to a really intense ass thrashing. He said it was for my own good and to motivate me for the speech "I WOULD" be making.

Do you feel you need a better sense of values? No.

Are you overly concerned about your appearance? No.

Do you go to the gym or do you work out regularly? Yes.

Were you taught it to be unmasculine to cry or to show emotion? Yes and no. I mean, my stepfather never admonished me for crying when he would pummel my ass with his leather belt. I think it was sort of a given that I would cry, show emotion when he beat me. I mean, it hurt after all. It was more with my teenaged peers that I did not show emotion or cry.

Do you wish you were more diplomatic? No.

Do you feel that you are an overly manipulative person? Not at all. One would think I would be at my place of work, given the position I hold but no, I am not a manipulative man.

Do you feel that you have to prove to others you can do better than them? Yes.

Do you feel that you are more creative than most males your age? Yes.

Were you often mocked or made fun of while you were in high school? No.

Do you often look down upon the actions of your friends? No.

What would you consider to be embarrassing? Losing my pants in a crowd.

Does it really bother you to lose or to do poorly at something? Yes.

What is one of your biggest fears? Being considered a failure.

Do you feel that your pride or ego often gets in your way? Yes.

At this time in your life, what do you feel you need the most? Money, sex and a promotion where I work.

Do you feel that you are an overly sensitive person? Sometimes.

Do you tend to blame others for your own misfortune? No.

Do you often feel disoriented? No.

Do you feel that you are often too eager to please? At times.

Do you often feel guilty and not know why? No.

What do you want to change the most about your present personality or self-image? That I can do it, that I can become a vice president and that I need to work at doing it.

Were you ever in, or did you ever want to be in the military? No.

Do you feel you can handle yourself well in "power" situations? I believe I can, yes.

Do you feel that you need new friends? Sometimes.

What do you want to change the most physically about yourself? Well, I'm in pretty good shape right about now so I suppose I just want to maintain how I look physically, which is why workout often.

Do you feel that you come from a dysfunctional family? Yes and no. I mean, my upbringing was pretty traditional…except for how my stepfather routinely reddened my ass.

Do you feel your short term goals are too high? No.

Do you usually feel sick or upset before a test, a confrontation, a new event, an athletic competition or performance? No.

Do you feel that you are a dull person…perhaps too dull? No.

At this moment, what are you most self-conscious or nervous about? What I'll be enduring when I come here for my "sessions" with you Master Jeff Sir…

As Terry recalled answering that last question on the first night he had met "Master Jeff" he realized as he finished his glass of water that there was now a new answer to that particular inquiry. At this moment Terry was most nervous about the thrashing he was going to receive via Master Jeff's large wooden spoon. As he sipped down the last of his cool water the high socked executive's cock churned and throbbed like a thing alive in front of him. His balls dangled low between his thighs, chock filled with his manly fear juices.

"All done Terrance?" Master Jeff asked. "Or would you care for another glass of cold water?"

"Thank you Master Jeff Sir, that's a wonderful offer but I'm done now," Terry replied.

"Good man," Terry's disciplinarian said, sounding prideful. "Now, go and place your glass in the sink and then return here…and when you return bring me my wooden spoon."

"Yes Master Jeff Sir," Terry said and got to his feet, holding his empty water glass in hand.

As Terry padded out of the room Master Jeff noted that the executive's dress socks had slouched down a bit around his calves during their session.

"And unless you want another extra fifty swats you'll pull your socks up Terrance," Master Jeff stated sternly, facing forward as he said it. "You know I want you tidy for our sessions…"

"Y-yes Master Jeff Sir," Terry said and quickly hiked his Gold Toe's up to under his knees after placing his water glass in the sink. "I mean, no Sir Master Jeff Sir, I do not want another fifty extra swats..."

Master Jeff smiled with satisfaction as he heard the water in the sink turned on and then the sounds of Terry washing his water glass...

When Terry returned to the living room Master Jeff was again seated on the spanking couch. Terry's ass cheeks and thighs were red as ripe tomatoes and as much as he hurt and stung back there the executive took a certain pride in what he had endured thus far this evening. As he stepped into the living room, his hard cock pointing the way he stopped midway and stood at soldierly attention before the man he had come to call "Master."

"Master Jeff Sir, I'm ready for the next part of our session," Terry said with the utmost respect.

"Good man Terry," Master Jeff replied. "Bring me my wooden spoon... and you know what else to bring..."

"Yes Master Jeff Sir, I know," Terry said, relaxed his stance of attention and proceeded to open a drawer in a nearby desk.

From the desk Terry produced a deck of everyday playing cards...

With the deck of cards held in hand Terry proceeded next to the coffee table where Master Jeff had his equipment lined up. With his other hand trembling Terry picked up the wooden spoon. This wooden spoon was a few sizes larger than the size of "mom's" stirring spoons and when one was walloped with one of them it hurt about fifty times more. Terry was no stranger to this fact at that point in time. Master Jeff's wooden spoon was about two feet long with the ladle part, or what Terry considered the spanking end about five inches long and two inches wide. After only about five or six strokes from the wooden spoon Terry often found it difficult to keep his butt still and his hands away and it was for those reasons that Master Jeff usually roped his hands behind him...JEEZ.

As Terry stepped to where Master Jeff sat he saw that his authoritarian was watching him intently. Like earlier with the leather paddle Terry kissed each side of the wooden spoon before handing it to Master Jeff.

"Your wooden spoon Master Jeff Sir," Terry said as he handed Jeff the spoon.

Master Jeff took the spoon from Terry....

Then, Master Jeff nodded "Yes" and Terry knew just what that meant. It was his signal after all. He handed Master Jeff the deck of playing cards and then lowered himself over Master Jeff's lap, his delectable red ass cheeks pointing straight up at the ceiling. Master Jeff marveled at how the crimson hue shone through the hairiness of his charge's butt cheeks...

A few moments later Terry's hands were bound tightly behind him as Master Jeff shuffled the cards a few times.

"Terrance, recite for me why I wallop you with a wooden spoon," Master Jeff ordered.

"Yes Master Jeff Sir," Terry replied, his head dangling at Master Jeff's feet, his wavy salt and pepper colored hair sweaty and dangling in his face at that point. "Ahem, even though the wooden spoon is associated with "Mom's" discipline it really is a very manly type of punishment. Being that you use an oversized wooden spoon makes it a more thorough thrashing than "Mom" used to give."

"Very good Terrance," Master Jeff said and the sound of the cards being shuffled filled Terry with dread as he lay splayed and balanced precariously over his master's lap, his hard cock pressed against Master Jeff's knees.

Terry squirmed a bit on his master's lap and pressed his socked toes hard against the floor in an attempt to maintain better poise. Being in this position reminded him too much of the times when his stepfather used to thrash his ass for him, the main difference here being that his stepfather never tied his hands behind him when he spanked him. At that thought his cock churned all the more. Master Jeff felt Terry's uneasiness at the position he lay in and did a quick maneuver with his legs. A few seconds later Terry felt his hard cock sandwiched between Master Jeff's thighs and then his master used his knees to move Terry's upturned ass a few notches higher.

"Tell me how the amount of swats you receive with my wooden spoon is decided on Terrance," Master Jeff ordered.

"Master Jeff Sir, something like earlier when you used the dice to decide how many swats I would receive this time out you'll be using the deck of cards you trained me to bring you," Terry recited from memory. "The number on the card that you draw will determine how many swats I will receive on my ass cheeks from your wooden spoon. If you draw a king, a queen, or a jack card I will receive twenty swats, as each of the picture cards are worth twenty, your rules. If you draw an ace of diamonds, clubs, or hearts I will receive double the amount of swats shown on the next number card. If you draw an ace of spades I will receive triple the number of swats shown on the next number card. If you draw a Joker card that is in my favor and I will receive no more swats for this session…not even from my stepfather's belt."

"Very good Terrance, very good indeed," Master Jeff said, rubbing Terry's red ass cheeks and sounding like a proud parent as he spoke. "Now tell me my executive, how many times have I ever drawn a Joker card since you started coming to me for sessions Terrance?"

"Master Jeff Sir, you have never drawn a Joker card," Terry intoned and clenched his teeth as he heard the deck of cards being shuffled one last time.

"We'll do three rounds only of this Terrance," Master Jeff said as he drew a card from the top of the deck. "The night is wearing thin at this point…"

"Yes Master Jeff Sir, yes," Terry said, sounding happy and disappointed at the same time.

"I've drawn a ten of clubs Terrance," Master Jeff announced and dropped the card to the floor in front of Terry's dangling face.

"A good number to start with Master Jeff Sir," Terry said out loud and to himself said, "For you but not for me…"

Master Jeff used a lot of shoulder strength this time with Terry. It was one way of making the punishment with the wooden spoon that much more intense.

WHAPPPP WHAPPPP WHAPPPP WHAPPPP was the sound as the rounded end of the large wooden spoon connected hard and harshly with Terry's already reddened behind.

"Count you numb nut executive," Master Jeff ordered.

"OWWWWWWWW, y-yes Master Jeff Sir, ONE, TWO, three, four…" Terry squawked loudly.

WHAPPP WHAPPP WHAPPP

"And…five, six, SEVEN, Master Jeff Sir!" the handsome and getting exhausted executive called out.

Terry counted true till Master Jeff reached the tenth swat with the wooden spoon…

As the no-nonsense executive lay splayed with his hands bound behind him across Master Jeff's lap he heard the ominous sound of the deck of cards being shuffled again. Terry clenched his teeth and sweated, a few beads of sweat pooling at the tip of his nose. He pressed his socked toes hard against the floor and his cock churned and throbbed between his master's thighs.

"OOOOOOO Master Jeff Sir!!" Terry bellowed as he felt his man juices boiling in his sweaty sac.

"Getting there finally eh Terrance?" Master Jeff teased his charge as he shuffled the cards.

"UH, y-yes Sir, Master Jeff Sir, I think I can feel it now," Terry squabbled.

"And you know what will happen if you shoot that load and soil my pants don't you?" Master Jeff asked.

"Y-yes Sir, Master Jeff Sir, if, if I shoot my load before you've granted me permission to do so I'll receive a bonus fifty swats with your trusty leather paddle," Terry panted as Master Jeff held up the next card he had drawn. "And I will also have to lick my seed from your pants."

"Very good Terrance, so I'm sure you're now using those self-control techniques that I've spanked into you over time, yes?" Master Jeff inquired mockingly, knowing how difficult it was for Terry to hold back shooting his load at this point.

When the topnotch exec had really done well, spank-wise, his elation always made him overly excited in the area of his crotch. It amazed the spanking master how even after all the pain Terry had endured so far he was able to get an erection. Master Jeff again had to wonder how many times a night Terry's wife wanted him. Smiling wickedly Jeff said he had drawn a six of spades.

"Yes Master Jeff Sir, a six of spades," Terry repeated.

Master Jeff raised the large wooden spoon high, pulling back far to gather strength into his shoulder. He then brought the wooden spoon crashing down on Terry's upturned behind.

WHAPPP WHAPPPP

"YOWCCHHH!!!" Terry bellowed loudly through clenched teeth and his bound wrists squirmed in their bondage. "ONE, two, Master Jeff Sir!"

WHAPPP WHAPPP

"RRRRRRRR!!! And three and four Master Jeff Sir!" Terry cried out, sniveling and feeling his erection betraying him between Master Jeff's thighs.

"Very good Terrance, but then again, it's not all that difficult to count to six is it now?" Master Jeff chuckled meanly and administered to Terry the last of the six swats, good and hard.

Terry screamed out the numbers five and six and panted madly as Master Jeff shuffled the deck of cards one last time for that particular spanking session. Even though Terry was glad that this area of his punishment would soon be over the most emotionally taxing was yet to come. His cock dribbled pre seed and Terry did his utmost not to lose his load...a bonus of fifty swats he was not looking forward to this night... It had been a rather long night at that he thought.

"A seven of diamonds Terrance," Master Jeff announced. "The cards have been very kind to you tonight I would say..."

"Yes Master Jeff Sir, very kind indeed," Terry said agreeably, recalling sessions with Master Jeff when the cards had not been as kind.

But even though the cards were being kind Terry's entire ass felt like it was the color of a red and overly tomato... He scrunched his ass cheeks together as he felt Master Jeff raise the wooden spoon... This time when Master Jeff walloped his tenderized ass cheeks the sound the wooden spoon made as it connected was more like...

SPLATTTT!!!

Terry reeled, screamed out the number one and cried like a little kid...

SPLATTTTT!!!

"OHHHHH Master Jeff Sir, t-two..." Terry reeled.

A short while later Master Jeff was done walloping his charge's ass cheeks with the wooden spoon. He commended Terry in a sarcastic tone about how well he had done in holding back shooting his load of pent-up juices. Terry thanked the man he called "Master" and quickly recalled a time when being walloped by Master

Jeff using the wooden spoon he "had" shot his load. The topnotch executive could not believe it, seeing as he was in blinding pain at that point…yet he was erect and HAD shot his load, right between his master's thighs as the man held his cock tightly between them. He had cum like a banshee to put it plainly. The first time it had happened Terry Dean Bradshaw could not believe the intensity of his orgasm. It was unlike any gusher he had ever experienced before…even with his very sexually apt wife. Master Jeff had explained that it was his over the top exuberance that had caused Terry to explode his juices. Knowing he had done so well in taking what his master dished out had caused the executive to ejaculate in a mixture of excitement and anguish. Master Jeff also explained how sometimes our emotions fly off the Richter scale, causing us to become erect when we think we could not possibly. It all made sense to Terry, until Master Jeff told him that they would have to work on some self-control techniques where Terry shooting his load while being walloped was concerned. Master Jeff had then ordered Terry to his knees to lick his "seed" from his master's trousers. Terry had never tasted his own cum before. Even when he was a kid and would secretly jack off he was never curious about the taste of his man juices. As he licked his cum off Master Jeff's trousers he discovered that he didn't taste all that bad. He had grinned, secretly thinking of the young lady he had dated when he was in his early twenties and how she had loved drinking from him, as she called it when she would swallow his seed. After he had licked his master's pants clean to his satisfaction Master Jeff then ordered the sock clad lug to his feet and told him that for shooting his load he would suffer an extra fifty swats with the leather paddle. Upon hearing that Terry was prepared to get dressed and leave Master Jeff's apartment but he had committed himself to this man…and inwardly he was only too thrilled to be back over Master Jeff's knees as the man leather paddle swatted him fifty times for shooting his load…

But this time, thanks to Master Jeff's constant attention and spankings Terry had managed to control himself and not shoot his load. His cock however was still rock hard and pulsing. Terry was aching to shoot his load at that point. It had been a long spanking night and the executive had done very well, *he knew*. In his deepest heart of hearts he knew he had pleased his spanking master. His feeling of elation was at an all-time high. As Terry stood now with his hands still bound behind him (Master Jeff did not want him rubbing his reddened and stinging ass cheeks just yet, he wanted his handsome executive to revel in the singing sting he was currently feeling) and as Master Jeff gathered him lovingly into his arms as he sobbed Terry's balls felt as if they were dangling just over his OTC dress socks…

"Oh Master Jeff Sir," Terry sobbed, his head resting on his master's shoulder as Jeff held him tight, moving his big hands over and over the executive's huge biceps, stroking his soft salt and pepper colored hair. "TH-thank you Master Jeff Sir!"

Terry allowed his emotions to really flow as he shook, heaved and sobbed in his master's arms.

"Easy Terrance, easy boy," Master Jeff whispered in his charge's ear, his lips grazing Terry's lobe as he spoke. "You did very well this session, very well... and I know you'll do well when we finish very soon..."

As Terry leaned down a tad more Master Jeff moved his hands over Terry's reddened ass cheeks. They were warm to the touch.

"Master Jeff Sir, I'm sorry for my stupidity upon my arrival earlier," Terry blubbered. "That will never happen again Sir!"

"I know, I know," Master Jeff chuckled as he slowly untied Terry's hands, feeling the executive's throbber pressing against him as he did so.

"As you said Sir, I am here for sessions, THERE WILL BE NO MORE EXCUSES or tries for reprieves," Terry went on. "I honestly don't know what I was thinking..."

Once his hands were untied Terry threw his arms around Master Jeff and the two men stood there embracing tightly, Terry still sniveling a bit and whispering "Thank you" over and over. Master Jeff pressed his lips against Terry's tear-soaked cheek and gently kissed him.

"Good man Terrance," he said softly. "But now you must prepare for the final ass thrashing for the night...and then you need to get home to your wife and children..."

Terry said, "Yes Master Jeff Sir, I'm ready..." and as he unfastened himself from his master's embrace Master Jeff kissed him once more on the cheek...

A few minutes later Terry emerged from the bathroom and quickly made his way back to the living room of Master Jeff's apartment. After a good discipline session Master Jeff always allows Terry five to ten minutes of bathroom time. Terry is permitted to do whatever his needs require...except to jack himself off. Master Jeff deems it that Terry must not lose his seed or his desire before his ride home. Terry Dean Bradshaw and Master Jeff have found that Terry's arousal is above average after he has been thoroughly thrashed. When he arrives home after a session with Master Jeff he and his wife go at it like rabbits...to coin Terry's phrase. Of course they go at it in the dark, seeing as Terry would be hard-pressed to try to explain to his wife why his ass and thighs are all red... It is partially that feeling of stinging redness on his ass cheeks (and sometimes his thighs) that seems to thrust Terry forward even more-so as he thrusts into his loving and beautiful wife...

As Terry emerged from the bathroom his mind wandered once more to the first night when he had met the man he would come to call "Master", the man in whose arms he would sob like a baby. The questions that Master Jeff put to him seemed to go on and on, but it was at the end of those questions that Terry Dean Bradshaw would make his life-changing decision. He recalled sitting in front of Master Jeff clad in nothing more than his black nylon OTC dress socks as the questions upon questions were put to him.

Do you often feel that you are too volatile? Sometimes I am, yes.

Do or did any of your parents have a drinking or substance abuse problem? No.

Do you believe in the axiom: "No pain, no gain? I do.

Do you have any tattoos or piercing which you now regret having done? None, I have none.

Do you like being under the control of others or being dominated by others? I uh, I like being in control most of the time, especially where I work. But I will admit to a secret and lusty part of me that wants to be dominated.

Picture yourself doing something creative. What is it? Painting.

If you are gay, are you comfortable about it? I am not gay, but if I were I am sure I would be comfortable about it.

Do you usually do what you are told without questioning? It depends on what I am being told to do.

Do you feel you are too gullible or trusting of others? No, I think I have a good instinct.

Do you often feel that you are too compulsive? No.

What type of situations make you feel uncomfortable? Sitting and answering questions while stripped to my dress socks.

Does competition generally scare you and make you withdraw? No.

Were you considered to be a dork, a nerd or a wimp in high school or junior high? No, being athletic the way I was I was pretty much accepted as one of the guys.

Do you feel that you are in a rut that you cannot get out of easily? Somewhat, but I think as of tonight all that is going to change.

Do you think you are more intellectual or more of a "free thinker" than many your age? A little bit of both I would have to say.

Do you feel your life is now too chaotic or too uncontrolled? A bit uncontrolled, yes.

Do all these questions I am asking you make you feel intimidated, uncertain or apprehensive? No Sir, I feel nervous and on display though the way you have me sitting here stripped to my socks.

Master Jeff told Terry that that was the end of the questioning part of their first session. He put the listing of questions down on the coffee table next to his "spanking" implements. As he spoke Master Jeff stood up and made his way over to his seated charge. Terry had not been told to stand or to get dressed so he simply sat there in his socks.

"Terrance, the next part of this meeting, our consultation if you would is now solely up to you," Master Jeff said and placed a hand on the back of Terry's neck and squeezed gently. "I have decided based on your answers to all those questions that *I want* to be your disciplinarian, your spanking master so to speak. *I want* to take you under my wing and under my paddles and wooden spoons and such. *I want* for you to submit to me Terrance. *I want* you to trust in me. But if you decide to accept me in that manner you must be daring, stoic and brave. Being spanked by me will show your endurance and pride levels, as well as how much you can take mentally and of course physically. This will teach you to think before speaking or acting and to concentrate. I will show you how it is you, AND ONLY YOU that is holding you back from achieving your truest potential in your place of work and career. *If* you give yourself to me in this manner you will learn to think under pressure and you will learn how much it can really bother you to be careless. An example of that is you will be punctual for sessions. If not you will learn lessons and what it means when you are *not* punctual. What I will dish out on you my tall socked and silk underpants executive is PURE BEHAVIOR modification techniques. Some of this is based on military training and/or fear of the unknowns. I gave you an example of fear of the unknowns when I brought you in here blindfolded. Being blindfolded you have already learned to trust me. You have already given yourself to me in the sense of humbling yourself before me in your near total nakedness at this moment. You will learn that real pressure, self-induced and other as well as punishment can occur here. Some people who have been spanked by me have cried; some have fainted Terrance Dean Bradshaw."

As Master Jeff recited he gently squeezed the back of Terry's neck and the executive found himself to be rage hard at the cock. He glanced down for a second and saw the pre seed that had oozed from his piss slit and slid down the sides of his throbbing shaft.

"Some have come here, been spanked by me and went through it all without any consequences," Master Jeff went on, taking his hand off the back of Terry's neck and stepping in front of his handsome prize. "It can be done Terrance, if you think and listen, and I assure you my executive, that is a big IF. It can be embarrassing. As you pointed out already you are embarrassed sitting there in just your socks. But the reaction that I see in your erection shows me excitement, perhaps a certain fear as well. Many men find themselves erect and pulsing when feeling fear. It can also be a little painful what I will do to you here, perhaps *very* painful at times, depending on how much discipline I feel you are in need of when at any of your sessions. I can see from the look on your face that you are also very curious Terrance."

For the briefest of moments Master Jeff ceased speaking, stood close to his seated charge and gently took Terry's chin in his fingers and thumb. Breathlessly he asked, "So tell me Terrance, tell me my handsome executive that fate seems to have brought to me tonight, *tell me*, are *you* willing to take the risk and challenge?"

"I'm willing Master Jeff Sir," Terry whispered and the tears in his eyes flowed down his cheeks.

Terry abruptly stood up and he and Master Jeff embraced tightly…both men knowing that a new and very special camaraderie, comradeship and friendship had just been born in that room…

"Let's go to the spanking couch Terrance," Master Jeff whispered as they hugged.

"Yes Master Jeff Sir, yes," Terry sniveled.

As Terry recalled that first trip to the spanking couch his mind was again jarred back to the present moment as he once more made his way to the spanking couch…where Master Jeff was seated and awaiting his charge. Terry padded on his navy blue socked feet to the coffee table where the man he called "Master" had his spanking implements lined up. It was time for the final ass thrashing…and it would be with Terry's stepfather's leather belt that he would suffer that final thrashing of the night. It was always the most emotional of all the thrashings as Terry's mind wreaked havoc on him with the memories of how his stepfather used to discipline him. Back then when he was a teenager Terry felt that the harsh discipline was a bit over the top…a bit not needed. But now, as an adult Terry knew in his heart of hearts how much he needed the kind of therapy that Master Jeff subjected him to. With his hand trembling Terry picked up his stepfather's leather belt and brought it to Master Jeff. For the briefest of seconds Terry saw his stepfather sitting on the couch instead of Master Jeff.

"Good man Terry," Master Jeff said as Terry stood before him with the belt in hand, his muscular chest heaving up and down and his erection pulsing as he fought his tears.

"Master Jeff Sir," Terry sniveled in a mixture of fear and joy. "I bring to you my stepfather's leather belt. It was the instrument of my punishment when I was a younger man, punishment that my stepfather doled out on me. Now it will be you using that same leather belt…Master Jeff Sir…"

Terry's erect cock stared Master Jeff in the face as he listened to his charge recite his litany. Terry then kissed the leather belt and handed it to his master…

Master Jeff gestured toward his lap and Terry lay himself down across it, his red ass pointing straight up at heaven…

WHAPPPP WHAPPP WHAPPP WHAPPPP was the stinging sound that filled the air and consumed Terry's already reddened ass cheeks as Master Jeff administered the final punishment for the evening. As Terry screamed, cried and counted he recalled how on the first night he met Master Jeff he had found himself in the same exact position, splayed over his master's lap, his delectable ass cheeks in the air…and being thoroughly and well spanked. It seemed in the ruggedly handsome executive's mind the two nights had come together on this night…and now as he was thrashed with his stepfather's leather belt memories of that man as well filled Terry Dean Bradshaw's mind…

As Master Jeff administered the final ass thrashing to Terry Dean Bradshaw's reddened behind the executive's mind once more returned to the first night he had met his "master."

"Yes Master Jeff Sir," Terry repeated again as Master Jeff sat down on the spanking couch and pointed to his lap.

"Over my knees and lap Terrance," Master Jeff said. "That is the position you will always assume here at the spanking couch," Master Jeff instructed the erect executive.

"Yes Master Jeff Sir," Terry said as his tears stopped their flow for the moment. "There will be other positions you will assume in this place, my apartment, but for the moment the one I want you in is over my knees and lap. The other positions you will learn as time goes on."

But as he was about to splay and humble himself over Master Jeff's lap Master Jeff held up a hand, halting Terry.

"Hand me my round leather paddle Terrance," Master Jeff said commandingly, pointing at the lined up items on the coffee table he sat in front of. "And before you hand it to me I want you to show the paddle your respect and thanks by kissing it on both sides."

"Yes Master Jeff Sir," Terry responded.

The stripped to his black socks and erectly throbbing executive leaned over and picked up the round leather paddle. As he bent over slightly Master Jeff took in the sight of Terry's well-shaped delectable ass globes. A chill crept up the spanking master's spine as Terry's crack gaped a bit. He watched as Terry picked up the leather paddle, held it in front of his face and kissed both sides of it. Master Jeff smiled with satisfaction as Terry handed him what would be the first instrument of his discipline.

"Now Terrance, for tonight I will spank you only with the leather paddle," Master Jeff said, pointing at his lap.

"Yes Master Jeff Sir," Terry said and got himself situated over Master Jeff's lap, his arms spread out in front of him, the palms of his hands pressed against the floor, his socked toes pressed against the floor behind him.

"Your job now is to count off the swats you receive," Master Jeff went on, rubbing the paddle against Terry's upturned ass cheeks.

"Yes Master Jeff Sir," Terry said.

"I will administer to you fifty consecutive swats for tonight Terrance," Master Jeff said. "This will be our getting to know each other spanking for you. If you jumble up the count by skipping a number or if you repeat a number we'll start back at the beginning."

"Yes Master Jeff Sir, I understand Sir," Terry piped up.

"Now, place your hands behind you and balance yourself on my lap you numb nut executive," Master Jeff said and Terry took a deep breath before doing as he had been told.

"You will always lay across my lap with your hands and arms crossed up behind you Terrance," Master Jeff stated. "If you try to move your hands down to rub your ass cheeks as I redden them I will proceed to tie your hands behind you. Is that clear?"

"It, it's clear Master Jeff Sir," Terry replied and as his cock slid between Master Jeff's thighs he felt his cum churning in his tightened up balls.

Master Jeff chuckled as he squeezed his thighs around Terry's erection...

"Begin counting Terrance, and be true in your count," Master Jeff said and raised his paddle.

WHAPPP WHAPPP WHAPPP WHAPPP

"AWWWWW SHIT, ONE, TWO, three, and four, Master Jeff Sir," Terry called out loudly, clenching his big hands into tight fists.

WHAPPP WHAPPP WHAPPP

"OOOOHHHH, I-I'm really bein' spanked here, JEEZ!!" Terry garbled throatily, a bit of triumph sounding in his voice. "F-five, six...seven...and eight..."

"And forty-two more to go Terrance," Master Jeff said gleefully and raised his leather paddle.

"Yes Master Jeff Sir, YES SIR!" Terry responded and received the next five swats, each one harder than the one before it.

Terry's cock throbbed between his new master's thighs and as he squirmed on Master Jeff's lap and sang out the numbers he knew he would shoot his load. He wondered what the punishment for shooting his load between his master's thighs would be...

As time went on Terry found out that shooting his load between his master's thighs would mean an extra fifty swats for that session...with the stinging leather paddle no less. Over time Master Jeff explained to Terry that his excitement over having done well and endured a hard spanking session was what made Terry erect and what caused him to cum as well. Master Jeff spanked self-control into his charge where this was concerned so that Terry did not shoot his load while being spanked, rather he was taught to hold his seed till he arrived home to his wife...just as he would now in the present...

As Terry recalled that first night, as he recalled his first spanking from Master Jeff his mind was jarred back to the present as he reeled out through clenched teeth the number "Fifty."

After being thoroughly thrashed fifty times with his step father's leather belt Terry stood and embraced Master Jeff. The two men hugged tightly, Terry's head resting on his master's shoulder as he cried and heaved in his arms.

"Good man Terrance, good man indeed," Master Jeff cooed gently in his charge's ear. "You did very well tonight Terrance; know that my executive, *you did very well…*"

"Thank you Master Jeff Sir, thank you, *thank you…* " Terry sniveled and hugged his master tighter as he looked at his step father's leather belt where it lay back on the coffee table. "Thank you so much Sir…"

"Let's get you some soothing aloe cream yes?" Master Jeff asked his charge and gave Terry's red as a ripe tomato ass a squeeze.

"Yes Sir Master Jeff Sir, let's do that," Terry replied and with his hands crossed behind his back followed his master like an obedient puppy to the bathroom.

In the bathroom Terry bent over and grabbed his socked ankles, putting his reddened ass cheeks and thighs on ample display for Master Jeff. Terry stood mortified and docilely still as the man he called "Master" rubbed a liberal amount of unscented aloe cream over his thrashed and wounded ass cheeks and thighs.

"Feels good Terrance?" Master Jeff asked as he reveled in his present chore, rubbing his aloe creamed hands over and over Terry Dean Bradshaw's bottom and over his delectable thighs.

"Yes Master Jeff Sir, very soothing, but I can still feel the sting," Terry replied. "And that's good Master Jeff Sir. Feeling the sting will remind me of my shortcomings and ineptitudes…"

"Precisely Terrance, precisely," Master Jeff said and just for the fuck of it slid an aloe cream slicked finger into Terry's bunghole.

Terry gripped his socked ankles tighter and gasped…

A short while later Terry was dressed in his suit, tie and wingtip shoes. He hugged Master Jeff one more time, said he would see him in two weeks and then left the apartment…

On his way home on the subway even though there was ample seating Terry Dean Bradshaw opted to stand…

(7)

Breaking Up is "Hard" To Do

(From the book: Milked)

For as long as I can remember I've always wanted to have sex on the beach, and I'm not talking about the drink called "Sex on the beach" here. The character of Paul Rogan in the story was modeled after a hunky guy in a red bathing suit that I saw while on the beach at a time that had to be many years ago at this point, seeing as I am no longer a beach going person.

I never thought how the character of Paul Rogan after having had his heart broken by the girl he was dating related to me in any way. After re-reading this story back to myself I realized how after Paul's girlfriend in the story broke up with him he wound up having anonymous sex with two men. In my own life I had dated a girl many years ago and after I had broken up with her I went out to a club and wound up having anonymous sex with two men. I wonder if I somehow drew upon my own experience of an ending of a relationship when I wrote this short story.

The one time I did go down to a beach at night time I was with my friend Joe and a guy we were visiting while we were on vacation in Florida. As we approached the water I suddenly found myself feeling the most intensely strange fear. When I saw the moonlit waves crashing on the beach and the sound of the waves themselves I was suddenly terrified. I decided to let Joe and our friend walk on the beach while I waited for them back on the boardwalk. When I wrote the story "Breaking Up is "Hard" To Do" and Paul Rogan walks down on the beach fearlessly I wondered *if that was my way of conquering whatever demon plagued me that night back in Florida.*

What's in a name? Well, in the case of Paul Rogan I received many e-mails from my readers saying how they loved the name I had given to the lead character in this story. It sounded sexy yet rugged at the same time. My readers also asked why the two men who feast on Paul on the beach were left nameless. I suppose my fetish for anonymous sex way back when I was a younger man came into play here.

I never said in the story that Paul Rogan was Gay. And he had just had his heart broken by a woman so that points to him being straight, yet he allows two men who find him on the beach to sex him over. While I can argue that point and simply say that the story was an erotic fantasy I will also say that Paul was so heartbroken and overwhelmed that his girl had left him that at that moment he was wide open to any kind of relief that happened to come along. I'm not sure that makes sense but perhaps some of my readers will think so.

I suppose one has to be very open minded when reading this particular story. I think what also influenced some of the scenes in this story (especially the scenes where Paul Rogan and the two anonymous guys were romping around in the water) was the music video of the song "Domino Dancing" by The Pet Shop Boys. The video depicted a lot of homo-erotic activity between a few well-muscled guys on a beach.

Being that Paul did not have a bathing suit of any sort with him he was either forced to swim in the ocean in his briefs or totally naked. I opted for him swimming in his briefs because of the ads I have seen of hunky models modeling white briefs in the waves of an ocean. It's very erotic and appealing to the eye to see a guy in a pair of soaked white briefs.

The way the story ends sort of leaves Paul Rogan wondering if the experience with the two guys really happened. I could have said that he thought he had been so brokenhearted over his girlfriend leaving him that he dreamt the entire thing, but I did not do that.

————————————

My name is Paul Rogan. I want to tell you about the most depressing night of my life, which then turned into the kinkiest night of my life. It happened about seven months ago. Till this day I still wonder if I recounted it all, it was pretty amazing. I had been dating Linda for close to a year when on that particular night she decided to tell me that she didn't want to go out with me anymore. She wanted to date other men. She wanted to feel free again. Needless to say I was crushed. My heart was broken. Linda was the girl I thought I was going to marry. I had been so sure of it. We had met at a dinner party given by a mutual friend of ours and from the moment our eyes met I knew she was the one…or at least I thought she was. We were both young, (I'm twenty two) college graduates, energetic and hard working.

I work for a bank in Manhattan as a computer systems analyst. We both enjoyed the same types of movies, music, and even Broadway shows. We began dating the night after the dinner party and it just seemed like everything in my life was perfect. Wrong, because as I said about eleven months later Linda decided to end our relationship. It was a warm September night and I drove around aimlessly after she had broken the news to me. It was after eleven o'clock at night. I thought about going to the twenty-four hour gym for a good hard work out to relieve whatever it was I was feeling (I work out four times a week and my body is really pumped up and muscular because of it) but really wasn't in the mood for working out at that moment. As I drove I realized that I had come to the street just before the boardwalk of Manhattan Beach in Brooklyn New York. I parked my car, got out, and walked to the boardwalk. I sat down on a bench and breathed heavily, tears in my eyes. I missed Linda already. As I sat there alone I listened to the sound of the waves of the ocean down on the beach. Whenever I'm feeling down or depressed I swim. It seems to relieve the ill feeling…sort of like working out does. I looked around to make sure no one was around and decided to take a swim. I took off my sneakers and sweat socks and holding them in hand I walked barefoot down to the beach. When I was a few feet from where the waves ended and broke on the sand I stripped down to my white briefs, piling my clothes up on the sand, laying my sneakers atop them to weigh them down in case of wind. The cool air caressed my muscular body and I was feeling better already. Slowly, I walked into the cold water of the ocean. It welcomed me like the arms of a lover. When I was up to my chest I leaned forward and swam out further.

"AHHHHH…" I sighed. "Feels great…"

The cold water invigorated me, caressed me, and made my nine inch cock hard as a rock in my briefs. I swam back and forth, trying not to think of Linda. As I was floating on my back, the moon shining down on me, I glanced at the beach and saw two guys sitting down on the sand. They lit cigarettes and seemed to be just relaxing. I was worried for a moment that they were homeless and would steal my clothes. My wallet and car keys were in my pants after all. The thought of having to report a robbery in just my wet briefs was not too thrilling. But the two guys just seemed to be minding their business, not bothering any of my stuff. A short while later I swam for shore. I was totally exhausted but feeling good and invigorated. I walked on the sand to where my clothes were and decided to lay down for a few minutes before getting dressed to head on home. I lay down and the white sugary sand stuck to the backs of my tree trunks like legs and muscular back. I would have to swim again to rinse off before getting into my clothes. I closed my eyes and relaxed, not thinking of Linda…and not thinking of the two guys who were now silently making their way over to me. My cock was still hard as a rock in my briefs. Actually, my cock is hard more often than it is not. As the cool breeze caressed me I suddenly felt it. My nipples were being sucked! My eyes shot open and I could not believe what I was seeing…and feeling. The two guys who I had seen earlier were stretched out on my sides, each of them sucking one of my big nipples, their arms then folded over my arms, holding me down on the sand. It had all happened so damned fast.

"H-hey…WH-what the fuck do you think you're doing???" I grunted, lifting my head up off the sand and looking down at them in disbelief as they sucked, licked, kissed and teased my nipples with the tips of their tongues. "OHHHHHH shit, that feels fucking awesome dudes…"

"Just relax…dude…" one of the guys said and gave my big succulent balls a squeeze through my sopping wet briefs.

He then resumed working my nipple. They ran their hands over my big rock hard chest, and ran their fingertips over the impression of my hard cock in my briefs as they continued working the fuck out of my nipples.

"OHHHHHHH fuck…" I moaned my head still lifted up off the sand. "I ain't a faggot you guys but I got to admit that that sure does feel great…fucking fuckers, working my big tits…YEAH!"

I lowered my head back down on the sand and looked up at the moon. Goose bumps broke out all over my body as the two guys went on working my nipples. In no time my nipples were erect and fucking hard. The two guys ran their tongues gently over them, running the palms of their hands over and under my huge male cleavage, my giant pecs. I saw that they were both dressed in bathing suits. I guessed that they had come out for some night swimming and found me as a bonus of sorts.

"OHHHHHH…" I moaned. "You two are driving me crazy…"

They slurped my nipples back into their mouths and gave them another good workout with their tongues. After a while my nipples were feeling a little sore but the two guys still chowed down on them. The mixture of pleasure and slight pain was totally invigorating…it was more than invigorating actually, it was fucking awesome! They had taken their folded arms off my arms, knowing by then that I wasn't going to try anything. Hell, why would I try to stop them or runoff? What they were doing to me felt great. Linda had never gone near my nipples in all our time together. This was like a whole new experience for me. I crossed my hands up behind my head and watched as the two guys delighted in servicing my nipples.

"My name is Paul…" I said softly.

They didn't reply by telling me their names…they just went on working my nipples.

"ARRRRHHHH yeah!!" I grunted and arched my back up off the sand. "FUCKIN' A!!!"

Then, one of the guys stopped working my nipple that he had in his mouth and moved his tongue over one of my hairy armpits.

"OHHHHH shit, what's this???" I asked breathlessly. "Fucking sleazy bastard licking my armpit…"

As he worked my armpit his buddy continued working one of my nipples with his mouth and the other one with his thumb and first finger, squeezing it, twisting it, and pinching it.

"OHHHHH yeah, fucking guys are making me batty," I groaned. "My goddamned girlfriend never worked on me like this…"

They stopped what they were doing for a second, looked at each other across my prone muscular body, smiled, and quickly resumed working on my nipples and armpits. The other guy moved to my other armpit and then they were licking, sucking, and kissing my armpits. My nipples had been sucked up past erect. They were as pointy as bullets and feeling just as hard. Goose bumps were all over me, I was sweating in the cool breeze, and my cock… GOD…my cock was harder than it had ever been before. It throbbed like crazy in my wet briefs, hard as a fucking rock, and oozing and oozing my pre seed like I can't begin to tell you. After a while they stopped working my armpits and I watched breathlessly as they moved toward my crotch.

"OHHHH yeah, go for it you sleazy fuckers," I gasped when I saw they were a tad reluctant to go near my hard manhood. "Suck my cock…"

They didn't need to be told twice. They reached into the fly opening of my white briefs and pulled out my hard, fat and throbbing sausage-sized cock, along with my big hairy balls. They looked at each other in awe, marveling at the size and girth of my huge meat. They each licked the tip of it a few times like it was an ice cream cone and then they took turns sucking it, pulling it deep into their mouths, and running their lips and tongue over the sides of it. They tongued my big balls, applying pressure to them, driving me wild, and making my head spin.

"OHHHHHH GOD!!!" I roared and my voice echoed across the deserted beach. "Fuckers…"

Then, as one of them sucked my meat the other one ran his tongue all over my balls at the same time. He pulled my balls alternately into his mouth and sucked them with real gusto. I sat up on my elbows and watched in awe as the two guys sucked my cock and lapped my balls.

"OH GAWD, this is fucking unbelievable," I grunted.

As I sat there in my briefs having my cock and balls worked on I ran one hand over my chest and squeezed one of my nipples. It felt hard and leathery between my fingers…from the workout my two new buddies had given it beforehand. When I felt myself getting close to shooting my load I laid back down on the sand, my muscular arms at my sides.

"Oh yeah you cock hungry fuckers…" I moaned breathlessly. "Getting close now…oh yeah get ready you guys…"

The guy who had my cock in his mouth at that moment took it out, grabbed it tightly in his hand, and held it as I shot my big creamy load…all over my chest, my stomach, and onto my nipples.

"OHHHHH yeah, yeah!!! FUCKING A you guys, fucking A!!" I roared as I shot globs of hot velvety jazz all over me. Fuckers, milking the tar outa me… FUCK!!!"

I bucked and writhed on the sand in sheer ecstasy as one of the guys held my cock and the other one continued licking at my balls…hard. When I was done and they had squeezed every possible drop of cum out of me I sat up on my elbows and watched as they eagerly licked my cum off my chest and stomach, sucking it off my now very sensitive nipples also. I moaned and groaned in a man's passion as they licked me like I was an ice cream cone.

"Oh yeah you two," I whispered. "Fucking turned the worst night of my life into the best night of my life."

At that moment I had completely forgotten Linda. A few minutes later I was on my knees in front of the two men, alternately sucking their cocks. Their bathing suits were down around their ankles on the sand as I, for the first time in all my life, sucked cock. I licked their pre seed off their piss slits as they pressed their hard throbbing cocks together in front of my lips. Fucking fuck, like I said, I had never sucked a man's cock before in my life, but, at that moment I was getting a damned good education in the art of it. My cock, still sticking out of my wet briefs along with my big gushy balls was again hard and throbbing, wanting to shoot another load. Can you believe that shit? And I had just cum not all that long ago. I ran my hands over the two men's legs, squeezed their thighs, and licked their balls as they stood over me, moaning and groaning in the moonlight. They squeezed each other's nipples and slapped each other's pecs as I went on alternately sucking their cocks, slurping on them, deep throating them one at a time. Every time they pressed their cocks together and held them to my lips I nibbled erotically at their slits and cock-heads. They reached down and caressed the back of my neck as I sucked and sucked them, sliding my mouth further over their cocks as I sucked. A few minutes later the first guy announced breathlessly that he was cumming and he erupted like a goddamned volcano, holding his hard cock in his hand, stroking himself all over my chest.

"OHHHHHHH yeah!!!" he crooned loudly as I leaned back in the sand and his cum landed all over my torso, stomach and nipples.

His friend wasn't too far behind. He shot his load a few seconds later, shooting a load just as big and creamy all over me. He moaned loudly in passion beside his buddy as he came and came also. As their cum dripped all over my chest, nipples and stomach I knew what without a guess I was in for next. When they were spent I laid back down on the sand without a word. I sat up on my elbows as they went to work licking their cum slowly off my chest, again slurping on my nipples like crazy, torturing them erotically at that point.

"OHHHHH you fucking guys..." I grunted and looked up at the moonlit sky. "Looks like I'm your cum buffet."

I ground my fingers into the sand as their tongues explored my huge chest, my pecs, my stomach, and of course my nipples. Damn, but those guys loved my nipples. It was as if they couldn't get enough of them. My head spinning again I laid back down on the sand. The two guys stretched out at my sides and continued slurping on me.

"I can feast on this fucking guy all night..." one of them whispered breathlessly.

I decided to do just that, to let them feast on me all they wanted. When they started taking turns poking the tips of their tongues into my belly button I cried out in a passion I never knew before. Not to mention that I'm ticklish as hell around my belly button. When they moved down to my feet I watched as they each took one of my big feet into their hands and sucked my toes one at a time. I sat up again and this time grabbed my cock in my hand. I stroked myself slowly as they sucked my toes and massaged my feet. I was swooning and sweating in an ecstasy all new to me.

"OHHHHH yeah, look at you two sleazy fuckers sucking my damned toes…" I said softly and felt myself cumming a second time as I milked my cock. "OHHHHHHHH yeah, yeah, you fuckers…feels great…"

I shot my load all over myself again and fell back on the sand on my back, panting for breath as the two guys went on and on sucking my toes. I ran my fingers through my cum all over my chest and new goose bumps broke out all over me as I squeezed my nipples. A short while later the two guys helped me to my feet and we all stood in a circle.

"Hot guy you are," one of them said to me and squeezed one of my nipples as I packed my cock and balls into my briefs.

"Let's all take a swim and then come back for some more," the other guy said.

"You two go ahead," I said. "I'll wait here for you two to get back…"

"Come on Dude, a swim will invigorate you and do you good," the first guy said.

Before I realized what he was about to do he scooped me up off the sand and slung me across his broad shoulders.

"UFFFFFF…strong fucker you are…" I said. "Okay, a swim it is then…"

He lugged me to the ocean followed by his friend and when we were out in pretty deep water he dropped me. I landed in the water with a big splash. He swam under me and came up with me sitting atop his shoulders.

"WHOA!!!" I cried out with a big smile on my face, quickly balancing myself as he lifted me high above the water.

We rough-housed for a while in the water and they took turns hoisting me and throwing me into the water. At one point they held me afloat by my arms and sucked on my salt water tasting nipples. When we had swam enough they carried me across their shoulders back to our spot on the beach. For the next couple of hours I lay there as they sucked my cock, my nipples, and feasted on every part of me again and again. I sucked them off again and by the time we were all spent it was nearly morning. I fell asleep on the sand as they walked off without a word…

When I woke up the sun was just coming up. I stood on the sand and scanned the area for my two nameless sex buddies. They were nowhere in sight… As my cock churned in my briefs I got dressed and slowly walked up to the boardwalk and to my car. I never saw them again but I will never forget that night on the beach…

(8)

Tickled Yuppie

(From the book: *Don't!! Stop!! That Tickles!*)

     This story, "Tickled Yuppie" was the first piece that I ever submitted for publication many years ago. (The late 1980's to be exact.) The first magazine that I sent it to was a bondage and foot fetish oriented publication. I never did hear from that particular magazine, but the story did find a home in the "Tickle Wagers" section of a hot website called "RopeJock.com." Peter Berg was an acquaintance of mine who, back in the late 1980's and early 1990's worked at the now defunct men's store, NBO (National Brands Outlet.) Because of his job as a salesman Peter always looked regal and sharp in his suits and ties. He had a smile that was beguiling and a laugh that could cut right through a person. It was those things combined, Peter's regal and sharp way of dressing, his exquisite smile and his infectious laugh that caused me to choose him to be the model and tickle victim for my story "Tickled Yuppie." I have not seen or heard from Peter at this point for many years, but I still thank him for being the perfect "tickled yuppie." Now, after all these years I have decided to give this story a re-write, some revisions, and to dedicate it to two special men in my (internet) life. The first is my good buddy, Timy, a definite tickle fetishist and superb role player and writer when it comes to this genre. Timy, I thank you for inspiration and friendship. You are a true (tickle) buddy. (Thanks to RopeJock.com I met Timy.) The second internet buddy this story is dedicated to is Vince. Vince, like Timy you are a superb inspiration to me and a wonderful role player for this erotic genre... (Because of Timy I know Will.)

I have my moments of exhaustion... doesn't everyone? I tried staying up late at night to write this one. It was before I had a computer so it was mostly done on my sister's typewriter when I could get to my parents' house and then in long hand while I was at home in the apartment that I was sharing with my friend Joe at the time. On some nights Joe would go to sleep and I would stay up writing into the wee hours. Sometimes a story will do that to me when I am writing it...just totally draw me in and rob me of sleep time.

When I see the story finally coming to an end I make sure to get enough sleep so that next time I work on it I can be totally focused and coherent. Like a lot of my other stories this one has a warped ending.

When I first wrote "Tickled Yuppie" I never thought that I would in time write so many other tickle stories. It was because of the website "Ropejock.com" that really seemed to push me in that direction though. Plus I do love seeing guys tied up in their dress socks so tickling them is a sort of bonus I would think.

Also because of "Ropejock.com" and this story appearing on that site it helped to form the friendship I now share with the real life person that is Timmy Backman, from a lot of my tickle stories. After he read "Tickled Yuppie" on "Ropejock.com" Timmy used the info on me on the website to e-mail me. From there we formed a great friendship and went on to co-write a lot of tickle tales together. So, from the look of things my first attempt at a tickle story really did bring me some very good luck in a way.

My name is Peter, Peter Berg to be exact. Christopher is one of my closest friends. He's also one of my kinkiest friends in the world. We've known each other for a lot of years but recently we got to know each other a little better. We're both twenty-six years old. I have light brown hair, brown eyes, and a pretty muscular body from working out regularly at the gym. I'm five feet ten inches tall. Christopher is slightly shorter than me. He has dark brown hair and brown sad looking eyes. His body is pretty lean from all the hours he spends on the exercise bike he owns. When Christopher called me at my office during the day and invited me over (after work) for some T.T. I had no idea what he was talking about; he would not even tell me what T.T. stood for. But because I was extremely curious I decided to accept the invitation. I arrived at Christopher's apartment wearing a Burberry navy blue business suit, a white shirt, a yellow silk paisley tie, and black wingtip shoes. Christopher greeted me at the door. He was wearing a pair of black shorts, a white tee shirt, and sneakers with no socks. He ushered me into the apartment and we sat down on the living room couch. Christopher handed me a cold beer and popped one open for himself also. We both took a long swallow of our beers and then I placed my beer can on the coffee table, removed my suit jacket, loosened my tie, and leaned back on the couch. I crossed one leg on my knee and looked at Christopher.

"Okay Friend," I began with a grin on my face. "You invited me over here for some T.T. and wouldn't tell me on the phone what T.T. is. Now, tell me, what is T.T.?"

Christopher smiled and put his beer can on the coffee table next to mine. He placed a hand on my ankle and moved his hand under my pants leg, toying with my sock. He looked into my eyes and said "tickle torture."

My eyes lit up and I laughed.

"Tickle torture?" I asked him. "You're going to tickle torture me?"

"Or maybe you'll tickle torture me," Christopher replied.

My curiosity was more than piqued.

"Okay, I'm game, but how do we decide who gets tickle tortured?" I asked Christopher anxiously.

Christopher moved his hand over my wingtip and toyed with the laces, tugging on them. He thought for a moment and then said, "We'll make it a game. The loser of the game gets tied up and tickled." Now it was my turn to think it over. Tied up??? I had never been tied up in my whole life and didn't plan to start now. I mean, even when I was a kid and my friends and I played cops and robbers I was always the cop. I never got tied up. But still, there was the possibility that I would win the game and get to tie up Christopher. Now that sounded like fun. I finally agreed and asked what kind of a game we would play to decide who would get tied up and tickle tortured. At that, Christopher took his hand off my wingtip (reluctantly it seemed), reached under the couch, and produced a deck of playing cards. He shuffled them a few times and placed them on the coffee table facedown.

"Okay," Christopher said as he was about to explain. "We each take one card out of the deck. The guy with the lower value card gets tickle tortured."

"That's the game?" I asked in shock.

"Yup Yuppie, nice and easy, and quick huh?" Christopher teased, tugging on my tie. "I can't wait to get started tickle torturing you Friend."

I put my foot down on the floor, and feeling pretty confident reached into the deck of cards and pulled out a card. Christopher did the same thing. We looked at our cards and then looked at each other expectantly.

"Let's do it together," Christopher instructed.

I nodded in agreement and we placed our cards on the coffee table face up. Christopher's card was an ace of hearts. My card was a king of diamonds.

"Wow," I said dejectedly. "For a whole second there I thought I would have won with that king."

"Nope, looks to me like you lose," Christopher said and grabbed my necktie and pulled me close to him. "Let's get started. I have everything ready in the bedroom."

I gulped as Christopher lifted my feet into his lap, untied my wingtips, and I didn't do anything as he yanked them off my feet. My heart pounded as

Christopher squeezed my socked feet a few times. At that moment I sadly realized what I had gotten myself into, I also thought about how very ticklish I really was, but shit, there was no turning back now. I had agreed to the rules of the game after all. Christopher and I stood up, facing each other. Christopher undid my necktie and unbuttoned my shirt. I stood there totally docile. In what seemed like seconds I was bare chested. I breathed heavily as Christopher squeezed one of my nipples.

"Been spending a lot of time at the gym eh?" Christopher asked me, my nipple pinched between his thumb and first two fingers as he looked at my big muscular chest.

"Yeah, I guess," I replied breathlessly as Christopher twisted my nipple a bit.

"Looks good," my buddy said and took his fingers off my nipple and proceeded to squeeze one of my bowling ball-sized biceps. "Now for your pants…"

I watched as Christopher undid my belt and unlatched my suit pants. They fell down around my ankles. As I grudgingly stepped out of my pants Christopher picked up my necktie.

"You have to be blindfolded," Christopher told me. "I didn't mention it earlier but it is part of the rules."

"I'll bet that if I had won you wouldn't have told me that," I said with a grin.

I stood still as Christopher stepped behind me and tied my tie over my eyes. That done, he held me by one arm and guided me slowly to the bedroom, noticing that my manhood was hard as a rock in my Botany 500 white briefs.

"Looks to me like you're enjoying this," Christopher said.

We got to the bedroom and Christopher stretched me out on the bed on my back in a spread eagle position. I felt the first rope being wound around my wrist and then tied to the headboard. My heart pounded like crazy in my chest.

"I want a chance to get even later on," I said.

As Christopher tied my other wrist he laughed at me and said, "With your luck you'll probably lose the game again and wind up getting doubly tickle tortured tonight."

"Maybe not…" I replied as I felt a rope being wound tightly around one of my socked feet.

"Do you really want to take the chance?" Christopher asked me as he ran a finger over the bottom of my now bound foot.

My leg jerked a bit and I chuckled.

"I'll decide for sure after you've had your fun," I replied.

Christopher grabbed my other socked foot and tied it to the bedpost on that side of the bed. I was now trapped, wearing only my white briefs and black socks. Christopher began running a finger over my nipples, my hips, and stomach areas. I chuckled softly at first and laughed harder as Christopher increased the tempo and the speed of his finger as it trailed over my nakedness.

"Having fun?" Christopher asked me. "It sure sounds like you are…"

"Go ahead," I laughed. "Ha, ha, ha, ha, my turn comes later…"

"Maybe," Christopher said as he began running his fingers over my crotch and thighs.

I whooped out my laughter and struggled furiously against the ropes as I laughed harder and harder.

"Glad you accepted my invitation Peter?" Christopher asked me mockingly.

I was unable to reply because by now I was laughing hysterically as Christopher tickled the bottom of one of my feet.

"This is nothing yet Friend," Christopher laughed. "Wait till I get the feather duster."

"Y-you wouldn't, ha, ha, ha, ha, ha, ha, ha, y-you wouldn't…" I said hysterically.

"Oh yes I would," Christopher answered. "Then I'm going to take your socks off your feet and run a dry toothbrush over them…"

I sputtered and saliva dripped from my lips as Christopher went to work tickling my other foot.

"We've only begun Peter," Christopher said. "Wait'll I flip you over onto your stomach. We're going to find out just how ticklish your ass cheeks are."

I could only laugh and listen as Christopher told me his fiendish plans for me.

Fifteen minutes later Christopher stopped tickling me. He told me that I could have a five minute break to catch my breath. He took the blindfold off me and sat down on the bed next to me. I was already drenched in sweat as I smiled up at my friend.

"I hope you're enjoying torturing me, because pretty soon you'll be the one tied to this damned bed," I said and tugged on the ropes.

"You keep saying that, but remember the rules my friend…" Christopher replied and squeezed one of my nipples hard, getting a good loud gasp out of me. "If you draw a losing card you'll wind up back where you started."

I licked my lips and asked for a drink. Christopher went to the living room an came back with one of the beers. He put it to my mouth and I drank.

"Thank you," I said.

I watched as Christopher put the beer down on a night table and then he reached under the bed and produced a large feather duster.

"Oh shit," I murmured.

Christopher checked his watch and told me that my five minutes were up. He blindfolded me again and began by tickling my chest with the feather duster. I let out a few sneezes in between hysterical bouts of laugher. A few minutes later my so called buddy ripped my briefs off me. My hard-on pointed at the ceiling.

"What a boner!" Christopher said jovially.

Before I could reply or even object to the fact that he had ripped my briefs off me Christopher was running the feather duster over my cock and balls and I was laughing and sweating profusely.

"Pl-please stop," I begged, laughing at the same time.

"No way," Christopher said. "The game must continue."

Christopher grew bored of the feather duster and tossed it on the floor. He then sat down on my huge muscular chest, straddling me.

"What now?" I asked him.

"Armpits," Christopher replied with a grin.

"OH NO!!" I yelled.

Without the slightest hesitation Christopher placed each of his hands under one of my hairy armpits and with his fingertips tickled them furiously. I squealed with sudden uncontrollable laughter.

"I-I can't take it!!" I screamed. "PLEASE STOP, ha, ha, ha, ha, ha, ha, ha, ha, ha, ha!!!"

But Christopher ignored me and kept on tickling and tickling me. I felt Christopher's hard-on against my chest. I knew then just where this was going to lead and why Christopher had really wanted me there that night. My thoughts were cut off however as another burst of hysterical laughter escaped me.

"Please stop tickling my pits!!" I begged.

"You should try to enjoy this Peter, because the time is coming close when I'm going to take your socks off you and tickle your bare feet with a toothbrush," Christopher said. "It's going to be much worse than having your armpits tickled."

Finally, Christopher did stop tickling my armpits. He climbed off the bed and picked up the feather duster again. He ran the duster over my thighs. I squirmed on the bed and laughed hard and loud.

"What'll you do to make me stop Peter?" Christopher inquired.

So that was it. I had known it as soon as I felt Christopher's hard-on. I answered Christopher's question with another question... "What would you want me to do?"

Suddenly, Christopher stopped tickling my thighs and leaned over my face. He lowered my blindfold.

"Let's start with a kiss," Christopher demanded, making suggestive movements with his lips and tongue.

I pulled my face away.

"Are you nuts?" I yelled. "I'm not queer!"

"Who said anything about being queer?" Christopher asked.

"I won't kiss you!" I shouted.

Christopher shrugged and picked up the feather duster.

"Oh well, looks like I'll just have to tickle you some more," he said as he blindfolded me again.

"Alright, alright!!" I said, not believing what I said next. "I'll fucking kiss you."

I could actually feel Christopher smiling. He leaned down and pressed his mouth against mine. To his surprise I responded by shoving my tongue forcefully and deep into Christopher's mouth. He put one hand behind my neck and squeezed gently as we kissed. Pre cum was oozing from my piss hole. When the kiss was done Christopher stood up and resumed tickling my thighs with the feather duster.

"HEY!!!" I yelped. "You promised you would stop tickling me if I kissed you!!"

"I never promised anything Peter," Christopher responded. "Besides, it'll take more than a kiss to make me stop tickling you."

Once again I was trapped in a hysterical bout of laughter.

Christopher finally stopped tickling my thighs about fifteen minutes later. By now I was breathless, sweaty, and thirsty.

"Let's take another break," Christopher said.

Once again he lowered my blindfold and gave me a few sips of beer.

"Having fun?" Christopher asked me.

"Tons of it," I responded sarcastically. "How much longer are you going to tickle me for?"

Christopher told me that we had a way to go yet. Then he smiled down at me and told me that another kiss might, just might, take ten minutes off my tickle torture time. Without any hesitation, I said, "Okay, kiss me," and opened my mouth. Christopher leaned down and we kissed long and hard again, our tongues exploring and probing in each other's mouth. When the kiss ended we looked at each other passionately and Christopher gently squeezed one of my nipples.

"What happens next?" I asked him.

Christopher regained his composure and walked to the foot of the bed. I watched as he untied my feet and slowly peeled my black dress socks off me, tossing them on the floor.

"Oh no," I whispered.

"Oh yes," Christopher said as he retied my feet to the posts of the bed.

I saw Christopher take a toothbrush out from under the bed and then he blindfolded me again. Christopher knelt at the foot of the bed and began running the toothbrush bristles over the bottom of my right foot.

"OH GOD, ha, ha, ha, ha, ha, ha, ha, please stop!!" I shrieked.

Christopher alternated from one of my feet to the other with the toothbrush. I jerked spasmodically on the bed, howling with laughter.

"What will you do to make me stop this time?" Christopher asked.

"Wh-what do you want me to do, kiss you again?" I asked in return.

The tickling intensified and so did my laughter.

"It's going to take more than a kiss to stop me this time Peter," Christopher said and tickled me some more.

"HA HA HA HA HA HA HA HA OHHHH GOD, tell me what you fucking want!!" I begged.

I knew at that moment that Christopher felt triumphant.

"Suck my cock," Christopher announced.

Christopher stopped tickling me, I stopped laughing, and the room was eerily silent all of a sudden.

Moments later, Christopher was sitting in a chair, naked. I was kneeling before him, sucking and slurping on his huge cock. I was untied and my blindfold was hanging loosely around my neck.

"Oh yeah, that feels so fucking good," Christopher panted as he caressed the back of my neck.

I sucked, kissed, and licked Christopher's cock and balls.

"Looks to me like you're enjoying all of this Peter," Christopher teased me.

I stopped and looked up at my friend.

"It's better than being tickle tortured," I said.

Christopher grabbed his cock and pushed it back into my mouth. I quickly resumed sucking him.

"You still have some tickling to endure my friend," he said. "Remember, I still haven't worked on your ass yet. The game isn't over yet."

Then, Christopher pulled his cock out of my mouth and shot his load, squirting his juices all over my chest. The cum was hot and it dripped slowly toward my stomach area and my pubic bush.

"What a hefty load!!" I remarked.

"Yeah," Christopher agreed, panting as he spoke. "Later on we'll see how much you shoot. Now, back to the game!"

In moments I was tied to the bed again, on my stomach this time, and blindfolded.

"Welcome to the end of the game Friend," Christopher said. "The tickling of your ass!"

"Please take it easy," I said.

Using the feather duster Christopher began tickling my ass cheeks. Once again I began howling and squealing with laughter. Christopher laughed as my sexy ass bounced up and down on the bed. He laughed even harder when I farted.

"Please stop!" I yelled. "Let's end the game now!!"

"Only when you tell me what you'll do to make me stop," Christopher replied.

I now knew what Christopher wanted. I told him to stop tickling me and to go ahead and make me cum.

"I thought you'd never ask," Christopher said.

He tickled my ass cheeks a little more and then it happened. He tossed the feather duster aside and reached under my crotch, pulling my cock and balls out from under me.

"AAARRR!!!" I yelled as Christopher lay down between my legs and took my hardness in his mouth.

He sucked my cock furiously and then I shot my load, squirting it all over the bed sheets.

"Congratulations Peter, you've survived the T.T. game," Christopher announced.

Sure, but I still wanted my chance to get even. After all, it wasn't everyday that I allowed someone to do this to me. Christopher untied me and took the blindfold off me. Later, we were both dressed and sitting in the living room drinking another beer each.

"That was some game," Peter said. "But how about my chance to get even?"

"Are you sure you want to take that chance Friend?" Christopher asked me warningly. "After all, you do know the rules."

A look of smug confidence came over my face.

"Shuffle the cards…Friend," I said.

Christopher did. We each drew a card. Christopher drew a three of hearts and I drew a two of clubs.

"Shit, shit, *shit…*" I whimpered as Christopher jumped to his feet and danced around the room, laughing mockingly.

"I cannot believe it!!" Christopher taunted me. "I cannot fucking believe your bad luck!!"

"Neither can I…" I muttered woefully.

"C'mon Peter, strip for me again, strip down to your socks and let's get started tickling you again," Christopher spouted joyfully.

Moments later I was stripped and blindfolded as Christopher led me back to the bedroom.

"Looks like it's going to be a long night…" Christopher said as he held my arm tight.

(9)

Timmy Backman meets Christopher Trevor and Vince (maybe)

(From the book: *Timmy and the Evil Dr. Von Vellicator*)

This is far from the oldest Ticklish Timmy Backman story written. Timmy appeared in a lot of my books from the beginning, the fourth book to be exact. I had even included some stories starring Timmy Backman in my fourth book before the book that introduced Timmy (Timmy's Ticklish Trials) was published. When I finally did have my book "Timmy's Ticklish Trials" published it was then that I thought about how the handsome ticklish character would make a great model for future tickle tales, sort of like the one I have included herein.

Even though this story is totally fiction it is written in the sense that Timmy Backman finally meets the author (Christopher Trevor, me) who has been writing all these tickle stories and submits to the man who has made Timmy his tickle muse in a way.

Besides being a total tickle submissive Timmy Backman is also very ambitious when it comes to business. Valerie Levi, a seductress from some of the earlier Timmy stories calls him her financial wizard. It's why he lives in his suits, shirts and ties, wingtip shoes and tall dark colored dress socks. But it's that ambition that also tends to get Timmy into tickle trouble, as is what happens in this story, predictably. But it's how Timmy gets himself into tickle trouble that is always so titillating. The guy is handsome and gullible, a very erotic combination when you stop and really think about it.

Timmy's beautiful wife Stephanie makes an appearance in this story as Timmy recalls his conversations with her before leaving for his trip to meet Christopher and Vince in a hotel in New York City. Somehow I and my readers and even the real life Timmy suspect that Stephanie knows about her husband's submissive side when it comes to being bound and tickle tortured. This shows in the scene where he calls the business he has to attend to "very ticklish." Yet Stephanie does not seem to mind her handsome husband being playfully captured and tickle tortured. So I think that if Timmy was not ambitious in business (he is a banker after all) he would be a gross monstrosity. Timmy's ambition and his tickle submissiveness just seem to feel natural and the two parts of the man work well together somehow.

This story also shows how even though Timmy is very ambitious and slick when it comes to business, how when it comes to his nature as a tickle submissive he can sometimes make really bad decisions. I think the scene in the middle of the story that takes place at the airport and the scene at the end of the story when Timmy goes to check out "the new Ronald's" bookstore give this statement credence.

When it comes to style I think Timmy has it nailed down. He is a sharp dresser that is for sure. But the image and the look that most readers of the Timmy Backman stories associate with him is him in just his white kangaroo pouch style under shorts and what Timmy himself calls his trademark Christopher Trevor black dress socks.

In my opinion even though Timmy's style is pretty conservative and usual the fact that he is such a tickle submissive gives that style new meaning. And I think it really shows in this story. Timmy's famous kangaroo pouch style under shorts and his dark colored dress socks are featured throughout the tale.

In a nutshell what caused this particular story to be born was the ongoing desire for Christopher Trevor and the real life Timmy Backman to someday really meet in person. Bringing my buddy Tickle Master Vince into the story made sense as he lives close by me in New Jersey and on the internet I brought him and Timmy together for some online tickle fun.

What would a collection of stories by Christopher Trevor be without a Timmy Backman tale thrown in?

"OHHHHHHH!!! OHHH YEAH, oh my word, oh my!" Timmy Backman bellowed in blindfolded darkness as he shot his load of Southern spunk, unswervingly and directly down Christopher Trevor's throat as he sweated and gyrated on the tabletop.

Timmy Backman, tickle hero, tickle star and constant unwitting tickle victim lay atop a cushioned massage table, stretched out on his ripped and muscular back, clad in nothing more than his trademark white kangaroo pouch boxer briefs and Christopher Trevor's trademark black nylon ribbed dress socks. For this special occasion however Christopher Trevor had opted for his tickle star to wear black sheer thick and thin calf length ribbed silk socks, what are also sometimes referred to as tuxedo socks or a guy's wedding socks. (The style of thick and thin silk socks is usually that the toe and heel sections are solid black nylon while the center of them are thinly sheer, sometimes ribbed, ribbed being all the more sexier.) The author claimed they were much more festive looking for the event...the event being that upon the release of the book "Timmy's Ticklish Trials", the author, Christopher Trevor himself, the CO-author and star, Timmy Backman in the flesh (and in the black socks of course) and Tickle Master Vince, a guy who if anyone *did* brought Ronald Greene (Timmy Backman's tickle captor and tormentor) from the book to life, should all meet, in person, finally. And meet they would in a hotel room in New York City to celebrate the release of this fateful tome that had brought three very much likeminded guys together. But Timmy had to wonder when Vince would be arriving, seeing as he and Christopher had been in the room for some time now that morning to afternoon since he had checked into the hotel...and the author had been killing time milking his star repeatedly...every half hour to forty five minutes to be exact. Not that Timmy was complaining, it felt great to be treated this way, even if he had to be tied up and blindfolded for it...even if Christopher tormented him a bit by putting tit clamps on his fleshy nipples for fifteen minute intervals, just to get Timmy real stacked up in the department of his manhood. But he also wanted very much to meet Vince in the flesh. After all he and the handsome muscular black guy had had many stimulating and ticklish IM conversations over time on the internet... HARDY har and har Timmy thought as Chris took the blindfold off him again. The way Vince had tormented him erotically on line made the tied up, tied down Timmy wonder just what the handsome African American master tickler would heap on him in person...*when* he arrived that is... Timmy recalled the tickle promises that Vince had made where he was concerned. Timmy's cock churned in his kangaroo pouch underpants as he thought of Vince's promise to kidnap him away from his family for some tickle time torments. He recalled Vince's dark proposition to tickle him crazy and then tickle him some more, once he had the handsome Southern laddy in his clutches that is. Timmy remembered the internet games that Vince had made him play, the consequences being that if Timmy won he would not be tickled...but if he lost, well, he didn't need three guesses to know how quickly he would be tied up and tickled, hardy har and har again the handsome Southern guy thought. Even while miles away from Vince when they would chat on their computers Timmy felt a certain submissiveness where this man was concerned. If Vince told Timmy not to touch his cock while he teased him in IM fashion Timmy found himself obeying perfunctorily. Being tied up there wasn't much poor Timmy would be able to do to stop the muscular African American guy from doing to him...tickle wise that is... and inwardly the handsome Southern gentleman had to wonder if he really would want to stop Vince. Oh decisions, decisions, Timmy had to chuckle to himself.

Vince, also known to submissive and ticklish Timmy as "Tickle Master Vince…" The tickle master who had, on numerous occasions challenged the ticklish laddy to numerous computer games…just to be inside Timmy's head and to see how the ticklish boy would react under pressure…

Christopher had met the handsome African American tickle master in person and had seen him at his tickling best with another buddy. The author knew that Vince would come to the hotel with all his equipment, his bag of bondage tricks as he called it. If poor Timmy thought he was tied up now he would not believe the positions and bondage he would suffer/enjoy when Vince arrived. But for the moment the author had his handsome tickle star all to himself, and he planned to simply feast on and enjoy him…he had waited long enough for this after all…

"Wow, how many times does that make now?" Timmy asked his captor as he lay with his shoulders hunched up off the table, watching as the author made his way to the end of the table, directly to his tied up black socked feet.

"I've lost count," Christopher said as he leaned down over one of Timmy's black socked and tied feet and slurped and licked at his solid silk covered toes.

Timmy wiggled his toes in ecstasy and chills engulfed him as his author buddy played suck and slurp with his feet…the part of his body that he seemed to treasure the most. Christopher held Timmy's foot by the sole with two hands as his head bobbed up and down as he serviced it. He also pressed his thumbs in a massage-like fashion into the balls of Timmy's black socked tootsies, sending definite feelings of ecstasy through his very special buddy. Timmy knew that Christopher Trevor adored his feet…the author also adored his big cock, seeing as he had once more left the beefy root dangling temptingly and invitingly out of the fly opening of Timmy's white kangaroo pouch style boxer briefs… And being that as it was the tied up handsome Southern gentleman knew it would not be long before Christopher was once more sucking him off…either that or Vince would arrive and the laughter would begin…his own Timmy thought woefully and hopefully at the same time… Timmy was never able to decide just how much he really hated/loved/loved/hated/hated/hated/loved/loved being tied up and tickled. His cock hung slightly erect, very slimy looking and stained with saliva and cum from his boxer briefs and Timmy, now with his eyes uncovered glanced over at the end table where the small pill bottle that contained the Viagra tablets and the pitcher of water and water glass were set. As his feet were serviced most lovingly Timmy laid his head back on the table and sighed contentedly.

"Dang it all, Viagra," he said to himself and chuckled. "Looks like this guy plans to make a meal or two out of my spunk…"

Christopher's mouth opened wider and he engulfed all five of Timmy's socked toes into his mouth. He sucked heartily and Timmy swooned atop the table, his tied up hands balled into fists behind his back. Chills traveled up the laddy's spine, up his calves and legs, into his thighs and into his pulsing and over-used cock. Christopher dribbled oodles of saliva onto Timmy's socked toes and sucked it up heartily, sending hyper-chills through the tied up guy. His muscular back arched and he crooned "Oh my word…" in his Southern sounding accent. Once more Timmy's root began to harden to full mast. He smiled thinly and wondered when Chris would clamp his man sized tits again…

"Oh my, oh my fucks," Timmy groaned.

The feeling in his spent cock was astronomical and he could not believe that he wanted/needed to cum yet again.

While he had been packing for his trip to New York City Timmy Backman somehow figured he would wind up in the weave of some tightly knotted ropes and a blindfold…not to mention on the ticklish end of a feather or some other infernal ticklish equipment that he was sure Vince would bring to torment him with. Timmy could not deny the churning in his cock and balls as he thought of his buddy Christopher and him finally meeting. He knew that the author would find some way to get him into a bondage and black sock situation. He smiled through pursed lips as he packed extra black socks in his luggage as he thought this. And sure enough, now, his hands *were* securely roped behind him at the wrists in a crisscross type of fashion, allowing the guy a tad of movement back there as he writhed and squirmed atop the table. His black socked feet were roped tight with mounds of white rope adorning his ankles, his muscular and sexy legs spread wide and his ankles tied off to the legs under the table. Timmy the ticklish laddy, as he was sometimes called found himself in a most vulnerable and sexy position…while in the clutches of his author buddy… He was a straight guy, a straight guy who loved and adored his beautiful wife, but there was no denying the effect that his author buddy, Christopher Trevor could have on him. Timmy knew in his heart that the author was crazy about him and being that as it was, he knew that Christopher would drink from him till his balls were drained…and then some.

When he was done packing Timmy slammed his luggage shut, just as his sexy wife Stephanie came into their bedroom. He breathed a quick sigh of relief. He was sure she would have questioned him on all the new pairs of black socks he had packed along with his other belongings. Most of the black socks were gifts for Christopher, but he knew also that he would more than likely be made to wear a pair of them or two…it was the author's most intense fetish after all. Throughout the tickle novel they had written, "Timmy's Ticklish Trials" Christopher had had Timmy's feet clothed in black socks more often than not. Granted Timmy did get his inner wish to be bare foot tickled at intervals in the story, but eventually the guy always wound up with his black office socks back on his big sexy feet. The sight of her handsome husband dressed in a suit and tie and wingtip shoes always sent the beautiful Stephanie over the edge. Ever since her girlfriend Valerie had introduced her to the finer, more erotic sexual practices she loved the thought of her executive husband stripped to his socks and briefs and at her mercy… It was amazing to her what a submissive nature her handsome and muscular husband had when it came to their sex lives. It also drove her wild how her husband always plumped up nice and big in his underpants for her whenever she decided to play her kinky games. The "Spinning Chinaman" device down in their living room had taken the poor Timmy on many a spinning journey while he was clad in just his socks and underpants, sometimes just his socks so that Stephanie could have some mean cock teasing fun with her darling hubby…and Stephanie planned to subject her hubby to still more…as soon as he returned from this impromptu business trip that he had to go on in New York City. It had come up all of a sudden and Timmy explained that there was just no getting out of it for him… Stephanie sidled up behind her husband in his Brooks Brothers navy blue suit and encircled her arms around him, pulling him close to her, pressing his shapely buttocks that she adored against the part of her that he adored. She swooned as she thought of the night before and how he had made the letters of the alphabet in her pussy as he ate her relentlessly…and right after that, *and right after* she had cum numerous times he told her about the business trip he had to attend to in the heart of the big apple.

As she held tight to him he turned around in her embrace and smiled the smile that always melted her heart…and hardened her tits…and made her pussy moist…

"So you're sure you're only going to be gone three days?" she asked him, straightening his tie for him as he held her tight.

"From what I know, yes," he replied, his hardness pressing against her through his suit trousers. "Like I told you Stephanie, *I have to go*…it really is a ticklish business thing that I have to take care of…"

She giggled like a schoolgirl, knowing how her handsome hubby hated yet loved being tickle tortured…

"Funny how you always use that word when it comes to these annoying little things that can crop up in one's life, ticklish that is," Stephanie cooed and tugged at Timmy's tie.

Now, as he lay tied atop a massage table in a hotel room in the heart of Times Square, Timmy recalled the way Stephanie had looked at him when he was done packing. He wondered what she would think now if she saw her handsome spouse and what kind of predicament he was currently in…

Blindfolded again Timmy sipped water from the glass to wash down yet another Viagra tablet that Christopher Trevor had placed on his tongue…after he had serviced Timmy's black socked feet for more than the usual fifteen minutes that time…

"OHHHHRRRR SHIT," Timmy bantered in the once more blindfolded darkness as he felt the tit clamps snapped onto the very tips of his hyper-sensitive man sized nipples. "Dang but that smarts Christopher…"

"Sure as hell Timmy my laddy," Christopher teased his CO-author and constant tickle victim, giving his dangling root a squeeze as it again hardened and reddened between his splayed legs. "But it also gets your core here nice and stiff. Admit it Timmy, you have real sensitive nipples for a guy…"

"Oh yeah, oh my, I do at that, I have real sensitive nipples for a guy," Timmy repeated nearly verbatim, the sound of his Southern accent driving his captor crazy with lust.

Being blindfolded Timmy could not see how Christopher Trevor was salivating just at the thought of once more drinking from the tied up guy's font. The author held Timmy's cock with one hand and then reached into the guy's kangaroo style boxer briefs and ceremoniously brought out his very plump kiwi-sized testicles. The tied down guy gasped breathlessly as his testicles were handled. Timmy's balls were all sweaty and musty scented. When he felt Christopher's tongue begin polishing them he swooned and tears of ecstasy soaked his blindfold...

He was enjoying himself so much...but he knew that all this sucking of his cock, the scoffing down that Christopher was doing with his seed, the servicing of his black socked feet and now the polishing of his balls would come to an end...and he would be tickle tortured. And he also knew that because he had shot his load a few times already how he would be ultra-ticklish when the time came. For whatever the fuck the reason Timmy always became more tickle sensitive after he had shot a load or two...or three...

"OHHHHH, or four..." he whispered as his author buddy once more slurped him into his mouth and started sucking. "OHHHHH my word..."

Timmy's clamped nipples tingled as Christopher Trevor worked him once more by the root...

"Ohhhhhh dang, what a way to go, what a way to be done," Timmy swooned and licked his lips.

When Timmy Backman had arrived at the airport in Atlanta Georgia he did not expect any tribulations or untoward occurrences to happen that might delay him or cause him to miss his flight. As usual the very organized, very structured executive had planned this trip like any other business trip...except that this was a tickle book related business trip, something that his buds at the bank he worked at just would not be able to relate to...but then again, one never knew Timmy surmised gleefully. As he climbed out of the cab he paid the driver and an airport bellman quickly tended to Timmy's one piece of luggage. He tipped the cab driver and the airport bellman, thanked them and as his luggage was moved onto the conveyer belt to be brought to the plane that would carry him to New York City our unwitting tickle hero entered the airport...

Looking at his watch Timmy saw that he still had an hour and a half before his flight took off. Since all the new security measures had been put into place at airports Timmy, like most other travelers knew that it was best to be at the airport at least an hour and a half to two hours before takeoff time. He sauntered through the airport with a slight bounce in his step, his cock at half-mast in his kangaroo pouch style under shorts that he was wearing under his suit pants. Timmy purchased a paperback book and a box of mints at an airport newsstand and figured at that point he would go through the security check and sit and relax in the plane's waiting area for his flight to be announced. Holding his paperback book and slipping his box of mints into his suit jacket pocket he approached the security checkpoint. He was the third in a short line of a couple of other business suited guys. Like the other two men before him Tim reached down to unlace and slip his wingtips off his feet. It had become standard airport procedure since September 11th, 2001.

"Damn, I hate taking my shoes off in public," the burly suited guy ahead of Timmy said as he turned and looked at Christopher Trevor's buddy.

"Yeah, I know what you mean," Timmy agreed, standing up straight, his shoes held in one hand and his paperback book in the other.

"It's always just my luck that I have an embarrassing hole in one of my socks or that my feet are all sweaty and everyone gets a whiff of it as I check through the scan point," the guy said to Timmy. "My name's Ronald by the way…"

A chill went up Timmy's spine as he said, "Nice to meet you Ronald, I'm Tim, Tim Backman," recalling another person he knew by the name of Ronald. He wondered if this was some kind of ominous omen where this trip was concerned. Ronald was the villain after all in the book he was headed to New York to celebrate the release of…the villain who had so brazenly kidnapped him in the story…

"Everything okay there Tim?" Ronald asked Timmy. "You look like you've just seen a ghost or something."

"Uh, yeah, sure, everything is great," Timmy replied and wiggled his toes in his navy blue nylon dress socks.

As he glanced down at Ronald's brown socked feet he said, "Well, no holes in your socks this time" and smiled at the football player shaped guy.

"Nope, and no stink either," Ronald chuckled.

"NEXT!!" came the sound of a demanding female voice, startling the two men out of their reverie.

"Whoops, looks like that's me Timmy buddy," Ronald said and dashed through the metal detector.

As Ronald was checked through and scanned by two very sexy, very curvy looking female security guards Timmy found himself sweating nervously. Ronald? A guy named Ronald? I've met a guy named Ronald at the airport Timmy asked himself incredulously. He tucked his paperback under his arm and loosened his tie a bit, wiggling his toes under his socks at the same time, his cock throbbing in his suit pants.

"NEXT!!" the blond curvy female security guard bellowed.

"Oh yes, oh, that uh, that would be me," Timmy gasped and walked through the metal detector after placing his book and shoes in the plastic basin provided by the airport.

The walk-through metal detector beeped slightly and the two women gestured for Timmy to approach them. Ronald was getting his shoes back on as the two female guards scanned Timmy with their rectangular shaped metal detectors. The first one, a tall curvy blond girl fitted into her security uniform like a glove, her short skirt, stockings and low heeled shoes driving the laddy into a frenzy. The second female guard was a redhead with beautiful green eyes and a body like a dancer. She too filled out her uniform most sexily. As he was instructed to do Timmy stood with his arms held out in a wing-span fashion as they trailed their scanning wands over him. It tickled slightly when they scanned his ribs and stomach areas and he squirmed on his thin socked feet. When the blonds' scanning wand trailed over his suit jacket pocket it made a loud beeping sound.

"Oh my, that's my fault," Timmy said in his Southern accent, sounding real sexy and macho at the same time. "I totally forgot to take my house and car keys out of my pocket."

As he reached down the redhead said to keep his arms where they were and that they would tend to his keys. Timmy did as he was told and the redhead reached with well-manicured fingernails into his suit jacket pocket, extracting his keys. She dropped them in the plastic bucket along with Timmy's shoes and his paperback book and then resumed scanning him along with her blond partner. Timmy noticed that two other security guards, both of them males had taken over scanning the passengers who had been in line behind him, to keep the crowd moving along he supposed. While he was in the clutches of the two beautiful women Timmy watched as other passengers were checked through with no problem, retrieved their shoes and other belongings and went along their way. His shoes however remained right where they were. Looking around he saw that Ronald was long-gone as well. As the two female security guards again ran their scanning wands over him Timmy squirmed a bit as they once more not on purpose tickled his ribs and stomach areas.

"No beeps that time ladies," Timmy said with a warm smile. "Guess I'm good to go huh?"

"No Sir, I think being that you caused the detectors to go off like that we should do a thorough search," the redhead, the more stern of the two guards said, holding her wand against Timmy's buttocks as she spoke.

"Uh, I'm sorry Miss, a more thorough search?" Timmy asked, slowly lowering his arms.

"Yes, it's all very routine you understand," she said, sounding reasonable yet strict at the same time. "How long till your flight?"

Timmy glanced at his watch and said "An hour and twenty minutes."

"Plenty of time for a thorough search," the blond security guard said and in a sweeping motion yanked Timmy's watch off his wrist and dropped it into the plastic bucket with his other personal effects.

She scanned his now naked wrist...

Then, a few moments later, carrying his shoes, his watch, his keys and his paperback book in the plastic bucket Timmy walked into a private security room with the two female security guards...

"I must say ladies, that was a bit humiliating for me, being brought here amid all the stares from people in the airport," Timmy said, sounding irritated as he set the plastic bucket down on a small table in the gray painted bare walled room.

The redheaded security guard explained that it was procedure when someone set off the metal detectors and that if he wanted he could complain to the airports upper management when they were done with him.

"Now Sir, your name please," the redhead said, picking up a clipboard and pen from the table.

"Tim Backman," Timmy replied, still sounding a bit irritated that this had befallen him, but unable to deny that the two sexy ladies in their security guard skirts and uniforms were making him tent up in his suit pants.

The redhead wrote his name on a blank sheet of paper along with the other information that Timmy recited for her, namely the nature of his trip, how often he flew, where his destination was, etc. As he spoke the blond security guard sidled up next to him and as softly as possible asked him to remove his suit jacket. Timmy complied and she hung his suit jacket on the back of a chair. The redhead put down the clipboard and asked Timmy to once again stand with his arms out in a wing-span position. He did as he was told and the two women trailed their scanning wands over his upper torso. But as they scanned his armpits area and his stomach and ribs he bent over slightly and squirmed, giggling a bit.

"H-hey, hee, hee, hee, easy with those wands ladies, I'm a tad ticklish here," Timmy said, sounding totally gullible.

The two security lovely's looked at each other across Timmy, rolled their eyes in their heads as if to say, "The things we have to put up with" and then the blond asked Timmy to please remove his shirt and tie and his under shirt, if he was wearing one.

"What?" Timmy asked as he lowered his arms, him sounding like he was in a state of disbelief now. "What is this, some kind of strip and tickle search?"

"Sir, Mr. Backman, I assure you, we are not here to tickle you, but yes, it is a sort of strip search," the redhead said and as Timmy reluctantly undid the knot in his tie he watched her pick up his suit jacket from the chair where it hung and she ran her scanning wand over it a few times.

No beeps or buzzes emanated from her wand as she scanned his suit jacket. He noticed how as he unbuttoned his crisp white dress shirt how the blond security guard was staring a bit transfixed-like at him.

"So uh ladies, you two know my name, what all are yours?" Timmy asked, practically blushing now as he handed the blond security guard his shirt and tie.

He stood before the two women now with his muscular bare chest on display, his big man-sized nipples totally erect. They both seemed to take in the sexy way his chest hair trailed down his ribcage and to his stomach region in a straight line.

"I'm Bonnie," the blond replied as she pointed at Timmy's belt. "And my partner here is Jane."

"Hmm, Bonnie and Jane, nice to uh, meet both of you," Timmy prattled on, his hands trembling as he reached to undo his belt.

Bonnie handed Jane Timmy's shirt and tie and like she had done with his suit jacket she scanned the shirt. No beeps or buzzes emanated…

"Say ladies, is this uh, is this really necessary?" Timmy asked as he undid his belt buckle.

"Very necessary Mr. Backman," Jane said, her wand held in her hand as if she were wielding a paddle. "You set off the metal detectors out at security check. What we're doing here is standard procedure. If you would prefer to have two male security guards conduct your strip search that can be arranged."

As she reached for her cell phone Timmy quickly bantered, "No, no, this is fine…" and shucked his suit pants down around his ankles. He stepped out of his pants and handed them to Jane. She held his pants up and when she ran the wand over the back pocket of them the device buzzed loudly.

"And what do we have here Mr. Backman?" Jane asked him as she reached into the back pocket of his suit pants while he stood there now clad in just his white boxer briefs and blue dress socks.

"It uh, it's probably just my wallet," Timmy said nervously. "More than likely my credit cards with the magnetic strips on them are setting off your wand."

Jane extracted Timmy's wallet from his suit pants pocket and looked at him as if he were totally guilty, but of what he was not sure. His cock was by now throbbing in the pouch of his boxer briefs in a mixture of trepidation and arousal as these two sexy women worked him over verbally.

"Why didn't you place your wallet in the plastic bucket at the security checkpoint Mr. Backman?" Jane asked him and dropped the wallet now in the bucket.

"It uh, it slipped my mind Jane, I mean, Miss, it slipped my mind Miss," Timmy bantered nervously. "Oh my word…"

"Please stand with your arms spread out while we do a body hair search," Bonnie said, rubbing her wand over Timmy's lower back as she spoke.

Timmy did as he was told and he knew that once he was standing in a wing-span position again his erection in his underpants would be beyond evident. The two women stood at his sides and when they trailed their wands over his hairy and bushy armpits he exploded into gales of loud laughter.

"WHOOOO, hee, hee, hee, hee, hee, hee, hee!!!" Timmy laughed loudly and instinctually lowered his arms and used his hands to block his ticklish pits. "Oh please, come on now, do you really think I have something tucked in my armpit hair?"

"Mr. Backman, do you find all this to be funny?" Jane asked him, holding up her wand. "Because we're trying to do this as quickly as possible so you can be on your way and we can get back to our posts in the airport."

"No, no Jane, I mean, no Miss, I do not think this is funny, not in the least…" Timmy squawked.

"Bonnie, please use the wire cuff to restrain Mr. Backman's hands behind him so that when we search his other areas he will remain positioned properly?" Jane suggested.

"R-restrain my hands?" Timmy bantered as the blond beauty produced a pair of plastic wire handcuffs from her utility belt. "Is, is that really necessary?"

"Hands behind you please Mr. Backman," Bonnie said and as Timmy did as he was told he saw Jane pulling on a pair of latex tight fitting gloves.

"Oh no, oh my word," Timmy whispered and his asshole seemed to contract.

The two women looked at each other almost fiendishly as Bonnie tied Timmy's hands tightly in the wire cuffs...

"OHHHHHHH..." Timmy moaned a few minutes later as Jane squatted behind him, pulled his underpants down in back and inserted a latex glove covered finger into his rosebud of an asshole. "ULLLPPP"

As Jane probed and dug in his hole Timmy stood facing Bonnie with his hands restrained behind his back. Bonnie had cleavage to die for and then some. As his hole was searched by the uncompromising redheaded Jane he could not take his eyes off Bonnie's chest, her nipples poking seductively against her uniform blouse.

"This is uh, rightly embarrassing I would have to say Miss," Timmy said to Bonnie as he arched his back and nearly hauled himself to his socked tiptoes, his biceps bulging as he tried to maintain his balance. "I mean, having my hole searched in such a fashion, you see what I mean..."

"It will uh, it will be over soon, we still have to search your socks," Bonnie said and with a grin on her face and unseen by Jane she kissed one of Timmy's nipples, giggling like a real blond as she did so.

Timmy's head spun and he wiggled his toes as Bonnie kissed his nipple again and Jane probed deeper in his hole... His cock churned in his underpants... Search his socks??? He wondered what the fucking fucks that was going to be like...

It wasn't long before Timmy found out exactly what Bonnie had meant about searching his socks and what it would be like and how he would laugh himself into a thither because of it...as the laddy found himself after his anal probe half on and half off the table in the private room. The plastic bucket with his personal belongings in it had been set aside on the floor and it was now Timmy atop the table on his lower back with his socked feet dangling off the side, his legs swinging back and forth. His hands, still restrained behind his back he had balled into a big fist and he laughed like crazy as the two female security guards were hunkered down at his dangling socked feet and were running the tips of their scanning wands back and forth against the bottoms of them. Bonnie and Jane each held Timmy by a calf to keep his feet steady as they scanned and scanned the bottoms of his feet.

"WHOOOOO, HAHAHAHAHAHAHAHAHA!!!" Timmy cackled crazily, sweating atop the table as the two bitch security guards seemed to be getting their jollies as they made him suffer.

"I ask you again Mr. Backman; do you find all this funny somehow? You think this is all a big joke?" Jane asked him as she held tight to his socked calf and trailed her scanning wand over and over the bottom of his foot.

"I-I don't think it's funny at all, poor me laying here with my danged under shorts pulled down in back and just my office socks," Timmy cried.

"HAHAHAHAHAHAHAHAHA! But with the way you two are a tickling the daylights out of my danged feet I can't help but laugh and laugh… HAHAHAHAHAHAHAHAHA!!!"

"Why do we get all the crazy passengers?" Jane asked Bonnie.

"L-ladies, I- I assure you, there is nothing in my danged socks," Timmy panted through his peals of loud laughter. "I am not trying to smuggle anything into New York City that way…"

"You would be surprised Mr. Backman the things that some people will do…" he heard Bonnie say as she and Jane did their dirty work.

"HOO, HOO, HOO, HOO, HOO, HOO, HOO, HOO, HOO!!!" Timmy laughed, sounding like a hyena as he did so…

"Okay, I think he's clean," he heard Jane say a short while later. "Let's let him get dressed so we can get back to our post."

"Th-thank you Jane, I mean, thank you Miss…" Timmy said, catching his breath as the two guards stood up, took him by an upper arm each and helped him off the table.

"Take the restraints off him and meet me back out at the post," Jane said to Bonnie as she exited the room, closing the door behind her.

"Well, I can see who's in charge," Timmy said with a boyish grin as Bonnie stood in front of him.

"She's just very job oriented," Bonnie said and looked at Timmy adoringly. "Sorry about the embarrassing tickling Mr. Backman…"

"It uh, it's okay Miss, just uh, please free my hands so I can climb back into my suit and be on my way, I don't want to miss my plane after all," Timmy said.

Bonnie looked at him for a moment more, kissed him on the lips once and then stood behind him to undo the wire restraints.

"Why'd uh, why did you kiss me first Bonnie?" Timmy asked as he massaged his wrists once they had been freed.

"I didn't think you would let me afterwards," Bonnie responded and walked out of the room.

Timmy chuckled, gave his erection a squeeze through his underpants, hiked his underpants back up over his ass, pulled his socks up and quickly got dressed…

"OHHHHHHH…" Timmy hemmed loudly yet again as his author buddy Christopher Trevor once more scoffed down his pearly white thick juices. "Oh my Lord never came so much in such short a period of time I must say…"

Timmy writhed and squirmed real sexily atop the massage table as Christopher drank him down yet again. The tit-clamps on his nipples started to drive the poor guy crazy, really making his man-sized tits feel real sensitive as he spurted his most recent load down his buddies' throat.

"Amazing, totally amazing what that Viagra stuff can do for a guy huh Christopher?" Timmy panted behind his blindfold.

"Sure as hell," Christopher replied a few seconds later after he let Timmy's soft cock slip from between his lips, giving the tip of it a few kisses as he did so. "God almighty, but your cum tastes so good Timmy."

As Timmy's once again spent manhood flopped to the side Christopher quickly took the clamps off his good buddies' nipples.

"OOOOOOOOOO..." Timmy swooned, his blindfolded head arched back as the feeling of the blood rushing back into his nubs sent chills through his muscular being.

"Yeah, I know bud, it feels real twisted when the clamps come off huh?" Christopher asked.

"You can sure say that Christopher," Timmy responded and if he hadn't been tethered to the table at the socked ankles he would have flown off it for sure when Christopher leaned down and slurped one of his jutted up nipples into his mouth. "OHHHHHH, oh my word of words...sucking my danged nipples now huh???"

"Got to do something to kill time till Vince gets here buddy..." Christopher said and quickly resumed suctioning Timmy's sensitive feeling nipple with his tongue, lips and teeth and gently squeezed and tweaked the other one with his fingers.

"Yeah, uh, speaking of that, when in tarnation is that guy going to get here?" Timmy asked Christopher as the guy sucked his nipple harder and harder. "I don't think you'll be getting any more milk from me buddy...least of all from my danged nipples...OH but my word that does feel good though..."

Timmy smiled behind his blindfold as he felt his buddies' hands roaming up the sides of his stomach area as he lay atop the table while his nipple was sucked and the other one was tweaked and squeezed...

After Timmy had gotten back into his suit, knotted his tie and tied his shoes he quickly dashed to the waiting area for his flight. As luck would have it he still had ten minutes before his flight departed and he saw that his fellow passengers were now boarding. He cursed the two female security guards for making him almost miss his flight...and he cursed Bonnie especially for not giving him the relief he was obviously craving in his under shorts when she had kissed him. Ah well the laddy figured, he was going to be meeting with Christopher Trevor and Vince the tickle master. He had no doubt that he would be getting more than his share of relief in his most private of areas, hardy har and har and thank you very much buds...

When Tim boarded the plane and headed for his window seat he was surprised to see his new friend, the guy he called "The new Ronald" sitting in the aisle seat next to his window seat.

"Well hello there Tim Backman," Ronald said jovially as he quickly stood up to let Timmy enter the seat and sit down.

"Well now, this sure is a surprise Ronald," Timmy chuckled, straightened his tie and got himself comfortable.

"Say, what happened with those two security guards back there Tim?" Ronald said as he too settled into his seat again.

"Trust me when I tell you man, *you do not* want to know," Timmy replied and saw that his seatmate was holding a trade sized paperback book on his lap.

"Hmm, that looks familiar," Timmy said, looking at the back cover of the book.

"It should, and it's the craziest thing," Ronald said and held up the book "Timmy's Ticklish Trials" by Christopher Trevor. "I feel like I've been plucked from the pages of a book Tim. The lead character's name in this book is your name, Tim Backman. And the guy who captured and tickles tortures him is named…"

"…Ronald…" Timmy said gripping the armrests of his seat as a look of disbelief came over his handsome face.

"Something wrong buddy?" the new Ronald asked Timmy as he stared straight ahead.

"Well, yes and no Ronald, somehow I think the omens are all making sense now," Timmy replied as he thought of Bonnie and Jane tickling his socked feet. "What uh, what's your last name? It's not Greene is it?"

Ronald chuckled and held up the book…

"You have read this haven't you?" the new Ronald asked Timmy as the laddy continued to stare straight ahead with a look of horror on his handsome mug.

"You might say that Ronald, you just might say that," Timmy said softly.

"My last name isn't Greene, it's Rosalie…" the new Ronald said and Timmy's Adam's apple was suddenly very prominent above his necktie knot as he swallowed hard.

So uh, Ronald, what are you all heading to New York City for?" Timmy asked his new friend, desperate to change the subject.

"I live there actually Tim, I own a bookstore in the village and I just recently acquired the Christopher Trevor books," Ronald said. "I was in Atlanta visiting a buddy of mine who owns a bookstore there. He said the Christopher Trevor books were selling pretty well so I decided to get them for my store too. What uh, what are you heading to New York for Tim?"

"I'm going to meet Christopher Trevor in person for the first time," Timmy said and he and the new Ronald looked at each other in disbelief.

Timmy was recalling that fateful meeting on the plane and his mind was jolted back to the present for the moment now while Christopher Trevor spoke on his cell phone as he cradled it against his ear on his shoulder. As the author spoke on his cell phone he was also tying Timmy's upper body to the table he was spread out on. No more being able to lift his upper body while being sucked off the handsome Timmy Backman thought as he was tethered tightly even more-so now.

"Yeah, okay that sounds great," Christopher said into the cell phone, Timmy watching with his blindfold now made into a makeshift gag, one of his own navy blue dress socks that he had worn with his suit for the trip crammed into his mouth with the blindfold now tied over it, keeping his musty tasting sock jammed in place.

Timmy was only able to lift his head off the table now as Christopher was obviously speaking to tickle Master Vince.

"Well, I'm glad you finally made it into Manhattan but what made you think it would be easy to find parking?" Christopher asked his tickle buddy.

Christopher smiled and listened as Vince was obviously telling him just how bad the traffic in Manhattan was.

"No, we'll wait for you here, it's no problem," Christopher said and looked into Timmy Backman's beautiful eyes as the guy watched himself being tied down at the upper torso. "You and I can go out to dinner later. We'll leave Timmy here while we're gone, tied up of course, ha, ha! He won't mind. We'll bring him back something to eat though. Timmy and I have been having some wonderful quality time together, haven't we Timmy? Here, say hello to your tickle master Vince."

Smiling mockingly Christopher put the cell phone to his tied down buddies' ear. Timmy heard Vince's deep voice saying "Hi Timmy, how's my ticklish buddy doing?" All Timmy could do in response was utter a feeble sounding "Mmmfff…"

"Yeah, I know just what you mean buddy," Vince replied and cackled meanly. "But keep your socks on, I'll be there soon enough and trust me you'll be doing a lot more than making muffled gagged guy sounds…"

"MMMFFFF…" Timmy responded again, chewing on his dress sock and the taste of it roiling down his throat, making his head spin.

He also could not believe what he had heard Christopher say, that he and Vince would leave him tied up in the hotel room later on while they went out for dinner.

"Ah yes my handsome Southern laddy, I can picture you right now," Vince cackled meanly in Timmy's ear. "I would be willing to bet a month's salary that my good buddy Christopher has you tied up real tight and I'll bet another month's salary he's got you wearing just those black socks he loves so much and maybe… just maybe your trademark kangaroo pouch style under shorts. HA!"

"MMMFFFF…" Timmy ranted into the cell phone as his cock dangling from his boxer briefs churned.

"Yeah, I bet I would win that bet huh my ticklish Timmy?" Vince laughed again as he drove. "My ticklish Timmy B…"

Timmy nodded a few times instead of making muffled sounds into the phone, realizing that he could not possibly communicate with a sock/gag crammed in his mouth. Christopher took the phone from Timmy's ear and placed it back against his…

Christopher said good-bye to Vince for the moment, hung up the cell phone and looked down at the tied up Timmy Backman, admiring his bondage handiwork.

"That was Vince," Christopher said and Timmy simply nodded in understanding. "He's here in Manhattan but he's having a difficult time finding parking…said it'll be another half hour or so at the very least before he gets here."

Timmy nodded again, aggravated that his buddy had gagged him with one of his own used socks. What a shitty thing that was to do to a poor guy Timmy thought. But then, he didn't have much choice in the matter, seeing that in a way he had handed himself over to Christopher for this trip…and to Vince as well it seemed… The two guys were going to make his weekend full of tickle madness, of that he had no doubt at all…

"So, it looks like we'll have to kill some more time before Vince gets here," Christopher said, looking quizzically at his handsome bound tickle star. "Got any suggestions on what we could do buddy?"

Timmy rolled his eyes in his head in disbelief, swallowed more of his own funky sock taste and wiggled his toes under his sheer thick and thins…

"I got it, how about another Viagra?" Christopher asked and whipped the gag off Timmy's mouth, followed by yanking the balled up navy blue sock from his captive's craw.

"Yeah, just what the doctor ordered huh bud?" Timmy asked, licking his lips to moisten them as his cock churned and Christopher a few seconds later fed him another Viagra tablet. Timmy gulped it down with a goodly amount of water as his buddy held his head up from behind. As Timmy drank down the Viagra Christopher pecked him lightly on the cheek and whispered "Thank you Timmy…"

While the Viagra took effect Christopher blindfolded his tickle buddy again and spent a few minutes sucking the laddy's socked toes…

While chills and thrills enveloped him Timmy's mind wandered in the throes of ecstasy…

"You're going to meet Christopher Trevor, the author of this very book, in person when you get to New York City?" the new Ronald asked his very perplexed and amazed plane-mate.

Timmy had to wonder what the chances were of his being tickle tortured by two gorgeous female security guards at an airport. But it had happened, it had happened bud. He also had to wonder what the chances were of meeting a guy named Ronald in line with him at the security checkpoint at that same airport… and what were the chances that that guy named Ronald would be reading the latest tickle book by his buddy Christopher Trevor? All this was too scary of coincidences Timmy thought as he pulled his tie down a notch as he sat next to the guy named Ronald Rosalie on the plane that was about to take off for New York City. (Ronald Rosalie???)

"Yeah, that's who I'm going to be meeting, yes indeed Ronald," Timmy replied.

"Jeez, so you're telling me here that you're Timmy Backman from the story?" Ronald asked aghast. "Do you mean to tell me that I'm sitting here with a fictional character made flesh?"

"Interesting way of putting it, but I suppose you could look at it that way Ronald," Timmy replied and ran his hand down his tie.

Then, the two men sat silently and enjoyed the feeling of liftoff as the plane barreled down the runway and were then airborne...

"Say, I have an idea Timmy," Ronald said, his eyes suddenly lighting up. "How about you come to my store in New York while you're there?"

"That sounds great, but somehow I think most of my time is going to be spent with my author buddy," Timmy said with a grin. "Somehow I get the feeling that I'm going to be real busy and tied up with all this book business..."

The two suited men laughed and Ronald handed Timmy a business card with his name, phone number and the address of his bookstore in New York City.

"Well, perhaps before you have to head back to Atlanta you could stop by for just a peek," Ronald said, sounding hopeful. "I have an awesome display set up for your buddy's books. Tell Christopher to stop by as well..."

He handed Timmy a second card...

"Hmm, now you really have my curiosity peaked Ronald," Timmy laughed as he took the second card from his new friend. "I think I will try to stop by your store at that before I head on back home..."

"Sounds like a plan to me...Laddy..." Ronald chuckled and a chill crept up Timmy's spine.

The two men settled back in their seats and read their books as the plane headed for New York City...

As Timmy recalled that meeting on the plane he now laid tightly tied down and blindfolded yet again as his author buddy feasted heartily on his newly induced Viagra erection...

"UHHHHHHHH..." Timmy grunted breathlessly, wondering when in hell Vince would finally be arriving, when the tickling tortures would begin and he wondered what the "Christopher Trevor" display of books at Ronald Rosalie's bookstore would look like...

That was one place Timmy intended to see while he was in New York City...but for the moment he could not see much as he felt his balls cooking up yet another batch of Southern Spunk for his buddy Christopher to chow down on...

"Oh my word..." Timmy panted and wiggled his toes under his sheer thick and thins.

After deplaning and collecting their luggage from the carousel Timmy Backman and Ronald Rosalie shook hands, said they would meet again and went their separate ways in cabs departing from the airport...

Timmy arrived promptly at the "Grand Diamond" hotel in the heart of Times Square at eight o'clock that Friday morning. He thanked his lucky stars that in the mornings the traffic in Manhattan was not as intense as it would be when Vince was arriving later on. Christopher had checked into the hotel the day before so his buddy was waiting for him in what would be their room for the weekend. Timmy tipped the cab driver, picked up his luggage and sauntered into the hotel lobby...

At the front desk he found out that Christopher was in room 1018 on the tenth floor...

As Timmy rode the elevator up to the tenth floor the handsome Southern gentleman had no idea what he would be in for. He did know that more than likely Christopher would have everything set up long before he had gotten there, bondage and tickle-wise that is, hardy har and har. At the sound of knocking Christopher dashed to the hotel room door and opened it. He took in the sight of Timmy Backman, his tickle hero, muse and constant story tickle victim standing there in the flesh, *finally,* in the flesh. Timmy, as Christopher was doing took in the sight of his CO-author and tickle buddy. Christopher was casually dressed in blue jeans, a pullover Polo shirt and slip on loafers. Christopher breathed in hard at the sight of Timmy; he was handsomer than his pictures did justice. And to really fit the scene he had shown up clad in a navy blue suit complete with a crisp white shirt, necktie and highly shined black lace-up wingtip shoes.

"Well now, and hello Mr. Author," Timmy said as he entered the hotel room, taking in the luxurious surroundings as he stepped in.

"And, I must say, this is very nice," Timmy went on as he put his luggage down on the floor and turned to face Christopher.

Timmy's salt and pepper colored hair and green eyes mesmerized the author. The two men held their arms wide open to each other and hugged tightly.

"At last we meet," Timmy said, sounding so sexy, so Southern, so Senator John Edwards to Christopher's ears.

"Yeah, my fictional character in the flesh," Christopher replied as he squeezed the back of Timmy's neck, his lips grazing the Southern guy's earlobe as he spoke. "My Mister Timmy Backman...my ticklish laddy..."

Christopher's eyes were filled with tears of joy but instead of crying he laughed a bit and then held his CO-author by the upper arms at arm's length. The author really drank in the sight of his star of so many tickle stories, and most especially the novel that started it all, "Timmy's Ticklish Trials."

"Is that what you're going to call me while we're here?" Timmy asked Christopher. "Your ticklish laddy?"

"Hmm, maybe I'll just call you Timmy Backman, my VERY ticklish laddy," Christopher replied and the two men burst out laughing together that time.

Timmy's laugh was booming and sexy sounding at the same time. It sent a true wave of lustful ecstasy through Christopher. As Timmy laughed he pulled the author again against himself and said, "It's really great to meet you Christopher Trevor..." Timmy's strong and muscular arms felt awesomely powerful to Christopher. The author could feel Timmy's bowling ball sized biceps against his back. Timmy was six feet one inch tall and he towered over Christopher's five feet nine inch frame. The author reached up and again ran a hand over the back of Timmy's neck, upwards then against the back of his salt and pepper colored hair.

"That hair that you're tousling and stroking used to be brown with blonde highlights," Timmy whispered in Christopher's ear, sounding unbelievably sexy and Southern once again as he spoke.

"It looks great," Christopher panted as he smoothed Timmy's hair, again fighting his tears that threatened to spill over from his eyes.

Christopher then boldly pressed his lips against Timmy's cheek and kissed him, something the author had been dreaming of doing since they had begun writing and since their on-line friendship had blossomed. Timmy didn't seem to mind so the author kissed his cheek again...

"You're my laddy after all Timmy," Christopher whispered in his special buddies' ear.

Timmy smiled and turned four different shades of red. Never before had he felt so special to someone, so valued. Actually Timmy had been the model for numerous erotic tickle stories that Christopher had written over time. It was something he had never given a thought to throughout his lifetime. More than just a model he was also considered a very sexy and erotic consultant on those tickle tales. As far as Christopher Trevor was concerned no one was better when it came to the tickle tales than Timmy Backman himself.

"Did you have breakfast?" Christopher asked. "I could have something sent up for you if you're hungry."

"Nah, I had something on the plane," Timmy replied. "I'm fine, but thanks still the same... Nice room you got for us...it's uh, really spacious..."

As Timmy looked around some more it was at that moment that he noticed the long sturdy looking massage table that was set up across the room, right next to the king sized hotel room bed.

"...yeah...really spacious..." Timmy said, taking in the sight of the table, slowly approaching it, noting also that a pile or white cotton rope was placed at the foot of the table. "Oh my word...so uh, is this to be my perch Christopher?"

Christopher laughed and took Timmy's upper arm in hand as his "laddy" seemed to be drinking in the sight of the table. Visions of the two lovely female security guards back at the airport flitted through Timmy's mind and his cock churned in his suit pants.

"I had the hotel send up the table," Christopher explained, holding Timmy's arm tight as he spoke. "The white cotton rope I purchased at "The Pleasure Chest" down in the Village area, along with some other things that I'm sure you'll find to be most entertaining. I learned years ago that when one is tied with white cotton rope it doesn't leave rope burns...no telltale signs of a person's bondage adventures..."

"I'm sure..." Timmy said and nervously tugged on his tie.

"After I checked in yesterday I went shopping in Manhattan," Christopher said and let go of Timmy's arm. "I figured if I won at the wager you and I will participate in very shortly I could use the things I purchased on you..."

"And if you lose buddy?" Timmy chuckled, him almost sounding as sadistic as Ronald in the tickle novel. "Remember, I may not be as unlucky in wagers as Timmy in the story was."

"Hmm, well, I suppose that if I lose the wager then the tables will have been totally turned here," Christopher said, mulling it over almost miserably as he spoke. "If I lose you and Vince, when he gets here will get to tickle torture the fuck out of me..."

Timmy laughed and said, "What a switch that would be huh? Christopher Trevor tickle tortured instead of poor ol' Timmy Backman."

Timmy shucked off his suit jacket, hung it in the closet and loosened his tie...

"So, speaking of Vince, when will that fiendish tickle master be arriving?" Timmy asked.

"Sometime today for sure," Christopher replied and tugged on Timmy's loosened tie, noting how sexy the laddy looked with the top button of his shirt undone and his tie loosened a bit. "He has some business to take care of and then he'll be here...so for the time being you and I have this hotel room to ourselves. We can uh, do our tickle wager and then have some fun until Vince arrives..."

"Fun...I have to wonder what kind of fun you have in mind for me if I lose that wager Mr. Christopher Trevor Author," Timmy said with a slight giggle.

"Let's just say your blindfold is ready Laddy," Christopher said and again tugged Timmy's tie.

Timmy's cock churned again and his balls felt like they were pulsing and Christopher prayed that he himself would win the wager...the present he had bought for Timmy at Bloomingdales was enough alone to make the author say this prayer. But if he lost he would enjoy the handsome Southern guy in the other direction... so be it...

"So what sort of wager do you have in mind?" Timmy asked with a grin etched on his handsome face.

"Over here please and I'll show you," Christopher replied, leading Timmy into a smaller room of the luxury hotel room, a room off to the side.

In the extra space of the hotel room Timmy saw two laptop computers set up on a table, two chairs facing the computers. On the computer screens were the graphics for the game "Electronic Hangman."

"So it's to be a word game then?" Timmy asked as he and Chris stepped over to the two laptop setups.

"Sure is," Christopher said. "First guy to lose three games is the tickle victim."

"Hmm, that sounds pretty fair," Timmy chuckled, his hands crammed in his suit trouser pockets as he rocked back and forth on his wingtip heels.

A few seconds later Christopher and Timmy were seated in front of the laptops and playing the game of "Hangman..."

"UHHHHHHHH!!! OHHHHHHH yes, oh my fucking word of words," Timmy panted in bonded and blindfolded darkness as his buddy Christopher drank yet another helping of thick white juice from his cock font. "That Viagra truly is the stuff of dreams...and nightmares, seeing as I'm the poor guy all tied up and being milked like this..."

Christopher had just the tip of Timmy's cock currently in his mouth. He teasingly swirled his tongue over the very sensitized tip of it, poked his tongue tip into Timmy's piss slit and scoffed down the last remnants of his laddy's latest offering.

"And you thought these balls of yours wouldn't be able to cook up another batch of soup for me Timmy," Christopher said with a grin once Timmy's cock was out of his mouth.

As Timmy heaved for breath under the binding ropes and his face contorted in ecstasy behind his blindfold Christopher could not resist once more moving to the laddy's sheer thick and thin black socked feet and playing suck and lick with them.

"I-I suppose that Viagra really does the trick then huh?" Timmy asked.

"And you as well Timmy, you as well," Christopher breathed as he held onto Timmy's feet by the arches and gently kissed his socked toes. "Vince should be here any minute now Laddy, so I think milking time is over for you...for the moment. I'm sure that I've pumped enough loads from you to make sure that every part of you is hyper ticklish at this point."

"Oh woe is me..." Timmy bantered behind his blindfold and it was then that Christopher trailed the tip of a finger upwards against the bottom of one of Timmy's sheer socked feet.

"WHEEEEEE, oh no, are we starting without Vince?" Timmy squealed...

After the two men had been playing "Electronic Hangman" for a good half hour Christopher had lost at just one of the word sessions while Timmy had lost at two.

"One more to go for you my ticklish laddy," Christopher chuckled as Timmy and he guessed letters for their perspective words of the moment.

"Don't get those ropes ready for me just yet buddy boy," Timmy said, his Southern accent pouring out real thick now, him obviously very nervous at that moment.

He guessed a letter and it was incorrect. An arm appeared on his hanged man on the computer screen.

"You only have one arm and two more legs to go Timmy," Christopher laughed as the letter he had chosen appeared in his current word.

Timmy looked at Christopher miserably as his opponent deliberately chose a wrong letter. An arm appeared on Christopher's hanged man.

"Just biding my time till you lose that session Timmy my ticklish laddy," Christopher said.

Timmy wiggled his toes in his wingtips and sweated as he moved his mouse toward yet another incorrect letter.

"Dang it all, what is that word?" Timmy seethed through clenched teeth, the feelings in his feet awful with tickle trepidation.

His cock churned and he felt glee filled as the next letter he chose was a correct one…

But then, a few moments later it was over…Timmy had lost three word sessions in the game of "Electronic Hangman." The handsome Southern guy slumped back in his chair and looked over at his fiendish buddy, his feet sweating in his shoes.

"Don't get too comfortable in that chair Timmy," Christopher said, reaching over and tugging on his tickle victim's tie. "I'm sure you'll be a lot more comfy stretched out on the massage table and wearing the gift I bought for you…"

"Says you…" Timmy said softly as he and the author got to their feet.

Back in the main part of the hotel room Timmy slowly undid his necktie and unbuttoned his crisp white dress shirt while Christopher took a gift wrapped box from his backpack.

"And what might this be?" Timmy asked as he stood bare-chested in front of his author buddy and took the box from him.

"I had them custom made for you by a tailor at Bloomingdales," Christopher explained as Timmy opened the box and then held up the pair of sheer thick and thin black silk socks.

"Oh my word, direct from our story "Timmy and The Hong Kong Tailor", Timmy said softly and his cock pounded in his suit pants.

"I trust you're wearing your kangaroo pouch style under shorts my laddy?" Christopher asked his buddy mockingly.

A short while later Timmy was stripped of the lower portion of his suit and lying atop the massage table on his back. He had changed from his navy blue nylon dress socks that he had worn with his suit to the ones that Christopher had given him as a gift. He lay looking totally sexy and vulnerable wearing just the socks and his trademark kangaroo pouch style under shorts with his hands tied off behind him while his author buddy slowly and methodically tied his ankles to the table legs. Christopher worked diligently and lovingly as he tied his buddies' feet…

As Christopher tied Timmy's sheer socked feet Timmy looked around the room from his bondage point now. He noticed the small pill bottle and the pitcher of water and the water glass.

"What uh, what's all that?" Timmy asked, gesturing with his head.

"You'll find out when the time comes, and you do too…" Christopher laughed, leaned down and kissed the bottom of one of his tickle captive's socked feet.

"Hmm, so what are we going to do until Vince gets here then?" Timmy asked and that was when Christopher, without a word, blindfolded his tickle buddy, helped himself to the succulent treat that the ticklish laddy kept stored in his boxer briefs and began what would be an all morning till afternoon suck and Viagra fest…

"OHHHHH…OHHHHHH my, oh my word…" Timmy panted at the ecstasy and squirmed under the binding ropes…

"So what do you think Timmy, is this a good way to kill time till Vince gets here?" Christopher asked and quickly slurped his buddies' huge cock back into his craw.

"OHHHHHHH…you won't get an argument from me on that Christopher," Timmy gasped as he was re-sucked into the author's mouth.

After Timmy had cum two times and Christopher ate both helpings the author gave the ticklish guy the first of what would be various Viagra tablets…just to keep his buddy on the ticklish edge for when Vince arrived…

Christopher was actually glad that Vince had delayed in arriving for their Timmy Backman tickle fest… It gave him time to feed off the laddy for a while and utterly drive him batty. Christopher knew that after Timmy shot his load his tickle barometer went upwards. By the afternoon Timmy had lost count of how many times he had spermed so Christopher was well aware of just how very ticklish his laddy was at that moment…

As Christopher drank in the sight of his bonded buddy they heard a knock on the door.

Vince arrives…

At the sound of the knock at the hotel room door Christopher quickly took the blindfold off his tied down buddy.

"So it would seem that Vince has arrived…MMMFFFFF…" Timmy squawked miserably as Christopher again filled his mouth with one of his navy blue nylon dress socks. "RRRMMMMMMFFF…"

As Timmy once more chowed down on his own musty foot scent Christopher walked to the door of the hotel room and opened it. Standing in the doorway Timmy saw one of the handsomest African American gentlemen he had ever laid eyes on. So that was Tickle Master Vince Timmy thought as his head spun and his cock churned. That was the man who had so tormented him internet-wise for over a year at that point Timmy was thinking as he drank in the sight of Vince. Timmy made mewling sounds of desperation behind his sock gag and squirmed under the tight binding ropes. From the look in the African American guy's eyes he was most definitely the fiendish tickler he made himself out to be…and then some Timmy thought as he struggled fruitlessly. The tied down Southern gentleman knew just at the sight of Vince that he would soon be laughing his head off crazily. He struggled harder to get loose…to no avail. Christopher quickly ushered Vince into the room and closed and locked the door, not wanting any passerby in the hallway to see that they had a guy clad in just his underpants and socks tied to a massage table in the room.

"Well, well, finally welcome," Christopher said as he and Vince embraced tightly.

Watching from his tied up position atop the table Timmy saw that Vince was six feet tall or better. Even though the handsome black guy was wearing a jacket it was obvious that he was well toned and very muscular. All those jokes he had made about "carrying" his ticklish Timmy away from his family for some tickle fun was obviously possible. Judging from the width and girth of Vince's broad shoulders he would have no problem whatsoever in picking Timmy up and carrying him off...just as Ronald had done in the soon to be classic tickle novel. Timmy could see also though that Christopher did not have tears in his eyes as he hugged Vince. For some reason he was glad for that as a pang of jealousy coursed through his tied up being...

"MMMFFFF..." Timmy bantered as he watched Christopher and Vince hug each other tightly.

Vince had rolled a large-sized luggage on wheels into the room with him. Timmy had no doubt that that luggage was Vince's bag of tricks, his tickle torture toys, his tickly implements that he had told Timmy about over their time of internet chatting...

"Sorry it took me so damned long to find parking," Vince said to Christopher as he held the author tightly in his arms, Christopher massaging the back of Vince's big neck as he spoke. "But Manhattan is not a good place to bring a car..."

"Well, I did manage to kill time while we waited for you," Christopher said with an evil looking grin and pecked Vince on the lips.

"Yeah, and I bet I can guess how the hell you killed time my favorite author," Vince laughed and pressed his lips against Christopher's once more, sniffing at the same time. "Your breath smells like Timmy B. cum...hee, hee, hee..."

At the sound of that "hee, hee, hee" a chill crept up the tied down Timmy's spine and he curled his toes back under his sheer thick and thin silk socks. It was the sound of his tickle tormentor, Tickle Master Vince's trademark sinister chuckle, a simple hee, hee, hee, but mind-bending nonetheless. The handsome laddy wondered what the fuck he had been thinking when he had agreed to all this. He swallowed hard and was treated to a mouth and throat full of his own sock taste, DANG!

"You've been milking that guy for a while huh?" Vince laughed and kissed Christopher again on the lips.

"A few times, yes, it's amazing what a pair of black silk socks, kangaroo pouch undies, tit clamps and a Viagra tablet or two will do for a handsome Southern guy," Christopher said and he and Vince disengaged their embrace.

Christopher gestured conspiratorially over at his tied up prize...

"And there he is, ticklish Timmy B. my handsome ticklish boy!" Vince squealed, shucked off his jacket, tossed it on a chair and with Christopher beside him made his way over to the table that Timmy was stretched out on and tied down to.

"HA, HA, just like I thought my ticklish laddy, just like I said on the phone," Vince said merrily, stepping behind Timmy's head and snaking his long dexterous fingertips through Timmy's soft salt and pepper colored hair. "Tied up, tied down, and wearing just your trademark kangaroo undies, Christopher Trevor black socks and gagged...gagged with one of your own dress socks I would guess... HA, HA, and hee, hee, hee for you my laddy. What a HOT looking display you make buddy..."

"RRRRRMMMFFF..." Timmy panted at Vince's touch, looking up at the guy in a mixture of awe, lust and fear.

As Vince's fingers played over Timmy's handsome face the tickle master leaned down and kissed him on his sock gagged mouth.

"MMMMMM...finally, *finally* my Timmy B. my ticklish laddy, finally, I get to torment you in the flesh..." Vince chuckled as he sidled his way down the side of the table, testing the tightness of the ropes that bound his and Christopher's tickle victim. "And trust me on this Timmy B. I am going to tickle your flesh till you're crazy with it. And look, just look at these ticklish Timmy B. man sized nipples, your man tits as you call them in the book. You guys weren't kidding when you said you had man sized tits Timmy B. Are they really as ticklish as you described in the book?"

"Mmmmffff..." was all Timmy could say in response.

Timmy watched miserably as Vince made like an operating room doctor and held up and open hand for Christopher. Christopher smiled wickedly, reached into his pants pocket and brought out two sharp tipped cotton swabs on sticks. The author handed the swabs to Vince.

"Time to do some quick experimenting my ticklish laddy," Vince said as he leered down at his tied up tickle trophy. "God, you're more handsome than your pictures will attest to Laddy..."

As Vince brought the tips of the swabs toward the jutted up tips of Timmy's nipples Timmy shook his head "NO" back and forth and sputtered against his sock gag.

"Been sucking these man sized nipples of his huh Christopher?" Vince asked as he then swirled the tips of the swabs against the tips of Timmy's nipples.

"RRRMMMFFFFFF!!!" Timmy squawked loudly and Christopher quickly took the sock out of Timmy's mouth.

The author knew never to keep a laughing guy gagged as it ran the risk of him choking.

"PWWWAHHHHHHHHH, ha, ha, ha, ha, ha, ha, ha, ha, ha, ha, ha!!!" Timmy laughed as Vince tickle/swabbed his nipple tips. "And hello to you too Tickle Master Vince!!! HAHAHAHAHAHAHAHAHA!!!"

The sight of the swab tips being spun over his nipples was unnerving for Timmy and Vince seemed to know just how to spin them and at just the right speed and tempo...

"HAHAHAHAHAHAHAHA, what a way to get started on me, t-ticklin' my danged nips!" Timmy laughed.

"Damn, his Southern accent is sooooo sexy," Vince said to Christopher after he stopped tickling the laddy's nipple tips. "You were so right about this guy…"

"He is a treasure," Christopher said as he and Vince stood at the sides of Timmy's upper torso. "Shall we Vince?"

"Oh yes, those man tits of his are too, *too* irresistible buddy," Vince said breathlessly.

Together, like two vampires Christopher and Vince leaned over the tied up Timmy's chest and helped themselves to one of his nipples each.

"OHHHHHHHHHH, oh my word, oh me, oh my…" Timmy grunted breathlessly as his two tickle tormentors made sport of sucking and slurping at his jutted up nipples. "Oh my, for a guy I really have sensitive man nips…"

As Christopher and Vince played suck and slurp with his man tits Timmy's cock and balls churned and he again curled his toes back under his silk socks…

A short while later Vince was strumming his piano player-like fingertips down Timmy's sides, tickling his ribs as he went.

"YAAAA, ha, ha, ha, ha, ha, ha, ha, ha, ha, ha, ha, ha, ha, ha, ha, ha!!!" Timmy cackled as Vince played Timmy's ribs with his fingertips while Christopher twisted and turned one of his nipples. "Oh you guys, what've I gotten myself into here today?"

"I warned you my handsome laddy, my ticklish Timmy B. I told you that my fingers were lethal tickle weapons," Vince mused. "Did you think I was lying when I said that I took extensive piano lessons when I was a child?

Vince strummed his fingertips up and down and up and down all along Timmy's tied down sides and ribs. A few times he leaned down and swirled his thick tongue tip into Timmy's belly button. That really got a few good hee's and haws out of Timmy Backman… To really make the handsome laddy laugh Vince used the tips of his well-manicured fingernails to tickle Timmy's sides and ribs. While Vince played Timmy's ribs with his long fingers and fingertips and teased his belly button with his tongue Christopher worked the tied up laddy's nipples with his fingers and thumbs. Timmy laughed and screamed under the binding ropes and his cock flip-flopped from side to side outside his kangaroo pouch under shorts…

"And just think Timmy B. all of this is just a warm-up, a quick experiment for what's coming later…" Vince mused as he trailed his tongue over Timmy's stomach region, kissing him a few times there as he went.

"OH my word, I get the feeling that I'll also be coming later…" Timmy gasped as his cock danced between his legs.

"Our dear author here is going to leave us alone for a while very shortly my ticklish tied up tied down Timmy B.," Vince laughed, looking over at Christopher. "Aren't you buddy?"

Christopher nodded in the affirmative and Timmy laughed louder as Vince did his work…

A few minutes later Vince stopped strumming Timmy's ribs and moved his hands over the sides of the tied up laddy's trademark kangaroo pouch undies, teasing him relentlessly.

"Oh man, just look at that juicy cock Christopher," Vince said sounding totally fiendish. "I would bet that that slit of his is real ticklish…"

"Oh no, oh my word, VINCE, you wouldn't," Timmy panted.

"Unless you want to chew on your sock again I wouldn't say things like that my ticklish laddy," Christopher said, dangling Timmy's navy blue sock over his nose and mouth as Vince took Timmy's balls in hand.

"MMM, nice hefty balls, and even though you've milked this guy a few times they feel like they're chock filled to the rim with his Brim," Vince chuckled, leaned down and slid his tongue liberally over and around Timmy's juicy balls.

"OOOOOOOOOOOOO…" Timmy swooned, arched his head back and goose bumps broke out all over him as Vince's tongue worked its magic.

It was obvious to Timmy how Vince was biding his time in getting to the prize he sought the most…Timmy's tied up feet…Timmy wondered if by the time Vince got to his feet Christopher would have left them alone. The thought of being alone and tied up and in Vince's clutches sent waves of chills of trepidation mixed with longing through Timmy's very being. Vince swirled his huge tongue all over Timmy's balls in their sexy sac. He sucked them alternately into his mouth, bathed them with his saliva and made sure they were well saturated. When he held up his long goose feather Timmy nearly screamed. But then, Timmy did scream, he screamed his laughter as the man he called Tickle Master Vince glided the tip of the feather against his wetted testicles.

"OOOOOOOOOO, HAHAHAHAHAHAHA!!!" Timmy laughed loudly, looking up at his author buddy as the guy continued to twist and squeeze his nipples. "HAR, HAR, HAR, HAR, oh my word, Christopher, he, he's tickling my danged scrotum…"

At the sound of the word that Timmy used to describe his sac of balls Vince and Christopher laughed meanly. Vince smiled wickedly down at the tied up guy and trailed his feather upwards against the underside of Timmy's cock shaft.

"HAHAHAHAHAHAHAHA!!!" Timmy reeled.

Christopher watched in awe as Vince worked his sadistic magic on his buddies cock and balls with the feather tip. As the feather strummed against his cock Timmy wanted to plead with Vince to jack him off. After all the times he had been milked by Christopher Timmy could not believe that he was fair game for milking yet again. Jeez, but that Viagra sure could make a guy his age a seventeen year old again Timmy thought fleetingly and laughed and cackled and screeched as Vince clamped the tip of his cock into his lips, pressed down hard and continued tickling the tied up guy's cock shaft. When Vince swirled his tongue tip into Timmy's cock slit while still holding the guy's cock-crown between his lips Timmy felt like he was in orbit…his head was spinning that much and his laughter sounded as if it were coming from someone else…someone very far away… As Vince teased and tickled Timmy the tied up guy heard himself pleading to be allowed to shoot his load…in between laughing raucously that is…

"Got him right where I want him," Vince said after letting the tip of Timmy's cock slip slowly from between lips. "He's totally horned up again… PERFERCT!!"

A short while later Timmy was alone with Vince in the hotel room. Christopher had gone out for a while to enjoy the city, leaving his two buddies alone to get to know each other better…or to be more precise and to the point…the author left Timmy and Tickle Master Vince alone so that Vince could reap his tickle magic on the Southern gentleman…

"OH NO, NO," Timmy crowed loudly as Vince took a pair of wooden stocks from his luggage (bag) of tricks.

"I just knew I should have blindfolded you my laddy," Vince said comically as he stood at the foot of the table.

He slowly untied Timmy's socked feet and then one at a time de-socked the executive.

"I know how much Christopher loves seeing you in your black socks buddy," Vince said as he dropped the socks to the floor. "But for what I have in store for you now requires you to be sock less…"

"OH MY, Vince, please, oh please man, don't lock my feet in those danged stocks," Timmy panted. "Please man, I'm so worked up from the Viagra and from being tickled and from the way Christopher milked me and from having had my man tits clamped off and on that I'm afraid I'll laugh so hard I'll make the ceiling fly off this place…OH ME…"

"Just what I'm hoping for my ticklish prince," Vince replied as Timmy prattled in the throes of ticklish ecstasy and set the stocks down at the foot of the table between Timmy's splayed legs.

"Oh no," Timmy whimpered as he watched Vince then encase each of his feet in the stocks at his ankles.

The bottoms of Timmy's soft meaty feet protruded through the stocks and his toes stuck straight up as he lay atop the table, feeling totally helpless and very sexy and very ticklish. The sounds of the stocks being closed and locked filled Timmy with the utmost dread…

"Now my laddy, let's see AND HEAR just how loud I can make you laugh and HAR HAR HAR for me, yes?" Vince asked his ticklish captive while at the same time reaching into his bag of tricks.

"Yes? Why, no, no Vince," Timmy pleaded miserably, cursing himself for having come to New York City in the first place.

When Vince held up the electronic manicure buffer Timmy nearly started laughing involuntarily. When Vince clicked the device on and the buzzing sound filled the hotel room Timmy nearly started crying…

With a maniacal looking grin on his face, with his pearly white teeth gleaming Vince stood at the foot of the table, at Timmy's bared feet in the stocks…

"Oh my laddy, prepare to go to the city of sadistic laughter now…" Vince said and with no hesitation whatsoever pressed the rotating tip of the manicure buffer against the bottom of Timmy's right foot.

"OH NOOOOO, NOOOO, OHHHHH WOE is me and my danged ticklish feet!!!" Timmy screamed. "HAHAHAHAHAHAHAHAHA!!! HAAAAAAAAAAAAAAAAAAAAA!!! VINCE, stop this, how about at least buying a guy a drink first before de-socking and ticking his danged feet??? HAAAAAAAAAAAAAAAAAAAAAAAAA!!!"

As Vince swirled the innocent looking manicure buffer over Timmy's right foot and then his left foot Timmy thought of his wife Stephanie and how many times he had gone to meet her in the salon after she'd been for her bi-weekly manicure. When he saw the row of ladies having their nails done, some of them having their nails done with the electronic manicure device he never once entertained thoughts of that sort of device being used on his ticklish bare feet…

"OHHHHHHH, if Stephanie could see me now," Timmy cackled crazily. "HAR, HAR, HAR, HAR, HAR, HAR, HAR, HAR, HAR!!!"

Vince watched with awe and his eyes opened nearly as wide as saucers as Timmy's beautiful feet flopped around in the stocks as they were tickle tortured. The tickle master would never be able to thank Christopher enough for having brought Timmy Backman to him in the flesh. After a good (bad?) half hour or so of having his bare feet tickled with the manicure buffer Timmy was sweating and panting atop the table as Vince released his feet from the stocks.

"I'll get you some cool water buddy," Vince said, sounding concerned.

But when Vince took the leather restraints and bindings from his bag of tricks Timmy wondered just how concerned the guy really was…GAWD…

A few moments later Timmy was finally off the massage table. Standing next to Vince with his wrists now locked behind him in leather wrist restraints Timmy slowly sipped the water from the bottle that Vince was holding to his lips. Vince marveled at the way Timmy's Adam's apple bobbed up and down as he gulped down the cool liquid. Actually, Vince was marveling over every part of this overly handsome overly ticklish guy. Timmy Backman was a tickle sadist's dream come true. Vince wondered how poor Timmy would feel if he knew that the water he was chugging down was laced with crushed up Viagra tablets. Actually, the ticklish guy would know very soon… He had been begging to be allowed to cum earlier while Vince was tickle torturing him. Now Vince could not wait to hear the guy plead in true earnest…

"So tell me Laddy, when was the last time you were hogtied with your bare sexy feeties pointing straight up while a diabolical guy like me lick tickled those said feet?" Vince asked his tickle captive.

As Timmy sputtered at what Vince just asked him Vince grabbed his arm and laughed sadistically…

The water trailed down the sides of Timmy's chin as Vince held him tight by the arm and forced him to scoff down the liquid...

"What all did you put in that danged water???" Timmy asked Vince a short while later when he was hogtied in the leather restraints on the hotel room bed.

By now Timmy was totally naked, seeing as Vince had taken his kangaroo pouch style underpants off him, telling Timmy he was taking them as a souvenir of this wonderful ticklish experience.

"Ticklish experience for me but not for you oh Tickle Master Vince," Timmy had cawed as he was de-under-pantsed.

"Are we feeling a bit worked up in the crotch my ticklish Timmy B.?" Vince asked his tickle hostage as Timmy now squirmed miserably in his hogtied position on the bed, his bare feet pointing straight up at the ceiling.

To tease the restrained guy all the more Vince stuck his long tongue out and swirled it seductively over his lips and near his prickly looking goatee.

"Oh my word," Timmy said softly as thoughts of that tongue and goatee tickling his bare feet filled him with dread. "But yes, I am feeling real worked up in my root man!"

"Amazing what a small dose of that Viagra can do to a guy eh Timmy my laddy?" Vince asked in reply and reached between Timmy's thighs from behind.

He pulled Timmy's sensitive feeling and bloated cock from between his thighs, along with his balls. Timmy's most private of parts flopped onto the bed and trickled pre seed.

"OH MY," Timmy cried out at Vince's touch on his cock. "You tricked me into drinking water laced with that damned sex potion that Christopher was giving me as well. Milking me like a cow, making me cum repeatedly just makes me all the more ticklish...but then I suppose that is what you guys would want where I'm concerned...OH MY WORD..."

Then, poor Timmy was off and laughing again as Vince licked and tickled his bare feet with his tongue and ran the prickly parts of his goatee over Timmy's feet as well. With his hand Vince reached down with his goose feather and tickled Timmy's visible cock and balls as they peeked out from between his tethered thighs...

"OHHHHHHHHH!!! HAHAHAHAHAHAHAHAHA!!!" Timmy reeled and cackled. "I for one cannot believe that Christopher left me here alone with you man!!"

"Keep talking in that Southern Senator John Edwards voice for me my laddy," Vince said. "It makes me want to tickle you all the more...and more...and more..."

As his feet and cock and balls were tickled Timmy wriggled like a fish out of water in his hogtied position. Vince was in awe once again as Timmy's delectable toes curled back and forth as he stuck the tip of the feather into his cock slit...

Timmy laughed in a high-pitched tone as Vince nibbled at his toes and kissed the sides of his feet, all the while using his goatee to tickle torture the guy's feet…

"HAHAHAHAHAHAHHAHAHAHAHAHA!!!" Timmy roared and wondered if he would survive the weekend in Christopher Trevor and Tickle Master Vince's clutches…

Then Vince switched tactics and used his goose feather to tickle torture the bottoms of Timmy's upturned feet with…

Timmy heee hawed and cackled and swore like a sailor as he laughed and laughed and laughed…. When Vince started sucking Timmy's toes one after the other while at the same time tickling his feet bottoms with the tip of the goose feather the Southern guy was bathed in a mixture of laughter and marvelous sexual sensations in his cock. Having his toes sucked always made the guy's cock hard. It seemed that like with his man-sized nipples, when they were played just right it affected the handsome laddy in the cock.

"I-I got, I got to cum, oh Tickle Master Vince, I REALLY got to cum…" Timmy cried out in between bouts of laughter. "HAHAHAHAHAHAHAHAHA!!! My cock feels like it's stalked up to the size of gargantuan…HAHAHAHAHAHAHAHA!!!"

A surge of emotion akin to high lust flooded through Vince's being as he heard Timmy call him by his rightful title of "Tickle Master." This told him that inwardly Timmy loved the role he was playing…even though he somehow hated (and loved?) being tickled tortured. Vince decided that throughout the weekend ahead he would work the laddy harder and harder. Smiling with two of Timmy's small toes in his mouth Vince sucked those toes hard and tickled the arches of the Southerner's restrained feet. As Timmy laughed and laughed and laughed his feet bobbed around beautifully in the leather restraints…

After an hour or so of tickling Timmy's feet with the goose feather, licking them and tickling them goatee-wise and sucking his toes Vince decided that the guy had suffered enough…for the moment. As he was releasing Timmy from the hogtie was when Christopher sauntered back into the hotel room.

"Anybody hungry?" Christopher asked. "I made dinner reservations for us down in the hotel's beautiful dining room."

"Sounds good to me," Vince said as he and Christopher watched the sexy Southern Timmy sit up on the bed, massaging his wrists and each of the men noticing the size of the stalk between the handsome laddy's legs.

"Oh yes, sure, dinner sounds like a very good plan," Timmy said breathlessly. "After all the tickling and milking that you two have done to me thus far I sure could use some nourishment…"

"Hmm, I see you stripped him of his socks and underpants," Christopher said as Vince sidled up next to his buddy.

"Yeah, I wanted those sexy feeties of his bare for my tickling tortures," Vince mused.

"So the hotel dining room sounds good to me..." Timmy said, getting to his feet and standing there naked and stalked up real sexy in the cock.

Christopher and Vince looked hungrily at the towering erection and low hanging testicles that the sweaty and tickled guy was sporting between his muscular legs. Timmy chuckled knowingly as Christopher picked up a pair of Vince's leather wrist restraints...

"HEH, heh, looks like dinner is going to be a tad delayed me thinks," Timmy said as Christopher yanked his arms behind him and cinched his wrists in the leather cuffs.

A few moments later Timmy was standing with his hands locked behind him in the leather cuffs as Christopher and Vince knelt at his sides sucking on his balls.

"OHHHHHHH, oh my, oh my word..." Timmy bantered breathlessly. "OH my, ticklers love my sweaty and mangy balls...can't wait till you two take sucking turns on my beet red cock down there..."

Timmy balanced himself on his bare feet and as he spoke in his Southern sounding accent it seemed that Vince sucked his testicle that he had in his mouth even harder.

Timmy hunched his muscular shoulders up, his eyes spun back in his head and his breath came in short gasps as his two tickle buddies licked, sucked and lapped at his balls. The ticklish guy hauled himself to his tiptoes and danced sexily as his balls were serviced most lovingly. Then, looking down he watched as Christopher and Vince seemed to really be tugging at his balls while they each held one in their mouths.

"OHHHHH, thanks for not blindfolding me for this Christopher," Timmy swooned. "I just wish you would get to the gusto and suck me off...you know how much you love the taste of my cum buddy..."

Looking up at Timmy Christopher squeezed the laddy's calf, shook his head "no" and let Timmy's testicle slip out of his mouth.

"WH-what no?" Timmy grunted as Vince also let his testicle slip out of his mouth.

"I think it best that I don't ruin my appetite before dinner," Christopher said snidely and stood up next to Timmy, taking the laddy's upper arm in a firm grip.

As Vince got to his feet as well Timmy looked at him expectantly.

"Don't look at me for that my laddy," Vince laughed and tweaked one of Timmy's jutted up nipples.

A chill sped through Timmy's being at Vince's touch and his well-sucked and dangling balls seemed to sway in their sac.

"Your buddy Christopher here holds the warrant on drinking down your sludge," Vince laughed.

"I'll have your slop for dessert when me and Vince get back from dinner," Christopher said and let go of Timmy's arm, quickly helping himself to a few more sets of leather restraints from Vince's bag of tricks.

"B-but I thought that the three of us were all going down to the hotel's dining room to eat together," Timmy said, his heart thudding in his muscular chest, him knowing very well the antics that Christopher and Vince would plan for him.

He cursed himself for having let the author bind his hands behind him while having his balls stimulated. Christopher knew just how to play him, DOUBLE DAMN!!! He knew he was not going to be made to cum at the moment...rather he was going to be made to wait...

"Change of plans my handsome ticklish buddy," Christopher said and then pointed at Vince.

Vince smiled fiendishly, scooped Timmy up off the floor and carried him in a position of a groom carrying his bride over a threshold over to the king-sized bed...

"Oh my word..." Timmy said sounding very frustrated at this latest development.

"Not to worry Timmy, we'll bring you back something from the hotel dining room," Christopher said and then he and Vince went to work overpowering and getting their ticklish captive secured to the bed...

"OH MAN, this is so not fair," Timmy huffed miserably as his wrists were released but then his arms pulled to the sides so that he could be restrained to the bed in a spread eagle position.

"And just think you handsome ticklish guy, the weekend hasn't even gotten started yet, all of this today was a warm-up to what we have in store for you," Christopher said as he cinched Timmy's left wrist to the bed board while Vince did the same with his right wrist.

Timmy looked from side to side as he was restrained.

"So, so you plan to leave me here all tethered and fettered while you both go for a nice leisurely dinner???" Timmy seethed, balling his hands into fists as his two buddies then got to work restraining his bare feet.

By now Timmy was laying on his back and his cock was hard and sticking straight up at the ceiling.

"We won't be gone that long buddy," Christopher said and when he and Vince were done Timmy was spread eagled on the bed, restrained tightly in leather wrist and ankle restraints.

After Christopher and Vince were gone Timmy tried to get as comfortable as possible but given the position he was in that was easier said than done.

"Dang, I can't believe they left me here like this," Timmy mumbled as he squirmed on the bed, his cock doing a dance between his spread legs.

But as he lay there he did find himself nodding off after a while. Timmy was exhausted to the point that eventually he fell into a deep sleep. He had been tickled that day at the airport and by his buddies Christopher and Vince. He had also been milked/drained to the point that only tickling him would more than likely bring him out of his slumber. The ticklish guy actually passed out...spread eagled to the four corners of the bed, naked as the day he was born...not even a pair of trademark "Christopher Trevor" black socks to wear at the moment. And because of all the sexual teasing, stimulation and the strong and constant doses of Viagra Timmy's cock was once again chock filled with his manly juices, rigid and standing tall. The height to which his cock was erect was accentuated by the flatness of his naked body splayed out on the bed.

When Christopher and Vince had left the room, as an afterthought and thinking it would be fiendishly funny Vince hung the "Room Service Please" sign on the doorknob. He giggled like a schoolgirl and pointed Christopher's attention to the sign as they walked away. Christopher also giggled...mostly at the prospects of Timmy being discovered by room service...whoever that might turn out to be.

As Timmy slept the tickle CO-author and tickle victim was lost to time. He was literally dead to world as he slept off the ticklish, teasing torments he had been put through for most of that day. So, he was totally unaware of the passage of time or that a floor manager had spotted the "Room Service" request sign and had alerted housekeeping of a job that needed to be performed. The request was answered promptly, because prompt service was a hallmark of the "Grand Diamond" hotel. A cute little Philippine maid in her crisp black and white uniform came bustling down the hall with her tool cart and entered the room using her master card key with no hesitation.

Once in the room she began to survey the situation to see what she needed to accomplish. She immediately saw that the room was a mess...clothes and stuff strewn all over. She even noted the crumpled pair of black sheer thick and thin dress socks. She instantly thought of a groom occupying this room. She swore under her breath, a new American custom she had picked up during her time in the states and headed to the bathroom to see what damage there might be there. As she trudged angrily through the spaciously large room she suddenly spied the sleeping form on the bed...a naked man...and from quick observation she saw that he was in a state of extreme sexual agitation. His male member was standing tall in the dim light of the room and it was swaying and pulsing with his rhythmic breathing. Slowly, the maid walked up to the bed to examine the handsome naked gringo, this naked American...she nearly lost her breath at the sight of the beautiful form laid out before her.

She noticed that he was obviously and very much alive...because she was able to hear his deep breathing and she loved watching the rise and fall of his muscular chest. He had nipples that were as thick as a woman's she thought. Her boyfriend would go crazy as he was a tit sucker to the extreme. Her own nipples tingled as she thought that. The maid also found that she was salivating a bit as she watched the gentle sway of his huge erect cock as he breathed. She moved down to his bare feet, touched his toe and said, "Sir?" Timmy did not stir. She grabbed more of the toe and squeezed, once more saying "Sir?" There was still no reaction from the sleeping nude man laid out before her. She then took note of the fact that his arms and legs were tied to the bed, pulling his limbs out in a spread eagle position. She also noticed all the paraphernalia scattered about the naked man and on the floor…feathers, brushes, pens, electric toothbrushes and the like. She noticed also an open bottle of pills. She picked up the bottle. The maid knew what Viagra was. She placed the bottle back on the nightstand where several of the blue pills were laying on the surface next to a pitcher of water.

"This is all so bizarre," the maid said to herself. "What in the world has been going on here?"

This time she jostled the naked man's foot. Timmy still did not react. He was still sleeping in an exhausted state. Then, the Philippine maid decided that she just had to call her cousin who also just happened to work this housekeeping shift at the hotel. Using the room phone she called her cousin's cell phone and told the young lady that she would not believe what she had found in this room…and for her to get there right away.

While she waited for her cousin to arrive the maid could not resist kissing Timmy's handsome face a few times and running her fingers in his soft and so sexy salt and pepper colored hair.

Shortly, the other Philippine maid arrived at Timmy's and Christopher's room and she was initially aghast at what she saw. Her cousin seated on the edge of the hotel room bed with a handsome, muscular, naked man tied to the four corners of said bed. Not to mention that his obviously excited cock was sticking straight up but with an angry red look to it.

"Milly!" was the only intelligible word spoken.

The rest was in Philippine.

"Lindy!" the first maid called back and then offered her own Philippine chatter to the mix.

Milly spoke, pointed and gestured at the naked, bound Timmy sleeping on the bed. Lindy chattered back and picked up a couple of the brushes. Then, as if part of her explanation Milly wiggled her bright red fingernails on Timmy's bare sole.

For the first time since Milly entered the room Timmy stirred and mumbled, "No, no! Christopher, no, stop, Vince, no…you can't…please stop." Then, his eyes popped open and he giggled. Timmy continued to giggle as Milly strummed his wrinkled wiggling soles with her sharp nails.

"WHAT…WHO the hell? Who…Don't…hee, hee, hee, hee!!!?" Timmy found himself saying as he struggled with this new and twisted turn of events.

Milly continued to tickle Timmy's foot closest to her and chatting in Philippine to her cousin. The cousin, Lindy, sat on the other side of the bed and grinning meanly she began using her nails on Timmy's other foot. Timmy's eyes were as a big as saucers as he took in the situation. GAWD, he had been found naked and bound on a hotel room bed by two beautiful and obviously very playfully sadistic maids. As his eyes opened wider yet the poor laddy giggled to the beat of the band. He could not seem to communicate with these two very beautiful Philippine maids.

At that point the door to the room opened and the floor manager stepped into the room. Although dressed in blue blazer, tan slacks and shirt and tie she was also obviously of the Philippine descent.

"Milly, Lindy!!" she called the two maids by name and then launched into what could be nothing other than an inquisitive tirade.

Even Timmy was looking at the floor manager. His laughter subsided as the two maid's attention had been focused away from him. The maid's chattered back and forth in their native dialect. Now Timmy began asking the floor manager for help. She quickly moved to the bed beside Timmy's head still chattering back and forth with the maids. Seemingly having heard enough from Timmy she clamped her hand firmly over his mouth. Timmy's eyes were still pleading with her however.

A little more chatter and then the floor manager looked back at Timmy.

"Sir, may I ask how you came to be like this…in this ticklish predicament?" she asked and she had to giggle herself at what was in front of her and what the maids had told her.

"Please, help me," Timmy pleaded as soon as he hand was off his mouth. "These two friends…no, guys, er, they kidnapped me. Yes, they kidnapped me and tied me to this bed. And they have been doing awful things to me…"

Timmy tried to sound as convincing as possible; wanting to be untied so he could at least jack himself off when the maids were gone…seeing as their only interest in him seemed to be to want to tickle him.

"Well Sir," the floor manager began and her hand reached out and began to move across Timmy's washboard abs. "This room seems to be registered to a Timothy Backman and Christopher Trevor. And from what my staff tells me they have checked out your wallet and you seem to be Timothy Backman. So, how could your friends kidnap you, hmm?" And her hand moved lower on Timmy's abdomen and her nails began to toy with his pubic hairs above his cock. Timmy giggled as her hand moved across his abs and he moaned as she found his pubic bush and toyed with his hair…his stiff cock lurched and began to leak. The steady diet of Viagra that Christopher had been feeding him had left Timmy in a constant state of overly sensitive, sexual excitement. His cock needed very little stimulation to begin oozing the clear, sticky substance everyone knew as a guy's "Pre-cum."

"OH, oh maam, please! Uh, well it may…oh…oh…it may be my room and the gentleman you just mentioned, Christopher Trevor's as well, but please, you're not helping…don't…please maam…" Timmy blubbered, trying to explain himself and get her to stop what she was doing.

Christopher and Vince had tickled and teased and drained his balls over and over…and yet…he was responding to this woman's teasing…and she really wasn't even touching his cock…just playing in his pubic hair.

The maid Milly chimed in but in Philippine. The floor manager was still toying with Timmy's pubic hair interpreted for him.

"Milly thinks that you have been subjected to quite a bit of tickling," the floor manager said and pointed out all the paraphernalia lying around the room. "Is that right Mr. Backman, hmm?

And as Milly the maid picked up a battery powered toothbrush that she found near Vince's bag of tricks Timmy moaned again and responded, "Huh? OH mmm, oh! What?" as the floor manager was still stroking his pubic hair, pulling at it to make him feel it in his erection and sweaty balls. But when Milly began to comb Timmy's armpit hair with the buzzing vibrating device Timmy's reaction was abrupt and violent. He leapt right from moaning to full nose blowing giggles.

"Eeeeeeeeeeee hee, hee, hee, heee HEEEEEEE!!! PLEEEEEAAASSE hee, hee, hee, hee, heee!!! Don't tickle me anymore! EEEEEEEEEEEEEEEE!!!" Timmy screamed shrilly.

Milly continued her toothbrush tickling of Timmy's armpit and jabbered to the floor manager. The floor manager responded, "Yes, I too think that the size of his erection does indicate that Mr. Backman here really enjoys this tickling activity. Don't you Sir?"

"EEEEEEEEEEEEEEEE hee, hee, heee, ha, ha, ha, ha, ha, ha, ha, ha OOOOOOOO, hoo, hoo, hoo, hoo, hoo, hoo!!!" was all the response she got out of Timmy.

Then, the other maid, Lilly, not wanting to be left out of this sexy tickling action picked up a ballpoint pen and began to draw all kinds of designs on poor Timmy's bare soles. Timmy's response was repetitive…but at a little higher pitch.

"EEEEEEEEEEEEEEEE, HEEEE, HEEEEE, HEEEE, HEEEEE HAHAHAHAHA, ha, ha, ha, ha, ha, ha, ha, ha, ha, ha!!!" was what Timmy screamed.

And all the while the Southern laddy's cock remained stiff and leaking and his balls rumbled in their sack. Timmy never could control his sexual response to being tickled. And even though Christopher and Vince had spent a great deal of time tickling and draining him Timmy was till full of Viagra and threatening to blow his cork yet again. So, while Milly and Lilly enjoyed tickling Timmy's armpits and feet…they even switched placed and switched instruments…the floor manager found an electric toothbrush of her own. It was amazing how much Vince's bag of tricks contained. She held it up in the air and tested it out…but, Timmy never heard the buzz. He never saw the evil gleam in her eye… He never saw the second toothbrush coming…But, he felt it.

The floor manager started out on Timmy's perineum. Timmy's eyes popped open and his breath left his lungs in a wheeze. She moved up and found his rumbling ball sac and buzzed his filling nuts…driving him closer and closer to becoming a nut. The floor manager was literally having a ball. Grinning, she moved the buzzing bristles around Timmy's balls…playing along the stretched tendons in his crotch, up through his pubic hair and then up and around his pulsing shaft. Timmy's cock was no longer the dry rod it had started out to be. Now it had a generous coating of pre cum, which was still pulsing out of his piss slit.

Timmy was howling and laughing and pleading, "OOOOOHHHHH PPLLEEEASE", and going crazy... Then, the floor manager began to work the vibrating toothbrush up the underside of Timmy's wet stiff cock. He was beside himself with laughter and lust as the three lovelies handled and used and tickled the daylights out of him. The floor manager worked the brush closer and closer to the head of Timmy's erection. She skirted the edge of the mushroom head...she even gave his piss slit a good vibrating...and the she slipped the buzzing bristles down his cock head and found the sweet spot where his cock shaft and cock head met with a little tuft of loose skin...and she brushed and vibrated this spot good. And she was rewarded with an explosion of cum and Timmy's nuts drew up and started pumping his man juice out once again...only this time Christopher was not there to scoff it down.

Just at that moment, as Timmy was spurting the last of his sexy mess all over himself the three women stopped tickling him and turned to meet the sound at the hotel room door. Timmy was still giggling and slightly squirting white gooey cum onto his chest and face as the door to the room opened. When the door swung open there stood the two Cheshire cats that had put poor Timmy in this predicament...Christopher and Vince. Christopher was holding a bag that contained Timmy's take-out dinner from the hotel dining room. The two men clucked their tongues and Vince was the first to speak as he said, "Well, well, well, it looks like Timmy couldn't wait for us and decided to call room service." Timmy looked at them miserably in his exhausted state as Christopher and Vince laughed and laughed. They thanked the floor manager and her maids for tending to the room and to Timmy while they were out. Christopher told her that they could handle it from here. As the women left Timmy was still wearing the freakish grin of a Halloween Jack-o-lantern...and he had a fresh coating of his cum dripping from his nose and chin. The women closed the door amid the chuckles of the two men as they took charge of the very ticklish handsome man they had found bound to the bed...

Before they un-tethered Timmy so that he could eat his dinner Vince came up with a ticklish idea for the poor laddy. Timmy found himself bent over in an upside down "U" shape position. His wrists were now bound to his ankles and as he balanced himself awkwardly in that position Vince used an electric toothbrush to tickle torment Timmy's exposed asshole from his standing position beside Timmy. In back of Timmy Christopher amused himself sucking the ticklish guy's cock... after he had squeezed the spent member through the crack of Timmy's muscular and shapely thighs...

"OH MY WORD, oh me, HAHAHAHAHAHAHAHA!!!" Timmy cackled as his two captors tormented him all the more.

Timmy's spent cock tingled as Christopher sucked it heartily. He did not cum that time but before he sat down to eat his dinner he was given a Viagra appetizer... For Timmy Backman that night proved to be the prelude to a very long and ticklish weekend of ticklish trials...

Epilogue

The weekend was at a close and Timmy Backman had survived yet another ticklish ordeal… As the cab he was in headed for the "Village Bookstore" on late Sunday afternoon the handsome and suited executive wondered just how the "Christopher Trevor" display at the bookstore would look. All during being tickle tortured while in Christopher and Vince's clutches the bookstore and the "new Ronald" were all Timmy could think about. Well, the bookstore wasn't actually all he thought about. He also thought about how long his two buddies/tormentors would tickle torture him during the intervals they had him tied up. But it was while he was not being tickled and not laughing his head off that he thought about the "new Ronald" and his bookstore. As the weekend drew to a close and his two so called buddies finally released him (rather reluctantly it seemed, seeing as Christopher sucked one last load from Timmy's cock while his hands were still tied behind him) Timmy called for a cab to pick him up earlier than when he was supposed to head for the airport. He never told Christopher and Vince about the "new Ronald", wanting this to be something for him and for *him only*…So many times now in his real life and his fictional life he had been the tickle victim and catered to the needs of so many others, so this time he wanted an experience that would not result in his being captured and tickle tortured. This time it would be for his own enjoyment Timmy mused delightedly as he rode in the cab, tugging his tie. According to the business card that "Ronald Rosalie" had given him the name of the bookstore was aptly "The Village Bookstore." It was located on a side street in the heart of the west side of Greenwich Village. He had called ahead to let the "new Ronald" know that he would be stopping by before having to head off to the airport and back to Georgia. Shortly, the cab pulled up in front of the "Village Bookstore" and Timmy, clad spiffily in a charcoal colored suit, a white shirt, black silk tie and black lace-up wingtips emerged from the cab, carrying his one piece of luggage with him. He paid the driver and as the cab drove off and he approached the door to the store the first thing the handsome Southern gentleman noticed was the sign hanging on the inside of the door that read, "Closed." Timmy wondered if perhaps "Ronald Rosalie" had had an emergency of some sort and had to run off. But as he was about to step away from the store the door opened and there stood the "new Ronald."

"Timmy, so glad you could make it to come and see my store, Ronald Rosalie said happily, standing in the archway of the entrance to the establishment.

"Oh, Ronald, hey there," Timmy said and held out a hand.

The two men shook hands vigorously, Ronald really pumping Timmy's hand.

"The sign on the door said "Closed" so I thought maybe our meeting had been called off," Timmy said as Ronald continued holding his hand after they had stopped shaking.

"Nah, well, yeah, I closed the store so we could have some privacy Timmy," Ronald said and finally let go of Timmy's hand. "Come on in, put that luggage under the front counter and I'll show you around."

"Thanks, sounds good to me," Timmy said and stepped into the store.

"Can I get you something? A coffee perhaps? I have a café area in the store as well," Ronald said as Timmy slid his luggage under the counter in the very front of the store. "I find that a lot of customers like to sit and sip a coffee after they purchase a book or two. This way they can get right into the story they bought..."

"Uh sure, a coffee sounds good Ronald, thanks," Timmy replied. "A little bit of skim milk, no sugar please."

"Coming right up Timmy," Ronald said and sauntered over to the area of the store where a sign hung over it that read "Village Bookstore Café."

While Ronald was preparing his coffee Timmy slid his hands into his suit pants pockets and looked around the place, moving slowly on his feet.

"Nice, nice place," Timmy said as he took in the rows and rows and shelves of books.

Like most bookstores each section was properly marked with a hanging sign over it, whether it was fiction, non-fiction, horror, romance, etc...

"Timmy stepped over to the section marked "Fiction" but did not find a row of the "Christopher Trevor" books.

"Here you go Timmy," Ronald said, startling Timmy a bit as he made him come out of his reverie.

"Oh, thanks, thanks a lot, it smells great," Timmy said, taking the medium sized container of coffee from his new friend, the "new Ronald" to be exact. "Say uh, nice store you have here Ronald, but I don't see the display of "Christopher Trevor" books anywhere."

"I have them in a section in back of the store," the "new Ronald" said with a sly looking grin on his face. "It's for adults only. I have a sign posted at the front counter that says you must be eighteen years of age or older in order to shop the "Christopher Trevor" section of the store."

"Yes, when customers order books from Christopher he insists on a letter stating that the customer is eighteen years or older," Timmy said and sipped his coffee. "Well, I can assure you Ronald, I am very well over eighteen years of age so please lead the way to the "Christopher Trevor" display of books."

The two men laughed good naturedly at Timmy's comment concerning his age...

"Wait till you see what else I have back there Timmy," the "new Ronald" said and pulled a long white handkerchief from his pocket. "You are going to be bowled over when you see this. Do you mind if I blindfold you for a few moments?"

Timmy breathed a sigh as the "new Ronald" without hesitation and without a reply from Timmy stepped behind him and tied the white cloth over the handsome laddy's eyes.

"Hold that coffee steady Timmy," the "new Ronald" said and guided Timmy by holding him by his upper arms toward the back part of the store. "I assure you, you are going to be amazed."

"Well, seeing as you blindfolded me for it I'm sure I will be," Timmy said and managed a chuckle.

He felt a tingle in his cock as he was led in darkness toward the back of the store... Holding Timmy's arms tight the "new Ronald" led the suited handsome guy through a door at the rear of the store.

"Okay, here we are Timmy," the "new Ronald" stated happily.

The "new Ronald" positioned Timmy facing the display and then put his fingers on the knot in his blindfold.

"You ready?" the "new Ronald" asked.

"I'm ready Sir," Timmy said and as the blindfold was whipped off him he took a hearty sip of his coffee.

Timmy could not believe what he saw...

The entire section at the back of the store was decorated and adorned ala "Christopher Trevor." Over a shelf of rows of "Christopher Trevor" books the "new Ronald" had hung a poster-sized portrait of the author himself. Timmy recognized the picture of Christopher as his author photo from the books. Around the poster of Christopher were poster-sized pictures of the covers of all of Christopher Trevor's books. Looking up Timmy saw the cover of "Timmy's Ticklish Trials." He smiled widely, took a sip of his coffee and his cock tingled more in his suit pants.

"Oh my word," Timmy said in awe as the "new Ronald" stood beside him, gloweringly thrilled that Timmy Backman was enjoying this. "I feel like a celebrity of sorts..."

But it was what was situated on the side of the shelf of books that truly mesmerized Timmy. It was an exact replica of the one he and Stephanie had at home, the dreaded device called...

"...the Spinning Chinaman," Timmy said softly and in wonder as he took a final sip of his coffee.

"Yep, the Spinning Chinaman," the "new Ronald" said as Timmy put his empty coffee cup down on an empty spot on the bookshelf and with his cock now at full mast in his suit pants he approached the device. "One of the many instruments of your ticklish tortures Timmy Backman."

"Oh my word, wherever did you get this?" Timmy asked as the "new Ronald" sidled up next to him.

"As you can see I have read the "Timmy" books very carefully," the "new Ronald" stated. I plan to even get a shoe shine machine with the tickly brushes in it to add to the other side of the bookshelf."

Timmy looked at the "new Ronald" out of the side of his vision, smiled thinly and tugged nervously at his tie.

"Did uh, did Valerie from the stories sell you this Chinaman?" Timmy asked as he took in the huge wheel-shaped device, complete with the leather restraints for wrists and ankles adorning it, the pin in the center in place to keep it from rotating at the moment.

"No, that would be funny though if she did," the "new Ronald" replied and saw the erection tenting Timmy's suit pants, but made no mention of it however. "Actually I had a buddy of mine build it from scratch. I had him read the Timmy books and he made it from the way it was described in the story."

"Well, I must say, whoever your buddy is he really got it down pat," Timmy said, running a hand over the side of the huge wheel. "...even down to the finest details..."

As the two men took in the sight of the device the "new Ronald's" eyes opened wide and he smiled from ear to ear.

"Timmy, I have a brilliant idea, if you're game for it that is," the "new Ronald" said and grasped Timmy's upper arm.

"I uh, think I know what you're about to say Ronald," Timmy said with a grin, his erection pounding now in his suit pants, it leading the way and his thoughts it seemed at that point.

"How about some pictures of you in the "Spinning Chinaman" Timmy?" Ronald asked and squeezed Timmy's arm tighter, coaxing him along it seemed. "It would be great publicity for sales of the "Timmy" books."

Timmy slid his hands into his suit pants pockets and grinned like a schoolboy.

"I don't know Ronald," Timmy said. "I have a plane to catch and all and..." Timmy began.

"It would take no time, just get yourself standing in the device for a few minutes, I'll snap the pictures and then you'll be headed for the airport," the "new Ronald" said hopefully.

"Hmmm, okay, I suppose that sounds reasonable and all," Timmy said as the "new Ronald" loosened his grip on his arm. "As long as the pictures would only be shown here and not posted on the internet or anything like that...I am a family man after all..."

"Of course Timmy, I'll even draw up an agreement paper, sort of like a contract," the "new Ronald" said. "How does that sound?"

Timmy considered it, clapped his hands together once and said, "It sounds like a good deal Ronald Rosalie."

"I'll get the camera, you get yourself comfortable in the Chinaman," Ronald said and headed for the door of the room they were in. "I'll be back in less than a minute."

"You uh, you'll want me in my under shorts and trademark black socks I'm guessing?" Timmy asked as he was undoing his tie and the "new Ronald" halted in his steps.

The store owner could not believe his luck...

He dashed to the front counter to get his camera and when he returned to the "Christopher Trevor" display room Timmy was shirtless and just taking off his suit pants. His shoes had been placed by the bookshelf and his suit jacket and shirt and tie were hung neatly over the shelf.

"Nice, looks like you work out pretty regularly," the "new Ronald" said as he took in the sight of Timmy in his kangaroo pouch under shorts and black calf length nylon dress socks. "That will make the pictures even better..."

What would make the pictures truly great thought the "new Ronald" was the towering erection that Timmy Backman was sporting in his trademark under shorts. If Timmy hadn't figured out that the coffee he had just drunk was laced with a powerful aphrodisiac he would know soon enough...when the "new Ronald" started edging him that is...

As the "new Ronald" put his camera down momentarily he stepped next to Timmy to usher him into the "Spinning Chinaman."

"Okay Timmy, just get yourself situated in there like in the story and I'll get the pictures taken as quickly as possible," the "new Ronald" said as Timmy positioned himself in an "X" sort of stance within the device, his arms and legs spread out as far as possible.

"Okay, how's that?" Timmy asked, looking real sexy and vulnerable already.

"So far so good," the "new Ronald" said as he stood next to the Chinaman and quickly fastened the restraint around one of Timmy's wrists.

"Oh, uh, I didn't think you would tether me to it," Timmy said and as he reached to release himself the "new Ronald" grabbed his other wrist from the other side of the Chinaman, having made his way over there at almost lightning-like speed.

In moments both of Timmy's wrists were fastened to the dreaded "Spinning Chinaman."

"I just want it to look as authentic as possible Timmy," the "new Ronald" said as he then squatted at Timmy's black socked feet.

As the "new Ronald" pulled Timmy's black socks up for him it was at that moment that all the warning signals went off in his head...and "OH MY WORD" it was too late yet again... His big cock churned and stiffened in fear in his under shorts as the "new Ronald" handled his black socks, pulling them up for him, straightening them about his muscular sexy calves... As he watched the "new Ronald" handling his socks thoughts of his other buddy Ronald Greene flitted through the handsome laddy's mind. Thoughts of what that original Ronald had subjected him to fill his tortured brain and his cock churned some more...OH MY WORD...

Timmy did not need three guesses to know what this "new Ronald" had in store for him as he fastened the restraints around his socked ankles...

"Okay, now *that* looks great Timmy my laddy, that looks really great," the "new Ronald said almost breathlessly as he took in the sight of the now scantily clad and bonded Timmy. "And I'm glad you left your black socks on, it'll be just like in the book when Ronald kidnapped you on that fateful night and you were wearing them, along with your under shorts of course."

At the sound of the "new Ronald" addressing him as "Laddy" a shiver of true trepidation crawled up the ticklish guy's spine.

"Okay Ronald, uh, how about taking those pictures and I'll be on my way, yes?" Timmy asked, sounding nervous as all hell.

He realized as Ronald snapped a few pictures of him what a mistake this had been. He had not told Christopher or Vince where he was headed when he left the hotel earlier than expected. He had not told Stephanie that he would be making a quick stop before heading to the airport. The store that the "new Ronald" owned was closed…and no one, NO ONE, knew he had ventured into this tickle trap. Well, so far it was only his own conclusion that he had walked into a tickle trap. The "new Ronald" had only fastened him to the "Spinning Chinaman" for picture authenticity, he hoped, *he prayed.*

"Oh man Timmy my laddy, these pictures will be awesome when it comes to selling the "Christopher Trevor" books, wouldn't you agree?" the "new Ronald" chuckled as he zoomed in for some close-up shots of Timmy.

"Uh, sure, uh, when all are you going to let me off this thing Ronald?" Timmy asked and his cock pounded fear hard in his kangaroo pouch style under shorts.

A few times the "new Ronald" snapped pictures of the tent in Timmy's under shorts. A few times he snapped pictures of Timmy's socked and bound feet.

"Well, I still have to get some shots of you rotating in that thing and then maybe even take a video of you spinning round and round in there…what do you think buddy?" the "new Ronald" asked and snapped a few pictures of Timmy's face as the twisted reality of this sank in.

"Oh my word," was Timmy's reply.

He knew then that what he had surmised was correct…he had been tricked yet again and this time he had walked into his own ticklish demise. It was slowly dawning on him that his plan had gone awry. This would not be an experience just for him. This would prove to be yet another ticklish experience and he would be serving yet another's twisted jolly needs… As his cock pounded harder in his under shorts he felt his balls shifting around involuntarily in their sexy sweaty sac. It was the same feeling he had gotten when Christopher had Viagra induced him over the weekend.

"Oh jeez, you slipped me a Mickey of some sort in that coffee Ronald," Timmy said as the guy again snapped pictures of his stiffening tented underpants.

"Sure did my laddy, and guess what? There's plenty more where that came from," the "new Ronald" said jovially. "I plan to keep you stacked up and erect for the duration. Ever experienced edging my laddy?"

"Edging, oh my word, that's when a poor guy is all worked up in the cock and he can't get the relief he craves," Timmy replied. "Christopher did the reverse of that to me during our time together this past weekend…"

"Lucky you, and him too," the "new Ronald" chuckled meanly. "But again, for while you're here I'm going to edge you till you're mad with it…"

"And just how long do you plan on keeping me pray tell?" Timmy asked through clenched teeth, it no longer a secret that he had been captured yet again for some ticklish devilry.

"Well, let's see, I'll want at least three rolls of film like this of you, then maybe a good couple of hours of video of you spinning in that thing. But not to worry Laddy I won't spin you for long intervals. I'll videotape you spinning for fifteen to twenty minute sessions until it all adds up to a couple of hours on video. I think that's reasonable, and of course the customers will get a charge out of seeing a model in the "Spinning Chinaman"," the "new Ronald" stated matter of factly as Timmy's jaw dropped.

"So I would think we're looking at, hmm, at least three days my laddy," the "new Ronald" said and smiled behind his camera and snapped off a few pictures of Timmy's look of horror as tears welled in the laddy's eyes.

"OHHHHH, oh my word!!" Timmy was bantering a few scant moments later after the "new Ronald" had taken the pin out of the "Spinning Chinaman" that held it fast and the ticklish guy now found himself spinning round and round in a clockwise direction.

And to Timmy's horror the "new Ronald" did not need to spin the device manually, rather he had an electronic hand-held remote control that controlled the rotation of the Chinaman.

With his fingers clenched into fists and his toes curled back under his black socks Timmy spun round and round in the Chinaman as the "new Ronald" snapped picture after picture.

"OH MY WORD of words let me off this thing Ronald!!" Timmy cried out miserably. "You all can't keep me here for three days man! I have a flight to catch in a couple of hours…"

"Sorry to burst your bubble Laddy, but that flight has been canceled," the "new Ronald" said and snapped a few pictures of Timmy as he spun upside down and then right side up again, round and round he went. "I'm sure your airline will re-schedule you though…once you're out of here that is…"

As the "new Ronald" chuckled he put his camera down on the shelf and a few moments later he was videotaping Timmy as he spun in the Chinaman.

"I-I'm startin' to feel a tad disoriented in here Ronald," Timmy complained, his strapped hands clenched into fists as he rotated round and round.

"Another of my specialty coffees will fix you right up Timmy my laddy," the "new Ronald" laughed meanly behind his video camera as he recorded the poor Southern guy's plight.

"Oh my, how do I always wind up in these danged predicaments?" Timmy chided himself.

After a good fifteen minutes of videotaping the spinning Timmy Ronald turned off the video camera, stopped Timmy rotating and set the guy in the Chinaman at an upright position, locking the pin in to keep it stabilized. Timmy did not even bother to ask again to be released as he knew it was pointless. He was the tickle hero of many a tickler and the "new Ronald" was his latest vanquisher. MY WORD!!!

"OOOOOOOOOOO HAHAHAHAHAHAHAHAHA!!!" Timmy was laughing and screaming a few scant seconds later as the "new Ronald" stroked his stomach area with a sharp-tipped goose feather.

Timmy squirmed miserably in the Chinaman and did a sexy sort of dance in his bondage as the "new Ronald" trailed the feather tip over his stomach region, his ribs, his pectorals and it was when he teased Timmy's nipples with the feather that Timmy really howled his song of laughter...

"Oh my word my laddy, oh my word," the "new Ronald" chuckled, sounding real sinister and imitating Timmy's Southern accent not all that well.

Timmy laughed louder and more and more uncontrollably as the "new Ronald" trailed the feather tip over his entire stomach area, upwards over his muscular chest and back down again and again in a circular-like motion...

The "new Ronald" then, about a half hour later had brazenly taken Timmy's erect cock and his sweaty balls out of the fly opening of his kangaroo pouch style underpants. Timmy bantered and swore like a marine at this latest invasion of his manhood, telling the "new Ronald" not to be helping himself to the good stuff between his legs. But Timmy's erection stuck out like a flag pole and his juicy balls dangled like low hangers and swung back and forth a bit as he squirmed and danced bonded in the "Chinaman"...as Ronald tantalized and tease-tickled his piss slit and the shaft of his towering cock with the tip of the goose feather.

"PWWWAHHHHHHHH HAHAHAHAHAHAHAHAHA!!!" Timmy screeched. "OH DANG IT ALL, not my cock Ronald, oh man, not my cock, oh my!!! HAHAHAHAHAHAHAHAHA!!!"

To add to Timmy's misery the "new Ronald" had tied Timmy's necktie as a blindfold over Timmy's eyes, thus forcing the poor ticklish guy to really concentrate on and enjoy his latest ticklish trials...

"OH MY WORD, HAHAHAHAHAHAHAHAHA!!!" Timmy catcalled as the "new Ronald" slid the tip of the feather into his piss hole and spun it, tickling the walls of Timmy's inner cock head.

The way Timmy's cock was stiff and sticking straight out made it all so easy for the "new Ronald" to penetrate the sexy piss hole with the tip of his feather. Beads of piss and oozing pre cum emanated from Timmy's cock hole.

"Looks like you have a bit of a problem in the area of your cock bud," the "new Ronald" teased Timmy. "Looks like someone needs to uh, cum..."

"You bet your danged bookstore and Christopher Trevor display someone needs to cum, *I got to cum*..." Timmy cried out in between laughing and laughing.

"All in time my laddy, all in good time," the "new Ronald" said and trailed the feather downward and then around and around and over and over Timmy's succulent balls. "We have three days ahead of us and tonight to get to all the good stuff Timmy... I do plan to milk you dry, I plan to play with those balls of yours... and of course I plan to have at those black socked feet of yours in pure tickle fashion… but for the next couple of days I'm going to keep you balanced on the edging edge, or to be more precise, balanced in the Chinaman…"

Scant seconds later "the new Ronald" had Timmy turned upside down in the "Spinning Chinaman." In blindfolded darkness Timmy looked upwards and laughed like a hyena as the "new Ronald" now tickled the bottoms of his upturned black socked feet, his fingertips strumming them together at the same time…

"YAAAAAHHHHHHHH HAHAHAHAHAHAHAHAHA!!! Ronald, PL-please stop, oh PLEASE STOP!!!" Timmy cried out laughingly and as he called out the name "Ronald" he recalled with woe once before, or many times before calling out that very name during his awful ticklish trials.

As his feet were tickled Timmy laughed and screamed…

His erect cock stuck straight out and his sweaty balls pressed against it as he lay in the upside down position, feeling beyond disoriented at that point… Droplets of piss and pre cum dripped onto his lips as he laughed and laughed…

Then, Timmy, back upright in the "Spinning Chinaman" once more the "new Ronald" forced his blindfolded captive to sip down a second coffee, this one doubly laced with his potent aphrodisiac…

Timmy made gluggling sounds as he swallowed the brew, the "new Ronald" holding the laddy's nose tight as he guzzled.

"There you go Timmy my laddy, down the hatch buddy," the "new Ronald" teased and Timmy grimaced when the guy pecked him on the cheek.

He somehow wished he had spent the remaining time with Christopher and Vince at the hotel, at least that way he would not be trapped and tethered to a replica of Valerie's torturous device…he would no doubt be being tickle tortured in some fashion but no way would he have been a "Real" kidnap victim…

When he was done drinking the coffee Timmy breathed heavily and gasped "Oh my" as his cock twitched big and long in front of him. When the "new Ronald" packed him back into his underpants along with his thickly filled balls Timmy again gasped at the guy's touch. He also felt a sense of woe as the guy was not going to give him a man's relief, a relief he desperately craved at that moment. OH DANG, where was Christopher to milk him when he really needed it???

Having been tickled and sexed up with yet another potent aphrodisiac Timmy was feeling very perilously balanced on the edge…

A few moments later the "new Ronald" wiped Timmy's lips clean of the coffee remnants and Timmy pouted as duct tape was wound round and round his mouth and neck, effectively gagging him…

"MMMFFFFF…" Timmy sputtered as the "new Ronald" said, "What a catch, Timmy Backman himself strapped into the "Spinning Chinaman" in my Christopher Trevor bookstore display…"

Timmy made another angry sounding "MMMFFF" sound as the duct tape was sheared at the back of his neck and was now stuck tightly to his lips.

"Yes, Timmy Backman in the flesh and in the socks and kangaroo pouch under shorts too…I'm sure that I'll sell a million dollars' worth of books over the next few days…" the "new Ronald" said happily.

Then, with a black spandex hood over his head Timmy nearly cried miserably as the "Spinning Chinaman" slowly spun, as Ronald closed and locked the display room of his favorite author…leaving Timmy alone for the time being…

(10)

Another Good Spin For the Tickle Torture Device (An ETUK inspired story)

The first new story for my anthology.

It can be said that this short story is a sequel of sorts to "Tickling Arthur's Feet", a story of mine that made its way around the internet but never in a book. The first place it truly found a home was on the website "RopeJock.com" and from there it seemed to have a good following.

ETUK is an online buddy of mine who lives in the UK and enjoys tickling the feet of handsome suited executives. He is also the inventor of the machine known as the "Executive Tickle Torture Device."

In the end, when it came to my story "Tickling Arthur's Feet" people seemed to narrow me down to a few story-writing traits. I had become this fiendish writer who delighted in tricking handsome men into devices that would tickle torture their bare and socked feet. When I wrote this sequel to "Tickling Arthur's Feet" I had never intended for it to see the light of day, it was just to show that the character of Ronald had moved on but was at the same time tickling other men's feet now. Also, I think that because people saw me only as a writer of tickle stories was part of the reason I branched out to other fetish type stories.

Being known as a writer is fun I am glad to say. But at the same time stories like this sequel and even its predecessor can invite some twisted people to stalk an author. I can honestly say I was stalked only once and it was pretty scary *when I found out who it was that was essentially using the internet to keep track of me. I felt totally violated. Some would think that because of the story "Tickling Arthur's Feet" and now this sequel that I would condone stalking, but what happens in fiction is totally different and totally removed from what happens in real life.*

Of course I want to be thought of as a good writer, but there is a lot of competition out there and there's always going to be another really good writer right around the corner. I like to keep my stuff as original and as outrageous as possible. At some point I would like to see my books entertaining a mainstream audience, rather than just the small niche I have been told about over and over who read my books.

When it came to advice on writing about guys being tricked into perilous tickling situations and being tied and tickled I cannot say that anyone offered any advice specifically. If anything I was given a lot of negative comments about what I was writing, how it was very offbeat and not for the masses. My responses to those comments were, "Well, I want my writing to be offbeat. That is what makes it and me unique."

Because of my writing I find that I don't have a lot of time for other things I used to do. I don't go out as much as I used to and I spend my time with some friends by talking with them on the phone. I like spending as much time as possible though with like-minded buddies when it comes to what I write about. I'm glad to say that I have a good assortment of friends who are into the whole tickling and feet thing. I also seem to have a lot of mentors and muses.

Looking back in my tickle stories I have to say that it's obvious, even to myself, how very much I enjoyed writing them. I didn't get sidetracked along the way, as some people thought when I started writing about other fetishes. For the most part I have always considered myself to be very down to earth. I mean, even though I am a published author I still do household chores and laundry and other menial tasks around the house. I do not spend all my time tickling unwitting gentlemen...LOL

———————

"I tell you man, I dunno why you're so anxious to show me this invention of yours Ronald," John said to me, sitting next to me in the passenger seat of my car as I drove toward my house.

"It's totally amazing man," I said to him. "It's the most ingenious thing, yet the most simple. I can't believe that more people haven't thought of it."

John smiled; his more than handsome face brightening up like sunshine and ran a hand through his wavy light brown hair.

"And you actually expect me to believe the story that you told me about the guy you sold your house to?" John asked, looking at me snidely as I drove.

"That's up to you buddy," I replied. "But ever since buying my new house I just had to build a second device, seeing as I left the original one in the house that I sold to that executive and his wife."

John looked at me and snickered, his big brown eyes filled with glee...

John works with me at the Real Estate office that my buddy Alex owns. John is a little shy of six feet tall, as I said more than handsome with light brown wavy hair and big beautiful brown eyes. He's a muscular guy in his late twenties and married to a woman as beautiful as he is handsome. I never thought to try to trick the guy into my devilish device. But when he came into work that April first (April Fool's Day to be exact) dressed in a light gray smart and spiffy suit complete with highly shined black lace-up wing tip shoes and charcoal colored socks my heart nearly leapt from my chest. I don't usually play April Fool's Day jokes but seeing the guy seated at the desk in front of mine, his feet entwined around the legs of his chair as he worked, his charcoal dress socks more than visible I could not resist. He would more than likely be pissed with me I thought, but once I explained that it was an April fool's joke I was sure he would understand...*hopefully*...

We got to my new house a few minutes later and John stepped out of the car first as I turned off the ignition.

"Nice place you got here Ronald," John said, standing there in his suit, looking at my new place.

Again he ran a hand through his wavy light brown hair, a habit of his that I found to be more than sexy.

"Thanks man, glad you like it," I said, getting out of the car. "The device is in the basement, just like the original."

Again John smiled and this time chuckled softly.

"From what you told me I have to admit that I have to see this thing," John said as I stepped over to him.

"Follow me buddy," I said.

We both took off our suit jackets and draped them over our arms. John loosened his tie and undid the top button of his white crisp dress shirt as I opened the door.

"Man oh fucking man, this is nice," John said in awe at the sight of the main floor of my house.

He walked into the main living room, looking around in sheer delight.

"Who decorated this place for you?" John asked.

"I did," I said, taking his suit jacket from him and dropping it on my black leather couch along with mine. "Come on, the device is in the basement."

Like an obedient puppy John followed me down the stairs to the basement, to hell...

The basement was one large room, which was still in the renovation process. My device however was done and ready for some action. Like the original it was situated in the center of the basement.

"There it is," I said, holding out an arm and pointing. "My baby."

"Whoa, look at this thing!!" John said, stepping over to my device, the device known as *The Executive Tickle Torture Machine.* "It's the craziest looking thing I've ever seen."

The device, my own creation, was actually two wooden straight back chairs facing each other. On the back of one chair dangled a pair of handcuffs. On the chair facing it was a pair of wooden stocks, cut by me and looking like they were right out of the seventeen hundreds, along with a pair of c-clamps holding the stocks to the chair.

On a small table in front of the second chair was an old fashioned record player. I had managed to get a second one from a dealer, not wanting to remove my device from the other house it was in. Hooked up to the turntable, which was tilted at just about sixty degrees, was a pair of wooden sticks attached to the spindle in the center. On the ends of the sticks were feathers.

"And you mean to say that this thing actually works the way you said it did?" John asked me, squatting down by the stocks and running a hand over them, his wedding band very apparent at that moment on his finger.

If his wife only knew what he was about to endure. If I played my cards right he would endure I should say.

"Exactly as I said it did," I said. "But come on, get in the chair here, stretch out your legs. You'll see exactly what I mean. You'll also see how comfortable being in it is."

John stood up; stepped over to the chair I was indicating, looked with dread at the handcuffs and again ran a hand through his light wavy brown hair.

"I don't know man," John said, looking at me intently now, tugging at his tie. "I mean, do you plan to turn this thing on while I'm sitting in it bud? I mean, I'll be real frank, my feet are real fucking ticklish."

My heart again leapt in my chest.

"Even through your shoes?" I asked him.

John smiled and pointed a long finger at me.

"Good point man, real good point," he said and seeing no harm in my intentions he sat down in the chair facing the one with the stocks on it. "Besides, my feet stink at the end of the day. So bad that my wife can't stand it."

"Roll up your sleeves buddy," I said, squatting next to him and moving the handcuffs toward his wrists.

Without thinking he did as I suggested and before he said another word I had his wrists locked in the cuffs behind him.

You didn't have to handcuff me man," he said with a grin, seeming a tad nervous now. "I would get the idea without them."

"Now for your feet," I said, ignoring his comment about the handcuffs.

John watched as I lifted his left foot at the ankle, slipped into one of the stock holes, did the same thing with his right one and then quickly pushed the stocks closed.

"There you go," I said, my hands resting on the tips of John's wing tips. "That's how a guy should be situated in what I have come to call the executive tickle torture machine."

"Executive tickle torture machine?" John repeated, looking a little more than worried now. "You called it a tickle device earlier bud; you didn't say that you called it an executive tickle torture machine."

Smiling meanly now I started slowly unlacing John's wing tips, one hand working each shoe.

"And you my good buddy are considered to be executive for sure in our office," I said, working at getting his shoes off his feet.

"R-Ronald, you wouldn't man," John said, realizing too late what he had gotten himself into. "Y-you said you wouldn't tickle me man! Oh God please don't take my shoes off me man."

"I said I wouldn't tickle you through your shoes," I said, holding up his wing tips, the scent from them wafting over my nostrils.

I inhaled deeply, squatted to put his shoes on the floor and got busy slowly getting his charcoal colored socks off his feet. The toes and heel sections of John's socks were solid black, a nice touch I thought.

"Oh God Ronald, you bastard, you tricked me man, *you fucking tricked me,*" John panted miserably. "Oh fuck man, don't take my socks off, please buddy…"

He watched in out-right misery as his nylon dress socks were slid from his feet, right through the holes of the stocks. Then, he still watched miserably, his breath coming in short gasps as I moved the feathers against the bottoms of his naked feet.

"Y-you bastard Ronald," he said through clenched teeth. "I'll get you for this man. Just why the fuck are you doing to this to me anyway? Y-you said you just wanted me to see the damned device, not experience it firsthand."

"April Fool's Day my good buddy, April, fucking Fools Day!" I laughed and switched on the turntable to the 78 speed.

"Oh no, ha, ha, ha, ha, ha, ha, ha, ha, ha, oh fuck," John squawked as his feet were helplessly tickled in the stocks. "I-I'm really being tick-tickled here… ohhhhrrrr fuccckkkk…ha, ha, ha, ha, ha, ha, ha, ha!!!"

He threw his head back and looked up at the ceiling as I got his thrashing feet secured against the stocks with the c-clamps over the balls of them. The rotating feathers did their evil work and tickled and tickled the bottoms of the handsome guy's feet. I got the guy blindfolded with his necktie and then with his smelly socks in my hand I slowly walked up the stairs and out of the basement…

As I sat in my dining room eating dinner the musical sound of laughter wafted up to me from the basement. I picked up John's socks from the table, my booby prize for the evening, sniffed them heartily and put them back down on the table. There is nothing, and I mean nothing, better than snagging a handsome guy's socks and tickle torturing the poor sap till he's crazy with it…

I kept John hooked up in my tickle torture device for four hours that night…
The next time he came over he wanted to see if he could surpass that…

(11)

Frustrating Rafael

The second new story for my anthology.

This story, short as it is centers around the fetish of cum control. Many have asked over the years just exactly what is cum control. It is also sometimes referred to as "edging." It can also be called cum denial and the reverse of this is enforced milking, to make a guy cum repeatedly, oh yes, it can be done, if done correctly and effectively. Enforced milking happened in my story "Milked Sailor", which appeared in my book "Milked."

An individual's ability to control when-and-if he cums, as is accomplished in this story by Rafael when he finds himself worked over by two gym members in the locker room of the gym where he works, is probably the most intimately personal thing imaginable (something we often take for granted to the extent that we don't think about it) – and when that ability is removed, and taken over by a Top, it becomes an intensely humiliating form of control, also which is something that befalls the character of Rafael in this story.

There is something wonderfully fiendish and unfair about using a male's urgent need for orgasm as a form of torture. The principle behind cum denial is simple: the victim wants to cum, but is somehow prevented from doing so. The more desperately he needs to cum, the more effective it is- and this becomes a torture when the Top sets about intentionally increasing the victim's need to cum, (This was also depicted quite well in my novel "The Jock.") while also making very sure that he cannot obtain the relief he so urgently needs.

There are many ways to accomplish this as there are victims, as each individual has his own turn-ons and fetishes- all of which can be used to excellent effect on him to make him progressively more and more desperate to cum, as is done to Rafael in this story. These methods may include physical things- the bondage itself; being hooded; the feel of leather, or rubber or some other fetish material; servicing the top perhaps or just plain taking orders, as Rafael in this story is very good at, as you shall see...but it can essentially be whatever really turns the victim on and gets him horny.

It may also include psychological things such as not knowing when he is eventually going to be allowed to cum- or even if; humiliation; seeing the Top; not being able to see the Top; wanting to touch the Top or even touch himself when he is steely hard, or not being able to touch The Top or himself for that matter; the list, as you can see is endless.

Apart from all of these, there is one other thing that is the most effective of all, which is, genital teasing. No matter what else a victim of cum control is into, having his inner thighs, perineum, ass- and especially his balls- worked on for a long period will almost inevitably make him want to cum. And then, of course, there is the center of his being, his cock. And when it comes to the cock many Tops will ask a potential victim to describe exactly- and in as much detail as possible- how he best likes to masturbate. Is he circumcised? Does he have a favorite position? Does he lie down or stand up when masturbating? Are his legs straight or bent? Are his legs together or wide apart perhaps? What technique does he use? Does he like fast or slow strokes? Does he like his whole cock teased or just the tip? What does he do with his other hand? Does he use lube? Does he require any fetish object or material? These are the questions designed to tell the Top the technique that he can use on the bottom which will make him cum the quickest, most effectively, and most intensely- and make him want to cum...but then not allow him to cum. More often than not the Top just wants to know the best way to get his victim close and then make him want to cum. And when the Top knows what kind of action the bottom is susceptible to, he will use it against the bottom to repeatedly bring him to the very edge of orgasm- and then stopping short, so that the bottom can't cum.

It was a Friday night and my buddy John and I had gone to a gym (where I have a membership) for a good hard work out before heading home after work. I had gotten John into the gym on a guest pass and after seeing the facility and working out like crazy he had decided to become a member. We were done with our workout and walking down the stairs toward the locker room when we saw one of the gym instructors locking up the front door of the place. Hearing us behind him he turned around obviously startled.

"Shit," he exclaimed softly. "I didn't know that anyone was still here. The gym is closed gentlemen."

He nodded toward the clock on the wall and John and I followed his eyes. Sure enough, it was ten o'clock.

"Man, we were so into our workout we didn't realize the time," I said to the instructor. "Just let us go downstairs to shower and get dressed and we'll be on our way."

"I'll join you," said the gym instructor. "I've been training so many clients today that I must smell as ripe as an overgrown grapefruit."

He took a hearty sniff of one of his underarms and we all laughed. As we walked past him I saw that his nametag read Rafael. He was tall with jet-black wavy hair and an olive complexion. He was wearing the black uniform of the gym, (black sweat pants, and black tee shirt with the gym logo on it and high top black and white sneakers) and I could tell that he was extremely muscular. He walked in front of John and me down the stairs leading to the locker room. His melon-shaped ass cheeks filled the rear section of his black sweatpants beautifully to put it bluntly. He looked like he had two round globes in the back of his sweatpants. Upon entering the locker room the smells of sweat, urine and other male odors assaulted us. It smelled like heaven to say the least. John and I walked over to our lockers and Rafael walked over to his, which was directly across from where ours were.

"Looks like we're in the same neighborhood," John said to Rafael with a smile.

"Sure does," Rafael said and shucked off his tee shirt.

He dropped it to the floor by his locker and stepped over to a full-length mirror to look at his bare chested body. His body was a work of art, to put it plainly. His arms, shoulders and chest were extremely muscular and looked to be rock fucking hard. He was almost hairless except for around his beautiful beefy and rubbery looking nipples. It was sort of strange and erotic at the same time the way dark hair grew around and over his nipples, causing a person to look at them instantly.

"Man, I have to work harder on my chest," Rafael said, sounding disappointed in himself as he looked in the mirror.

He ran a hand over his big chest and squeezed one of his nipples.

"Your chest looks just fine to me," John said to Rafael after opening his locker.

We both turned to look at the hot gym instructor.

"I don't know, I'm just never satisfied with the way I look,' Rafael said, still looking at his reflection and rubbing his chest. "I guess I'm just a little insecure…"

John and I looked at each other, smiled and walked over to Rafael as he turned his back on the full-length mirror.

"Like I said Rafael, I think you look fine," John said to the gym instructor. "Especially this chest of yours…"

John boldly reached out and ran a hand over Rafael's rock hard chest, knowing that the guy had been teasing us from the moment he stepped in front of the full length mirror bare chested. When Rafael didn't object to what John had just done I took a chance and squeezed one of those nipples of his that was driving me crazy. It felt soft and rubbery at first between my fingers but then as I squeezed it some more it hardened at the tip. I squeezed it again and Rafael moaned contentedly.

"Yeah, nice nipples too Rafael," I said breathlessly, squeezing and twisting his nipple gently.

John and I looked at each other again and Rafael leaned his back against the full-length mirror.

"Go for it guys," Rafael said softly, yet breathlessly and placed his hands up behind his head. "Just listening to the two of you oooing and ahhhhing over my body is turning me on..."

John and I didn't hesitate for a second. We both leaned down, stuck out our tongues, and each of us slurped one of Rafael's big nipples into our mouths.

"Ohhhhh yeahhh, that feels great you fucking guys," Rafael panted.

He closed his eyes and his dick made a big bulge in the crotch of his sweat pants as we tongued, slurped and licked his nipples for all we were worth. We sucked, licked, bit, chewed and kissed Rafael's nipples, both of us getting hard in our gym shorts. We drooled over the hair on Rafael's chest and sucked up our saliva, feasting on his muscular pecs. We spit liberally on his nipples a few times and lapped that up as well.

"Ohhhh man, you guys are driving me fucking wild!!" Rafael exclaimed. "I feel like I'm goin' to pop a load any fucking second now..."

That said Rafael brought one of his hands down toward his bulging and twitching crotch. I quickly grabbed his hand and placed it back up behind his head with the other one.

"Not yet," I said with an air of authority in my voice. "Not for a while..."

"Ohhhhh man, you two are going to frustrate the shit outa me," Rafael complained.

He didn't seem to mind being frustrated though. I truly got the feeling that the muscle boy really wanted to play this game. He simply stood there with his hands up behind his head, his muscles in his arms flexed, doing as he was being told. He could have swatted John and me away from him with one hand but instead he chose to go along with what we wanted at that moment. And what we wanted at that moment was to feast on his hot muscular body till we couldn't feast anymore. As we continued working Rafael's nipples we ran the palms of our hands over his sweaty, smelly and stinky armpits. They were moist and felt great as we explored them with our hands. At one point we each held one of Rafael's nipples in our fingers and thumbs while we licked, slurped and kissed his rancid armpits.

"Ohhhhh fuck, yeah you guys, eat my hairy and stinking pits," Rafael grunted, pulling his hands further up around his head, really exposing those armpits for us. "*Fuckers*, just love teasing my tits too..."

When we stopped slurping at his pits and sucked his nipples back into our mouths the muscle boy again made a move to his bulging crotch. I quickly grabbed his hand and without being told what to do he placed it back up behind his head. By now the gym instructor was more than frustrated.

A few minutes later Rafael was standing in the center of the locker room wearing just his white sweat socks, which were pushed down around his ankles. John and I had stripped him because we wanted to get at his dick at that point. And what a dick it was. Rafael had at least eight inches of prime thick beef between his legs. It was long, fat, thick and throbbing hard when it popped out of his briefs. Droplets of thick pre-seed oozed from his wide sexy slit. He stood there in just socks squeezing his nipples as John and I took turns sucking, licking, and chowing down on his giant tube steak. A few times one of us would tongue bathe Rafael's balls as the other sucked his big dick. Rafael's balls were big and hanging low in his nut sac. They were filled to the max with his man juice and ready to explode with it. The way they were twitching every time we worked his dick in our mouths told me just how packed up with his juices his balls really were. We poked our tongues into Rafael's piss slit a few times and that really got him begging us to let him cum, pleading with us practically. Still, we told him to keep his hands anywhere he wanted to, except near his pulsing and throbbing dick. When we saw just how close he was to shooting his pent-up load we stopped sucking his dick and tongue bathing his balls. He huffed miserably as we stood up straight at his sides and ran our hands over his chest and stomach region.

"Fucking hot guy you are Rafael," John said into Rafael's ear and licked his earlobe.

"Please guys, *please,* I'm so fucking hot and horny right now," Rafael said pleadingly. *"Please get me off..."*

"Soon man, real soon," I said and kissed one of Rafael's nipples. "Hands back up behind your head, now."

"Fuckers, just love my damned nips, kissin' them and everything," Rafael grunted and did as he was told, as John and I resumed sucking his nipples again.

They were hard as buttons and very erect as we smothered them with our mouths.

"Ohhhhhh you fucking guys," Rafael moaned passionately.

Rafael's dick was hard and totally throbbing in front of him at that point. Thick droplets of pre seed oozed from his wide slit and dripped onto the locker room floor. John and I knew that the muscle boy wouldn't be able to hold out much longer at that point. God almighty if anyone were doing to me what we were doing to him I would have shot my load long ago. The kid had good staying power that was for sure. Rafael leaned his head back in a virile swoon and moaned loudly at the ceiling as we continued working his nipples more and more and more. The sounds of slurping and sucking were music to all our ears...

Finally, I took Rafael's big meat in one hand and slowly stroked it as we went on working his nipples.

"Ohhhhhhhh yeahhh, fuckin' a man, stroke my meat pole," Rafael exclaimed in a high pitched tone of voice. "Gads, nothin' feels better than shootin' your load when two mugs are playing suck and slurp with your tits, *fuck!!!*"

It didn't take long and Rafael shot one of the biggest loads of creamy jizz I had ever seen in my life. He screamed and grunted in manlike passion as thick ropes of sperm shot out of his giant manhood and landed all over the floor in front of us.

"Ohhhhhh yeah man, yeahhhhh, don't fuckin' stop guy!!!" Rafael roared. "See what the fuck happens when you frustrate me, FUCK!!"

It did seem to go on and on as the muscle boy shot that fucking giant load of his. When he was done John and I stopped working his nipples. He looked at us and we all smiled.

"Man, what a mess of jizz," John said in astonishment, looking at the floor.

"Don't worry about it man," Rafael said. "The cleaning guy will mop it up in the morning. It won't be the first time he's had to clean up a mess of man juice. Now, how about those showers?"

John and I stripped out of our gym clothes as Rafael pulled his sweat socks off his feet. We all walked naked to the shower room and stepped into one stall together. As the warm water cascaded over our bodies John and I leaned up against the walls of the stall as Rafael sucked and slurped our nipples alternately and stroked our hard ons…

(12)

The Human Barbell

The third new story for my anthology.

It's pretty obvious that what inspired this story from the outset were professional bodybuilders. With that in mind what also played a major role in inspiring the idea for this tale was a short video I saw on you tube. In the video a muscle guy is carrying two other muscle guys slung across his shoulders around a gym. To the viewer it at first looks and sounds like it's some sort of punishment being heaped on the guy carrying the other two guys. And from what one of the guys on the muscle guy's shoulders calls out, "If you had stayed facing the wall, this never would have happened!" makes one wonder why the muscle guy is being punished in this most unusual fashion. What kills the idea that it's a form of punishment for the carrier is the fact that all the men in the video are sporting semi erections in the Speedos that they are clad in. When I saw that video on YouTube I thought about how a guy could actually be turned into a human barbell.

There actually are assortments of guys out there who enjoy seeing another guy being lifted. The over the shoulder carry is used in the military for PT (Physical Training) wherein one buddy has to lug another over his shoulder at a high speed as if his buddy was injured while in combat and he has to be carried to safety. Then there's the carrying of a teammate on the shoulders of a fellow baseball or football player or players when one of their teammates makes a great play, hits a homerun or scores a touchdown. The way a baseball or football player is carried off the field is majestic for the guy in a way, really spotlighting him for the fans. Sadly in the *world of baseball carrying a winning team member off the field seems to have been replaced by hitting him in the face with a shaving cream pie.*

The character of Rick "Powerhouse" in the story "The Human Barbell" was inspired by those old beefcake magazines from the 1950s.

It's obvious that "Powerhouse" likes his body. He takes pride in it and he's not ashamed of it. Sadly the guys that capture and chain him up and use him as an unwitting and unwilling human barbell like "Powerhouse's" body too.

"Powerhouse" is sexy and masculine at the same time. One has to ask, how could he possibly avoid something like what happens to him in the story befalling him at some point? It's the essence of him to be sexy and yet vulnerable in this story.

I like seeing big muscular tough guys at the mercy of someone less strong and smaller than them.

Back in the 1990s I knew a guy on the internet who had a fetish for seeing other guy's (and perhaps even himself) carried around on another guy's shoulders like a king of sorts. Me and this guy, his name was David, if memory serves me correctly, had a lot of really cool and interesting chats concerning this often unheard of subject.

"Powerhouse" is an awesome example of a man who works at not being self-destructive. I think he is also a good example for wannabe bodybuilders. Like I said earlier he embodies the images of those old fashioned beefcake magazines from the 1950s...and then again, he also embodies the image of the muscleman of the 21st century.

———————————

"Fuck man, goddamn it all, *I don't believe this shit!!* Fuckers, this is some damned fucked up shit you're doing to me here!!" I seethed heatedly angrily as the junior body builder named Ronald lay on the weight bench, holding me, the tightly snugly chained up body builder in a prone position by one muscular arm and one of my tree trunks like legs, literally bench pressing me. "Fuck man, put me down already, good Gods, usin' me like I was a damned human barbell or something!!"

"Heh, well, to put it bluntly "Powerhouse", that is exactly what we've turned you into at the moment, a real live human barbell," the blond lanky guy named Alex said jokingly, looking hungrily at me all chained up as his buddy Ronald hoisted me up and down. "Come on Ronald, get that third set done and then it'll be Brian's turn with the big lug."

"Arrrrhhhhh!!!" Ronald roared mightily as he hefted me, all two hundred and thirty sheer muscled pounds of me above his chest and held me there for a few seconds. "Th-three more reps you guys, I can do it!! *I can fucking do it!!*"

Alex, his buddy Brian and the short stocky and muscular guy named Howard all watched as Ronald lowered me slightly, the chains wrapped tightly and tied around my muscular body jangling with his effort, the small weights dangling off hooks that they had hung on me. Ronald then gripped me tighter as he would a regular weight bar and hoisted me again, holding super-tight to my upper arm and leg. I grimaced miserably as Ronald, being the most muscular of the four junior body builders was having the time of his life showing off his strength.

"Huhhhhhh, he, he's starting to get heavy you guys, get ready to grab him from me," Ronald suddenly piped up breathlessly as he held me only slightly aloft at that point. "G-goin' to do this last rep with him and then he's yours Brian."

"Sure I'm getting heavy you blasted mug," I barked loudly. "It's two hundred and thirty sheer pounds of muscled body builder you're hoistin' here!! And talkin' about me like I really was just a piece of equipment here in the gym is real shitty and un-sweet I gotta tell you, ya mug!"

The other three guys cheered Ronald on as he hoisted me, Rick "Powerhouse" Bradley up and above his heaving chest.

"AYYYYYRRR!!!" Ronald roared mightily, holding me hoisted for a few seconds and then lowering me slowly back down, my semi hard and exposed muscle pipe dangling down beside one of my thighs.

Alex placed his hands on my chained up shoulders along with Howard while at the other end of me Brian, the guy who was up next to use me as a barbell gripped my sweaty moist and stinking bare chained up feet and ankles.

"Okay you guys, on three, one, two, three," Alex counted off and together the three mugs that had snagged me real good lifted me out of Ronald's grip.

"Bastards, put me down already!! When the hell are you mugs planning on releasing me?" I ranted miserably as I was held balanced in an upside down position, my bare and stinking feet pointed straight up at the ceiling, as if I was a weight bar being held by a dude taking a break between sets. "Punks, this is no way to be treating a body builder of my caliber!!"

My muscle pipe hung straight down against the area just below my stomach region. I was now just about fully hard and oozing pre cum.

"Okay Brian, your turn," Ronald said as he got up off the weight bench. "Three sets of twelve reps of hoisting the big guy then it'll be Howard's turn."

"I think we'd better take some of the weights off him," Alex said, holding me tight by my knees as I stood on my head, feeling ridiculous. "Brian, you're not as strong as Ronald.

Looking upward I watched as the guys took some of the small weights off the hooks they had attached to several of the chains wrapped around me, stealing strokes and pulls on my erect manhood. And then I was being handed to Brian as he took up position on the bench. Once again I was being hoisted up and down once again being used as a human barbell. As Brian took his turn with me I fleetingly thought back to how I had come to wind up in this more than fucked up predicament… How I had come to be a human barbell…

My name is Rick Bradley my weight lifting buddies at the gym call me "Powerhouse." The guys who compete against me in weight lifting competitions call me all sorts of things, none of them nice enough to mention. Ha, I can't recall the last time I lost at a weight lifting competition. Probably way back when I started doing this professionally. But now, at the age of twenty-eight I was known in the weight lifting circles as one of the very few body builders who never lost a competition. I'm just about six feet tall, give or take an inch, I have short cut black hair, brown eyes and my smooth hairless body is more than totally muscular and well proportioned. I began seriously working out when I was eighteen years old. I have shoulders as wide as a goddamned doorway, biceps that are more than sixteen inches around and *still* growing bud, my forearms and hands are strong enough to punch holes through walls and my legs are like two tree trunks. My massive chest is forty inches around and I have (literally) bouncing massive sized steel-like pecs, adorned with two of the sexiest very pointy and meatiest man tits you've ever seen on a guy. I have a washboard six pack like hard stomach and my calves are strong enough to crack coconuts between, if I chose to do that with them that is. All totaled I weigh in at two hundred and thirty pounds of sheer iron like muscle. I've lost count of how many trophies and medals I've won for weight lifting competitions at this point. I've been photographed and modeled for more than a few Men's Exercise magazines. I've been approached to do some nude layouts but up to now I've declined those offers, not that I'm ashamed of the size of my damned muscle pipe, fuck, more than eight inches of pure thick beef I've got between my muscular thighs bud let me tell you. But for the moment I want my career to be known as a professional weight lifter, a spokesperson for some of the products sold in health stores and as an occasional trainer for body builders in training. Being an occasional gym trainer is what got me into a real mess recently with some mean joke playing dudes who wanted to find out just how well they could do at some *real* "Powerhouse" weight lifting. I'll get to that very soon I promise. It started while I was competing in a recent competition at the gym that my good buddy Leo owns called "Leo's Iron Gym." Leo frequently closes the gym to the general public and invites only the best of body builders, magazine reporters and some junior body building fans to watch the competitions he hosts at the gym. Doing this keeps his gym in the press and thus scares up some good business for him every time he hosts a competition. Fucking excellent businessman that buddy Leo of mine is. This time out I was competing against a real brawny and muscular guy named Bruce "Big Pecced" Dawson. Bruce had heard about the competitions that Leo hosted at his gym, he knew about me from magazines he had read and asked Leo if he could set up a competition. "Big Pecced" Dawson was more than sure he could beat "Powerhouse" Bradley in a weight lifting competition. Leo told me that the guy had been real cocky about it and all too. Hearing that I readily agreed to the competition. Now, laying there on a weight bench, clad in just a pair of onion skin white gym shorts, ankle length white sweat socks and sneakers my chest heaving I lifted three hundred pounds above my massive chest, more than my own body weight. I listened with a slight smile on my face as the announcer of the event spoke into a microphone at the podium set up in the center of the gym.

"Rick "Powerhouse" Bradley needs to lift that weight bar twice more and he will again be the winner of yet another competition," the announcer said softly.

The fans who had come to see me clapped loudly, my buddies with me hooted loudly, yelling for me to get it over with as I lay there gripping the heavy bar of weights.

"Goin' to give you a victory ride "Powerhouse" old buddy," my best friend Ross called out to me from where he was standing with my other good bud Steve; although at that moment I didn't know just what the guy meant by a victory ride. "Come on "Powerhouse" finish this up buddy!!"

Bruce "Big Pecced" Dawson stood off to the side, the handsome Afro American muscular guy sweating from competing against me, his hard muscles glistening. Clad in a pair of blue silk gym shorts, navy blue ankle length sweat socks and blue sneakers the guy watched as I clenched my teeth. The look on his face told me he knew that it was over for him. With my teeth tightly clenched I gripped the weight bar tight and hefted it slowly forward and over my chest.

"I repeat, "Rick "Powerhouse" Bradley must lift the bar at least two times to win the competition," the announcer said as I began lifting the bar over my chest.

I pretended to struggle as I lowered the bar and slowly hefted it a second time. Bruce "Big Pecced" looked hopeful for about all of two seconds. But then I hefted the bar way up above my chest, winning the competition. The look of hope faded instantly from his face.

"Arrrrhhhhhhh!!!" I roared triumphantly as my two buddies rushed to my sides to take the weight bar from me.

They got the bar onto the support racks behind the bench I was lying on and then I sat up on the bench amid the clapping and cheers from the audience gathered at the gym.

"Thank you!!" I called out, sweating and breathless, getting to my feet.

Bruce "Big Pecced" Dawson came over to me, shook my hand real tight and thanked me for competing against him.

"You're welcome man," I said to him as people went on clapping. "Better luck next time huh?"

"Yeah, I hope so," he said, let go of my hand and walked off.

"You did it again man, fucking "Powerhouse!!" Steve said, standing at my side while Ross sidled up behind me.

Suddenly, without even telling me he was about to do it Ross squatted down, got himself between my legs and the next thing I knew he had me hoisted and I was sitting up on his broad shoulders.

"WHOA!!! Hey bud, good move!!" I laughed as he gripped my thighs tightly, holding me balanced up on his shoulders.

Looking down I waved at the crowd of clapping people and I leaned down to shake hands with people as they reached up to me.

"Rick "Powerhouse" Bradley has won yet another weight lifting competition here at Leo's Iron Gym," the announcer said into the microphone and then stepped away from the podium.

Ross began walking slowly through the gym with me up on his shoulders.

"Hey man, I know you've been working out pretty diligently, and lifting me like this sure proves it," I said with a chuckle as my feet dangled over his chest.

"Enjoy the moment buddy," Ross said and I placed my hands on the top of his bald sweaty head as he carted me around the gym.

Suddenly, I realized that my cock was hard as a fucking rock in my onion skin shorts. I prayed that Ross wouldn't feel it pressing against the back of his big neck. I ran my hands over his bald sweaty head and my cock throbbed harder. Fuck, I felt like I was a toy up there while Ross carted me around the gym…

Ross carried me around the gym on his shoulders for all of six minutes and then it was time for me to chat with the magazine reporters and set up some photo sessions along with anyone who wanted to schedule a training session with me. That's where the real trouble started. After Ross put me down I was besieged with questions from reporters, the usual how long have you been working out bullshit to when can you do an exercise photo shoot for my magazine. When things had finally quieted down, about an hour and half later was when the four junior body builders approached me about a training session.

"Mr. Bradley?" I heard my name called out from behind me, just as I was finishing setting up a photo shoot with a men's exercise magazine. "Powerhouse" Bradley?"

"Yeah?" I replied, turning to see four young junior body builders standing there, figuring they wanted autographs or some other memento of the event they'd just witnessed.

"Hi, I'm Alex," the blond lanky said, stepping forward with his hand outstretched.

"Good to meet you Alex," I said, taking his hand, gripping it tight and shaking it.

"My buddies and I here were hoping that we could set up a weight training session with you at some point," Alex said. "This is Ronald, this is Howard and this handsomer than handsome dude over here is Brian."

I shook hands with all of them, taking in the sight of their pumped up muscles under their tee shirts, but noting that they still needed work. All four of the young guys looked to be in their early to very mid-twenties.

"Yeah, sure, sure," I said to Alex, him seeming to be in charge of setting up the session. "Let's talk to my buddy Leo who owns this gym and see if maybe we could set something up. Whenever I train more than one person I like to have the gym all to us only. Makes it easier to pay attention to the trainer, know what I mean?"

"Good deal," Alex responded, sounding hopeful.

With a towel draped over my shoulders I led the way to Leo's office.

"Got to tell you "Powerhouse", that was some competition you just won," Alex said, walking next to me. "Congratulations to you."

"Thanks man," I said, smiling from ear to ear to hear the dude calling me by my nickname.

"And the way that buddy of yours hoisted you on his shoulders after you'd won, *man, that was fucking awesome too!!*" Alex went on. "I mean, he had to be practically as strong as you to do that, right? I mean, lifting you can't be an easy chore after all."

Listening to the guy mentioning my buddy Ross hoisting me was having a tingling effect on my muscle pipe, once again, just thinking about that I was getting hard in my onion skin shorts.

"Well, sometimes when a person has been training professionally for more than a while they're eventually able to lift more than their own body weight," I explained. "And I don't weigh all that much more than Ross."

"I see, so he used you as a sort of human barbell I guess you could say," Alex said with a smile when we got to Leo's office.

"Yeah, I guess you could say that," I replied with a smile, holding the door for Leo's office open.

"Wow, a fucking human barbell," Alex mused and we all walked into the office.

As luck would have it Leo said we could use the gym that Friday afternoon for the training session. The four guys split the rental fee between all of them and we were set. For Friday afternoon until closing time we would have the gym entirely to ourselves…

After we were done setting up the preliminaries of the training session I said good-bye to the four guys, telling them I would see them that Friday afternoon around four PM. I thanked Leo and then headed down to the shower room to get cleaned up and dressed. My muscle pipe was still hard in my onion skin shorts as I headed down to the shower area. I was glad to be alone in the locker room when I peeled my shorts off, seeing as I was harder than hard at the moment. God almighty, just hearing that guy Alex mentioning the moment when Ross hoisted me to his shoulders got me all hard and bothered. I got my sneakers and socks off and headed to the shower area. Walking with my meat stick erect and pointing straight out in front of me, a towel draped over my shoulders I entered the shower area and turned on the hot water in one of the stalls. Looking down at my throbbing hard on I wondered what was up with that shit, being aroused by some bud lifting me to his shoulders… I'm straight as a fucking arrow and could not figure why the thoughts of being hoisted like a toy was so damned arousing to me. When I recalled running my hands over Ross' sweaty baldhead my hard on throbbed even bigger and harder. I hung my towel on a hook, stepped into the shower stall and the hot water instantly helped my tired and overworked muscles to feel relaxed.

"Ahhhh, nice, real fucking nice," I said out loud, soaping myself up liberally as the water drenched me, my muscles glistening. "Should have set up an appointment for a massage."

Standing there, soaped up, I grabbed my hard muscle pipe and as I started stroking myself saw myself being easily hoisted by my buddy Ross. As thoughts of my feet leaving the floor flew through my mind I felt the orgasm building in my big juicy balls. Seeing myself perched up on his shoulders, him carrying me around the gym my meat stick twitched like crazy. I stroked myself faster with my soaped up hand... I thought about running my hands over and over Ross' shiny sweaty baldhead...

The sounds of my orgasm echoed in the deserted tiled shower area as my sloppy mess of sperm splashed against the shower stall wall and circled down the drain...

On Friday afternoon I was back at the gym by myself at three forty-five in the afternoon. I figured I would give myself fifteen minutes or so to get ready for the training session. In the locker room I got myself stripped to a fresh pair of white onion skin gym shorts and a pair of sneakers. Training guys while dressed real scantily is good inspiration for them. Seeing my muscular iron-like body in all its robust glory is enough to make any guy work harder at weight training. I locked my locker and then dashed up to the main entrance of the gym. At five minutes to four the four guys arrived.

"Hey guys, good to see all of you again," I said, shaking hands with them as they filed in. "Are you all set for a good hard work out?"

"Sure as hell man," Alex said anxiously.

They were all clad in gym shorts, tee shirts, sweat socks and sneakers, all of them carrying big gym bags.

"You can put your stuff downstairs in lockers and then we'll head up to the gym area and..." I began.

"That's okay, we'll hold onto our gym bags," Alex said, his three buddies nodding their agreement. "It'll save us time that way."

"Okay, if you're sure it's not a problem," I said.

"Not a problem at all," Alex said with a smile.

Had I insisted that they put those damned gym bags away it would have saved me a lot of trouble...

"I can't fucking believe that we're about to be trained by fucking "Powerhouse" Bradley, the best fucking body builder in the gym circuit," Ronald said enthusiastically, seeming to be drinking in the sight of my massively muscular body. "You know man; I worked out a little yesterday, just to get up some strength. You see I have a big surprise for you "Powerhouse.""

"Really?" I asked him with a grin. "And what might that be?"

Without responding Ronald stepped behind me as his three buddies watched with hopeful expressions on their faces.

"Okay, now just stand like that," Ronald said, giving one of my upper arms a squeeze. "Legs slightly parted."

"Yeah, sure, but what," I started to ask and then, just as Ross had done on the day of the weight lifting competition, this time Ronald hoisted me and got me propped up on his wide shoulders. "Whoa, holy shit bud, not bad for a junior body builder!!"

Alex, Howard and Brian clapped loudly as Ronald stood there looking totally triumphant with me up on his shoulders.

"Told you guys I would be able to do it," Ronald said turning and facing his three friends. "Alex, take my bag, I'm carting "Powerhouse" to the gym area."

All the guys clapped some more, including me as Ronald carried me across the reception area and into the gym, the gym where just a few days prior I had won a weight lifting competition. As Ronald carried me my muscle pipe was instantly erect in my shorts...

"Fuck man, like a human barbell," Alex said from behind as we entered the gym.

In the gym Ronald put me down and I led the four guys over to a long weight bench. Beside the bench was a tall rack with variously weighed barbells and dumbbells stacked up on it. I had set up everything prior to the four junior body builders' arrival at the gym.

"Okay, we'll start with some bench pressing for the chest and pecs area as a warm-up," I said.

All the guys nodded in agreement, placing their gym bags on the floor around the bench.

"Basically what you want to do is stretch yourself out on the bench on your back and heft a bar of weights, three sets of twelve reps," I said to the four guys. "We'll begin with stretching our arms and then our chest areas."

I made the mistake of turning my back on the four junior body builders to demonstrate the arm stretch.

"Okay, arms pulled up straight and long, stretch 'em out straight, hold 'em like that for a few seconds and then down to your sides," I said, demonstrating the technique. "And then of course, repeat the action."

As I stood there with my back to them Alex and Ronald quietly got their gym bags open and produced a long length of chain each. They nodded at each other while Brian and Howard looked hopeful. I got to say those guys were good. I mean, I didn't even hear the chains rattle once as they took them from their gym bags.

"You should stretch your arms like this between each exercise and..." I was saying, just placing my massively muscular arms at my sides for the third time when it happened. "ULLLLPPPPPPPPPP!!!"

Suddenly, and before I even realized what the fuck had happened, two long lengths of medium width heavy chains were looped around my upper body and being yanked tight.

"H-hey, *wh-what the fuck???*" I garbled and made the mistake of turning around to face the jokesters, wrapping myself still more in the chains. "Wh-what are you mugs up to here???"

"Like I've been saying "Powerhouse", a real fucking human barbell," Alex said with a grin as he and Ronald circled me in a clockwise and counter clockwise direction, chaining my upper body as they went, wrapping me tight, pinning my arms to my torso.

"*Stop this shit now!! Get these damned chains off me you punks*!!" I ranted angrily through clenched teeth.

As they chained me tighter and snugger with each turn I struggled madly, my mammoth-like muscles flexing involuntarily.

"Fuck, just like Hercules in that old movie," Brian said, squatting down and opening his gym bag.

"Yeah, but Hercules was able to pull free," Alex laughed as he and Ronald began looping their chains together behind my back, literally binding me up tight. "Powerhouse" here doesn't stand a ghost of a chance of getting himself free."

"Fuckers!! What's the point of this?" I seethed, arching my back my chained up massive chest heaved forward, my nipples making a nice showcase with the chains looped over and under my pecs.

"Just having some real weight lifting fun with you "Powerhouse", Ronald replied and from behind me gave one of my hard buns a tight squeeze.

"Fuck, you guys are faggots!!" I ranted.

Then, Howard produced from his gym bag a set of iron wrist manacles. The dark haired stocky muscular guy stepped in front of me and pushed my wrists together above my belly button.

"No, no," I garbled in a huff as the guy manacled my wrists locked in front of me.

Alex and Ronald pulled the chains tighter and my manacled wrists were now trapped in front of me. The handsomer than handsome guy named Brian squatted in front of me, shucked my sneakers off my feet and did the honors of chaining up my ankles and thighs, thus hobbling me real good.

"I don't believe this fucking shit," I whispered, shaking my head from side to side, looking down, and watching as I was chained up good and fucking tight. "Fucking bastards, *I'll fuck you guys up for this*!! See if I'm kidding!!"

When they were done with their dirty work the four guys stood around me and looked me over.

"Good job, if I do say so myself," Alex said. "Now we've got ourselves a real human barbell."

"*A human barbell*???" I barked at him. "Just what the fuck is up with this human barbell shit???"

In response Alex grabbed one handful of the chains around my chest area and a handful of the chains around my stomach area. With a mighty effort he hoisted me up off my feet and to a prone stretched out position.

"H-holy fucking shit and tarnation!!" I grumbled as the guy hoisted me up and down, using me to curl his biceps. "Oh God, *I'm a human barbell!!! You mugs have turned me into a goddamned human barbell!!!*"

To prove his point Alex curled me more than a few times and then put me down. After having been hoisted by Ronald and carried into the gym and now having been curled by Alex my muscle pipe was a little more than semi hard in my onion skin shorts. Although none of the pranksters had made mention of it just yet. It seemed that for whatever the fuck the reason, being hoisted by another guy got me all hard and hot in the crotch! Standing there again I was totally helpless as the junior body builders hung small hooks onto the chains binding me. I didn't need three guesses to know what would be hanging off those hooks.

"Okay Ronald, you get to go first, seeing as you thought of this little escapade for us," Alex said, grabbing my upper arms as Brian squatted down and grabbed my chained up feet.

"Oh shit!!!" I garbled as they hoisted me off the floor while Ronald positioned himself on the bench, ready to press me.

Ronald gripped me by one upper arm and one thigh as I was literally handed to him.

"*This is fucked up shit*!!" I seethed as Ronald got a good tight grip on me and began hoisting me up and down and up and down above his chest. "Strong fucker you are dude!"

"Thanks for the compliment "Powerhouse", Ronald replied. "Lifting you is a real honor I got to say."

The four guys laughed meanly...

Ronald finished his first set of twelve reps and Alex and Brian lifted me from his grip. They stood me up balanced stupidly on my head, holding me tight by my knee area.

"Okay Howard, hang some five and ten pound weights on him and then I'll do the second set," Ronald said, looking up at his buddies from the bench as he lay there.

With my mouth hanging agape I watched as Howard hung two ten pound weights on the hooks hanging near my shoulders and two five pound weights on the hooks on my thighs.

"What is this shit man?" I barked in Howard's face while he was squatted down at my shoulders while I was standing on my head. "Do I look like some kind of weight rack to you?"

In response Howard gave each of my big nips a hard tweak each.

"Fucking faggot," I seethed, but then Alex and Brian were again lifting me. "Holy shit, and here we go again!!"

They handed me down to Ronald, this time me weighing thirty pounds more with the weights hanging on me. Ronald held me aloft this time by the chains at my massive back. I looked up at the ceiling in a tight stretched out position as Ronald pressed me up and down.

"Entertaining experience wouldn't you say "Powerhouse?" Alex asked me, standing over me, watching intently as Ronald pressed me up and down.

"Entertaining nothing you blasted mug!!" I spat up at him as Ronald lifted me high. "This is no way to be treating a body builder of my stature!"

In response Alex gave one of my nipples a firm tweak and a nasty twist.

"OWWWWW!!! Get off my man tits you faggot!" I ranted as Ronald lowered me to his chest area.

But then, what I had been dreading happened.

"Hey you guys, I wasn't sure before but I am now," Brian laughed, stepping over to my crotch area as I was hoisted up and down. "I noticed it before when I was squatted down to chain up his thighs but I wasn't one hundred percent sure then. But I am now. Fucking "Powerhouse" has a hard-on in his shorts!"

"Yeah, looks like the big lug is enjoying all this crap after all huh?" Howard added stepping next to Brian, looking intently at the stain of pre cum on the front of my onion skin shorts.

Together, while Ronald had me hoisted high Brian and Howard each grabbed the front of my shorts.

"No, no, oh God, *you faggots!!*" I sputtered madly as they literally shredded the front of my shorts off me, tossing the tatters to the floor. "Ohhhh you fuckers!!"

My muscle pipe was hard as a fucking crag and sticking straight up like a flagpole.

"No, no, leave my damned baby maker alone you bastards!!" I ranted as I was hoisted a few more times and Brian took my hard on in hand. "Ohhhhhhh no, no, this is beyond mortifyin' now!!"

As Ronald lowered me and raised me the last few times through his last set Brian held tight to my throbbing and pulsing penis, literally jacking me off.

"Ohhhhhhhhh, g-goin' to make you guys pay for this shit!!" I panted.

"We already paid for the session "Powerhouse", Alex laughed, giving one of my nipples another tweak and twist. "All of this is just an added dividend."

Then, as Ronald did his last rep, lowering me Brian stroked me twice. That was all it took as he held tight to my hardness. My over-sized juicy and succulent balls churned between my legs and I felt the orgasm beginning in the base of my hardness.

"Ohhhhhh fuccckkk, perverts, goddamned faggots, makin' me shoot my load of slop!!" I grunted throatily and then let loose with a torrent of man juices. "Ohhhhhh fucking A you bastards!!!"

Ronald struggled at that point to hold me aloft as Brian squeezed every possible drop of my mess out of me, my cum splattering all over my chained up chest area, splashing onto my nipples and stomach region. The last droplets of the good stuff oozed from my wide sexy slit and dripped into my nest of pubic hair.

"Fuck man, never saw a guy cum that much," Brain said in awe, letting go of my muscle pipe once I was done spewing my mess. "Looks like ol' "Powerhouse" really is enjoying all this after all."

Alex, Brian and Howard hefted me out of Ronald's grip and stood me up straight this time between sets.

"Fuck it all you mugs, never had no damned guy jack me off before," I seethed, looking down, watching my mess drip down my chained up torso. "*Gods...*"

So now, since Ronald had finished up his three sets of hoisting me, the damned human barbell, Brian was on the bench, pressing me. And once again my baby maker was hard as a fucking rock, if you can believe that shit...

And once again I was going to be made to cum as I was hefted up and down and up and down, this time courtesy of the stocky muscular guy named Howard...

"Ohhhhhhh no, no, oh fuck, not this you bastard!!" I roared as Howard leaned down and slurped my hardness into his mouth. "Fuck man; don't be suckin' my muscle pipe!! I'm no goddamned faggot!!"

But, as I was hoisted up and down and my penis slid in and out of Howard's craw there was no doubt at all that I would soon be spewing another mess of my slop for the four pranksters."

"Hoooooo, st-stop sucking me so soon after I've just shot my load you bastard," I panted. "I'm all sexy and sensitive down there right now!!"

But then, as Brian hoisted me for his last rep in his first set I shot my second load of soup.

"Ohhhhhhhhhhh fuccccckkk, fuck it all, and holy crap!!" I gasped, shuddering and all goose pimply in the tight bondage. "Got me fuckin' cummin' again you guys!!"

Howard held my hardness tightly in his mouth, swirling his tongue around and around my shaft, suckling down my mess, swallowing every drop of me...

"Fucker, stealing my power spunk!!" I grunted.

When I was done shooting my second load Alex, Howard and Ronald lifted me from Brian's grasp so he could rest between sets of lifting me. While Brian sat on the bench catching his breath Ronald used me to curl his biceps a few times, standing in front of a walled mirror, holding me by a handful of chains at my chest and thigh areas, really giving his biceps a good workout...

"Fuck, fuck, *fuck...*" I seethed as I was curled up and down and up and down...

When Brian was ready for his second set the three guys hoisted me and handed me back to him. He pressed me, holding me by the chains around my massive back and over my round coconut shaped ass cheeks.

"Hooooooo I-I'm goin' to report you mugs to Leo, the owner of the gym for this," I garbled stupidly as the ceiling came into view as Brian pressed me up high.

"Oh yeah, and what the hell are you going to tell him "Powerhouse?" Alex asked me teasingly. "That four clients managed to chain you up good and tight and used you as a human barbell?"

All the guys laughed meanly, including Brian as he hoisted me down...

When Brian was done with his last sets on the bench with me it was Ronald and Howard who did the honors of getting me hooked up, *literally*, for the next round of my being used as a "human barbell..."

"Arrrhhhhh God, you fuckers!!!" I roared more than angrily when I was precisely hooked up as a chained up hanging "lat-pull down" bar. "Got me hanging like a damned side of beef in a butcher's freezer!!"

I was hung straight out, stretched tight, facing downward blindfolded, in a prone position from the hooks of the lat-pull machine.

"Fuck, he makes a much better looking bar than the one we replaced with him," I heard the stocky muscular guy named Howard say, reaching up and giving my slimy semi hard on a good tug, sending chills and thrills through me.

"ERRRRRHHHH GOD, leave my damned muscle pipe alone ya pervs, shit, don't know why you felt the need to blindfold me now," I complained miserably.

"Looks like it's my turn to work out," Howard said.

Then, with a pair of tit clamps clipped to my man tits and handles hooked onto the sides of the chains around my chest and knee areas Howard sat on the bench of the machine, his arms raised, his hands gripping the handles on me. The fucking guy yanked me down, slurped my semi hardness a couple of times and then slid me back up, using me as the lat-pull bar.

"Ohhhhhhh f-fuck, n-never knew a guy to suck my cock while he lat pulled," I groaned.

Howard yanked me down again, the chains rattling, the tit clamps tugging on my man tits and again slurped me into his greedy mouth. He held me there for a few seconds before letting me out of his mouth and sliding me back up again...

"Fuck, goddamned pervs," I whispered, my meat stick betraying me by getting harder each time Howard yanked me down and slurped on me.

A few times while he had me yanked down he nibbled teasingly at my cock head and I felt tongues darting and flicking over the bottoms of my bare smelly feet.

"Ohhhhh G-God," I muttered as Howard slid me back up, holding tight to the handles hooked up to my chains.

When Howard reached the twelfth rep of his first set I shot my third load of body builder soup as I hung there like meat in a freezer.

"Arrrhhhhh f-fuck, fuck, got me creaming my goddamned load *again* you blasted mugs!!" I ranted as I hung there after being sucked more than a few times by Howard while he'd yanked me up and down.

I shuddered as I hung there, my load splattering all over the floor below me, as I seemed to spew more and more. Alex took my blindfold off so that I could see the mess I was making. The four mugs cheered me on, reaching up and giving my manhood a few last strokes when I was done, getting some good loud grunts of forced passion out of me...

"Ohhhhh God, wh-when are you guys planning on lettin' me go?" I ranted, hanging there as beads of piss oozed from my slit, my clamped man tits smarting a hundred times more now that I'd shot my load again.

In response, Howard sat back down on the bench, reached up, grabbed the handles on me and yanked me down, beginning his second set. When he slurped my now more than sensitive manhood into his mouth I reeled and ranted crazily...

Howard completed three sets of twelve reps of using me as the bar for the lat pull-down machine. I next found myself being hoisted up and down by Alex being used a "shoulder press bar." The blond lanky guy held me tightly and aloft by the chains at my middle back as he hefted me up and down and up and down...

"Uhhhhhhhhh!!!" I grunted my legs splayed down at the knees, my feet dangling and my chest area arched back as Alex sat on a bench pressing me up and down above his head, working his shoulders.

While Alex lifted me and brought me down my cock remained semi hard, beads of piss oozing from my slit and landing in my pubic bush....

When it was over all the guys had taken a turn at using me as a "human barbell." I then stood balanced on my chained feet in the center of a rubber mat, screaming bloody murder as Alex and Ronald, the meanest of the four guys hooked small three-pound weights onto my fleshy man tits.

"No, no, *oh God no,* wh-what is this shit now???" I bellowed furiously, looking down miserably as the weights hung on the chain attached to the tit clamps and pulled down unforgivingly on my poor nipples.

"Well "Powerhouse", we all worked out pretty hard," Alex said teasingly, pulling on the chain on my tit clamps, making the small weights pull down on them even more. "Now it's your turn."

"Fuck man, if you dudes hadn't chained me up like this I would've given you more than a real workout," I ranted at Alex. "You guys didn't work half as hard as I would have had you done."

"Up and down "Powerhouse," Ronald said, stepping to my side and curling a big hand around one of my massive biceps. "Come on you big lug, let's see you work those big ol' tits of yours..."

The four guys laughed meanly and clapped, slapped me on the ass and hooted as I bent down and pulled myself back up slowly over and over, really giving my poor nipples an unneeded workout...

When they hung a five pound round weight from my balls I nearly went crazy, but not being in much of a position to argue I continued hefting the weights hooked up to my tit clamps...

The next Morning...

Leo opens the gym every morning promptly at six AM. On the morning after my session with the three junior body builders Leo was there like clockwork to get the gym open for his members. His earliest clients usually showed up as early as six fifteen. Leo likes to inspect the gym quickly before any of his members get there, thank God for that is all I can say bud. When Leo walked casually and as usual onto the weight floor of the gym that morning the first sound he heard was a loud and angry, "MMMMFFFF!!!" Leo at first could not believe what he saw, but then, with his eyes opened wide in shock made his way over to me. The four guys had left me chained up tight and gagged with Ronald's rancid sweat socks. One sock was crammed in my mouth while the other one was tied snugly over it, jamming it in place. Not only had they left me chained up, but also they had left me stacked up with the other weights on the weight-bar storage rack. I was hung on my side in the center of the weight rack...

"H-holy Shit," Leo said as he got over to the weight rack. "P-Powerhouse, what the fuck is this all about?"

He took the socks out of my mouth and still stacked up there on the rack I told him most of what had transpired at the gym with the four joke playing junior body builders, leaving out the parts where the dudes had made me shoot my load. I was glad that my mess of cum on the floor had all dried up during the long night.

"Fuck, they used you as a human barbell?" Leo asked when I was halfway through my story, glancing over at the lat pull-down machine, not believing that I had been hung there like a side of beef.

"Yeah man, fucking dudes really put one over on me let me tell you," I said to Leo.

"Stripped you too huh bud?" Leo asked, giving my exposed manhood a quick shake.

"Yeah, yeah, fuck man, but I got to piss," I said breathlessly. "Come on, get me off this rack and then unchain me buddy. I need to get out of here and get to work and all that. Man, I hardly slept either."

"You know "Powerhouse" seeing you this way gives me a great advertising idea to drum up business for the gym," Leo said.

"Wh-what?" I asked him nervously.

"Yeah, imagine using pictures of a muscle god like you all in chains as a way of promoting some real heavy duty advertising," Leo said, scratching his chin as he mulled it over. "Just like Hercules in chains in that movie. We could even do some shots of you breaking free."

"Yeah, that would be great right about now bud," I said to Leo. "Free would be better great, it would be awesome!!"

Smiling, Leo, a body builder himself lifted me off the weight rack and held me in a prone stretched out position.

"What say we go to my office and talk about it huh "Powerhouse?" Leo asked me with a grin.

"Leo, put me down man, come on, put me the fuck down!!" I ranted as he carried me toward his office. "Oh fuck man!!!"

(13)

The Bathhouse, Charlie, and the Chubby Chaser

The fourth and final new story for my anthology.

This story has to be the one that truly is an escape for me. In any of the stuff I have ever written I never included a scene in a bathhouse. I suppose the reason for that is that I came out during the times of the beginning of the AIDS scare when most bathhouses were being closed down. I remember how the government ordered bathhouses closed down in an effort to stop the spread of AIDS. It was enough to frighten the tar out of any naïve eighteen year old just making his way out of the closet.

Instead of bathhouses I have used gyms as settings for certain stories I have written over time.

Charlie, who appears in this story is a real person and was the consultant for this story as well. He is also the person that I dedicated my book "Love Torture and Redemption" to.

Most Gay men prefer a guy with a supple or muscular and well-toned body. But this story can be true in that there is a sub-culture of Gay men out there that prefer a heavier weighty man; these men are called "Chubby Chasers." I am not sure if the term "Chubby Chaser" has become politically incorrect at this point in time. I think the term that a lot of heavy men prefer is "Bear", although I think "Bear" is a term that heavy and very hairy men like to use to describe themselves.

When Charlie first told me about this experience of his at the Club baths bathhouse I was glad to hear about the guy named Tony who had a fetish not only for heavy men, but for big feet as well. Once again I was able to combine a couple of fetishes into a story. That always seems to work well for me I am glad to say.

I myself have never been to a bathhouse. My only experiences with bathhouses were the stories I have heard from others and the movie "The Ritz." In the movie "The Ritz" one of the more flamboyantly Gay characters is a chubby chaser. I remember that my friend Charlie loved this movie and the way the guy with the fetish for a heavy man was portrayed.

Even though Charlie is a heavy man he was never ashamed of his body, and even though he was what a lot of Gay men called a "chubby" he never had any shortage of sexual encounters.

Charlie told me about his experience with the guy named Tony at the bathhouse after I had told him about my foot fetish. Admittedly my fetish for feet is different from Tony's, only in that he preferred bare feet where I like feet that are clothed in dress shoes and dress socks.

Charlie often wonders if the guy named Tony that he met at the bathhouse in this story is still out there somewhere.

While the story is essentially true I did add some of my own "Christopher Trevor" spice to it. I find that I am pretty good at listening to another person's story and then spicing it up just a bit. I never lose the original essence of the story though, I always make sure to keep the person's original synopsis intact at all times.

Back in the 1970's before AIDS the hottest places for me to go were the bathhouses in New York City. On a week-end I was able to score at least four or five times in one night alone. The story I want to tell you about happened back in 1977. I was thirty four years old. My name is Charlie. I have wavy brown hair, light eyes, and I weigh close to three hundred pounds. At the time the story I want to tell you about happened I was approximately two hundred and fifty pounds. From the time I was a child I was always a heavy person, a chubby. Anyway, it was 1977, I was thirty four years old, and on a Friday night after work I went directly to the Club baths bathhouse which was on Second Avenue between first and second streets in Manhattan. I was tired from a hard day at work on the shipping dock where I shipped heavy packages all day long. At six thirty PM I arrived at the Club baths. I paid the admission charge to the cute guy who was working the front desk that night. If I remember correctly his name was Joe or John. He handed me a large towel and a key for a locker where I could lock up all my personal stuff. He asked me if I would need a room. I said I would and he handed me a key with a number on it, indicating which room I should go to. I thanked him and walked away from the front desk. After putting my personal stuff in my locker I proceeded to room number five ten, carrying the large towel slung around my neck. In my room I stripped my clothes off, tied the towel around my forty four inch waist, and left my room holding my room key in my hand. I walked up and down the hallways, looked in some rooms where some guys had left their doors open and were just sitting and relaxing, others were looking for someone they found attractive to pass by and invite in, and some were lying down on the small beds that the rooms were equipped with. As I passed by a room where a guy of about average height, dark hair, and a muscular body was sitting I stopped and looked at him for a second. He was beautiful, absolutely exquisite. I guessed his age to be around twenty three or twenty four. When he saw me looking at him I thought he would just look away from me, indicating that he wasn't interested.

"Hello," he said to me and smiled.

"Hello," I replied and returned his smile. "Are you uh, looking for company?"

"Yes, as a matter of fact I am," he said happily. "Come on in."

I went in, closed and locked the door behind myself, and looked at him in awe.

"My name is Tony," he said and stood up with his towel tied around his waist as mine was.

He was looking at me hungrily. I had stumbled upon a hot looking chubby chaser.

"I'm Charlie," I replied breathlessly.

God, just looking at him was driving me wild. His chest was muscular, well-toned and smooth. His nipples were small, brown and real pointy. What a beauty he was. Together, we both took our towels from around our waists and dropped them on the floor. We were both hard as rocks and throbbing, our cocks oozing pre cum already. We stepped close to each other and began exploring each other's bodies. Tony ran his hands lovingly over my big pot belly as I squeezed and twisted his nipples, then giving them a few sucks and slurps each.

"God, you're delicious," I whispered, my hands cupping Tony's hot buns, holding him close to me, practically lifting him off the floor. "I could just eat you up."

"I bet you could at that you hot chubby man," Tony sighed and pressed his mouth against mine.

He sucked my tongue into his mouth and worked it like it was a cock. When I thought I was going to shoot my load I eased my grip on him. I didn't want to cum yet, not too soon. I wanted to savor the time with this beautiful man I had met. Tony sat down on his bed as I stood over him, my cock hard as a fucking diamond. He placed the palms of his hands on my love handles and leaned forward. He stuck out his tongue and ran it over and over my stomach, in my belly button, sending chills up and down my spine. Goose bumps broke out all over my body as he licked my fat stomach like crazy.

"You have such a nice large stomach," he exclaimed breathlessly as he went on and on licking my tummy, squeezing my love handles, and poking his tongue in and out of my belly button. "Why don't you lie down so I can play with your big feet?"

He licked my stomach for a few more minutes and then I lay down on the bed. He began handling my feet, squeezing them, and even massaging them.

"My God, you have big fat toes," he said, squeezing one of my big toes. "What size are your feet?"

"Ten and a half triple E," I responded and he looked at my feet in awe.

"Your feet are the fattest I've ever seen," Tony said, still toying with my toes. "Can I lick your large feet and toes?"

I nodded that he could. He put a towel over his hard cock and pressed his cock against the arch of my foot. Slowly, he rubbed his towel covered cock against my foot, slowly jacking himself off.

"Oh yeahhhh, fucking big feet you got you hot chubby," Tony said breathlessly. "Oh fuck, I'm getting close already now…"

Then, Tony took the towel off his cock and shot his load, shooting torrents of hot creamy jazz all over my foot.

"Ohhhh yeahhh, yeah, you hot fucking chubby man," Tony gasped as he came and came and came.

When he was done my foot was drenched with his cum. Tony leaned down over my foot and slowly licked all his cum off it.

"Ohhhhh yeah, lick my foot clean you pervert," I whispered in passion.

When Tony was done licking his cum off my foot I stood over him. Without a word I plunged my hard and throbbing cock into his mouth. I fucked his mouth like crazy and Tony eagerly deep throated my cock a few times.

"Ohhhhh yeah," I gasped as I gyrated my heavy hips, fucking his mouth like an animal in heat.

When I exploded Tony gulped down my cum as fast as he possibly could, not letting a drop of it escape his mouth.

"Ohhhhhh God, ohhhh you fucker," I rasped in a high pitched tone of voice. "Swallow my cum you cock sucker, ohhhhrrrr yeah…"

When I was done Tony gave my cock a few last sucks, causing even more chills to climb up my spine. I ran a hand through his beautiful hair as my cock slipped out of his mouth. We looked at each other and smiled.

After that I saw Tony several more times at the Club baths bathhouse during the late 1970's. But then, one night I went there and he wasn't there, nor was he there the night after that, or ever again. I'm now fifty four years old. It's been twenty years since that first night with Tony at the Club baths bathhouse and I have not seen him since. Tony, if you're out there I still think of you and remember you well.

Charlie, your number one chubby…

ABOUT THE AUTHOR

Christopher Trevor was born in July 1963 and grew up in New York City. As soon as he was old enough to know how he began writing fiction and has been writing gay erotic/fetish stories for the past ten to twelve years at this point. He became an avid reader as well from the time he knew how and reads everything from fiction, to non-fiction to biographies of interesting and unusual people, people who have made a difference or who have paved the way for others. Christopher attributes his writing artistic inspiration to artists such as Etienne, Tom of Finland, Tagame, The Hun, and most notably Joe T, who Christopher has had the pleasure of speaking with and  even meeting over the last few years. Christopher states, "Joe T encouraged me to write about my fetish because I was embarrassed about it at the time. Joe T said that when we are embarrassed about something that makes it even more enticing somehow." Christopher totally agreed and never stopped writing in this genre. Erotic writers who inspired Christopher Trevor were: Tom Shaw (author of "That Day at the Quarry), C.S. White (author of Big Sur), Larry Townsend (author of countless erotic novels), and Mason Powell (author of the classic story "The Brig.")

Christopher discovered that not only did he enjoy writing erotic tales but that after his first bondage experience he had a genuine flair for it. Writing to erotic oriented magazines about his first bondage experience truly opened the floodgates for Christopher where this style of writing is concerned. Christopher thanks the handsome and muscular "Greg" for that experience way back in time. Christopher took "Creative Writing" courses every semester during his high school years and while other friends of his stopped writing what they loved to write about as time went on Christopher never let a day go by when he didn't write something... "I feel that if I don't write every day I will die," Christopher has said many times over.

Foot fetish stories and all things related; spanking fetish, erotic shaving, muscle bondage, tickle torture, and hardcore stories are just a few of the areas of gay eroticism that Christopher enjoys writing about and inspiring in others as well. As one internet buddy said to Christopher where the black socks fetish is concerned, "Until I started talking with you I never gave a thought to my socks when I got dressed for work in the morning. Now when I pull my dress socks on every morning I get a chill up my spine."

Christopher is proud of the erotic effect he has on people...

Christopher Trevor is also the author of:

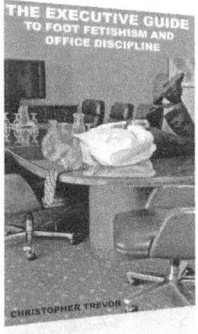  

  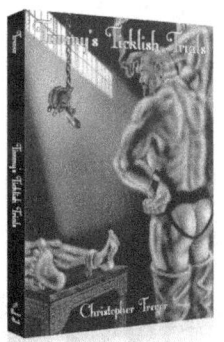

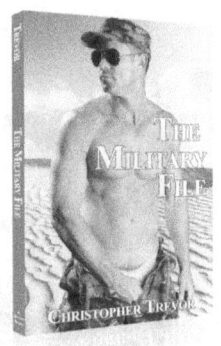

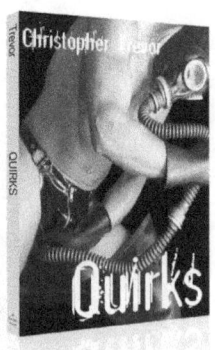

**Look for them where you bought this book,
Amazon.com, or TheNazcaPlainsCorp.com.**

www.ingramcontent.com/pod-product-compliance
Lightning Source LLC
Chambersburg PA
CBHW071827020726
47502CB00004B/1271